"BEC STARED OUT AT THE MOON. 'WHEN I DANCED, I SAW HIM EVERY MINUTE, AS IF HE STOOD THERE AND WATCHED ME.'"

THE DAUGHTER OF HELEN KENT

BY

SARAH COMSTOCK

AUTHOR OF
THE VALLEY OF VISION, ETC.

FRONTISPIECE BY
JOHN ALONZO WILLIAMS

GROSSET & DUNLAP
PUBLISHERS   NEW YORK

Made in the United States of America

CONTENTS

PART ONE

PART TWO

PART THREE

CONTENTS

PART ONE

THE DAUGHTER OF
HELEN KENT

CHAPTER I

THE DANCING PSALTRESS

I

MORNING lay upon the city.

The sky had been grey, and the shadowed faces of the skyscrapers had glowered like sombre gods out upon the waters. But as the sun began to break through, it silvered the countless aigrettes of steam that tossed on high, it fell upon the slate-coloured water like handfuls of broken crystals spattering light as they struck. With the sun came a sense of buoyant promise.

From the first hint of day the city had been drawing insatiably from all directions. Early milk wagons had clattered over cobbles, vegetable trucks had lumbered in, funereally swathed, workmen had come running to catch boats and cars. As the morning advanced, the flow had increased, and now the city was fuming as it greedily sucked in life from everywhere. Ferryboats packed to the gates plodded across the rivers, emptying load after

3

load, returning to be filled again. Shrieking trains disgorged their passengers, crying, "Here are more, more, more!" From stations high above the street, streams of people poured, and from the bowels of the earth others scurried up like ants from their holes—all drawn to the ravenous creature, all impotent to resist. Whatever they possessed—wares, brains, hands, gifts, youth—these they brought eagerly, to fling to the hungry maw.

By nine o'clock the sun had gained full possession, driving every cloud from the sky, touching the city with a rainbow-hued brilliancy such as rare potteries attain at the hand of the master ceramist. The rush of travel was at high tide; one might have thought the entire world to be assembling here. And yet it was but one day like all other days.

A lumbering brown ferryboat detached itself from the Jersey shore, and made for the iridescent city. Its passengers huddled indoors, cowering from the smart whips of the December air; a young man pacing the forward deck was obliged to address his remarks to a horse in default of other companionship. The horse, harnessed to a pickle-maker's wagon, waited restively during the brief period in which his load was shifted to that other aged beast of burden, the ferryboat.

"You and I," observed the long, lean, strolling young man, "are the only passengers that appreciate the hygienic value of fresh air. Or is it the esthetic value of this vista that brings you here? For myself, I am led by both. I should like to compare your motives."

Upon this the horse shook his head sharply and uttered a reply that sounded like, "Nei-ei-ei-either."

"I see." The young man drew his collar almost to his hat, gave a weather-defying swish of the long brown overcoat he wore, and drove his hands more deeply into his pockets. "Neither the hygienic fad nor the artistic impulse moves you, but solely the prompt delivery of— Pickles. Yet who shall deny that Pickles may be the highest motive of the three? They lend a piquancy to life; they lift it above the sordid bread-and-butter plane (which art often fails to do), adding a zest such as fancy adds to fact——"

At this moment his observations were broken off by a sense of something sweeping in upon his consciousness like a fresh wind. The door of the crowded cabin was flung open; out upon the deck a girl came rushing, with a laugh of sheer delight, calling to someone who followed:

"Oh, it's glorious out here! Come on, Helen—hurry! Feel it! It feels rosy!" She pressed her hands to her cheeks, and the words, the gesture, somehow became one with the vivid sting of the air, the joyous colour of the new day.

"What are those lines?—something like:

'. . . Earth is a wintry clod:
But spring-wind, like a dancing psaltress, passes
Over its breast to waken it. . . .'"

flickered the young man's thought.

"And look, Helen! Look at the city!"

The other smiled with indulgence in her more sophisticated eyes. "The bags are inside," she said, however.

"Bother the bags!" The girl seized her wrist. "Come and look! Don't waste a minute! Oh, it's *to-day*, Helen darling—do you realize it? To-day, of all days! The day we enter our new world! Ours, our very own, dearest! Oh, Helen, Helen, are you nearly *bursting* with joy?"

The other, still smiling with indulgent maturity, let herself be led to the very gate, out where the wind lashed their skirts wantonly to the form of their lithe bodies, while their eyes were stung by the glittering winter sunlight, and the girl's hair was whipped to a foam of gold.

The young man covertly observed. What he saw was merely a girl of perhaps eighteen or twenty, and a woman of, say, twice those years—strangers, ferryboat passengers, ships such as, in the swarming waters of New York, pass by the thousand and seldom even speak each other in passing. But for some unknown reason he felt a curious indelibility in these two.

Both were young. So-called "middle age" being an abstract point nowayears, from which a woman may project her line in either direction she chooses, this woman distinctly projected hers toward youth and arrived there. She was in full control of her tall, supple figure, of her alertly dominant carriage. Her tailoring was smart, her manner and expression brittle. A fantastic comparison occurred to him as he waited: "She suggests," he thought, "one of those tapering, perfectly groomed blackbirds that arrive early, looking so scornfully capable—perhaps it's her sleek blue-blackness—or that jetty, cynical flash of her eye, which may be slightly malevolent, but what humor! Holy smoke! What a dinner companion she'd be!"

His eyes rested for moments longer upon "Helen," then traveled to the girl.

"And she suggests—" he began, rambling on in agreeable confidence to his highly interested self—"she suggests——"

He halted. No simile came. Perhaps she suggested nothing that he had ever seen; or perhaps so many things. . . . Again the lines flickered, like bars of a forgotten tune recurring at the touch of some association of ideas:

> ". . . Spring-wind, like a dancing psaltress, passes
> Over its breast to waken it. . . ."

"Bah!" He shook his head disgustedly. "Horrible word, that 'psaltress'! Sounds like some kind of cracker. And Browning at that—as 'Helen' would say, 'He lies with the crimson rep and the marble-topped bureau, not even obsolete enough to be revived.'"

He paused at this. It occurred to him as odd that he should be attributing remarks to "Helen" in imagination, when the sole utterance he had heard from her lips was, "The bags are inside."

"How tame the gulls are! They come as near as our own California gulls," he caught from the girl just then, as she turned to watch the grey creatures dipping in curled flight.

"Wherefromabouts located," the young man observed, with satisfaction.

And of a sudden he saw what he had seen once in a hurried month of travel years before: Hillsides afire with flame-coloured poppies, swaying down to the folds of fruit-bearing valleys where the rose of almond blossoms, the white of prune blossoms, rippled into one another like blushes and pallors. . . . Miles of this thing, a vast, fearless opening of life, he recalled his impression—sheer life, the untrammelled, undoubting burst of it. . . . Yes, now he knew. That was the girl. She was the essence, the very embodiment of the spirit he had found in California; life so intensely eager and so unafraid to live, to fulfil itself, as he had found nowhere else in his wanderings. More like ancient Greece, he had always fancied, than anything else we have nowadays. . . . Yes, the girl was all this, and yet there was something more, something that didn't quite jibe. California had seemed so gloriously, so wantonly, pagan; California was an instinct, like possession, or love, or hate, or sex—"splendidly soulless," he had once said. . . .

"I am drivelling," concluded the young man. "I have gone so far as to attribute a soul to a young lady conversing of caramels."

II

She was. "I do wish they liked candy," she regretted now, as her caramel cast upon the water failed to find favor in the sight of the gulls. "I'm so happy myself that I want to feed something!" The overflow impulse was at high tide. With an open candy-box in her hand, she glanced about at random, and her eye lighted on the horse.

"He is pining for some!" she asserted, and made a rush toward the animal. She had stripped several caramels of their paper and was about to offer them, when she noticed the young man. His attitude beside the horse suggested possession.

She drew back. "Oh!" she said. Then, "Do you mind

if I give him some candy? He looks such a gentle old
dear. And candy is very nutritious—that is, it gives heat
and energy, I believe——"

The young man lifted his hat. "Let me express for
him his appreciation of your thoughtfulness. He feels
that heat and energy will be of great advantage in his
line of work. As a matter of fact, he is merely a chance
acquaintance of mine—I happen not to be the pickle-
maker——"

"Oh! I didn't——I thought——" The girl broke off,
stammering, as she grasped the situation. Her cheeks
were teased to crimson by the young man's whimsical
manner. He seemed to be laughing half at her, half with
her; after hesitation, she decided to recognize the latter
half only, and she laughed frankly.

"Then, as the owner isn't present, and the horse agrees,
here goes," she declared, and the acquisitive lip gathered
a handful of caramels from her palm.

"Helen," strolling and amused, had followed.

"He is so delighted!" the girl informed her. "I don't
believe he ever had candy before in his poor, tired old
life. Think of being doomed to drag a pickle-wagon day
in and day out—who wouldn't turn to the sweeter side
of life?"

Helen's smile, that quick glance of hers that suggested the glint of polished jet, met the young man's in
adult comprehension. In that smile he caught a strange
blend of cynical insight and fatuous doting. "Isn't this
new-born creature delightful?" it inquired of him. "It
no more recognises the struggle that life is than does a
colt in a pasture. We know, you and I, that the pasture

is surrounded by bars, and that whip and harness lie in wait."

And the young man's loafing, whimsical brown eyes responded, "We know, of course. But why spoil the illusion of a limitless and eternal pasture?"

They all turned at the sound of a sharp whinny. The horse had just discovered the difficulty of mastication peculiar to caramels; his jaws wouldn't work properly, and he mouthed in indignation.

"Poor fellow! He isn't used to caramels!" The girl's hand went out impulsively. It happened to be bare, having snuggled in her muff; and the rosy palm which had proffered him this strange torment caught the resentment of the horse. A jerk freed his jaws; his next move was to snatch angrily at the hand.

Just what the young man did never was exactly discovered, even by himself; the only significant point was that he did it. That loitering purveyor of leisurely philosophy became on the instant as taut as a swaying, ease-loving hammock suddenly jerked to tension by its rope. The girl had gone white and shut her lips without a sound; her companion had made a futile snatch at a strap as the horse jerked its head. Then there came one swift, precisely-aimed movement, and the girl found herself staring at her unharmed hand. The young man was stuffing his own, with elaborate unconsciousness, into his pocket.

"Let me see it." "Helen" was as restrained and authoritative as a nurse.

"Nonsense! A mere nothing!" He had gone slack and smiling again, like the hammock that once more sags in comfort the instant its rope is released.

"Let me see it at once, please." Laughing, he complied. She examined it carefully. "Good! Bruised, but no skin broken. So I'll shake it, with thanks. The thing that interested me," the lady continued, deliberately, "was the way your energy came up out of your laziness so"— she snapped a finger. "Like a bolt. You'll do something yet, young man."

The girl was profuse. "It was so brave of you! And I didn't deserve it. I'm always getting into scrapes, and I ought to pay the price!"

"Even if you ought—which I don't admit," the young man responded, "one article of my creed is the preservation of all things beautiful, there not being any too many of 'em as it is. Forgive my impertinence—but I couldn't help noticing the finger-tips in question, even before our greedy friend, here, the horse, took a fancy to them. I was merely living up to my belief. Had they been a different kind, he might have swallowed them without a protest from me. So don't thank me, I beg of you."

The girl flushed, newly unfolding as she was to the world's atmosphere of cross-currents to which we become so accustomed later on that we rarely feel the need of a wrap. She faced this tingling challenge to her poise without a flinch, however.

"All the more to your credit, then, if you lived up to a creed. That's more than most people do—even when they say very long, solemn creeds!"

"Bravo, youngster!" "Helen" acclaimed, and again that glance of pleasurable adult amusement passed between her and the young man. The experience of her years met the experience of his sex; there was mutual comprehension.

And yet something was puzzling him: something in the frolicsome laugh with which the girl had said "very long, solemn creeds!" making a *moue* such as might a pixie peeping in at a church window. It wasn't mere commonplace irreverence; it was more the point of view of some elfin being who had never known reverence and thought it droll. . . . And just then she took a little dancing step, unconsciously, as if she naturally moved by dancing rather than walking, and it gave force to the elfin impression—"a jolly big elf, though!" . . .

The journey by water was drawing to its close. Involuntarily they all pressed forward and stood silent, facing the city. At last the sun was complete master. High against the east rose the jagged outlines of the city, irregular squares sawed out from a burnished sky. The buildings loomed, towering above the travellers, frowning upon them formidably as if challenging their approach. But over all shone that wonderful iridescent glory, the splendor of the new day, as yet unpolluted.

It was the girl who at last broke the hush. Her whisper came tense, between indrawn breaths:

"Oh, I'm in such a hurry—such a hurry—to live!"

She stood at the very prow, in advance of the others, and she seemed to the young man like a ship's figurehead, eager to breast the waves, pressing on to the adventure.

He glanced toward "Helen"; she was still observing the skyscrapers.

"And 'to live' means——?" he ventured, in response to the girl.

She turned to him, and their eyes met. And at that instant something happened—something more than the

mere meeting of young eyes. He had a curious consciousness of something important occurring; something
very, very important; and with it came the consciousness
that the girl was similarly conscious; and yet it was all in
a flash——

"To live," she said, slowly, and their eyes did not part,
"may mean heaven or hell, I suppose. But whatever it
means for any one of us, we've each got a right to try it
for ourselves, I think."

Perhaps it was the unexpected maturity of the girl's
manner that made "Helen" turn so suddenly; at any rate,
her glance darted swiftly from one to the other, then fell
across the meeting of those other glances like a severing
blade.

Her voice was sharp. "We've each a right to sables, a
limousine, and plover—which we shall possess when we
claim them. Come, youngster!" she said. And "good-
byes" followed.

III

With a rude embrace the pier received its ferryboat;
the landward rush was released. The young man erased
himself promptly, in full recognition of the conventions.
Nevertheless, while assuming no right to accompany, he
maintained the right to observe. From a discreet distance
he kept the two within his range of vision.

They walked briskly, the elder woman in the lead and
purposeful. She gave over the bags to a porter who had
singled these out as travellers used to the attentions that
make for self-respecting ease. They were both far better

able to swing off with their own suitcases than was the little drab, spinsterish person just beyond; but in some way this "Helen" conveyed the idea that she did not intend to carry her own bags and therefore would never have to, while the frail spinster, tilting to one side against the weight of hers, plainly accepted the burden and so invited it to remain.

"Find me a taxicab," the young man heard "Helen" give instruction.

"Yes'm. Right this way, ma'am."

He found himself borne on by the speed of the pilot porter, and he hurried, endeavouring to keep the precise distance that combined discretion and observation. But the crowd hindered him. There came a swift eclipse, as streaming commuters blotted out the two—he darted the wrong way—caught again the glint of the girl's hair— followed, rushing wildly—there was an obliterating curve, despair—then of a sudden he found himself almost upon the two, who had halted.

"But I want a taxicab," the older was protesting.

"Too bad, ma'am. I dunno why, but the' don't seem to be nothin' 'round but them two haansom caabs."

The lady shrugged, and accepted the situation with contempt. The girl clasped her hands.

"Oh, I'm glad! I love these jouncy, stuffy old coops! And the way they smell is exciting, like the smell of train smoke! It makes me feel that I'm going somewhere. 'Want a hansom, hansom, hansom?' " he heard her voice mimicking as the cab door banged upon the two.

Suddenly an idea, born of their change of plan, halted the young man stock-still upon the pavement. After all, they were not being whirled from his sight at taxicab speed; they were jolting sluggishly off. . . . He plunged a hand into a pocket, rummaged, drew forth a half-dollar, a quarter, a dime. That was all.

One cab still remained. Its driver, a solemnly impressive person, met his questioning eye.

"Fatherly by nature, and an ex-professor of—well, say classical literature, to judge by appearances. Therefore he should comprehend the finer feelings." The young man beckoned.

"This is at present my entire fortune," he informed the impressive person, displaying his few coins. "What would you advise me to do: keep it that I may lunch to-day, or employ you to follow the cab containing those ladies? It would be your gamble—you might drive ten blocks or ten miles for the sum."

Only an instant did the impressive person reflect; then he lived up, and fully, to the judgment formed of him.

"If it comes to a choice between lunch and a lady, sir, and I'm asked to give my advice on the point at issue, would state—" the cabman paused to make sure, and gathered that he was to continue— "that there's something—something about a lady, sir, that you'll remember when even the most superb menu has long faded into oblivion." And he held open his cab door.

The young man plaited his lean length within the cab.

"The main difference between him and me lies in our direction," he observed. "On the road toward Better Days I meet him coming away. We hail in passing—exchange a few coins for a ride and a bit of philosophy, and clink invisible glasses to the Eternal Feminine."

Then he sat up abruptly. Again that surprising tension occurred, as of the swaying hammock suddenly jerked taut. For the cab ahead, which had never once escaped the corner of his eye, had given an unexpected lunge into the seething traffic, and was disappearing.

He leaned forward, tense, sharp. "Follow! If it means a smash-up!"

IV

With a crack of his whip the impressive person plunged into the crowd, following like a sheriff in the wake of a murderer, and now the chase became desperate. Through congested blocks it led, around swift corners, wending, zigzagging. Now the cab ahead would vanish utterly, now it would flash into sight, only to be snatched again into a new vortex. At Thirty-Fourth Street it crossed; as its pursuer was about to do the same, a blockade of delayed trolley-cars pressed forward, halting all traffic.

"Make it!" cried the young man, and he was on the verge of leaping to the seat and snatching the lines himself.

"I will, sir—trust me!" came back to him, like the voice of omnipotence. And as a small opening formed itself between two of the cars, the impressive person drove straight into it, despite the shouts and wavings of a policeman—wedged his vehicle in, wormed it through, extricated it, and was at the chase again, lashing like a chariot racer.

In a cross-street a few blocks further north, and near Fifth Avenue, two ladies were seen descending from their cab. They entered a hotel, and bags followed.

The young man's tension scattered as quickly as it had gathered. "Thank fortune!" he sighed, in a long breath of relief. "Saved! And I might have lost them forever!"

He unplaited himself with luxurious slowness from the cab's confinement, and once more the garment of imperturbability fell over his shoulders.

"Bravo!" he praised the charioteer. "My paltry coins are poor reward for your heroic effort. But such as they are—" and he proffered them.

Then occurred one of the most amazing incidents recorded in the history of the Metropolis. For the impressive person, bowing, refused the coins.

"It has been my privilege to assist in an affair of the heart, sir," said he. "And I would state that this fact alone is sufficient recompense." With which expression of sentiment he drove off so promptly that the young man had no opportunity to insist, but was left dumfounded at the curb, his money gaping back at him from his extended palm.

"It's incredible. It's an hallucination," he muttered. "A New York cabman!" Still dumfounded, he turned and went slowly on. "Is it, I wonder," he questioned the unseen powers, "a day when the earth rocks and the heavens fall?" He shook a pondering head and strolled on past the hotel.

The whereabouts of the two was established. No need for haste now. In fact, discretion advised delay.

He wandered off toward Fifth Avenue, strolled aimlessly, conversed with his thoughts. "A bit of a caprice, this pursuit of mine," he reassured them, blandly. "I'm a whimsical chap, you know, and there's no accounting for my impulses." In fact, he strove earnestly to give his challenging thoughts the impression that he might do this sort of thing any day.

It was two o'clock before he realised that food might be refreshing and that he still had the price of it. "A shame to lunch at the Professor-of-Literature's expense," he thought, "but I didn't even get his number. So here goes!"

He sought a *table d'hôte* and lunched at his leisure, with that enjoyable dallying that denotes assurance. He set down an empty coffee cup at last, and lighted a cigarette. Yes; it would be safe by now to proceed with his "whim." Smoking and sauntering, he approached the hotel.

Carefully he ran his eye down the arrivals of that date.

A man and large family, two married couples, three lone men, one lone woman—no other names.

"But," he protested, staring at the clerk, "two ladies arrived this morning——"

He scanned the page again.

"Yes, but they didn't stop. They found a message from a friend, and they left for her home."

That was all. No name recalled, no address left. . . .

So vivid had been the young man's visualisation of another meeting that this unforseen whirl of chance left him confounded. Slowly he turned away, and walked heavily back to the Avenue.

Absurd, he told his thoughts—the mere bubble-burst of a ridiculous boyish whim.

Yes, absurd.

He repeated this adjective at brief intervals for several minutes, emphasising it from time to time by such adverbs as "utterly," "supremely," "preposterously," "consummately," "assininely." In fact, there were no words properly to express the absurdity of the whole situation.

What had he expected to do, anyway? he demanded of his absurd self. To rush in upon two ladies with whom luck had scraped for him a transient acquaintance, and greet them like a long-lost brother? He had pursued them as if life depended on the pursuit, had waited in anticipation of a meeting which would probably have won for him a pair of cool nods. . . .

He continued, unknowing, to walk on and on up the Avenue.

Absurd, chimed his brain, absurd, absurd, absurd!

And still as he continued to wander, there persisted before him a picture; it rose determinedly between his eyes and the mere physical objects that confronted them. The picture was disorderly in its parts, like some disturbing dream in which one thing slips into another, all a jumble of photographs imposed upon one plate, but from the jumble two figures emerged.

There was the woman, who made one think of a cynical, handsome, cocksure blackbird, and who would not be easy to disobey.

And there was the girl. At the prow of the old brown ferryboat he saw her: a slender figure, all light and tingle like the morning . . . pressing forward, too, like the morning . . . yes, in such a hurry, such a desperate hurry was the girl. Again he saw the skyscrapers frown-

ing down formidably, challenging approach; beyond and
amove their sternness shone again that wonderful iridescent glory, the splendor of the new day.   And again
that tense whisper like a prayer, uttered to what gods
he could not guess:

"Oh, I'm in such a hurry—such a hurry—to live!"

CHAPTER II

CALIFORNIA DAYS

I

A BRITTLE winter sunlight glittered in at the afternoon windows of a small uptown apartment, and met its spirit of bright vigor halfway. It discovered one occupant poised on the top of a step-ladder and tweaking a picture's wire; the other standing below, her head cocked, her long fingers pressed downward against her long hips, in an attitude of critical observation.

"Down on the right——there——no, that's too much, Bec. I can't see through you, child! Duck!"

Bec crouched upon the step, protesting, nevertheless.

"You're so particular, Helen darling! What if it is just a teeny, weeny crooked——"

She sprang upright again, and fluttered by some miraculous movement to the floor—a movement that seemed to spurn descent by steps—and alighted like a wide-winged butterfly.

"I'm too happy to care whether a picture is straight or crooked! What does it matter?" Her arm encircled the other's waist, and she whirled. "Helen dearest, isn't the whole apartment simply *wonderful*? Don't let's work any more to-day—let's just gloat!"

The other laughed in her indulgent way. "Which means, 'I'll run away and play, and somehow the work will do itself'." Again that odd mixture of cynical insight and fatuous doting noted once by a young man on a ferry-boat. "All right—run along. Anna will help me."

"But I didn't mean to crawl out! I'll stay, dear—truly I will!" Penitence inspired a violent embrace.

"No—go for your walk, before dark. And to tell the truth, I think I may get on more expeditiously with Anna." Helen drove the girl off—much like driving a capricious butterfly, the task was; as when a winged creature dashes here, there, everywhere except out the door that you hold open, and returns to hover, and flutters in your face till you are distracted, and then of a sudden darts straight out where it might have escaped in the first place, and with one brightly vanishing wave of its wings is gone beyond recall.

Helen turned back to the task of "settling." The rugs were down, the furniture in place, some pictures hung. A precious table of teakwood gleamed ruddy-black; a few other good Oriental bits brought from California, such as an antique Satsuma bowl, a rare old Japanese charcoal-burner, stood about. The atmosphere of good taste and charm was even now making itself felt in the little living-room and the adjoining dining-room. But many books still lay wrapped while empty shelves awaited them; and yards of yellow drapery stuff still lay uncut into cur-tains. Helen lazily passed it through her fingers. Its very touch was exquisite.

"It will keep me poor for weeks," she reflected, with

satisfaction. And still she caressed the curtain-stuff, and still she did not summon Anna from the kitchen.

She crossed the room and stood looking down into the street. Bec emerged from the building, craned her neck toward this high window, saw, waved her grey squirrel muff. Helen watched her winging on toward the riverside until she was out of sight.

Already the short winter day was waning indoors. Out there it burnished the river to copper, it flamed behind skeleton trees, throwing them into sharp relief; it cast a strange glamour over the bleak wheels and chutes of a summer playground atop the Palisades, turning these forsaken toys to mirage-like spires and domes. Even a stern battleship took on a moment's brilliancy.

Helen watched the copper lustre dull slowly. The mirage faded. The river dimmed from copper to grey, and a sombre light supplanted the brief ruddiness behind the winter trees.

II

Helen had turned from the window. Although the outer world was still lighted after a glimmery fashion, the room was now shadowy with dusk. She glanced at the work awaiting her; but she did not take it up. From the kitchen came the faint, insect hum of Russian Anna; from the avenue a block away rose the dim, sea-like roar of home-going vehicles. Here around her, stillness brooded. She was in a nest of stillness. She lighted a cigarette.

She leaned back in a deep chair. Her crossed knees

revealed trim stockings and smart pumps.   The sleek
tailoring of a plain black gown encased her as his plum-
age encases the slender blackbird.   All this the young
man of the ferryboat would no doubt have observed, had
he been present.   But he was not present.   Helen Kent
was alone—agreeably alone, with a genial cigarette's glow
for company.   Now and then she uncrossed and recrossed
her knees, turn and turn about, in such manner as her
own mother, that fastidious lady of an earlier generation,
would have deemed deplorable.   She blew reflective rings,
and leaned back still more deeply, and tapped off an ash
into the little brass tray at her elbow.   A love for finish,
for the order that is beauty, made her as fastidious concerning her ashes or a picture wire as she was concerning
her dress.

Soon it would be time for Bec—the girl would come in
like a sun scattering mists.   How she was plunging into
this new world, delighting in its novelty!   To be sure, she
frankly disliked the school where Helen had placed her;
but "you shut your eyes and swallow it quick and it's
over," she philosophised.   Neither the detested studies nor
a strange metropolis could squelch this splendid Cali-
fornia-born-and-bred young pagan.   As well try to squelch
a mountain brook, or a humming-bird, or a sea wind,
or a firefly.   The creature simply wouldn't squelch. . . .

Good heavens, how she loved the child! suddenly struck
across Helen's mind, and the realisation came like a blow,
as if it were a new thought.   Those who love are subject
to these sudden realisations and know the sharp pain they
bring—the sense that some vague but dreadful portent
lurks behind them.

It wasn't as if there had been anybody else, anybody in the world, Helen mused. All her eggs were in one basket. . . .

There rose, in that shadowy room, a picture that often rose—of a yellow-haired little girl picking up ripe apricots under the trees, and holding their downy copper cheeks to her own to feel how warm they were from lying in the sun, before she plunged her small white teeth into them. Somehow ripe apricots and sunshine and Bec's babyhood seemed inextricably tangled in her memory. Perhaps because all that period had been so hotly branded that its least detail was more vivid than yesterday's happenings. It covered her earlier years of California life. . . .

III

Helen herself was but an adopted daughter of the Golden State. In fact, she had never known any home except New York until a short time before her marriage. Her childhood had been stamped as unique by a doubt of God and a love for pickled olives—a natural love, in itself as unnatural as the doubt is supposed to be in one reared in a proper atmosphere of church-going. She was the product of a moderately prosperous lawyer's family of the old-fashioned type, of a long-established church, of precocious and omnivorous reading, of an inclination to do more thinking on her own account than was comfortable for family traditions, and of the most disagreeable but most stimulating climate on

earth.   Being what she was, at seventeen Helen Clifton
went to visit cousins in California.

She was ready for college and determined to enter,
but resistance was strong in the family circle.   College
girls always became so "strong-minded," her parents
contended, in the language and prejudice of conservatives
of that day.   But a way now presented itself.   A great
university had flung open its doors in the West, to young
men and women alike. . . .   Somehow the thing was
managed.   A doctor made the fortunate error of finding
something the matter with her—California climate was
prescribed—the cousins begged that she live with them,
near the university—reluctant family consent was the
upshot.

So it came about that Helen Clifton was a college girl
of the end of the nineteenth century.   It was a crucial
period, and girlhood was at a crucial point.

Here in America three factions of thought were entering into controversy: one representing those who, as the
phrase went, "clung to religion"; those who were all for
"science," and those who caused much head-shaking
among the first, much sleeve-smiling among the second,
by "trying to reconcile science and religion."   It all looks
pitiful and rather funny to-day in retrospect, even though
barely a quarter-century has elapsed to produce our
vantage-point, as we recall this tortured effort to "reconcile" elements that in their fundamentals at least have
been one since the dawn of eternity, and that only man in
his queer perverseness could ever have contrived to separate in appearance. . . .   And this young university,
free from the traditions that moored older institutions,

was plunging courageously into the new current of scientific explanation, letting who would follow.

There was no urging whatsoever. The young craft that preferred quiet harbours where their forbears had lain peacefully at anchor, found such harbours provided. They could attend chapel; they could join religious associations; there were frequent opportunities to praise in lusty chorus the promised joys of "Beulah Land, My Beulah Land," and to proclaim satisfaction in "How Firm a Foundation, Ye Saints of the Lord." They could rest undisturbed by such problems as "origin of species" or "inheritance of acquired character." But the more daring young barks, tugging at their moorings, found a certain small faculty group leading quietly and steadfastly on into the perturbed waters of biology and evolution. Those that tugged hard enough broke at last and followed. Helen Clifton, entering early maturity at a period when both religious thought and femininity were growing restive, was prompt to join them.

She had been born with scepticism peeping forth from under the lids that were like tent-flaps, tilted far downward at the outer corners of her bright dark eyes. She had always looked as if she didn't quite credit anything, even in her cradle—had examined her teething-ring critically before she would put it into her mouth. The scepticism had grown more sure of itself, had occasionally asserted itself strongly, as her lower teeth—firm, white, regular, charming teeth they were, too—had gradually established their position slightly but fixedly in advance of the upper row. This and other irregularities in no way spoiled the well-cut lines of the alert face; they only individualized it the more.

For all her scepticism, she had drifted on, while at home, in the old New York church where the Cliftons had engaged the first pew set up generations ago. In this pew representatives of the family had sat on fifty-two Sabbaths of every year since. Helen was wont to sit at attention until the sermon began, when she would settle back with a comfortable sigh and proceed to "plan clothes." Just why the sermon hour should be so productive of fashion dreams among young females has never been explained, but every woman knows it to be so. Probably the roving glance, alighting on so many "Sunday bests," brings stimulus to the inventive mind. At any rate it is a fact that the number of gowns and hats designed between text and "finally," would fill innumerable fashion books and leave innumerable zealous pastors amazed, indignant; perhaps, occasionally, self-searching.

Helen approached her college years with an open mind. More open, by far, than anybody suspected. The family had heard her affirm once of the stately pastor that "Dr. Mouser was an awful old bore," and although they saw to it that the statement was never repeated, they were quite conscious that her opinion had not changed. But that she was secretly conceiving of certain orthodox tenets as "howlingly funny," they never dreamed.

Her young, vivid, incisive, scornful intellect was racing on, breathing with gusto in an atmosphere where old-school orthodoxy panted and wheezed. But the lean hand of tradition was raised in warning, and she saw it over her shoulder. It bothered her now and then. It would shake a finger at her.

The warning hand was driven off at last. "At least science can do one thing for the young mind: it can brush away cobwebs, and give it a clean room to furnish afresh," one of the vigorous new-trend professors of the western university was wont to say. It took this vacuum-cleaning process less than one semester to leave Helen Clifton's mind as scoured of creed-remnants as an empty room of litter, and herself ready to arrange whatever furniture she could find according to her liking. The aged hand nevermore cast its shadow.

And, turning to look about, she found such furniture as she had never seen, avid reader though she had been. Wonderful! Darwin, Wallace, Huxley, Spenser—and the Germans, those wielders of terrible might in thought, that *schrecklickheit* of the brain — Schopenhauer, Haeckel, Nietzsche! The brutal pessimism of these, a certain fearless facing of so-called "truths," laid hold upon her formative mind. As yet neither she nor the world guessed the hideous portent that lay behind the fallacies of their doctrine. She seized upon her new-found authors at random, read them late at night as another girl might have read French novels, with her flame-colored negligee falling apart over a lace petticoat and a box of chocolates at her elbow. She plunged into the laboratory, avowed herself a believer in nothing that could not be demonstrated therein, and revelled maliciously in the electric shocks she gave her roommate, who was a member of the Epworth League, and who always hummed, depressingly,

"Work, for the night is coming,
. . . When man's work is o'er."

while doing her hair in the morning.

"I think it's dreadful," the roommate said. "When our President sits up on the platform during prayers in chapel, he doesn't even shut his eyes. He sits there and looks all around, and doesn't listen to a word!"

The disconcerting Helen inquired:

"How do you know?"

The roommate stammered, and broke a celluloid hairpin. "Well, I just opened my eyes once, to see where the draught came from, and I—I happened—to notice——"

Already Helen had formed the habit of watching Prexy's roving eyes during prayers. The reason she sat through them herself every Sunday was her curiosity concerning various creeds—now a Bishop of High Church formalities would preach; then a staid Presbyterian; next some famous revivalist of the shoulder-slap type; once a rabbi, and even a Vedantic teacher. This fearless, clear-seeing young university made a practice of giving its students a chance to hear all and judge all—no sealed orders here. The atheistic Helen revelled in this opportunity to compare all "the funny things people believed." The morning that she entered its broad-minded chapel to listen to the Swami, with his head swathed to a white ball, his silken robe trailing, she realized that, by Atlantic time, her family were already arising from a roast chicken dinner, blessed before and after, recuperating from one Sunday service and preparing for two more. Heaven alone could have sustained them had they seen her now!

Such ideas as these became her daily diet:

"There is no such person as God. Ridiculous! A man with a long white beard! Like Santa Claus! I know now that I never really believed all that, only I hadn't brushed out the cobwebs, and I didn't quite know what I did believe. There's nothing but cold-blooded Law. In the long run it makes for survival of the fittest, and that's fair. Our business is to be the fittest if we want to pull through."

Again, "Aren't people funny that they pray? What do they think they pray to, I wonder? How can you pray to Law? You might as well pray to a great mechanism, like an engine, to stop, or run the other way, when it's been adjusted and set going. It's silly! There couldn't be a 'special dispensation' for one little individual. It would upset all the machinery."

Helen's conception of truth would often have surprised these doctors of science and philosophy, for its pessimism was her own. The natural scepticism, which had been part and parcel of her temperament from teething-ring days, seized with instinctive relish upon the idea of chopping up old creeds for kindling-wood. Unfortunately, she missed her teachers' vital point: namely, that this kindling-wood was capable of creating a new fire, warmer and more wondrous than any fire of yore. Her professors were not to blame if she perverted their teachings into destructive rather than constructive belief. It was a matter of temperament. The contents of her kit, which she was packing for use later on, were, in brief: a firm conviction of no merciful God; an assurance of dust-to-dust and only dust-to-dust; a scorn for prayer as "silly"—like kneeling and asking for presents from a stone wall; and a cock-sureness that man is but a body containing a highly complex system of cerebration which he absurdly flatters by calling it a "soul."

It was with such a mental background that she entered matrimony.

IV

It may be imagined that she entered it by some scientific path, finding it to be economically expedient or eugenically valuable to the race. Indeed no. Neither economics nor eugenics concerned her one whit. Romantically, rapturously, Helen Clifton fell in love. When Vernon Kent came her way she plunged headfirst in love with him, within twenty-four hours after he had taken the initiative by plunging in love with her. It seemed as if the same intensity with which she had entered into philosophical controversy now turned itself into the channel of her passion. There was that wonderful rush that we see only now and then in a workaday world—the rush of wide-winged youth flying to the meeting. Helen had lately passed her eighteenth birthday, and it was spring in California.

Spring, in the valley where this university lies, comes shyly up in February, holds out a nosegay of buttercups, pleading softly to be admitted, coaxes with caressing winds, and by March gains assurance and enters high-handedly to the golden blare of poppies. There were weeks . . . Helen would be picking pale cream-cups while Vernon lolled in their midst, or strolling beside him across fields of poppies, the stems parting in supple avoidance back from her skirts. There were glittering blue skies, as vivid, as intensely blue as a cloissonné bowl; tumbled clouds which piled in from sea over the mountain range like rollicking fat boys, pushing each other, shoving for room, by and by romping off in rowdyish chase. Spring, youth, love, California—these combine in the headiest mixture that can be distilled in this land of ours— in the world, indeed, with the possible exception of Italy and certain parts of North Africa.

From the first it all moved with that rush which had marked the meeting. Young Kent, a San Francisco chap, was spending a few days at the university when he met Helen at a "frat-house" dance. Those were the days of waltz and two-step; she was accomplished in both, but Vernon thought he had never seen anything to beat the way she two-stepped to a Sousa march—that trimmed-close way about her—figure, movement, face, utterance— she snapped, like a long, graceful lash. Simply, he *had* to meet her and get a chance to do it with her. Just watching her made him feel as if he were marching to the whip of music. She wore some sheer black gown that night—the sleeves and skirt were crisply distended after the fashion of the nineties—and there were flecks of flame-color, as if her throat and breast had caught fire. And the way she put a foot out, long and pointed in its slim black slipper (that was the day when shoes were worn two or three sizes too long, in AA width, and the toes stuffed with cotton)—it was that curved, deliberate, fastidious movement with which a tall bird steps forward.

By the end of that first two-step together it was all up with young Kent. He had to marry the girl, that was all about it. He had never failed to get anything he wanted in his twenty-one years, and he wasn't going to begin by missing the most desirable thing yet. He had been born with a silver spoon in his beautifully cut, smiling, occasionally petulant mouth. He had laughed his way through life with those rollicking blue eyes that drew everything to him; he had played tennis and danced and yachted—how the girls always fell prostrate before him in his white yachting togs, with those blaze-blue eyes of his and that crop of yellow curls above the manly tan of a skin far darker than the hair, which *would* stay blond as a boy's! It had all been so easy for Vernon Kent. Things that were not easy he had dodged—college, for instance. And this new matter was being made easy for him, too—all there was to it was to fall in love with the girl, run down every few days to see her, tell her you'd got to marry her or die in the attempt—and then, he assured himself, do it.

There was not a reservation in her love. As if with wide-flung arms she received his, giving way utterly to the rapture of it all. There was that in her fibre, which would not let her feign coyness, half escape, vacillate between fleeing and yielding, play fast and loose. She was too proud for such pretense; it would have been "silly." She loved him with every bit of herself, she dreamed of him day and night during every hour that she was not with him, she could feel his kiss like fire on her lips for days after they had parted—why feign, indeed!

The very fervour of her passion increased his. Hers was not the love to cloy a man; rather, to madden him on with

its own leaping flame. He grew distracted until he could
arrange for the marriage. The distant family had to be
won over, Helen said; so he began, with a facility which
in later years bore more significance for her than she had
then comprehended, by winning over Helen's California
cousins. Enraptured, they wrote her parents that this
was the match of a lifetime—excellent family, money,
simply delightful fellow, and *promising!* Although what
he promised they did not explain. They said among
themselves that he had never *done* anything as yet, but
he was so young, and even if they *had* heard he'd been a
little wild, what was the use of writing that? Marriage
would settle him down.

But the New York family closed its mouth like a purse-
snap and made austere remarks about "youth," "folly,"
and "not knowing one's mind." Wherefore, to prove that
they did know their mind, youth and folly, aged eighteen
and twenty-one, got married anyway, and did without the
distant family's consent. The marriage took place in
early summer; so there was no pause in this miracle-year
of Helen's, when her first California spring and her first
love had come up the valley hand in hand, and were leading on, through weeks snowed under by cherry-blooms;
more weeks, lying heavy with roses; into the summer of
darkly gleaming mystery that hung now like a midnight
sky.

The only explanation of a nature as sceptical as Helen
Clifton's accepting love with such complete abandonment,
lies in the paradox that there is no one as credulous as
the doubter when once he gives way to belief.

V

Dreaming weeks followed the wedding—weeks that drugged the senses, steeping them in the perfume of southern gardens, the seductive plashing of southern waters, the sapphire-black velvet of night skies, the warmth of silky sands on a lissome beach, the rustle of palms on a moon-frosted air. They drifted from Santa Barbara to San Diego, loafing at every point of beauty between. Helen bore from all this associations never to be broken— for instance, the dull scent that petunias give off in a hot sun was ever to bring back to her the pacing of Padres at Santa Barbara. Orange blossoms called up for her not a wedding—she hadn't worn them—but a certain walk through a grove where the heavily perfumed flowers and the fruit, like lighted lanterns glowing in dark foliage, hung side by side. It was in that walk that Vernon gave way to a burst of confidence. He said:

"I've been a bit of a devil with women. I'd rather you knew. Seems squarer. But that's over, Helen mine. Good and over. It's one woman now and ever after, you'd better believe."

She did believe. In fact, she almost ignored his confession. It seemed not to penetrate the trance in which she was wrapped. Afterward she remembered it, and the oppressive sweetness of orange blossoms was ironically bound up with the memory forever.

Long after time had erased all sense of other contacts—his arm around her, the warm clasp of his hand, his kiss on eyes and lips, his man's cheek that felt so hard against her own—years after these sensations had crumbled to dust, she was still to remember the feeling of his absurd, irresistible blond curls—her hand pushing them back, her long fingers tangled in them. . . . Nights upon nights, it seemed in memory, æons of nights, eternal nights. . . . If the baby, little Bec, hadn't had exactly the same tumble of gold atop her head—more spun-silky in texture, of course, more gleaming, but as nearly the same as a tiny girl's and a big man's could possibly be—Helen might have forgotten that contact along with the others. But Bec's hair kept his alive. Even now Helen was sometimes startled by that sensation of her hands stroking and weaving through his curly tangle. With it always came the dull banging of surf beyond a window, the scratch and rustle of palm leaves like giant fans in silhouette, the gulping blackness of shadows that swallowed swords of moonlight. . . . Such had been the nights. . . .

The week following that walk and talk, up turned one of the women with whom he had been a bit of a devil.

VI

Even yet Helen did not stir in her trance. From her hotel window one day she saw him talking with a dressy person (green and white plaid silk frock, the person wore, and hyper-golden hair) on the palm walk, where he had gone to wait while Helen dressed. When she came down he was alone. She asked him lightly who the dressy person might be. He hesitated. Then he chose frankness.

"I used to see something of her in San Francisco. But I shook her. I can't help it, Helen, that she happens to be here, and trapped me into speaking to her, but for heaven's sake don't imagine——"

"Dearest, I don't imagine anything."   She laughed carelessly; so utterly had she surrendered to faith! "Come on to the tennis court."

It lasted a year. A year seems, for some obscure psychological or astrological reason, to be about the average time allotted to illusions. Helen's went with a crash that was cataclysmic, when her husband returned at five one morning. He had been growing more and more irregular, but her belief in Vernon's excuses had been as stubborn as her disbelief in God's acts.

Hearing a cab at their San Francisco door, she looked out to discover a helplessly intoxicated husband being assisted out by the driver, while a hazy female voice back in the cab gave directions.

"Tha's right—hoisht him up shteps—can get in hi'self. I'd help, but daresn't show my fair face. Tha's th-ticket —buck up, old boy, there—there y'are! See you t-morrow night."

It was the end. Where another type of woman would have scolded and whimpered and pleaded and kissed and forgiven and begun all over again, until a fresh outbreak, Helen did none of these things. She didn't shed a tear. She didn't say a word. She went down and helped Vernon to the library couch in dead silence, covered him with an afghan, and left him; then went back to her own room and walked the floor the rest of the night, as white as her nightdress, her lips drawn to a hard drab line, her eyes burning.

The earth had caved under her feet. Such a thing as

half-belief, that sop of diluted credulity which a weaker woman holds out to her thirsting infatuation, was impossible to Helen. It must be all or nothing. She had believed utterly—wreck on the track ahead had delayed his train, he had said once—again, she mustn't expect him the following night—he had to run down to Burlinghame to see about that piece of land he was buying for their country house—and so on. And now she credited not a word he uttered.

The country home never came to pass. By the end of another married year, when the baby was six months old, the break came outright. He had "braced up," as he expressed it, over and over, but the bracings didn't last. Vernon Kent had never had a fair chance in life, as a matter of fact—he had never been given a start by poverty or injustice or cramped environment or lack of love. And yet he did try.

"There's something good in me after all," he said once, with unconscious pathos, after one of his repeated slips into debauch. "Save it, Helen!"

"How?" she scoffed.

"By believing in me."

"Believing! What can I see to believe in?"

"That's just it. In this world you've got to keep on believing in what you don't see. It's the believing makes it come true."

Probably he himself was not fully aware of the mystic depths lying beneath his own words; and to Helen they were sheer madness. And madder still she now saw the emotion that had bound her senses for that period of belief in love. During it, she had admitted no evidence against him. But from the hour of waking, she had been herself, her full self again—scoffer at illusion and delusion, steeled sceptic. The glamour of belief had parted like a mist. She saw—clearly, at last, she said.

"Now I am as hard as nails!" she told herself, with a queer sort of bitter exultation. "I know all that life is, all that men are, all that love is not."

Love, indeed, she paused to contemplate.

"Romantic love and God! They're the two prime self-delusions of this world's fools. If there were such a thing as love, real love, this would have happened, wouldn't it?" she sneered to invisible listeners. "And as for a 'loving God'—what he loves, apparently, just now, is watching me writhe!"

Helen Kent had reverted completely; she was once more the caustic disbeliever. And here was disbelief with the addition of a new immeasurable bitterness. The brief period during which she had been swept away by a force more potent than any other force in all living creation was over. Along with God and the orthodox tenets she now sent Love crashing down from the pedestal—that Love which poets have immortalized and mortals died to win.

A crisis of debauch, involving drink, gambling, and the hyper-blond person, brought even the ostensible union to an end. Helen took her baby and left Vernon. A lawyer urged her to sue for divorce, but she scorned the idea.

"What for? Only to throw tidbits of gossip to the harpies. We couldn't be any more divorced than we are. As for alimony, I wouldn't touch a dollar of his!"

"But for your child's sake——"

"I'll fight for my child, and I'll win, too! And with no help from him. She's mine. He's forfeited all right to her. She and I will fight it out together."

Vernon Kent entered no claim and left the two undisturbed. He might have been dead for all he meant to either wife or child.

The death of Helen's father and mother had given her, the only heir, a small income—very small, for the family property had turned out to be in a desiccated condition —but by careful management she contrived to make out until the baby was old enough to be left for awhile each day in another's care while she went forth as bread-winner. She had taken a pretty cottage near her university, and at first she coached a bit, but her mind was riveted upon the business world. Business! That was to be her life. The ambition grew into an obsession. Business meant money.

The relatives to whom she wrote of this intention raised horrified hands. Helen could see the hands as she read the letters with a grim smile. Business! they cried in shocked clamour. A lady—one of the Cliftons! In business! Could she not find a ladylike way in which to support herself and child?—fine embroidery, or china painting, or teaching, or even taking a few paying guests? But a *business* woman! Really, the Clifton traditions must be considered!

Helen's smile passed from grim to sardonic, and she consigned the Clifton traditions to a climate more tropical than that of California. "Time one of us smashed 'em," she observed. "I'm going into business because business makes money. It's money I'm going to have—for myself and my child. Money, not illusions, will bring her happiness—nothing else will." And she set her teeth like steel.

And meanwhile—in the wonder-world where sweet-peas grew higher than a big man's head, where geraniums and fuchsias clambered to the porch roof, where rose-vines choked the windows and had to be cut away like weeds, where fruit trees pelted you with great red and purple plums, coral cherries, golden peaches, coppery apricots—little Bec grew, and turned into big Bec.

VII

She grew like everything else in California. She leaped toward the sun; ran with the wind flowing back from her like a garment. Life springs, rushes here; need not crawl and struggle and strain into being. The wand touches, and there it is. There was Bec.

She had been named for Helen's mother, Rebecca Clifton, and in the days of blind bliss it had been agreed by Vernon and Helen that the little girl (they were bound it was to be a girl!) should not be weighted by anything as suggestive of Puritanism as the English form of this name. In the South they had been charmed by a lady of Castilian lineage bearing its Spanish form—Rebequita.

"A perfect compromise!" Helen had cried when the Castilian lady's name occurred to them. "We'll make our child the California granddaughter of my puritanical mother—Rebéca—Rebequita. Sounds a trifle shocking, like a wicked eye peeping through a fan and a dagger in the dark. Poor Mudder—wonder what she'll say?"

And so this gold and rose creature bloomed under a

name as black-eyed and fire-brandish as old Spanish California. She grew to laugh at the joke of it, but Rebequita she remained. Helen tousled the name about—Rebéca to-day, Bequita to-morrow, always, to everyone, little Bec.

She rushed on, from babyhood to childhood, to girlhood, growing tall and strong and always lithe, always imbued with that instinctive grace of movement which made dancing in her a natural form of expression. She danced her feelings, her thoughts, as some children tell them to their dolls, as others sing them. Some called her beautiful, others disagreed; certainly the face fell far short of perfection; but her remarkable grace no one denied. Indeed, Helen often thought that the one thing she embodied was motion; she was never still, always hastening on, flying forward, swaying about, the pliant body seeming one with the eager mind. She darted, like light; she quivered, like water; she swayed, like trees; she floated, like clouds; she ran, like wind. There was a strange underlying truth in all these comparisons, profounder, infinitely profounder than the mere pretty poesy of them. In some almost mystic way this young life seemed a part, the very offspring of elemental forces, of the great free womb of California. Helen Kent watched it, with a love that was feline in its pride and its fierce protectiveness. And, watching it, she formulated her resolve.

"She's to have the best there is for a girl, if I have to hold up Life and take it for her at the muzzle of a revolver. She's to have clothes, and fun, and luxuries, and beaux, and money to play with, and *no man* in her life to wreck it. Oh, it's a pretty enough little game, is living, once you get the hang of it, and know it to be just that and nothing more. Trouble begins when you start chasing illusions. Men are all very well in business relations and friendship; but no love-nonsense, no marriage, no illusions of any kind for Bequita."

It was the regimen that was to control her child's mental and moral diet; that regimen being the outcome of innate scepticism augmented by years of brooding over her own life's disappointment. In her embitterment, Helen Kent was reasoning from the particular to the general; because love had failed her, therefore love was a failure. Unchecked, her morbid outlook upon this phase of life had grown with the years; it had become an obsession, distorting her vision, dominating her doctrines. Masterful by nature, she set out from the first to implant her abnormal views, like strange poisonous growths in the child mind.

Bec was taught, therefore, all about that gigantic fraud called love. Thus, armed to the teeth with warnings, she remained fancy-free. She laughed at her lovers —at Robert, most of all, when he recited to her the beginning of his poem:

> "How fair thy golden locks do shine,
>   Like snares to lure me on.
> How ruby are thy lips like wine
>   My eyes do feast upon."

"I didn't mean anything—anything familiar about your lips, Rebequita," he explained, crimson. "Of course I—I wouldn't think of—of—unless you let me. And of course our family are strictly temperance, anyway." He was overwhelmed with embarrassment at this juncture. "Only it's so hard to find rhymes!" he admitted. "I'm hunting

now for one for 'Bequita,' and all I can find is 'mosquito.'
I'm afraid it'll have to do. I'll recite the rest to you
when it's done."

Bec shouted in heartless glee, and told Helen. And
the others—Tomas, that scion of an old Castilian family;
good, honest Stephen, a man at twenty, who loved her
too deeply to be quite laughed at; jolly Dennis Ellery,
and Van Payne—"Fudge!" was her brief summary of
their emotions. She was completely frank about them all,
and obviously untouched. Helen nestled in her own secret
security.

As for the other fraud—that preposterous Santa Claus
called "God"—Bec had been taught from the beginning
the absurdity of that delusion. She grew up looking
upon church-goers as a bigger child looks upon those
who still listen for reindeer bells, chuckling gleefully at
their "funny ideas." And was evidence lacking to con-
firm this atheism? For Bec had been only a child when
told in full of her mother's experiences.

She thought of her father with horror, as the creature
who once had made her darling Helen so frightfully unhappy.

"But, dearest, I'm here now!" she would cry with an
enfolding rush.

"Yes, you're here, and I've weathered it. But my
daughter shan't go through what I did! Never! When
some handsome loafer comes along and swears that you
are the one star in his heaven, you'll inform him that
the stars are not to be plucked. Think of it, Bec!" She
would break off from her cynical lightness to drive home

facts. "The man who swore undying love for me lay
in a drunken heap before me a year after our marriage,
while the woman—also drunk—with whom he had spent
the night drove away from my door to await the next
night's meeting!"

So she stripped the canvas of its last veil, and left the
picture naked for young eyes to see. It was an ugly
picture. Bec would shudder. And Helen would point
out baldly every detail. For the girl's own sake, there
must be no sparing her knowledge. She was to know life;
was to visualize it at its bitterest; was to be on her guard
for every pitfall.

When Bec was fifteen, she read a newspaper item to the
effect that Vernon C. R. Kent, formerly of San Francisco,
had been killed in a drunken fight with an Indian in north-
ern Idaho.

She carried it to her mother. To her surprise, Helen
went white, and the paper rustled with the quiver of her
hand.

"Look at *that!*" In steely detachment Helen indicated
her hand. "Nerves. They never get over such experiences. More fools they." The last bond was severed,
then. In due time Helen received notice of the death from
Vernon's relatives, with the not surprising statement that
he had died penniless.

Helen was now a trim commuter, going to business in
San Francisco each day, earning a good salary in a responsible secretarial position, and she had long been seeing farther. When Bec was eighteen, she laid definite
plans for moving to New York.

"It's a broader world there. It's the best our country offers. The body grows out here—but your body had better not grow any more," she laughed. "The East offers an intensive training one can't get here. The East is to the West what Europe is to America. There's a sharper edge put on the tool, a finer tempering."

Helen herself had never lost that finer tempering, had always been recognized as an "Easterner". And it glinted, in a way, too, through Bec's more abounding physicalness—by heritage, perhaps, or by home contact.

"What are we going to do in New York?" Bec asked one day.

"Do, child? Have fun, of course. Which involves getting rich. That's what counts. I'm going into business of some sort. Big business. I've outgrown this work in San Francisco. My brain is an uncommonly able organ." Helen was as detached in regarding her brain as if passing on the merits of an employé. "I shall establish myself, and later on draw you in with me. You'll have to begin by learning the drudgery of office life as a man does—thorough grounding. I shall put you in a first-class private business school. That will bore you, but it won't last long. And then you can start with me on your life work."

Bec's eyes wandered to distances of their own. Helen noted the fact sharply.

"Couldn't—couldn't I study dancing?" Bequita's voice was both timid and wistful. "Dancing is so wonderful," she went on. "The finest kind, that is. Like sculpture, and music——"

Helen rounded the girl's words up with one lash of her eyes, drove them into a corral where they cowered. "We've thrashed that out before," she replied. "And settled it."

So, indeed, they had, and always to the same end. Helen would listen to no suggestion of a dancer's career. Dancing now and then for play was all very well—she encouraged it, in fact—but an artist's life! "Not practical," was the reason she gave Bec; that was enough for the girl to know. Her profounder reason was her own affair.

And so, outwardly at least, the matter was dropped for the time. When Bec was nineteen the move to New York was accomplished. Volatile youth and the excitement of the change swept her up, she fell in with Helen's plans. Like lads conspiring to adventure, the two set forth.

"Oh, it's all so wonderful, Helen mine!" Bequita cried day and night. She cried it from the bottom of a trunk, over the edge of which she doubled like a long hairpin, or from high in a closet where she rummaged, or from her bed after sleep time should have begun.

"It's as if you had rubbed a lamp, darling, and made things come true! To think that we're going—really, truly, almost starting!"

"Almost starting," Helen smiled.

"Dearest, we're going to be rich as Mrs. and Miss Crœsus, and ride and buy clothes and have fun—and we're going to find *life*, aren't we, Helen mine?" with an exorbitant embrace.

And the green slopes that had given tenderly to her romping baby feet, the Pacific that had swung her girl-

hood on its wide breast, the flowers that had flung themselves, myriads, lavish, to her plucking, the fruits and
trees and winds and sunlight of her great mother-world,
California, held silence while she turned from them and
hurried away, arms open, to find "life."

CHAPTER III

THE FIRST REBELLION

I

THE doorbell snapped the long string of Helen's reverie that afternoon, and the varied beads of it rolled away. She rose, waiting, while Anna shuffled down the apartment's long hall to answer the bell.

Helen thought: "I must teach that girl to walk. She sounds like a sack of potatoes being rolled to the door. Never mind—soon I shan't have to keep a cheap maid." Her love for the finished, the perfect, made of Anna a thorn in the flesh.

"Mr. McNab!" she exclaimed, as Anna ushered in a brisk, short, and rotund gentleman of thirty-five. He was essentially the man of the business world, living up to the code that preaches "Look prosperity." He carried himself with that defiant erectness assumed by some short men, as though they perpetually demanded, "Who's that said 'Sawed-Off'?" Upright he bore one of those long, vaguely-shaped tissue parcels that a woman always detects as flowers.

"You're the person I've tried to get on the telephone four times to-day!" she told him.

"Good enough!" Mr. McNab evidently found great

50

satisfaction in the fact. "Sorry I was out. But mighty glad you were after me. Hope it means my good luck?"

"That's for time to prove. But it does mean that I've decided to accept the position, and I'll start in as soon as you wish."

"Good e-nough!" the gentleman repeated with fervor. "That's the ticket! If I'd known you'd already given in, I needn't have wasted perfectly good flowers, eh, what?" And he presented the tissue parcel.

They laughed together, in excellent good-fellowship. "Daffodils!" Helen cried, as she unwrapped them. "The first I've seen! Thank my luck I missed you on the telephone!" She held up the flowers with a very keen delight. Life had been rather sparing toward her of late years. She made McNab comfortable in an easy chair and went for a vase.

"Now we can talk." She settled down at last, opposite him.

"We sure can." He extended his trim shoes a trifle by way of ease, and revealed a gleam of silk hosiery as he gave each knee a pluck. In the same glance that showed him his own well-clad feet, he took in Helen's; with that swift appraisement of material values so characteristic of the commercial world, he silently approved the quality of her black silk and dull kid. "Show me a woman's feet well dressed, and I'll take the rest of her dressing on trust," was one of his maxims.

"Now then," he went on, lighting the cigarette she gave him, "to business! I'm to understand, am I, that you agree to our proposition? In other words the Monroe Mutual Life Insurance Company, one of the greatest in the United States, creates a job for you—just according to your scheme—installs a women's department, contrary to its fixed ideas—upsets the whole business, just to let you experiment, and make ducks and drakes of as many thousands as you can get away with—and at last, after mature deliberation, you condescend to accept this arrangement?"

"I condescend. And also, remember, I am offered, for the present, only a very modest salary! Until I make good." Friendly understanding smiled between them.

"Well, we'll risk it, anyway! We sure will see something doing." In an excess of satisfaction he fell to, laying plans.

II

When Bec burst in, the two were so deep in these plans that they did not hear her impatient burring of the doorbell, her rush down the hall.

"Helen, feel my cheek! The weather's gloriously cold!" She had flown to her mother with one brilliant cheek proffered as testimony to the weather before she realized another presence.

"Oh!" she cried on the instant that her own rose cheek and Helen's olive-white one came in contact. She was giving a vigorous rub, with the energy of a young colt; she stopped with embarrassed abruptness. "Oh!" she repeated. But her disturbed "Ohs!" were less at the fact that a stranger had surprised her than at the extremely frank and admiring gaze of that same stranger.

"This is Mr. McNab, Bec—you know all about him.

My daughter, Mr. McNab. She's a foolish creature, who doesn't know how to do anything but dance. It never occurs to her that bread and butter is needed, while she devotes herself to the jam of life. In short, she's a mere trifle," Helen concluded, with her usual incongruous look of fatuity and cynicism resting upon her offspring.

"*Some* trifle all the same, eh, what?" approved Mr. McNab. With difficulty and a sigh he removed his gaze at last, preparatory to returning to business.

"Bec, Mr. McNab and I have been making our final arrangements for me to enter upon my career. I'm to go to work next Monday. How will you like that?"

The gold and rose trifle—a very sizable trifle, forsooth, the gentleman must have thought!—was evidently in full cognisance of the plan, whether or not she held the correct valuation of bread and butter. She shone upon the news. "It's all so exciting, isn't it, Helen? I'll miss you, of course, dear—away all day—but I'm so busy now, too. We're sort of partners, you see, more like sisters," she explained soberly to Mr. McNab. "We came to New York to seek our fortune together, you know —I suppose Helen has told you. She's more practical than I am, but we're hoping I'll come to it in time. She wants to be connected with some great business like yours, some very big field, where she can deal with hundreds of people and feel herself a part of progress. Won't that be glorious? Then, when I'm ready for it, she's to draw me in with her. I'm beginning at the bottom now —taking lessons in shorthand and typing, so that I'll have a solid foundation—and some day we're to be great

women of the business world, and frightfully wealthy. I
think it's a splendid idea, only I'm so stupid at Pitman.
Somehow I don't seem to be made that way."

"What way are you made?" inquired Mr. McNab with
lively interest.

Bec had thrown off her wraps and seated herself between the two, completing an intimate circle. "What way
am I made?" she pondered aloud. "Of very flimsy material, I'm afraid, according to Helen. She laughs at
me when she catches me reading poetry. How do you
feel about poetry, Mr. McNab?" she appealed with disconcerting suddenness.

Mr. McNab looked troubled. "You've got me," he confessed. "Might as well ask me how I feel about the
Pyramids of Egypt. I don't suppose I've read a poem
through since I went to school, and the teacher made me
learn 'selections'——

> " 'Cannon to right of them,
> Cannon to left of them,
> Cannon in front of them
>   Volley'd and thunder'd!' "

he bellowed, and thumped his projected chest with a pudgy
hand in reminiscence, while the ladies laughed apprecia-
tively.

"But it strikes me," he went on, and a surprising softness, almost a musing look, passed over his alert countenance, "that poetry's sort of like religion, and a man's
mother, and the pies she knows how to make: we're too
darned busy to see much of 'em, but it makes us feel
good to know they're there."

"Halt! Halt! I allow no one to break into my methods

of training!" Helen protested, with gay violence. She felt a secret surprise at this note struck by a hard-headed business man.

"Now look here. I constitute myself a committee of one for the Protection of Young Ladies That Want to Read Poetry. You call on me whenever you want help, Miss—Miss—Bec."

Bec rippled with delighted laughter. "Oh, thank you! And I'm to report to the committee every time she laughs at me?"

"Every time. She'll be fined, too."

"Good! I'm going to begin now, and read a dozen sonnets all at once, under the protection of that threat!" She snatched a volume of Rossetti, another of Keats, tucked one under each arm, and retired to a corner, while laughter followed her and the play broke up.

How exciting it all was! This new life, so intensive where the California country life had been so spreading! So full of quick play and stimulus, so teeming with new persons, new situations! What fun to toss balls with this handsome young sister-mother and the new friends they were already finding! She liked this lively, frank Mr. McNab—he was so jolly and honest, he had so much "pep," and he didn't treat her as a "kidlet!"

Bequita, tingling with the game, was only pretending to read the poems while her mother and Mr. McNab talked on, seriously now. They were once more engrossed in business. Bec's mind and eyes roamed—to Helen's long, talkative hands, to the little fat, immaculate ones of Mr. McNab, then passed on—the daffodils caught them——

"What beauties! Did you bring them to my mother, Mr. McNab?"

"I did. I hadn't met her daughter then."

"I'm so glad!" Bec was very earnest. "You see, I'm likely to have more flowers than Helen, so it's nice these came to her."

"Don't be too sure." Mr. McNab tacked the other way now, with quick diplomacy. "Your mother may decide not to hand over the trophy to you, and if she makes up her mind on any point, look out, I say!"

Bec caught the ball and tossed it back. "Of course I know I can only win by default, but if my opponent chooses to default, I have a right to the prize, haven't I?" Her blue eyes sparkled black; her own words excited her, they sounded to her like the things people say on the stage, or in a book. How the cards were beginning to flick and snap upon the table of this new life!

She crossed to the mantel and stood examining the flowers with intent interest, pulling one from the vase, holding it with her head cocked, her eyes narrowed, while she scrutinised blossom and stem. The yellow petals brushed against her yellow hair as she reached up to the vase; instead of paling it by their more emphatic color, they contrived to enhance it, discovering the greater delicacy and finer texture of its gold.

Mr. McNab watched her, then cast a glance of fervent summary at Helen. He lowered his voice discreetly—so discreetly that she could not hear all he said, but one metaphor, no less than reverent in its utterance, reached her ears:

"*Some* peach!"

III

The two busy schemers, once more lost to outside matters, had not noticed that Bec had carried the daffodils into the adjoining room, her brow knitted while she studied the flowers, quite as preoccupied as they. An outburst roused them.

"Helen, dear! I'm sorry to interrupt, but if you'll only play for me a few minutes! Just one little air! Please, darling, and I'll dance a daffodil!"

Bec stood in the doorway between the rooms, the flowers in her hand, and around her was swathed the yellow stuff, yards of the warranted-not-to-fade fabric destined for curtains.

"I've been trying my neck in the mirror, and I've got it at last! Hurry, dear, do—I *must* see if it dances-out! Some little polka will be best—daffodils are a polka, don't you think so, Mr. McNab?" she appealed in desperate earnestness.

Helen glanced at that gentleman, who was evidently overcome with delight but too puzzled to reply. She laughed.

"It's only one of her whims—she 'dances-out' everything that appeals to her, as some 'act-out' their ideas. You'll see." She went to the piano, ran over some music hurriedly, and tried a light polka.

"Yes—that's exactly what I want!" Bec's eagerness tugged. "It tosses, that quick way that daffodils do outdoors.

"'Ten thousand saw I at a glance
Tossing their heads in sprightly dance.'

Yes—the music's just right—go on, dear. Now!———"

Forth from the doorway she burst, her yellow draperies thrown out with one fling as if a sharp breeze had picked them up. There through the little rooms she nodded, she flickered, she sprang, she alighted. A prance—then arrest, and a long, supple bending, a bending like that of a stem pressed almost to the breaking point by a ruthless wind—helpless instants in which the lithe body seemed all but prostrate. . . . A sudden up-spring, a toss again, a nod, a fling, and the dance ran mad once more.

McNab, who had hurriedly scuttled piece after piece of furniture back out of the way, and had even crept into the next room, hugging the wall like a cat, until he could reach the dining-table and roll that into a corner, now stood back in dumb admiration. His dumbness broke at last in two muffled words of awe:

"By George!"

Helen's amused eyes shot over her shoulder while she played, watching both dancer and spectator. McNab approached the piano.

"Say, but look at the way she handles her neck!" he whispered.

Helen turned further about, while her hands played on. Yes, used as she was to Bec, she knew this to be wonderful—the girl had caught that abrupt forward tilt of the flower's head, and all the while she danced the poise of her head carried the suggestion of the daffodil's posture in a way that was subtle to a degree.

"By George, how does she do it? She looks like it

and she moves like it!" he marvelled. "Never saw anything to beat it!"

The last ray from the sun darted in at the window,
caught up the yellow of Bec's hair, of her draperies, of
the flowers in her hand—tossed them into every shadow
of the room—then vanished, and dusk descended. The
merry tune broke up, the dance fell as if she had been
a flower from which the gay breeze had suddenly departed. Breathless, she panted up to her mother:

"You were a sport about the curtain stuff, darling.
I didn't hurt it so *very* much. Was I a daffodil?"

"You were," Helen smilingly approved.

"Well, I guess yes," McNab sighed heavily. So deeply
moved by admiration was he that solemnity reigned upon
his usually cheerful countenance.

Solemnity gave way at last, however, to the McNab
instinct within him. (His father, he had told Helen, had
begun with a tobacco shop so poor that it had waited
three years before it could buy its Indian—and now look
at Charles Mack McNab!)

"Well," he began on the brisk note of enterprise, "what
about it?—this dancing proposition. How are you going to cash it in?"

Bec had thrown aside the tangled yards of curtaining,
and was seated between the others again, flushed, and flapping herself with her handkerchief. The flapping stopped
suddenly, and she gazed at McNab in vague bewilderment.

"I—I don't know. Cash—" she murmured.

Helen picked up the question crisply. "This 'dancing proposition'—nonsense! We're all for business in this

establishment, my friend. This dancing is play, nothing
more. No life of art here!" Her eyes met his on the
defensive, saying to them, "Dangerous suggestions strictly
forbidden on these premises, sir!"

He pursed his lips reflectively. "I don't know," he
demurred. "Nothing the matter with art if it represents an A-number-one cash value, is there? Dancing's
one of the best selling lines in the country just now. And
a high class article, too. Of course, I'm not considering
the line they've showed us for years in the restaurants:
every kind of animal and fowl trot, and all that. I mean
this strictly refined and exclusive sort of thing they call
'interpretative' and 'esthetic.' I don't understand it very
well, but I know they take some highbrow piece of music,
and go waving around to show you what the music means
—you don't always know so much more about it when the
show's over, but it's good-looking, all right. Strikes me
I'd think twice before I let that kind of goods"—the gesture of his chubby hand supposedly indicated Bec's talent—"lie on the shelf while the demand exceeds the sup-
ply."

But Helen tightened her lips. "No art in this partnership!" she declared with asperity. "It's all the same
—music, painting, sculpture, dancing—they're well
enough for pastime, but once they absorb the life they
become corrosives." A shadow of bitter passion crossed
her words as she drove on. "I've been at pains for nearly
twenty years to produce as finely tempered a bit of metal
as was possible, and I'm not going to have its hardness
and its brightness eaten into by art!"

McNab regarded her with narrowed eyes of scrutiny,

but shrugged with an air of "It's your affair." He turned
to Bec. She had been following the conversation with
widening eyes and parting lips; now she met his glance
with a breathless, half-afraid question:

"Oh, do you really, really believe, Mr. McNab——"

"*Non-sense!*" Helen's voice clipped off the question
with its flashing scissors. And the discussion ended.

Mr. McNab departed soon after. "All the same," he
remarked in an undertone to Helen, "you're closing down
a gold-mine that's ready for operating on a big scale, in
my opinion." He shook hands cordially. "See you Monday—and here's luck to us!"

IV

"Isn't Mr. McNab great fun?" Bec cried as she and
Helen were making ready for bed.

"Time for you to quiet down for the night."

"I don't feel like quieting down. It's all so exciting.
When he comes to dinner some day we must have charlotte russe. Fat people always like charlotte russe—
maybe that's why they're fat—anyway, I've noticed it.
. . ." She paused; her thoughts wandered and sobered.

"Helen," she began after awhile, "he's a practical business man, isn't he?"

"Certainly. Why?"

"He didn't think my dancing all foolishness!"

"Well it is, whatever he thinks." Helen compressed
her lips and closed the topic. When she did that, no
use trying to discuss further! Bec flitted off.

Her Japanese dressing-gown was adorned with wide

storks embroidered upon its heaven-blue; as she spread her wing-sleeved arms in flight down the hall, it seemed that the very birds themselves gave a flap of sympathetic glee. "It's all such fun!" they might have been echoing her cry.

She continued to roam at large in the dressing-gown, with that freedom which women occupying a manless dwelling ever enjoy. But eventually she "quieted down." So quiet did she become, in fact, that Helen went to look for her.

"What on earth are you doing here in the dark, child? You'll take cold."

The living-room lights were out, its radiator turned off; a ghost against the west window, Bequita stood looking out where the Hudson gave off the moon's radiance from its fluted surface. Ice-clear, the night sparkled in cold beauty.

She stood without turning, and made no answer.

"Come on, you moon-struck goosey!"

Bec turned at length, slowly. "It's so beautiful," she sighed, "I can't bear to leave it." Her voice was soft now with fatigue; the excitement of the evening had passed like a wind and left her drooping.

"I was just wishing——" she began on a wistful note, and broke off.

"Wishing what? What more do you want, my dear? Here we are, twin Lochinvars come out of the West, with brilliant prospects shining ahead."

Helen dropped into earnestness. "This is the most important opening I've found, Bec; the salary isn't large at present, but the outlook is tremendous, if I make good, and develop the women's department of this great insurance company as it ought to be developed. And after awhile, when you're thoroughly grounded in the drudgery of business, you can start in with me. We'll be rich women some day, my child; I haven't spent half my best years yet, and you have all yours before you. It's for us to make ourselves modern women of the highest type, Bec; self-dependent in the fullest sense, not man-bound by so much as a hair of our heads! Man shall never concern us, except as a jolly comrade or in our business."

Her earnestness had risen to fervor. "We're going to be free, Bec!" she cried. "Free to prove what a woman's life can be when she dares cut all bonds of sentimentality and forge ahead as she chooses. I burst my shackles long ago!" Her gesture was triumphant. "And yours shall never be forged!" She flung an arm of comradeship about the girl.

For all her doting motherhood, the physical caress was infrequent on Helen's part, and Bec's more sensuous and unrestrained youth usually leaped to response. But now her slender body remained passive in the embrace.

"Yes," she murmured doubtfully. "Yes. It's wonderful, isn't it? We'll be very rich, of course. And that will be such fun—to have a great ruggy, cushiony apartment, and a sunken bathtub, and more maids, and our own car. Yes," she mused on, strangely remote for the accessible Bec. "I love soft things—like oriental rugs, and a warm bath that the maid has ready and violet-smelly, and all the towels you can use and throw on the floor—the way Cousin Ress has it. I love it. But somehow. . . ." Her remoteness was increasing, as if she

spoke from some other world, the dream-world of adoles-
cence. "It's fun. And the fun side of me loves that
sort of thing. But the other side——"

A vague disturbance was contracting Helen's brow.
She stepped in alertly.

"What other side is there, silly child?"

A pause, then determination.

"The other side," Bequita said, ignoring the snap of
lash in air, "the other side is the *me* side of me. It doesn't
seem to care about—things that cost money. It just
wants, oh, it aches, to be *me!* It—oh, I don't know how
to express it, but it's as if it had something to tell, and
it would burst if it couldn't tell! It—it tells itself when
I dance! Oh, if I could only study dancing, and give
up everything else—make it my real work! Mother!"
(The almost never-used name startled Helen.) "Why
can't I? It isn't all foolishness! Mr. McNab said so,
and he knows what's practical if anybody does! So that
ought to make it all right—with you." Bec was quite
unconscious of the stab of those two words. "And at
the same time," she went on, "the *me* would be happy, too."

Anger and pain blazed and froze at once within Helen's
mind, suddenly given over to upheaval. What did all
this reveal? her thoughts clamored. It was something
behind the girl's words, rather than the words themselves,
that was causing her disturbance. It was no longer the
childish wistfulness that formerly had begged for dancing lessons; here she felt not only a clearly-thought-out-
wish, but a repressed rebellion. What was its depth?
she wondered. And its threat?

"You've been satisfied enough with our prospect of a

successful business life," she retorted with banked heat, "until the idle flattery of a man-of-the-world went to your head."

"His flattery didn't go to my head. He started me thinking harder, that's all. I've never done anything but want it. It's the very highest and finest interpretative dancing that I want. But you didn't approve, because you thought art wasn't practical, and so I crammed my own wish down, and of course I've been interested in our plans to get rich. But there's been something down under all the time—something that ached in the deep-down of me, even when I was happy."

"At nineteen one analyses one's own emotions with as exquisite a joy as a youthful surgeon feels in dissecting his first guinea pig," sneered Helen.

But to her surprise the girl was not withered by the scorch of this. Instead, it brought her head up with a fling; it steadied her stumbling expression to a temporary maturity.

"I don't feel any 'exquisite joy.' I feel something that wants, and wants, and is going to keep on wanting, if it has no opportunity to be set free and express itself. I don't know what it is; but it's been there from the time I was born, I think, and I suppose it will keep on until I die. . . . Good night, dear." The "dear" was crisp, a mere form; Bec's steps passed down the hall; Bec's door closed.

And Helen Kent was left to realize that this puerile creature, her offspring and handiwork, had brought the debate to an end upon its own authority!

Helen turned and went slowly to her room. There she

flung herself into a chair, gripping its sides, as though to steady herself against the two overwhelming surprises that had sprung up armed before her.

The one, that Bec could rise against her in an opposition both heated and self-contained. (Despite her own retorting anger and roused alarm, Helen could not resist a certain sneaking pride in this fact. The girl would be able to hold her own, then, when she should meet the world!)

But the other! The surprise that this creature of her vigilant moulding had been secretly struggling toward another mould of her own choosing! Instinctively she realised at last that this was not the childish whim she had always taken it for, but a far more serious and brooding desire. For the first time she woke to the fact that the child had actually taken her dancing seriously, had secretly craved what erotic youth loves to call "self-expression"!

How easily she had always believed those wistful requests to be snubbed by a curt reply! And now at last it dawned upon her that they hadn't been snubbed! Phrases started up out of memory—phrases laughed at when uttered!

"Years and years of practice wouldn't tire me, if I could learn to dance-out everything I feel at last," Bec had said once. And,

"When I dance, I seem to know things that I don't know at other times, and feel things, and wish things, and say things. I'm myself when I dance."

And now it came to Helen—did she only imagine it? —that there had been brooding moods of late, behind the more apparent exhilaration. So! The secret ambition was taking root! Art, indeed!

Art! The very word roused Helen's sentinel soul to a prickling attention, a hot defense. Art! Her alleged objection to it as not "practical" was but superficial. In fact, she knew what McNab knew, that the girl's gift was marked enough to warrant moneyed returns, and those to be reckoned with. Far deeper lay Helen's real reason for fighting this art impulse to the death. For she knew only too well the relation of art to all that emotional life from which she was guarding the girl with every weapon at her command. Art, indeed! What was it but fellow-conspirator with that passion which she was holding off from her daughter's territory as if it were an invading enemy, seeking to destroy? All her experience of life, all her mother's instinct, all her feline love for the child she sought to protect, cried warning in her ears.

Yes, she knew the secret of protection. Once fill the girl's mind with the cold, steadying influence of the business world—let her be hedged about by ledgers, desks, typewriters, the talk of "endowment policy," "paid-up insurance," "probability of life," "first-class risk," and she would be safe. The business world, its jargon, its accessories, were death to romantic dreamings. Plainly, she must lay still more stress upon these, must rouse interest in them more vigourously.

How mad she had been to let this dancing go on even as play! Why, she had actually encouraged it, never dreaming that she could not check its influence at the

snap of a finger! But now she was awake to the danger.
No more of it, play or no play!

Helen cast off her clothes with angry flings and went
to bed. She lay there for hours, rigid and awake, scowl-
ing her resolve into the darkness.

v

While Helen lay awake, Bec sat in the little white
willow chair at her own window. She, too, was in darkness, but she looked forth from it upon the moonlighted
river, for Helen had insisted upon giving her the apartment's one outside bedroom, where her youth, healthy
though it was, might grow even healthier in the best air
obtainable. To the last detail, Helen's maternity spared
nothing to bring forth the perfect product.

Bec had undressed no further, although it was long
past her bedtime. The folds of the Japanese gown still
fell about her relaxed body. She was shaken by the conflict through which she had passed—a conflict infinitely
more violent on both sides than its words indicated. So
absorbing was the mutual devotion of these two, so rare
any more than a trifling difference between them, that
every utterance of this altercation had been like a blow,
wounding, shattering, as can only be between those who
love intensely. Bec still felt her breaths come short, her
heart thump; she pressed her hands against burning
cheeks.

"Oh, I wonder if Helen's asleep? I want to go to her,
and put my arms around her, and tell her I do love her,
oh, I do! I want to kiss the hair above her ears, where

it's so black and slippery!" emotional habit cried in torment.

But something choked her as she almost rose.

"Yes, I do love her—oh, how I do! But I couldn't tell her I'm sorry. Because really, truly I'm not. I only told her the truth, and I can't be sorry for that. I want to learn to dance, so that I can dance-out everything I think—beautiful thoughts, and poems, and songs.

"There's a way to tell everything in a dance. Not just jolly things, but the sad ones, too, and the dreadful ones even. Yes—even that ship—" her eyes dwelt upon the looming grey object. "How terrible and stern and proud and cruel it is, like this——"

She rose, and her flexible body drew itself erect, a calm that was almost majesty breathed coldly from her, a slow, austere gesture suggested the movement of the great destroyer.

She sank back into her chair. "All I want is to be *me* —how I long just to be *me!*" she breathed painfully. "And besides—I don't understand it, but the dancing seems to have something to do with—with——"

She stared out at the moon's streak across the river. "No, I don't understand at all," she thought on, "but it's as if the dancing were all one with—with—that other thing inside me! When I dance, I somehow feel close to *him!* When I danced the daffodil, it wasn't fat little Mr. McNab I saw at all; I saw Philip every minute, as if he stood there and watched me and liked it. I think that if I could dance—if I could only dance-out every-thing I'm thinking—oh, then, I feel that somehow I could find him, as though I were dancing my way to him, wherever he is!" A dry sob of impotence suddenly shook her.

Could Helen Kent have seen these thoughts she would have been struck dumb. The strength discovered in the girl's art impulse had been shock enough; but here at the gate, armed and ready to enter, stood the other passion, the very enemy itself, the foe against which Helen had erected every fortification for almost a score of years. Here, summoned by the fewest of memories, urged by the many-est of dreams—here stood love!

Long before, when Helen vowed in her morbid bitterness that love should never enter her child's life, she had known that she pitted herself against nature. But she believed in nothing more securely than in the dominance of Helen Kent. She never doubted her power to rule her child's emotions as she ruled her daily routine of sleep and meals and study and play. What she termed a "sane" life—freedom from romance constituting sanity —would dissipate emotionalism as the sun a fog. So long as body and brain were kept busy with wisely-directed exercise, no "harm" could come. Dam the current back, was her doctrine, and in time it would vanish—evaporate, sink into the soil, scatter in forgotten tricklings. She was astute, and her natural astuteness was augmented by a rare mother-love; but the obsession born of her own tragedy blinded her. That she might be increasing the pressure of the current by this process of damming back, never occurred to her imperious, self-sure mind. That the inner life of this child of hers might be an unknown world to her, was utterly unsuspected by the masterful Helen.

From the day of her arrival in New York Bec had been two Becs: the overflowing, jubilant, impetuous, enthusiastic creature that her mother saw; and another being, known to herself alone.

During all these weeks her hours of solitude had been again and again engrossed with thoughts her mother never suspected. Every day she had watched—she would start at the sight of a long brown overcoat, peer at some face in the crowd which had suggested a resemblance, turn eagerly at the sound of a lazy voice—always to meet disappointment. Was she never to find him again —never—never—in all this crowded world? Had it been but a moment of speech to break eternal silence—silence, and forever dreams—of a lean, brown, twinkling, overcoated young man on a Jersey ferryboat?

"If I could dance, I feel that I could find him!"

Whimsical enough, the fancy; and yet behind it lay a dim perception of the law that Helen understood; the law of that psychic bond between art and the emotional life.

The turbulent thoughts beat her into a weary sleep at last, and she sank back in the little white chair. A crumpled, fragrant heap, Bequita slept on. The moonlight played upon her hair, her neck. Groping hopes, longings, the young agony of life repulsed but nevertheless clamoring still for its expression—these filled Bequita's dreams.

CHAPTER IV

FACES IN THE CROWD

I

ORNING brought a reaction of ardor between Helen and Bec. Shocked, pained upon recalling last night's incident, they hurried with their wounds to the healing waters of reconciliation.

"Good morning, little girl! Don't you want some new violet soap for your bath?" rang from Helen's room— she knew Bequita's wanton delight at "breaking into" cakes of expensive French soap. And,

"Top o' the marnin', Helen darlin'!" burst in at her door with a Bec that was all bear-hugs and kisses.

Helen's angry fright of the night before had vanished. How could it have taken such hold of her? she wondered, disdainfully amused at her own weakness. The young thing was wet clay in her hands. Thank fortune she had caught the warning in time, while yet the clay *was* wet!

At the close of a merry breakfast, "Dearest, let's do each other's rooms, for lovingness!" Bec cried, and was off, swooping up her mother's pillows, beating them to a fluff, patting the beautiful embroidered bedspread into orderly beauty, rearranging the heavy silver toilet

72

pieces upon the dressing table—treasures cherished from earlier years, kept intact by Helen's exquisite care.

Their relations shone brighter than ever before, like a flower that is not one whit beaten, only refreshed by the storm. Rejoicing quite as eagerly as Bec, Helen hurried with an indulgent smile to the little blue room that overlooked the river. With lingering hands she hung away the dressing-gown and its incorrigible storks; she drew up shoes and slippers in regimental rows within the closet; she aligned the books on a hanging shelf; she made loving, useless motions as she touched the white brush and comb, the mirror and buffers and emery and orange-wood sticks. With such motions had she once handled the small white utensils in a puffy, lacey, foolishly adorable pink baby-basket. . . .

How she loved the child! stabbed her once more.

And again, a half-hour later, as she stood at the window to return the wave of the grey squirrel muff, how she loved the child! She would give her all, she would sell her last chance of happiness, for Bec.

II

Bec waved her muff, and turned toward the river and her own thoughts.

The day was keen, it made her thoughts tumble impetuously. There—wasn't that a long brown overcoat just coming around the corner? Yes, and a very long, lean person within it—her breath caught—but now the person turned. He was at least fifty, and dyspeptic at that.

So it went. Day after day she watched, waited, sought faces in the crowd, hoped, was disappointed. It had become automatic now, this action of her eyes and brain. They searched absurd places, scanned impossible persons.

A green bus came lurching down the Drive, and she mounted. Presently she would be at her daily routine within the secluded cloisters of Miss Timmons' Private Business School for Young Women. But for half an hour Bequita, atop the green bus, would be wistfully scanning every long masculine figure she met.

"One might go on like this for years upon years upon years!" sighed Bequita.

III

Helen, having set the household machinery to running for the day, started downtown. She wanted to look over the office before taking up work on the following Monday. But first she visited the near-by shops in person, instead of using the telephone; no hit-or-miss marketing in her efficient methods. She selected her small Delmonico roast as fastidiously as during the far-away period of prosperity when she had directed a number of servants and entertained on a lavish scale. Her lettuce, oranges, pears for baking, green peppers for rice stuffing, were all chosen under her own inspection; and the tradesmen with whom she dealt expended more pains upon her very small orders than upon those of her neighbors who bought five times as largely. Mrs. Kent's fastidiousness seemed to infect them, her quick displeasure and equally quick approval stirred their effort to please.

"Even after I take my position, the housekeeping shan't suffer," she resolved. In its simple way her table was perfect; critical taste demanded this, but far more urgent was her insistence that Bec should have the most nutritious, the most carefully balanced menu. With a final satisfied glance at her pearly-green lettuce hearts, she hastened to the subway.

The great insurance company occupied a vast suite of rooms in the lower part of the city. There were reception rooms, and private offices where the imposing representatives of the company crossed velvet carpets and passed rubber plants *en route* to corpulent mahogany desks. There were spreading rooms where sat rows upon rows of girls, young and old, all, whether young or old, wearing their hair in a trifle more than the latest fashion. Spectacled and unspectacled young men sat at desks or came and went, a large majority showing indigestion in its early stages. But, young or old, man or woman, all hurried, hurried ceaselessly. One felt a high blood-pressure in the veins of the very business itself; its pulse seemed driven at top speed by a heart that demanded more and more expansion.

"Expansion—that's the word!" McNab said to Helen, as she stopped for an exchange of greetings. "That's why we've fallen for you. We look to you to help us do it. You expand us and we'll expand you—get me? This shop doesn't pretend to be any school of philanthropy, but good business helps everybody all 'round—am I right? So—we'll start off with one of our best suites—reception room and private office—and you'll get more room as soon as you need it. Is that square?"

"That's all I ask," she told him. "Oh, but I like it!"
She looked around, over the bigness of it, the hurry of
it, the urgent prosperity of it all, and her eyes snapped.
"It's been my dream for years. It spells *life*. Now—
where is my domain?"

"Next to our company doctor's, and communicating,
so you'll find it handy to confer. Miss Muldoon and I'll
show you the way." He called the young stenographer
who was to assist Helen; "pretty, and potentially intelligent, but sentimental," was Helen's mental appraisement.
"However," she promised herself, "it will not take long to
develop the muscles of the intelligence and amputate the
sentimentality."

Thus unknowingly did Miss Muldoon's long-lashed
glances and full red poutings march to a threatened doom.

"Pleased to meet you," said Miss Muldoon in response
to the introduction, and dreamed not that the surgeon
waited.

McNab led on through the corridor for some distance,
and halted. "Here you are—sunny side, outlook toward
Broadway, plenty of room, mahogany, peacock-blue deco-
rations—what'll you bet we make a hit with Mrs. Kent
when she sees it, Miss Muldoon, eh?"

"Hit? Well, I guess yes!" And the two beamed upon
Helen like a pair of happily conspiring Santa Clauses.

McNab stepped ahead, opening the door to lead the
way in. The others were behind him in the hall; they
heard his hearty, "Why, hello, Doc, you back? Heard
about the new neighbor we've got for you while you were
in Boston?"

In reply came an outburst of rage. It was, to be sure,

in a deep, rich voice, a voice that bespoke cultivation; but neither deep richness nor cultivation concealed its wrath.

"I'll have nothing to do with this affair! A women's department, indeed! What is the Monroe Mutual coming to, I should like to know? A dignified, conservative old company—for fifteen years I have been proud to be connected with it—and now it disgraces itself——"

Helen saw McNab's pudgy hand steal to the door behind him and push it almost shut. With Miss Muldoon, she waited; and she heard.

"Oh, come, Dr. Aspden, you're treating us rough!" Thus the conciliatory McNab.

"Disgraces itself, I say and I mean! A women's department, indeed! Frills and furbelows and chocolate creams! The company's doomed, as far as any decent standing goes!"

"Oh, look here, Doc, you ought to have married—that's all that's the matter with you! When a man stays single too long he gets sort of out of the habit of appreciating women. They aren't so bad—they make things lively, so to speak." McNab still maintained his soothing drawl, which apparently acted as red rag.

"Make things lively! Lively! Yes, sir, this new women's department of yours has made them lively to the extent that you may look for another physician to the company! Here I return to town, enter my old suite, stroll into these rooms as I used to do when they were occupied by the out-of-town agents, to be told that an interloper, a *woman*——"

The pudgy hand closed the door hastily at this, with

a click. Helen could hear the murmur of what was probably McNab's protestation; then a sharp crescendo:

"I tell you, I shall sever my connection at once——"

Helen laid a perfectly gloved hand firmly upon the
knob; turned it; entered. Miss Muldoon, following, dumb,
scared, and wondering what on earth was going to happen, saw McNab step forward with a distressed, "Mrs.
Kent, just a minute, if you'll excuse us—"; saw Dr.
Aspden clamp his lips and stand defensively staring at
the "interloper" with an air of outraged dignity; saw
the "interloper," graceful, suave, extend a hand to him
with a self-possessed smile that flashed a twinkle of relish.

"So this is Dr. Aspden? I have to plead guilty to
one crime—that of being a woman. Otherwise I'm not to
blame for this situation. The company has chosen me
as a representative, and is putting me into this suite.
But the fault of being a woman rests wholly with me.
I always intended to be a man, and I simply failed, like
any other weakling, to live up to my intentions."

Dr. Aspden's hand had gingerly received hers, and
withdrawn in haste. Helen, looking a considerable
distance up, saw an austerely erect man of some forty-five
years or more; firmly and finely chiselled features; grey
eyes under straight brows——

"Don't disturb yourself about me, I beg of you," he
replied icily. He showed embarrassment; but there was
no intention of yielding his indignation or his ground.
"My ideas are conservative, it happens. Since this company is taking up new fads, it is better for me to sever
my connection at once. Good morning." And he snapped
the door of his office behind him.

"I say, don't mind him, please don/t, Mrs. Kent!"
began McNab in a fume of anxiety. But Mrs. Kent
met his eyes with a nonchalant smile.

"I don't!" she replied, and proceeded to settle herself
at ease before her capacious desk. "Now, Miss Muldoon, you and I will put our house in order." And she
smiled a charming dismissal to the very red and very
perturbed McNab.

It was just before she left at noon that a tap was
heard on the door through which Dr. Aspden had departed. Irritation lay in the very tap.

"Come in!"

As she looked up at him now, she was struck by a
weariness in the Doctor's whole aspect. It showed in
voice and movements, despite the irritation; it was enhanced by the greying of hair, the thinness of figure.
It was borne out by a certain carelessness of dress, con-
trasting oddly with the surgical immaculateness of the
man; linen scrupulously white on the one hand; on the
other, a homely brown necktie badly frayed, a drab business suit in need of pressing, hair tousled as if fingers
had perpetually rambled through it. "Exquisitely clean
and abominably untidy," Helen's observations recorded
mentally.

"I just stepped in to mention what you may not notice—that if your desk is turned this way—" he seized
and moved it—"you will get the best light and air without a draught. And I have told my secretary to bring
you the window ventilators I had made for my office—
they are especially good, and can't be bought. Good
day."

"But you will need them——"

"No, I shan't," he protested with annoyance. "They wouldn't fit windows in any other building. *Good day!*" This time he escaped. There was no opportunity to thank him.

Miss Muldoon stared after. "Ain't it the funniest thing? Mad as a wet hen—I never saw him mad like that before—and all the same he wouldn't be Dr. Aspden if he wasn't doing something for somebody. Yes, take it from me, that's Dr. Aspden. . . . My, but ain't he mad to-day!"

Miss Muldoon opened the lavatory door, upon the inside of which hung a mirror. With reverent touch she patted into shape a little pad of hair above each ear.

"I never saw him so mad," she repeated, musing. "I'm awfully sorry, though"—pat—"that he really—" pat, pat—"is going." Pat, pat, pat.

"You need not be," replied Helen, in her neatest, surest, most deliberate articulation, and smiled faintly and diagonally. She adjusted her hat. "He will not go," stated the surprising Mrs. Kent.

Miss Muldoon turned suddenly, with a sharp glance of inquiry. For the moment curiosity got the better of secretarial restraint. "Why—— Do you know him?"

"No, my child, I have never seen him before." Helen picked up her muff, and smiled a trifle more carelessly, more diagonally. "I do not know Dr. Aspden. But I do know his sex. And some day," she added, pausing in the door, "we will have a little talk about that same sex, you and I. . . . Monday, Miss Muldoon—at nine sharp,

please, so as to get a good start.   My cousin, and a lady
whom I have met at my club have asked to take out
policies as soon as the department opens—Miss Clifton,
and Mrs. Gwendolen Elise Hobson.   Remember the
names, won't you?   That makes for good business.   And
now, good-bye.   I'm sure we shall get on very nicely."

IV

The winter told off its weeks, and still two Becs dwelt
within the charming nest of Helen's feathering.   So widely
did they differ, that only the passionate pendulum in
which youthful moods ever swing could explain their
divergence.

The Bec that Helen saw was, as ever, all flash and ripple, like the surface of glad water.   This Bec shone in
the "good times" they were having—new friends, a weekly
theatre treat, occasional restaurant dinners, and that
unfading delight, "bus-riding," kept her in a state of
happy sparkle.   Helen smiled with sagacious satisfaction;
no more mutiny here!   Yes, she had caught the warning
in time, again thank fortune, before the clay had dried!

Never once since the outbreak had Bec danced, even
in the most casual way.   So Helen had been spared the
disagreeable duty of having to squelch that form of
"self-expression"!   No doubt the child was heartily
ashamed of her sentimental nonsense!   And she had not
once again complained of disliking the Business School.
Yes, she was indeed "coming around" at last to a sane
viewpoint.   What a simple matter it was, as it proved,
to stamp out these diseases of youth!   As simple as it

had been to carry the baby Bec through her light attacks
of measles and whooping-cough!

And the other Bec, unseen, unsuspected, though dwelling all the while within that intimate nest, dreamed and
longed and ached on. Day after day, as the weeks grew
into months, that eye and brain, trained to ceaseless alert-
ness, watched. Still they scanned every long masculine
figure; still they would start, would flash a swift message of hope back to the longing heart, then another,
equally swift, of failure.

In shops, theatres, restaurants; walking, "bus-riding";
in company and alone; still they watched without ceasing. And still, dreaming out from her west window toward
the darkly shimmering river, Bec would sigh:

"In this great city, among millions of people, how can
I ever find him? Any day I may pass him—brush against
him—and never, never know! Oh, it could go on for
years and years, long, dreadful years, silent years, years
that would make me old—and grey! And after awhile
the years would come to be—forever!"

V

The days were very busy now. Bec attended morning
and afternoon sessions; Helen spent long hours at the
office, having lunch downtown. She had swept up the
new work, was carrying it before her with incredible
vigour and success.

On the Monday when she officially entered her new
department, she had knocked at McNab's door with a
smiling request.

"Will you be so good as to have that door of mine leading into the other suite fastened permanently?"

McNab had looked slightly surprised.

"You mean the one that was the Doctor's door?"

"Yes. I suppose there's no telling just how that suite will be used now, and anyway, I've a liking to command my own privacy."

"Sure! Anything to please you! Ask the Company to move to Yonkers and we'd probably do it!" McNab had jested good-temperedly, and a carpenter had that afternoon sealed the door.

For weeks the neighboring suite had stood empty, and the Company had worried along without a physician of its own. No one could be found to replace Dr. Aspden; the management was missing him desperately, but it would not listen to Helen's offer to resign that he might return.

It was not until a late February morning that Miss Muldoon conveyed a piece of news.

"Dr. Aspden's coming back next month," she told Helen.

Again that faint, diagonal smile crossed Mrs. Kent's face, and her eyebrows arched ever so slightly.

"Yes?" was all she said.

"He sent word to Mr. McNab that he'd come if—if the door between the suites was permanently fastened." Miss Muldoon struggled with a rising giggle.

"And Mr. McNab?——"

"Wrote him that it had been done already, as the women's department insisted upon commanding its own privacy," reported Miss Muldoon. And the giggle had its way.

VI

And the winter months approached their end, and still Bec vainly scanned faces in the crowd.

CHAPTER V

THE IMMORTAL HOUR

I

HELEN! Oh, Helen, it's snowing! Beautiful tiny stars, and blossoms, and ferny whorls, and feather rosettes—all over my window sill!"
The uncommonly mild winter was at an end, and now, in a sort of death-bed repentance for its neglect of duty, it was hurrying to produce a snowstorm. Helen glanced up with a smile.

"So, my young California ignoramus is to have her initiation at last, is she? Better hurry out before it melts."

She realized the thrill of this event, practically Bec's first experience of snow. Once the child had made an excursion to a perennially white peak in her native state; but that was ever so long ago, quite in kidlet days, Bec reminded her; in fact, she hardly remembered it; and she had always supposed that snow was hard: it looked hard on Christmas cards. Watching the fluffy stuff fall, swansdowny and warm-looking, she had never dreamed it could be as beautiful as this!

"Darling, must I do my room now?" she pleaded at the end of a gulped breakfast. "Don't you think," it occurred to Bec, "it would be better for the bedclothes to air longer?"

Helen smiled with her customary expression of amused clear-seeing.

"Run along, youngster—I'll attend to your room—this once," she added, to reinstate her discipline in her own opinion.

And, as always, at the window to return the wave of the grey squirrel muff—how she loved the child! her thoughts cried with that ominous, indefinable pain of motherhood.

II

The streets were dismal, as always in a storm; but presently Bec's brave gait brought her to the upper end of Central Park. Here, as she entered, a hush seemed to fall; so early in the morning the Park was as deserted as the forest primeval.

She walked on, rapt in wonder at the miracle, almost tiptoeing as she penetrated the depths of those woods so marvellously secluded by the wizard who laid out the paths that the outer world seems to have vanished at one touch of the wand. Now she heard only the dimmest sound of the city, as low as a distant and forgotten sea; from the spot where she paused, no buildings could even be glimpsed through the trees; the effect of a sudden magic removal to a remote forest was complete. Light abundant snow was piled upon branches; it lay at rest in the stillness of the air; it shone unscarred upon the ground. Once a small brown bird alighted and disturbed a branch with the commotion of its wings, spilling a thistle-down of snow to the ground; so absolute was the peace that even this tiny incident cleft it for the moment like a thrust.

Bec's steps, growing more and more awed as she advanced, stopped at last, and she stood as if before a shrine. The beauty almost frightened her; and it hurt. She had never felt that hurt before. It was as if at some time, ages past, she had known just such a place, such beauty; and as if she had lost it, and had always missed it since, and must always go on missing it, could never hold it but for the escaping moment. . . .

A pair of acquisitive eyes confronted her, and she dived into her big coat pocket. She had not forgotten the graham cracker so highly approved by that little gourmand, the New York squirrel.

"First and last call for breakfast!" she warned him. The animal peered at the scattered bits, started toward them, made pretense of disdain, at last yielded to his fleshly appetite.

"You greedy scamp!" While she rebuked him for his gormandizing, she continued to pander to it with larger and larger bits of cracker. He was gluttonously stowing them away, when from behind a snow-swathed clump of bushes was tossed a peanut. With one beady glance of valuation, the squirrel basely deserted his hostess, who was offering her best, and turned where entertainment appeared more to his liking.

Bec looked toward the bushes but could see no one. Apparently the peanut-purveyor was in the next path, and they were completely screened from each other. She heard the person's voice, however; it was masculine, a bit drawly, deep, husky, and nice.

"What royal little beggars you city squirrels are, to be sure!" the voice was saying, and more peanuts accompanied it. "Here you are, totally dependent upon our alms; and yet you pick and choose, you demand and criticise, as if you were lords of the land. You are mere hangers-on at the club of life; but any stranger might think you were the patrons. Here, sir, is a fine fat nut; and another. . . ." They pelted upon the snow.

Bequita's breath caught, she stood tense, her eyes fixed upon the concealing bushes. She was conscious of a desperate desire to rush to them and pull them aside and see who stood behind them; and conscious at the same time of a compulsion to stand perfectly still and wait for the owner of the voice to find her out—or pass her by. She did not know that the impulse and the conflicting restraint were as old as cave days; that all her womanhood was bound up in them.

Her thoughts beat like wild little wings against bars: "It sounds like him—his voice was low and lazy, exactly like that—oh, *how* it sounds like him! The kind of voice that knows it can wake up perfectly well if it wants to, but it doesn't waste any energy till there's a reason." Bec was "not Nell's daughter for nothing, when it came to sizing-up a chap," an uncle of hers had once observed.

"He talked just that way," her thoughts continued. "Sort of laughing inside all the time, and yet liking the person he was laughing at. Oh, *can* it be anybody else and still sound so like him? It can't, it can't possibly——"

The voice entered once more. "Life must at times be no more skittles and beer to you than—to me, for instance, but I believe you'd perish before owning to the fact. I know your type of *poseur!* 'Of course I have merely to ring for a meal to be served,' your swagger seems to say. Fraud that you are! And, do you know, I like you for it! There was a decayed Kentucky colonel Dad used to bring home—on his uppers—averaged a meal or less a day—and yet, when a meal did come his way, and he couldn't help falling on it lustily, he always explained his appetite by saying that he had just walked ten miles to reduce his flesh produced by overeating. 'Joke on me, sir, ha-ha, that it starts me overeating again!' he would roar. Bluff, sheer bluff. But there's something game in the hypocrisy."

The tail of an overcoat swung into sight. It was— yes, it was a brown overcoat, a dark mixy brown, and of heavy, rough goods! Bec's throat was so tight now that she felt as if a cord were around it, and being drawn in, in——

"There! You've emptied my pockets, you little beggar! Good-day to you!" The end of the brown overcoat swung out more boldly into view; the toe of a boot appeared. . . . Bec was scarcely breathing at all. The speaker had bidden his adieu; the next instant he would step forth, they would be face to face. . . .

A queer sickly fright spread over her like something cold and trickling: that fright which comes at the consummation of any event long waited for, for which every nerve has been strung taut in readiness, from a lovers' reunion to a hanging. She backed wretchedly against a tree; an astonishing desire to run and hide numbed all her faculties, which a moment ago had tingled with the eagerness of hope.

"I'm a little idiot," she whispered, indignantly, shutting

her teeth in determination. "Every day for a month I've
pined for this moment, and now when it comes I'm scared
to death! I'm a little idiot, I say; a little *id-i-ot!*"

She refused her poltroon feet permission to stir from
the spot where they were firmly planted beside the path.
Her hands, reaching behind, caught some current of
valour from the aspiring tree they grasped.

"There's nothing to do but wait—wait perfectly still,"
she instructed her coward self, "until he steps out and
comes this way. He can't help having a good look at
me; and then I'll see—I'll see—if—he remembers——"

Straight as the high-hearted tree she stood against it,
her eyes riveted to the clump of bushes behind which the
overcoat's tail had once more swung back. Under the soft
grey fur of her neckpiece her slightly rounded young
breast beat in a storm of agitation. A tiny flaming spot
of nervousness burned in each cheek; for the rest, Bec
was paler than usual. It was significant that, as she felt
the opening burst of chords approach, that opening burst
for which every instrument in the orchestra of her nature
had been tuned and waiting, she made no move toward
any of those petty preparations of dress, that artificial
composure of feature, so instinctive with a multitude of
women. Short locks of hair had fretted themselves loose
above her ears, but she did not touch them; a glove had
come unbuttoned, but she ignored the fact. She rubbed
no leaf of *papier-poudré* over her nose; she squinted into
no tiny mirror to adjust her hat. Now that Bequita's
moment drew near, it was her soul, not her costume, that
she put in order.

The moments were passing, and the brown overcoat had

not appeared again. "Funny!" She frowned anxiously and strained her eyes harder toward the clump of bushes. But all was still; the surfeited squirrel had departed, seeing that the feast was over; the voice had vanished, no rustle or step could be detected.

"It *is* funny!" Bec pondered. The only path leading from those bushes was the one that passed her; she had therefore taken it as a matter of course that the young man would come her way. And now, apparently, he had departed; for surely he wouldn't be standing still forever behind a bush!

Many, many minutes now had escaped, and Bec relaxed her hold on the tree, and stepped forward along the path. She could see behind the bushes now; yes, the young man had disappeared as completely, as soundlessly, as some Prince of the Arabian Nights spirited away from his tremulously awaiting Princess.

III

There went his footprints, blurred already in the powdering snow. They had ignored the path. Her eye traced them on—she walked for a few yards thus hopelessly tracing them—until they lost themselves in the wheel-tracks of the road.

Something within Bec tumbled down, down, thudding as it went. "Oh, why must it always be like this?" she whispered, her lip quivering. "One day I think I see him on top of a stage—it looks so like him—and then it turns out to be a stranger. Or in Riverside Park, or at a restaurant, or in a shop. But this time—it wasn't fair, this time!" she suddenly accused Fate. "This was really Philip—I know his voice and his make-fun! It was like holding him out and then snatching him away! It was playing a practical joke on me! I call it unfair!"

Alone in the still temple of the snow Bequita thus brought her charge against the unseen Powers. But as ever, since the first man and woman did likewise, these same Powers defended themselves behind a screen of inexorable silence.

"What can a girl do?" she demanded. "A girl can't go and seek. And in this great city how does one ever happen to meet anybody? I might be beside him in the crowd—right beside him—a hundred times—and never know it!"

She paused, struggling with her lip. "Oh, if I were the man," she broke out, "I'd go forth and seek! I'd seek day and night, on every side; I'd never give up till I found her! But the girl—the girl just has to stand still and wait, and wait, and keep on forever waiting—in vain, I suppose. . . ."

All at once something hushed her frantic spirit. It seemed to be the peace of the place. Not even a squirrel or a snow-bird brushed that peace now. It was like a strong, quieting hand. Bec could almost fancy it wanted to make her listen to something.

"What if," slowly came an idea (it seemed to approach slowly, gradually to be growing more distinct), "what if there were some way that a person could *make things come true while keeping still and waiting for them?*"

She was very still after asking this question, as if by listening acutely she might make out an answer. And she had a queer sense of the answer being in the air all about her, like those vapours of which they teach you in the laboratory; if only she knew how to gather and condense this vapour she could have it in tangible and usable form.

So Bequita, groping, did not know as yet for what she groped. But still there remained that queer sense of something like an answer, a higher knowledge, a solution, and, with the solution, peace. It was something that seemed to hover, almost as if trying to help her.

Helen Kent was at that moment sitting at ease in her swivel chair, dictating her morning's letters, placid and unsuspecting. And here in the solitude of the snow this mystical succour hovered perilously near Helen Kent's carefully guarded daughter, reared in the shelter of all her mother's atheism. Could it be that the delusion so watchfully held off from without might find its way from within?

IV

Despite the bitterness of disappointment Bec was conscious of some unexplained easing of that bitterness. She strolled on, roaming as idly among these winter trees as though they had been sheathed in white blossoms; there was no whip in the air, so mild was the day that the snow seemed no more than a down puff to snuggle the world to warmth.

"You see," she explained to that undefined, invisible listener who accompanies each one of us on our solitary travels, "one thing that made me think it was Philip was his talking to the squirrel. He likes animals, and he dis-

cusses matters with them as if they were human beings. I
saw that, with the old horse on the ferryboat. And then
the brown overcoat—exactly like his!

"Suppose I had found him after all? I wonder—oh,
I wonder!—what we each should have done!

"Suppose he had said that he had been looking for me.
Should I have owned that I have looked, too? Girls don't
tell those things. That is, they're not supposed to. I
wonder," mused Bequita, "why? Is there really any
reason? I should have to be very careful, and only say,
'I'm glad to see you again'; but I'd like to be honest, and
say, 'I've thought of you every day.' But girls say it
isn't modest, and that men don't like you if they think
you like them too much. I'd ask Helen, but——"

For the instant Bec's eyes swam in tears. All of her
ignorant, above all, self-ignorant youth was crying for
the guidance it craved.

"Helen would laugh at me, and quote something sar-
castic from her little red 'Book of Days,' like 'Love is a
passion that removeth the understanding, a thing without
reason, without order and stability.'"

But the moment's pang passed. The snow was falling
again, scattering its marvelous designs upon the blacky-
blue velvet of her cuff. No two alike! And all as soft as
the stuffing of a baby's pillow!

"Like this it comes down!" her thoughts cried, and her
supple arms extended, lowered themselves in a series of
soft falls that suggested the fluttering descent of flakes.
"Light as thistledown, lighter, lighter yet!" she insisted,
repeating the delicate movement, perfecting it.

Next, "Oh, that's jolly, the wind is coming!" She was

exclaiming aloud now, so solitary was she that she had lost all recollection of anyone but herself in existence.

There in the heart of the thronged city, like some bird of the forest which, on open wings, tosses forth its joy in the mere sense of being, Bec "danced-out" the snow. To her it was a discovery all her own: that spirit of winter which had only to-day entered her life. She did not know that the snow-play is as old as the drama-dance of Japan, that it is incorporated in the very childhood's expression of more than one ancient race. She was telling her own version of the story and it was new, as each human life and its reactions are new. The snow of her dance flickered in the wind; it frolicked; it drooped, falling gently when the wind departed. It tucked in the flowers; rocked them to sleep; in her arms Bec soothed an imaginary blossom, folding it warmly, crooning:

"Tucked away, tucked away, sleep till the spring."

The pantomime dance moved on. And as it moved on, that feeling within her grew: the feeling she had often known when she danced, of being "somehow close to him. As if he stood there and watched." As if she "could dance her way to him."

Again the wind rose, her dance rose with it, the steps romped madly to picture the moment of the wind's height; wind-blown locks escaped and tossed; there in the isolation of the white woods she poured forth the wild play-mood of the snow. It escaped; it returned mischievously; it was off again, eluding capture, fleet as virginity——

In a long brown overcoat with a sprig of pussywillow

in his buttonhole, the young man of the ferryboat stood before her.

v

Now that the thing had really happened, the thing that, in mere anticipation, had set her very thoughts reeling; the thing that, expected, had driven her feet to implore for flight, her arms to cling for support—now that this thing had taken on form and occurred, all panic slunk away as if ashamed in the face of the moment's serene greatness.

She drew a long, marvelling breath. And this Bequita, who had pondered as to whether she must be "modest," and not permit the male creature to "think that she liked him too much"; Bec, who had resolved to be "careful," and merely say, "I'm glad to see you again"; this same Bec was bigger than her resolve. She met her great moment not falsely, with lying eyes and prudishly untrue lips, but gloriously, head up, eyes alight, voice newly rich with all that lay unuttered behind her words.

"You've been so long!" she said, simply, and it was not one hand but both that reached forth to him in welcome.

He stood without moving, his eyes driving straight into hers, asking, exulting, doubting, agonising, hoping, longing, in one eternal moment. Afterward, again and again, Bec was to re-live that moment, and to realise that it was one of the half-dozen that amount to the sum-total of our span here below. "It was as if," she told herself long after, "he had thought he was dead, and then had sud-

denly waked up alive, and had looked around and couldn't
believe it and wouldn't believe it, and yet he wished with
all his longing that it could be true."

For what seemed minutes upon minutes he stood there,
challenging his heaven to prove itself to him; silent, terribly silent in his challenge. Then with one long stride
he reached her, as if he would seize hold upon his vision
and put it to the test, whether it was to dissolve, a mirage,
to his touch. The movement was bold, defiant in its incentive; but the hands extended toward hers were tim-
orous; they even shook as a man's hands do but once or
twice, perhaps.

They touched her own. Not until that moment did he
utter a word.

"They're real!" His sigh was sharp, the sigh of tortured tension loosed. "Now I defy all the gods to snatch
you up into the air, or cause you to be swallowed by a
yawning earth, or to melt into vapour, or crumble to dust!
Let them dare try their little game on me a second time!"
The whimsical funning that Bec remembered so well
tweaked his words to playfulness; but behind them his
eyes burned into hers; they again demanded assurance,
wondered, longed, feared.

"Have — have you truly—been thinking——?" she
breathed, her own eyes never leaving his.

"Have I been thinking——!" He charged on with his
assaulting eyes toward the very entrenchments of her
mind's fortress. "Have I ever stopped thinking! I've
wondered and guessed every waking hour, and examined
every feminine being I met, and dashed around corners
whenever I caught a glimpse of light hair or a grey muff,

ruthlessly bowling over old ladies and children. The cas-
ualties in my wake will greatly swell the mortality figures
for Greater New York, especially as I couldn't take time
to render first-aid while the hair or the muff were still
in sight."

Thus the whimsical chaff, a screen spread to cover the
soul that the male creature battles so savagely never to
reveal. And the female creature, as has been the way with
his mate since Eve smiled tenderly aside at Adam's surly
protestations, barely saw the screen for the ill-concealed
truth that met her loving and therefore all-understanding
eye.

He asked at length, and now his tone was timid and
without banter:

"Did—you wonder—too?"

"I—wondered—" (he had to bend the least bit, so
frightened at itself was her voice) "and I looked, too.
Every single day."

They stood without any physical contact; their hands
had met in but the lightest, the most faintly lingering
friendly pressure. And yet it was as if they rushed together after long waiting; as if the immortal thing within
each claimed its own, in some sublimated form of embrace.

At last, "Let's walk, and tell each other about it!" he
proposed, boyishly.

"Let's!"

"You begin—at the very beginning!"

"No! You!"

They turned to the winding path that slipped so shyly

away into the forest, and there in the snow they strolled as lovers stroll on a mid-summer holiday.

"You see, my pursuit of you was based on a logical hope, until I learned at the hotel——"

Her eyes had widened. "Pursuit?"

"To be sure. Didn't any little bird ever whisper it to you? I snatched a cab and came driving after, that morning we met, goading my poor charioteer while he goaded his horse——"

She was breathless. "Truly? As if I'd been a Cinderella?"

"Precisely. Cinderella with all modern inconveniences. For the up-to-date young woman is far too efficient to scatter any valuable articles, such as slippers, while she flees. She understands conversation; knows that the cost of shoe-leather is high; and there isn't so much as a heel left behind for a clue."

"But Princes should give a hint of their intentions. You don't suppose the original Cinderella, with all her thrifty training, would ever have permitted herself such carelessness if she hadn't received an inkling?"

"I accept the rebuke and bow under it. But what was I to do? Frankly, I didn't realise, until I saw Cinderella disappearing forever from my sight, that my courage could rise to the occasion. Courage surprises one in the hour of despair."

"Then why—why didn't you——"

"Someday I hope to tell you the touching tale of my cabby, whose sympathy was of a material sort. But now I'll hurry on. When I saw Cinderella disappearing with her coach, I gave an agonized groan and fell upon the pavement like one stricken.   Again I rose, however, snatched my fallen sword, leaped astride a galloping hansom, dashed through the streets of Manhattan in hot pursuit."

"You ridiculous boy!"   She laughed a long ripple of delight.   Strangely, it was as if he had chaffed and she had laughingly protested through years that they had been growing up together.   And not once did it seem to occur to either of them that this was most astonishing; that in fact they scarcely "knew each other," as Bec would have phrased it; that they had met but once before, as mere fellow-passengers for a ferry trip's length. By magic known to the subconscious mind alone, they seemed to have grown into each other's knowledge during the months of absence, so that now they met at a stage of acquaintance as far advanced as if they had spent it side by side—or who shall say that it was not even further advanced, by those unhindered processes of silence?

"I succeeded in keeping your cab in sight.   The chase had its thrilling ups and downs, under the auspices of my remarkable driver, and I managed to follow until you were landed at a hotel.   Then I retired, perfectly at ease, and strolled and lunched at leisure.   In the afternoon I planned—well, I'm not sure just what I planned— that was rather hazy—but somehow, I determined, I would present myself.   At two o'clock I went to the hotel office to learn that Cinderella had been spirited away almost as soon as she arrived."

Bec raised her hands in dismay.   "And if Cousin Ress hadn't snatched us up to her home the minute we arrived

I might have—it might have been—all this time——"
she stumbled in sudden self-consciousness.

"Yes. All this time, oh, heartless Princess, it might
have been!"

"Say rather, 'ill-fated Princess.' "

"Would that I dared believe you mean it!"

Her smiling eyes replied to this. "Anyway, it doesn't
matter now," she reassured him.

"Nothing matters now."

This bore down too significantly with its tone and look.
The maiden within her took alarm. She had met him in
splendid fearlessness, but now the caprice of sex, the
instinctive darting to cover, had become alert. "I
mean—it's nice for good friends to get together and talk
things over," she murmured, and her eyes sought flight.

He did not press the pursuit then. "Talking things
over should not be one-sided," he responded, with imper-
sonal kindness. "Now it's your turn."

"Yes, I'll tell you all about myself," she said, with
relieved briskness. "In the first place——"

"In the first place, would you mind our revealing our
names?"

She turned to him in astonishment. "Why, we haven't
either of us told, have we? I didn't know we didn't know,
because I did know—that is——" She broke down, her
ideas having become like feet tied together and trying
to run; "that is—you're Philip, aren't you?"

He stopped with a jolt. "How on earth did you
know?"

As she faced him they both stared, not so much at
each other as at the fact, in utter astonishment. "Isn't

it funny! But I did! I've always thought of you as Philip. I just knew, somehow. But not the rest."

"The superfluous part is 'Rodney Oliver.' A brief sketch will suffice. I dwell in a modest room in the quaint old downtown, my close companion being a highbrow Boston terrier named A. D. T., a person whom I wish you might know. Since I returned from my small share in damaging *boches*, I fear I have been too much of an idler. It is thanks to idleness, however, that I happened to stroll back this way!"

She tingled with excitement at these flashes of revelation. "You were in the war? Truly? Oh, tell me——"

But he waived it. "We haven't yet finished the subject of names," he reminded her.

" 'Mr. Philip Rodney Oliver,' " she read from the card he had given her, with his address. "That's awfully nice. Names are very important, don't you think? Mine," she went on, "is—oh, I wonder if you are going to like it?"

"I couldn't help liking it. Say that it's Keturah, Keziah, what you will, it shall be the title of my first sonnet."

"You're the most rid-diculous boy! I'd like to say 'Keturah,' and see you crawl out! But it really isn't as bad as that. It is——" Bec paused, prolonging the suspense. Oh, the excitement of this "getting acquainted"! The thrill of that first voyage upon the uncharted seas of a new companionship, whereon we are destined to sail! The discoveries of blossoming isles, of changing tides, of perilous reefs, of consoling harbors!

"My name is——" said Bec, and halted in suspense

at his suspense. To utter it would be flinging open a gate, and her hand lingered at the latch.

She said at length, "*Rebequita.*"

Philip's tawny skin flushed with delight. "It's the very nicest I ever heard!" he declared. "It sings, and dances! And by the way—you have told me nothing yet about this dancing fairy of the snow, whom I surprised, and who is almost as wonderful as Miss Rebequita!"

Then followed the history of all the long years of "dancing-out" thoughts and stories and longings. And the ambition—if only Helen would let her have lessons!——

"You must have them! A gift like that can't be wasted! If only Zélie Barrajas could teach you!" he exclaimed, impetuously. "She lives in Bittersweet Alley— no, no!" he corrected himself on the instant. "Impossible!"

"Zélie *what?* Oh, do tell me—is she a dancer?"

"A blundering slip of the tongue," he said, as if greatly annoyed at some inadvertence of his own. "It's out of the question. . . . Won't you tell me how you came by the Spanish name of Rebequita, and what follows it?"

So the talk sped on. They were magic moments, immortal moments, but they fled. With them fled something never to be recaptured. Whatever of intenser passion or profounder devotion may succeed, that first voyage upon the sunlit, luring waters of the unguessed can never be traveled again. Thereafter never comes quite the same thrill of surprise. It is as if the lips of the spirit met for the first time, and the future, alas, holds only the first meeting of fleshly lips with which vainly to attempt its reproduction.

Bec swung around in the midst of her narrative with a violent start. "Oh, what time is it?" she cried in alarm, and snatched forth her watch. It pitilessly reported ten-fifteen.

"How perfectly dreadful! What will the Obelisk say? She gets very angry—icy-angry. I must fly!" She was hurrying along the path, chattering her alarm like a fluttering bird, almost running, so nearly escaping that he strode his longest to keep up. "I must get that bus!" she cried, as a reeling green vessel came lurching. She waved distractedly. "Good-bye, good-bye!" she called to Philip.

The commander of the vessel was snatching her aboard—there was a pause, for the hoisting of two old ladies——

"Good-bye!" Bec called again from the pirouetting staircase.

She saw him springing to reach a hand up to her. "But you're not—not going to vanish again?" he panted. He looked as frightened as if the earth were opening to swallow his all. "Without—" he hesitated, then gulped his hesitation—"without telling me where you live? Mayn't I know?"

"You—you want to?" The swift pink flooded her face as she had felt it come and go a dozen times that morning. She leaned over and gave him the address. "You—you will come—soon?" In the marvel of all that was happening her voice went low, almost below hearing. But, being a lover, he heard.

"May I?" The second old lady was being hoisted all too quickly.

"Do! And my mother will be delighted. She likes my young friends. Come very soon!" The vessel was setting off in earnest now.

"Very soon!" reached her. She saw him standing where she had left him, on the asphalt, and not until a honk pierced his ear did he jump for life and limb to the sidewalk.

From her seat atop she waved a grey muff. His hat was waved in response. But for all the gaiety of gesture there was a certain despondency in his attitude: as if the lunging vehicle bore from his grasp something that he might never again hope to hold.

VI

Miss Timmons, the "Obelisk," was indeed "icy-angry." She conducted her small private school on as rigid a basis as Helen could desire, and she made severe though brief comment on Bec's tardy arrival.

"I'm so sorry, Miss Timmons! I'll do twice as well as usual, to make up!"

Bec plunged headfirst into the dictation being given, and her dots, dashes, tendrils and corkscrews trooped valiantly forward and lined up on her notebook's page. Following the shorthand exercise, her typewriter ticked and clattered as never before; line after line was rung off by the announcing bell; over and over she swept back the carriage with strident burr as of a harsh wing, and began a new flight across the page.

But the vigour lapsed. Miss Timmons, finding her class absorbed in practice work, had relaxed into a book on the psychology of salesmanship. Bec's finger-taps grew less forcible, less rapid. Her brisk staccato fell into a lingering touch, suggestive, at length, of wistfulness; one felt that, had there been a soft pedal, her foot would have been touching it; one almost heard minor chords in the tenderly hushed tones of the instrument. Her eyes were straying; they brooded now upon the snow-heaped fountain in the apartment building's court. Her fingers, clinging to their minor chords, fell away completely, sank at last into her lap.

In the clatter made by eight other pupils all bent upon improving the shining hour to their utmost advantage, Miss Timmons, beneath the towering coiffure which had tempted Bec disrespectfully to name her the "Obelisk," read on at ease. Something of a thinker was Miss Timmons; she was intensely interested in the author's discussion of "the business world's psychology."

"Profound. Subtle," Bec heard Miss Timmons murmur to herself, as she pressed her lips to an emphatic line and nodded her carefully netted pompadour. She turned to a fresh page.

And Bequita's instrument, like a piano whose chords have wrought dreams to steep the player's own senses, lay silent and forgotten; Bequita's thoughts, albeit only two feet and seven inches lay between the golden head that contained the thoughts, and the keyboard, had, paradoxically, never been so far from it. For she had passed into her own world: the same world of dreams and

longings in which she had for weeks been dwelling; but
now she looked about it, startled, marvelling. For a veil
had fallen from her eyes. It was the veil of girlhood.
The unveiled eyes which now looked forth were those of
woman.

VII

Mr. Philip Rodney Oliver walked slowly through the
thawing snow. To all outward appearances he was walking according to the normal functioning of muscles. To
his own inward sensations he was passing through up-
heavals, overturnings, leaps, vaultings, breathless rac-
ings, paralyses. Blocks passed in this manner; halting
at last, he found himself at the entrance of a small restaurant.

"If I can sit down, I can pull my brain together and
talk things over with myself," he realized, and went in.

In a remote corner, unobserved by the few tardy break-
fasters at other tables, Mr. Philip Rodney Oliver ordered food that he did not desire, left it standing before
him untouched, and delivered himself to himself of
thoughts which ran somewhat in this wise:

"In the first place, Oliver, you don't deserve her. But
of course that knowledge won't in the least hinder you
from trying for her—it never hindered a man yet, in all
of history.

"Therefore, since you're determined, as I see, to make
the try, there's just one instruction I have to give you—
which is, although you miss it by the distance of earth

from high heaven, come as near to deserving her as you
can.

"You're a loafer. You're a picker-and-chooser. You're
a procrastinator of the deepest dye. Here you are, possessed of high training for a fine profession, sound of
mind (except temporarily) and body, free and unham-
pered, and yet you've got time to walk in the Park in the
forenoon. To-day, of course, that was written by the
Fates; but don't let it happen again.

"What's the reason for your idleness? Simply that
you've spent these months since returning from France
in congratulating yourself on what you did over there and
thinking about what you are going to do over here—
some day. You've had positions offered you and you've
turned them down because they weren't good enough.
You deserve to be obliged to take a job instead of a
position.

"Yes, it's put-off-ish-ness that's the matter with you.
You're always just going to do things.

"But in spite of all your failings, I've noticed, from
the time when, at ten years of age, you rose in your wrath
and earned a bigger sailboat than any of those that the
other kids had been bragging about, that you had one
trait worth cultivating. Although you took longer than
anybody else to get ready to do a thing, when at last you
made up your mind to roll up your sleeves, you did it—
and *then* some."

The ruthless self-contemplation paused. At that
moment there flashed through the young man's memory
the words of a critical lady:

"The thing that interested me was the way your energy

came up out of your laziness so"—with a finger's snap—
"like a bolt. You'll do something yet, young man."

"Cling to her prophecy as to a life-line, Oliver," said
the young man, rising and looking at his watch. "I'll
give you, you darned loafer, just five hours to find that
job."

CHAPTER VI

A CRY IN THE DARK

I

HELEN'S Cousin Ress was to lunch at the little apartment on the day of the snowstorm. Helen had arranged to leave the office early and take the afternoon off, but Ress had already arrived when she reached home.

Miss Resignation Clifton, many years older than Helen, was the one member of the family who had warmly welcomed their shockingly enterprising relative from California. This wealthy and high-spirited old maid—such an old maid as only the twentieth century has learned to produce—bore the ancient family name of Resignation "by way of a little joke," she explained, "never having been resigned to anything except the inheritance thrown in with the name." She was frightfully stout, with a wheeze; bluntly good-tempered, as the stout and wealthy often are; had a passion for large-figured dress-goods and novel adventure (she had been one of the first of her sex to ascend as an airplane passenger) ; and a perverse delight in making especial pets of these two relatives from the West, all the more because the other Cliftons disapproved.

"Anna seemed to be having all sorts of trouble getting lunch," she told Helen, "so I just pitched in and made the French dressing to boost things along."

"Worked in the kitchen, forsooth! I always said you did not deserve your lot! You are not patronising, or inconsiderate, or idle, or indiscreet—in short, you don't know how to avail yourself of any of the privileges of wealth."

"Helen Kent, you ought to be drawn and quartered for suckling that adorable child of yours on such cynicism! Hold your tongue! Here she comes now!"

It was Bec's slam of the door; it was Bec's rush, like flight, down the hall; but Bec's shout was stilled. Always it had been, "Hello, hello, Helen darling!" or, "Aren't you ravishing glad I'm home?" or some other extravagant nonsense. But now, by that subtle process which telegraphs a mood on the instant and without a word uttered, Helen became aware that Bec's silence was more piercing than a shout.

The girl paused in the doorway. She did not see Cousin Ress for the moment, and her eyes glowed toward Helen's with the burning excitement of her news.

"Helen, I've got the most wonderful thing to tell you!" Her voice was low with the marvel of her thoughts. "Dear, what do you think? You could never guess, Helen mine——" It was then that she saw Miss Clifton, and fell dumb.

"Well, infant, what's the good word? Gracious, she looks as though she were seeing things! What is it, my dear? Arabian Nights?"

"Yes," Bequita murmured. "It is—Arabian Nights."

It was not until she slipped away after lunch to school that she whispered, "When we're alone I'll tell you, Helen—oh, it's all so surprising you can't believe it, and all the while it isn't surprising at all!"

"The youngster looks as if she'd been falling in love, Nell," Miss Clifton observed, as the two settled down to black coffee. "And what's more, you might as well make up your mind to face the music. With a girl like that, it's got to come sooner or later."

Helen sipped at luxurious leisure. But behind her movements was the tension of tight-drawn cords.

"It's coming neither sooner—nor later," she asserted, deliberately.

"How are you going to help it?"

Helen extended a perfectly manicured thumb. Its lower phalanx was long with logic; its upper broad, startlingly broad, with will.

" 'Sooner'—I shall keep her under *that*," and she riveted the thumb upon the table. "And 'later'—she will have learned to steer safely herself."

With steady deliberation Miss Clifton surveyed her younger cousin.

Now Miss Resignation Clifton was nearly sixty, and she belonged to a generation which had not discussed inhibitions and obsessions, neuroses and psychoses. She did not, therefore, pronounce upon Helen's case in the terminology of the complacent modern, who sometimes knows less than he thinks. But Miss Clifton possessed, if not modern psychology, at any rate what she herself would have termed "good old-fashioned common sense."

She gave over her survey at length, and leaned back in portly comfort.

"Nell, you're a fool," she observed affectionately. "And a damn fool at that."

II

The later afternoon found Helen alone and reflective. "All Ress's nonsense!" she rebuked her thoughts, as they flung back at her, over and over, certain words. That phrase, "The youngster looks as if she'd been falling in love," was curiously persistent. It was true that the girl had shone, somehow—but how absurd to fancy such a thing!

The doorbell rang. After her peculiar fashion, Anna ushered in a young man, and Helen rose to greet him. This was no one of the new friends who had been coming to the house of late, nor anyone concerned with business. And yet something in his long leanness, his dark face, struck her as familiar.

"Mrs. Kent?" the young man was murmuring, questioningly, though not timidly. It was as if he inquired, with a charming deference, what his welcome was to be; but without fear of the answer. "I suppose your daughter has prepared your mind for my call. She was kind enough this morning to command me to come very soon, and I have obeyed to the letter." His smile both made fun of his own zeal and begged forgiveness for it.

The slow voice, the whimsical eyes, fluttered at large for a moment in Helen's memory, then alighted. To be sure she recalled him—the young man of the ferryboat!

He had never been mentioned; he had not crossed her thoughts since that day of meeting; but personality always left its record in her well-ordered mind. And along with the recognition came a puzzled astonishment.

"My—daughter?" Wild impossibilities thronged forward, blocking her thoughts, as always in that stupid first moment when a situation surprises us. Had Bec been meeting him secretly? Was there some clandestine friendship? And then, breaking through the blockade, her thoughts found their way to Bec's "wonderful" news.

"I had the good fortune to run across her this morning in the Park," he explained. If the lady's surprise had surprised him in turn, he was bearing off the situation with excellent grace. He told, briefly, of the accidental meeting; there had been a delightful chat, he said. and he had brazenly asked permission to call.

During this narrative they had stood, Helen listening alertly and eyeing the young man in silence. Ah, the light in Bec's eyes, the throbbing hush in Bec's voice! her thoughts cried now. The sentinel within her sprang to attention, stood rigidly on guard.

"My daughter is not at home."

"Then I won't detain you."

"No—don't go." She smiled at last. The tent-flaps at her eyes' outer corners were lowered to more than usual reticence, but the dwellers within the tents peered forth with more than usual awakeness. She offered him a chair, seating herself. He hesitated, however.

"Had I better?" He met her glance. "I find I am rather afraid of you."

She laughed. "Am I so formidable?"

"You defeated me once. The vanquished always fears the victor, even though in secret, does he not?"

"Defeated you?"

"Not only defeated me, but, for all I know, jeered at me, after riding off victorious." He paused, respectfully but rather shrewdly scrutinising the lady in his turn. He seemed debating some problem within his own mind.

Then, with a gesture that suggested decision reached at last, he said resolutely:

"Thank you, I will remain. Long enough, at least, to ask you whether you could possibly have guessed what I did not—that I should pursue the Princess? And so have snatched her from my sight on purpose? Were you clairvoyant? Because it is true that I did pursue her, first in a cab, later astride my galloping thoughts, and have done so every day since first I saw her, and none other but her do I adore."

It was playful in word but deadly earnest in purport. For some reason of his own he had evidently resolved to take the game into his own hands, and now he drew himself erect in his chair, arms folded high, with a look that said, "Madam, we meet in the open. You may choose to sting my face with the lash of your terrible eyes; or you may deliver yourself of some excoriating satire; you look capable of either. But at any rate, I have played high-handedly; that fact brings its consolation."

If the crash of his avowal stunned Helen's nerves, she did not intend that he should know it. There was a sharp wince of one eyelid and the corner of a lip; there was an instant's gripping of the chair-arm; but no stranger would have noted these signs, so swift was their passing.

Vernon Kent had known them; time had been when he used to evoke them deliberately, watching for them with a mad desire to torture where he could no longer stir love. But her smile now became more vivid, although narrower.

She waived the questions. "You have my condolences, poor Number Nine—or are you Ten?—let me think." She spread her fingers as if to count. "There was Robert—and Stephen—and Dennis——" She became murmurous, like one telling beads.

The young man did not flinch. His chin grew stiffer, his eyes graver. Under the playfulness of his next words Helen felt something tautening like steel wires.

"Enter me on the card index under *O—Oliver, Philip Rodney*. Born in Oneida County twenty-four years ago. Father, a small-town banker, too honest to do more than moderately well. Mother dispensed with all servants in order to educate three of us, which we came to realise after it was too late to buy her a rest." His face tightened painfully for an instant.

"To continue—said P. R. Oliver graduated as an architect, but as he had to give his attention to cellar plans in France for a year or two, his real career has only now begun. It began at two-thirty this afternoon, when he secured a humble position with Frost, Timlow Hunt." (Evidently the lady recognised the name of one of New York's greatest firms of architects.)

"This same P. R. Oliver confesses to having dilly-dallied a good deal since returning from France. Want of incentive kept him from rolling up his sleeves. But he met the incentive in Central Park this forenoon. And, now that his sleeves *are* rolled up, he stands a good chance

of being rich some day—chiefly because he has always
been so poor.

"In brief, this is Oliver: a young man with no background of wealth, distinction or influence—only the sim-
pler aspect of American life—that of the gentleman's,
gentlewoman's home in a typical American small town.
I believe it to be the most representative American life
we have. Our large cities and our farming districts draw
from Europe; but the small town is American to the back-
bone. It cherishes the simple old virtues, such as patriot-
ism, home-love, loyalty, cleanness—the stuff of which our
first colonists were made. This young man doesn't pretend to live up to its ideals; but he does lay claim to
hitching his wagon to the star of those ideals."

Helen, playing with a shining chain of jet that fell to
her waist, and intently watching its glitter, followed
Philip Oliver with close attention. There was silence
as he ended; he, too, fell to watching the jetty gleams.

She said at length, "And you have told me all this
because——"

"Because I come to you as a total stranger. In my
short chat with your daughter, I did not tell her even
what my profession is. So I am laying myself before you,
asking leave to be your friend and hers."

"If I am not mistaken, you mentioned 'adoration'——"

"And you, I suppose, are suppressing the statement
that I am a young fool for falling in love at first sight?"

She nodded. "Yes—a young fool," she said, compos-
edly, and fell to laughing. It was a laugh that seemed
to glitter and tinkle with the same hard sheen and sound

as the jet falling through her fingers. She saw him wince at it; he went on, however.

"My answer to that is: no one could fairly be condemned for falling in love with *such* a Princess, even precipitately. Moreover, my declaration was made by way of dealing honestly with her mother. It never occurred to me to press my suit with the young lady as yet, while I am a hall-bedroomer, struggling with difficulty to support a Boston terrier." With the return of his whimsicality he recovered complete poise.

"Then laugh at my presumption if you will!" he politely defied the terrible lady, and she felt in the atmosphere an unuttered threat.

"I do. For you half confess to some ulterior purpose."

"I have one. Like the model youth in the Victorian novel, I beg a parent's permission to win the hand of her daughter when I shall have earned the right."

Helen leaned further back and surveyed him insolently. "Possibly, my dear boy, you hardly realise that home-making in America to-day is expensive. It needs a solid financial foundation. And a good income to keep up even a modest establishment. Plus something for the ornamental side of life. You know what Love does when Poverty rat-tats at the fashionable brass knocker!"

"There, my dear Mrs. Kent, is where I am not a young fool. Again, like the Victorian youth, I am prepared to work and wait as long as necessary!"

That slow, cool, firm voice stirred ever a sharper alarm within Helen. How lightly he jested upon the surface; and how deep she felt the undercurrent to be! She recognised in him a precocious self-command, that of a man twice his years.

"I am willing to believe you," she said, with a candour as deliberate as his own. "In fact, I think you will probably make good. And I like you. But you see, love has no part in my scheme of life for my young daughter."

"You don't mean that you expect her never to fall in love?"

"That is exactly what I expect. And intend. 'Love,' Mr. Oliver, is a disease of youth—nothing more than measles. Poor boy! I'm deeply grieved that you should have fallen victim; but you can't blame me for shielding my child from infection!"

A glance at the clock reminded her that Bec's return might be at any moment. She rose, and the young man, looking baffled and distressed, was obliged to obey the tacit command.

"I am sure I could find someone to furnish a conventional introduction——"

She brushed aside his protest. "Entirely unnecessary! I should accept you without it if I chose to accept you at all. But—well, infection sometimes carries, despite all precautions—so we must forgo the pleasant friendship." And Mr. Philip Oliver found himself bowed out. "Good luck, and a speedy cure!" followed him in Mrs. Kent's most suave utterance.

With a snapping of nerves Helen flung herself upon the couch. The blood swept up to her forehead at the release of tension. Who would have believed it? She, Helen Kent, played out by an encounter with a lovesick boy!

What should she tell Bec?

The truth, of course, was her natural impulse. But, suppose Bec should be left merely to believe that the young man never reappeared? Would not her roused emotions die, then, an easy death? Would not she thus be spared greater suffering? Bec's speedy and easy cure was the point at stake. Helen must spare nothing to effect it.

Bec's ring of the bell brought her to a decision.

III

"Helen! You poor tired darling! You look dead —absolutely dead! You're so dreadfully flushed—is it one of your horrid headaches?"

Helen was enveloped in a hug, and the cushions behind her were chastised into fresh order.

"I noticed you didn't eat much lunch, and you're always preaching nutrition to me! I'm going to make you some tea myself." Bec whirled away to the kitchen, and Helen lay back in weary silence until the steaming pot arrived, with a plate of slightly erratic sandwiches.

"I'm not very good at slicing bread—I'm sorry. My knife always cuts on the bias. But you'll forgive them for being a little bit sloping, won't you?" Helen mustered a smile and murmured her especial partiality for sandwiches of a sloping conformation.

The tea revived her rapidly. "You look like a new Helen already!" Bec cried. "Now we can talk. I have my wonderful news to tell!" (Ah, that light in the eyes again!) "But it's so wonderful that it must be kept for the last! So you tell first, dearest. What have you been doing to give you such a beastly headache?"

"Nothing—nothing, that is, to account for a headache." There was a curious note of annoyance in Helen's voice. She hesitated; then, "I have done nothing except receive a call from a gentleman," she stated, and her narrowed eyes fixed themselves upon Bequita.

"A gentleman? Oh, Helen, who? Was it nice, fat little Mr. McNab? Was it anybody exciting? Anybody new? Someone that I know?"

Inability excused Helen from answering five questions at once, so she made her selection.

"No. It was not Mr. McNab."

"Who was it, then? Any friend of mine?"

Helen paused before answering, and absently twirled her wedding ring. Then her gaze narrowed again upon her exuberant daughter.

"He is—no friend to you," she stated deliberately at length. "He is a young architect, pleasant, but not to be added to our list of callers."

Bec's face puckered a trifle, as she tried to guess her way through her mother's reticence. "A young—architect," she pondered aloud. "And what—what did you talk about?"

Helen regarded her daughter now with head tilted back and sidewise glance piercing from under drawn lids.

"We discussed," said Helen, "problems of building. Naturally the subject interests an architect. We talked of—foundations. And superstructures. The sort of structure suitable to America to-day. And to what extent decoration is of value. And that old question of entrance by doorway versus exit by window. . . ."

She rose, and stretched her long arms above her head. "I must go and dress. Thanks for the tea, dear. It did me good. I feel," said Helen, "that I have the whip-hand over my forces again."

IV

Bec, left alone, gazed about the room wonderingly, as though its walls could answer her vague and troubled questions. What had Helen's eyes meant by those black, shining glances? And her mysterious replies—especially all those queer remarks about foundations and super-structures, exits and entrances, that sounded like the things the Oracle used to say to perturbed young Greek heroes. Something, somebody had upset her—that was certain. She had been wrought up to the point of one of her rare headaches, and there was something strange and dark about it all; something she was holding back.

And then that tight, hard smile—and she had gone! Without so much as a query regarding Bec's wonderful news, saved till the last because of its wonderfulness!

It was very strange for Helen to be indifferent to any interest of her daughter's. Bec had been certain that she would remember the young man of the ferry-boat, and be excited over the miraculous accident of meeting him again, and be delighted to welcome him as a friend among all the friends that came to the jolly little apartment. Thus one Bequita presented the matter to the other Bequita. The plausible apologist within

her mind never called attention to the constraint that
had prevented her mention of him during all these weeks.
It never hinted, either, that Helen might have seen a
marvellous new light shining in her daughter's eyes, might
have heard a voice lowered to throbbing hushes. "He is
my friend, and she likes me to have friends," explained
the plausible voice.

"I'll run and tell her," an impulse cried, but somehow halted. Helen had smiled such a tight, hard smile,
and had closed her door so firmly. It was almost as if
she had forgotten the wonderful news on purpose!

Bequita rose and wandered restlessly about the room.
She paused at the west window. Who was this young
man that had so disturbed Helen? her thoughts asked
over and over, and found no answer. And why was
Helen so funny and mysterious about him?

She turned away perplexed, turbulent with many emotions. She was restlessly in need of action. She picked
up books, opened them, laid them down. She played
broken bits, standing before the piano. She rearranged
flowers, reordered her hair before the mantel mirror.
She roamed down the long, narrow hall—a small table
stood there in the dark end near the outer door, a table
where callers sometimes left their "things," or a card——

A tiny object lying upon it now caught her eye. She
picked it up. It was a sprig of pussywillow.

And now Bequita knew.

Never once had her heart dared guess such a rapturous guess as that he might come *to-day!* Never once
had a gleam of suspicion crossed her thoughts—how

could she have suspected such charming audacity? But she picked up the pussywillow. At once she knew.

For a moment she could only raise the sprig to her cheek with a stiff movement as if she were a little stunned. She felt the short velvet pile against her cheek, her lips, like the velvet that grows at the base of a kitten's ear. She grew very white there alone in the dark hall, did Bequita; white, and queerly dumb and numb, while a vague hand kept passing the grey pussies over her cheek, over and over and over.

Then the inertia of shock passed. A fire flamed up in her eyes, flushed her face; she seemed very tall, very cold, very hot. With a rush like the sweeping of angry wings she was at her mother's door—knocking imperatively—bursting in——

"This!—" she panted, holding up the sprig of willow. "This—— It was he! He came when I was out! And you weren't going to tell me! You sent him away!"

Helen stood there in a Chinese coat of flame-coloured silk in which Bec had always told her she looked wicked; and now the shallow, burning colour and the oriental suggestion seemed more than ever to enhance that oblique gleam of her jetty eyes.

"Well," observed Helen with careful *insouciance*, "now you know!"

"Yes, I know! I know all of it! I never dreamed it was he, so soon, but I've found out. And I've found out about—about——" For a second the charge caught in Bec's throat, but only a second. She plunged on.

"About you!" she cried. "How you were trying to

deceive me. You weren't going to tell me—ever to let me know that a—a—friend——"

Helen's eyebrows rose to the highest of arches. "What a tempest in a teapot, forsooth, to be roused over a mere 'friend,' and one picked up on a ferryboat and in the Park, at that!" It was her clearest, most delicate articulation, which Bec had always feared. But now she feared nothing.

"You know very well, you can see for yourself, that Philip is no ordinary young man——"

" 'Philip'!" mocked that delicate articulation.

Bec gasped, startled at her own use of the name. But she was too obsessed by fury now to stop.

"Yes, Philip is his name. And he is my friend. And I tried to tell you all about meeting him, and I never dreamed but you would be glad to welcome him, as you do my other friends. And instead, you treat him cruelly, and conceal it from me that he came, and I might have gone on forever, never knowing——"

"Why do you say 'cruelly'?" Helen inquired with a careless smile. (Oh, she smiled, cried Bec's thoughts, like a cat that keeps a mouse in torment!) "Really, I think I was rather polite to the youth!"

"You practically admitted that you sent him away —'not to be added to our list of callers.' You must have given him to understand that he was never to come again!"

"My child, I regard that as a kindness. It was of a curative nature."

Bequita's fists involuntarily clinched. She trembled in enraged torture.

"Then he will never, never come again? That is true?" Even the terrible verification was better than the tormenting ghost of a hope.

Helen turned to her dressing-table. Deliberately she raised her heavy silver hand-mirror and surveyed her glossy French twist.

"I think he will not disturb the equilibrium of the household again," she said, and adjusted a jet comb with exquisite precision.

Bec stood behind her, and in the mirror their eyes met. The girl was ablaze, and her words came in panting breaths.

"Then he came—and you sent him away—forever—and I'm never to see him again—as long as I live."

She stopped, as if strangled. A great choking sob held back her words for a moment, but no tears came. At last:

"Helen Kent, do you expect me ever—ever, to my dying day—ever to—to——"

She almost broke down, but her rage gathered up her forces for her and she concluded:

"Ever to love you again?"

She was in her own room. With a clatter, she had locked her door.

v

It was a night of tempest.

For the first time in Bec's nineteen years she was learning the agony of adult passions. The moods of her girlhood had been flitting whims, for the most part, light as moths; and she had taken a youthful pleasure in thrusting through them the pin of adolescent self-interest; in watching them wriggle and die, while she classified them. There had been among the lot, "tiny mads" and "big mads"; but now, from the plane of her new maturity, she looked back upon them as the caprices of a child—her own child, that past of hers, to be humoured and pitied and forgotten.

That morning she had entered womanhood—the grown-up world for which she had yearned. And all within one day she had discovered the throb of its sharpest longing, the sheer precipice height of its joy, the pit of its despair, the sinister ugliness of its rage.

Since locking herself in with her thoughts in the afternoon, she had not left her room. Anna had tapped and announced dinner; Bec had briefly replied that she didn't want dinner, and no further message had come. She found that she loathed the thought of food; the violence of anger was sweeping her like a disease. She did not trace cause to effect; she only knew that her head ached like an anvil and that she wanted never to taste food again.

All night her head ached more and more thumpily, her feet grew icier, her face hotter, and her brain more madly wakeful from the need of food to draw the blood from it; and all this physical disturbance, roused originally by the mental, now reacted in its turn upon her mind. Her woman's emotions had sprung into being full-grown, and as yet she had no more control over them than a child. It was as though she were tugging at runaway horses with toy ribbon reins.

As her fury grew more and more feverish, it shrieked certain phrases in her ears:

"She has snatched my life's happiness from me." Over and over her fury cried this. So final is event at nineteen!

"She is trying to kill all that is real in me." "She never could have loved me, and let me be so unhappy." "She pretends to want my happiness, and she thwarts it at every turn." And once a strange question entered Bec's mind:

"I wonder," she asked of the darkness, "if my father had lived, and been with me, if he would have done the same?"

It was the first time that Vernon Kent had ever entered his daughter's mind except with a shudder of horror. To her he had always been the brute who had wronged her Helen. But now this strange new hostility toward her beloved had flung her, in imagination, toward the other parent for sympathy.

And invariably, after minutes of storm, would come the horrible conclusion:

"There isn't anything ahead but blankness. Like the Mojave desert. Years upon years of life, just like the desert, all grey sand, and every little while a cactus. Grey sand. A cactus. Years upon years. Grey sand. A cactus."

The years loomed eternal. She could not—no, she could not face them.

Bec sat upright in bed. The covers fell away, and her thin nightgown fell low on her neck, and she shivered without knowing it. The room was very black now; it was that terrible hour just before dawn.

For minutes she buried her face in her hands, resting them upon her raised knees. Then of a sudden she flung her bare arms wildly upward into the blind darkness.

"God, don't let it be forever! Don't let it be! Bring Philip back to me! Don't you see, God, I can't live and bear it—forever!"

Her arms fell. Bequita sat staring, amazed, almost terrified, into the darkness.

"Why! I—I prayed!" she gasped, in a sort of wondering fright. "Just as if—as if there were someone to pray to!" said the daughter of Helen Kent.

PART TWO

CHAPTER VII

COFFEE FOR TWO AT THE SPINDLE

I

THE long reception room of the Spindle Club was crowded to suffocation on a Sunday afternoon in late March. The Spindle's Sundays were always popular; and to-day its guest of honor was Mr. Cyril Sinclair, the dramatic critic from London, who was the fashion in New York. He was talking delightfully but not briefly on "Dramatic Expression in the Twentieth Century."

From where Helen stood (chairs being at a premium) she could watch Bec's face, and she was finding in it a satisfaction that quite took her mind from "Dramatic Expression." "Thank heaven, the child is interested in something at last!" she caught herself almost groaning aloud.

At last, indeed! For the past weeks had been a prolonged wretchedness to Helen. Not once since the night of tempest had Bec stirred from the overwhelming depression which had settled, black as despair, upon the gleaming buoyancy of other days. On the morning following the storm, she had come from her room, surprisingly quiescent; had never alluded to the quarrel and its cause;

had dully moved through her daily routine of home duties
and school work; had shown no more spirit of revolt
than a tornado-stricken land. Yet all the while—through
the girl's passive acceptance of duty, during the quiet evenings when her book would fall into her lap and her
eyes gaze into vacancy, in the midst of merry-making,
when she would slip away from the other young people
and sit staring out at the black river—Helen had been
conscious of depths that she could not plumb.

Helen had confessed to herself that it was wearing her
own nerves thin. "I'd rather she'd rear and buck again.
I can master a show of temper. But there's something
in this docility that I can't get hold of to fight. Well
—it's up to me to give her new interests, keep her away
from her thoughts."

She had taken her to the theatre more than ever, had
invited in young friends, had insisted upon the girl's
accepting every invitation, although she often made excuses to avoid parties. It had all been futile. The
cloud had hung black and persistent. But to-day, oddly
enough, at this club of women artists and professional
and business women to which Helen belonged, and to
which she had brought the child merely to keep her from
brooding alone, the old Bec had suddenly flashed into
being. There she stood, drinking down every word that
Mr. Sinclair uttered; her whole face was kindled.

"Why on earth such a talk should rouse her, when
dinners and musical comedies have failed, I can't imagine;
but it's enough that it does!"

So engrossed was Helen in Bec's awakening that she
had quite lost track of Mr. Sinclair's discourse, which

had meandered along a path of mellow wisdom to the revival of the ancient art of the dance.

The talk came to an end. People crowded around the speaker, chattering to him, twittering thanks and congratulations. Helen saw Bec struggling through the crowd, straining toward him; she saw the distinguished gentleman glance past the crowd of tiresome chatterers as if that fresh, eager young face presented an oasis; he reached forth a hand to hers; "Oh, I'm so longing to ask you a million questions!" panted Bec.

Had Helen listened further, the sentinel within her would have sprung to its post. But she was drugged with satisfied delight; she was glad to turn away and leave the child to paddle her own social canoe. And just then, as Helen turned into the breaking-up throng of members and guests, a masculine figure caught her eye—she saw the back of the head, strong in modelling, decidedly wider than the erect neck; lean, resolute shoulders—hair touched with grey——

"Can it possibly be?" wondered Helen, unable to see the face. "Incredible—and yet so like him!"

The throng was surging downstairs now, to crowd the dining-room even more suffocatingly than it had crowded the upper apartment. Women chattered, and gathered crêpey draperies out of the way of treading feet upon the stairs, and called back to those behind them, and leaned over the baluster rail to greet others below with little screams and fluttering hands. Men guests, who numbered one to six, and were for the most part those docile spouses known as "club husbands" to this feminine organization, were borne along with the softly rippling current of Georgette crêpe and taffeta toward the stimulating aroma of coffee which lured below. Bec, along with the few other young people present, came after like a swirling spring gust, shamelessly to descend upon "the eats." Yes, for to-day at least, the Bec of sunshine and laughter had been conjured back, indeed!

Helen's mind was at rest after long perplexity; but her body was weary. She fell in with the noisy throng, but in the lower hall she paused. Suddenly it had come over her that she could not stand that dining-room crowd to-day. It pushed and snatched, though in a veiled and deprecating manner. It ate and ate. It talked incessantly, and her head ached—she had been losing sleep outrageously of late, a fact carefully concealed from Bequita. If only she could get a cup of that coffee, yearned Helen, without going into the dining-room. . . .

The crowd had passed her, she was left alone in the hall. She heard the voice of Mrs. Gwendolen Elise Hobson addressing a guest.

"I'm really distressed that you must go—and without even a sandwich!" Mrs. Hobson rang with the resonance of deep sorrow. "And we pride ourselves on our Spindle sandwiches—they are fascinating! I'm sure they must entice you to stay, even though *I* fail!" she pursued archly.

Mrs. Hobson was quite the most ornate member of the club—a writer of dramas which were never produced; instructor in dramatic art which she did not possess; highly adorned as to person; smelling of sandalwood; fifty-five; and excessive. There were days, reflected Helen, when she couldn't stand Mrs. Gwendolen Elise Hobson,

and this was one of them. She was starting to take her
aching head out of range of the temperamental voice,
when she caught sight of Mrs. Hobson's escaping guest.
He was the tall person she had almost recognized upstairs, and now she fully recognized him.

II

"*Je suis désolée!* But, as woman ever must, I submit!" mourned Mrs. Hobson with bovine playfulness,
and gave her guest a clinging hand. She sank back into
the dining-room tide, he seized his possessions in the
cloak-room, and was hurrying toward the outer door as
if to make sure of escape before recapture, when Helen
became conscious that an imp had leaped into her own
eyes and waited there in ambush. It was not her doing;
the imp acted of its own volition. Such haste was the
gentleman making that he had almost passed the lady
standing shadowy against the wall when the imp, flashing forth, arrested him.

"Ah—good afternoon, Mrs.—Mrs.——" ("I won't
help him out!" Helen inwardly chuckled.) "Mrs—ah,
Mrs. Kent!" he recalled at last.

She held out a hand of greeting. "So Dr. Aspden
flees from our hospitality?" she challenged, while the imp
fairly gloated in amusement at the gentleman's ignomini-
ous retreat.

It was only within the past fortnight that the Doctor's return to his old suite had been effected, and, oddly
enough, Helen had not once chanced to meet him. On
the day of his return there had occurred a great rattling

of the door between the suites—evidently its security was being well tested. Miss Muldoon had caught Mrs. Kent's eye and had buried her giggle in a handkerchief; and there the matter had ended.

"A busy doctor can't give himself even Sunday off for pleasuring," he began his apologies. Plainly, the unexpectedness of the meeting was causing him embarrassment. "I—I—rarely take time for teas—" he muttered, edging away.

"You mean you detest them," Helen finished for him. "I should have known it. Anyone should have known it. Mrs. Hobson should have known it." (Helen observed to her thoughts that Mrs. Hobson's tactics of pursuit had outdone themselves to achieve this capture. Already she had traced the steps—Mrs. Hobson, as a policy-holder in the Monroe Mutual, had contrived to meet the distinguished physician, and her usual pressing invitations had ensued, pressed to the point where refusal was impossible.) "My acquaintance with you has been restricted to one sole and very brief occasion, and yet I know precisely your opinion of teas."

At that moment something within his eyes gleamed, and she saw it. It flashed in sudden response to the imp within her own. With that gleam his irritable embarrassment melted. "At least," whispered her imp to Helen, "he's not trying to get away just now."

In the moment's pause, she observed him swiftly. How distinguished he appeared, she suddenly realized—somehow he towered, by mere personality, above others. The carelessness of dress which she had noted on an office day had disappeared; he stood before her, a fine and dignified figure, conventionally attired, perfectly groomed.

"Perhaps," he said, still with that gleam, "I may have given you reason to think of me as a churl." It was not apologetic; it was amused.

"I think of you as a man. By which sign I know that you would enjoy a cup of that coffee"—she sniffed the air in suggestive enticement—"if you could get it in some quiet spot where you would not be trampled to earth, and where you would not be chattered at by ten at a time, and where you could sit comfortably at a table. It's in man's nature to resent having to poise a cup and plate in midair, while accepting a sandwich with one hand and cake with the other, like a Japanese juggler manipulating his balls."

She saw the swift response in his eyes. It flashed at her as if she were temptation incarnate for that instant. Then he wavered——

"There is a little tea-room upstairs, never used during these big functions," she pursued softly. "You will be safe there from discovery—a maid will bring us coffee —really, I am in need of a cup, and my headache refuses to face that crowded room. There are times when I can't mingle with a throng of humans without realizing that they don't differ one whit from any cage or pit in the Bronx Zoo at the feeding hour. And now I appeal to your sympathy as a physician to see that I have my coffee in quiet——"

Small-talking, she had led the way down a side hall, and into an automatic elevator. Dr. Aspden was following. Upon his lips, moving again and again to speak, there appeared protestations; but the protestations failed to find their opportunity.

Helen summoned a passing maid. "Bring us coffee—sandwiches—everything there is—for two. In the tea-room." And the little elevator sprang into flight at her touch.

Minutes later they faced one another from deep-cushioned chairs across a small table. Speech tarried; but imp met imp in eyes.

"Well?" Helen opened at last.

"Well, indeed! I, a middle-aged physician with a reputation for integrity, having already bidden my original hostess good-bye and hastened away from her hospitality, find myself here!"

Her elbows were on the table, her chin rested in her palms. A slender mirror behind Dr. Aspden showed Helen herself in panel framing; the sketch vividly incisive, an impression of impudent eyes and earrings jettily twinkling between upcrowding furs and forward-tilting hat. A vision of Dr. Aspden's original hostess rose, a moment's imaging of that lady as she would appear did she know the truth—florid, flurried, cacklingly indignant, shrill with outrage—and Helen saw her own imp in the mirror fairly putting thumb to nose.

"But now that you *are* here," she said, "now that you've signed your contract with Mephisto, and *are* here"—— she waved a hand that took in the alluring room with its half-dozen restfully vacant tables, the gay draperies delightfully carrying out the color scheme of a tall screen, the cheery plate shelves, the windows overlooking old and ordered gardens—"now that the die is cast, confess," ordered Helen, "that you like it!"

"That I like it is, I believe, what is disturbing me most." And across the table the two imps, more perilous imps by far than those that wigwag from younger eyes, made signal of mutual and delectable wickedness.

"Don't let it disturb you! The sign of the true epicure in sinning is that he never foretastes his repentance while the sin is still freshly plucked and sweet."

"Believe me, I'll not spoil the flavor of this fruit by any foretaste of repentance! Perhaps, on second thoughts, my disturbance comes from the knowledge that I'm never going to repent."

"You can drown even that in the cup." Maid and tray were at the door. The burnished pot with its slender spout gave forth a steam of pungency; dainty cups were set forth; sandwiches and cakes were placed at hand, and the two were left alone once more.

And now he suddenly relaxed, as if giving way completely to the seduction of it all. "It's shameless and it's jolly!"

Filling his cup, "There's a curious effect these nervous headaches of mine always produce," she informed him. "They make me shameless. I have never yet come through one of them without blackening my record to a still inkier shade. And now, to eclipse all former sins, I have abducted the guest of a fellow club member!"

"To say nothing of adding the burden of his sin to your own."

"Adam!"

"My utmost flattery is to retort by calling you 'Eve.'

I have always felt Eve to be the primary argument for
suffrage, the great original proof of woman's power of
initiative. It was she first knew a good thing when
she saw it; it was she had the courage to take
it; and she was generous enough to pass it on.
It was sporting of her, too, not to throw back
Adam's words at him; she could have called him a liar,
could have declared that he passed the apple, and there
would have been only his word against hers——"

"But hers wouldn't have been credited. Being a woman,
her statement would never have been believed."

"Not believed, but accepted. It's a matter of courtesy to accept a woman's statement against a man's.
Eve must have known that—every woman knows such
things. So it comes to this: she simply refused to avail
herself of the privilege at her husband's expense."

Helen mused. Then the panel sketch flashed back at
her a sudden audacity, flashed mischief——

"How then, is it," she inquired, "that, cherishing so
great an admiration for the first Eve, you have never
succumbed to any of her successors?"

He was spared an answer. The sound of approaching chatter came up the stairs. There were deep male
voices in the background, and against them, in bright
relief, the soprano laughter and ecstatics of women.

"Dear me!" Helen became uneasy. "I thought a South
Sea island couldn't be safer than this to-day! This
floor is never used except on week-days. The other rooms
are rented for studios"—the voices were drawing ever
nearer—"It sounds—" She gasped, and rose, catching
her breath—"It sounds like—like—Mrs. Hobson——"

Dr. Aspden also rose. "It—*is* Mrs. Hobson," he breathed.

III

They stood opposite, staring in blank fellow-confusion into one another's face. And while they stared, the voices—above all, that one voice—approached nearer and nearer, like doom.

"Charming little studio," they heard her down the hall. "I use it for my classes in dramatic expression. So inspiring—that view of the rose arbor and fountain—so quaint—a fountain!" Murmurs and exclamations approved the fountain.

Helen leaned forward across the table. "A second more," she whispered, "and she'll be upon us!"

Dr. Aspden too leaned forward, until their eyes were separated by only inches.

"Eve," his whisper demanded desperately, "have you no resource—no trees of the garden amongst which we may hide—*this* time?"

For a wild moment her eyes beat against the four walls of perilous captivity. Then, "There's nothing less banal," she told him in horror, "than the screen!"

He glanced at it, lifted his hands in a gesture of martyred helplessness that seemed to groan, "And Fate heaps this insult upon the dignity of a sober middle-aged man!" But he bowed to the yoke.

"Time-worn farce shift, I submit!" he murmured. He paused. "But this?" and he pointed to the abandoned feast for two.

"Leave that to me." She clapped shut the screen's fold upon him, and only in the nick of time. Mrs. Hobson's party descended.

"And this is our bewitching tea-room," that lady guided. "Oh—why, Mrs. Kent! So sorry! I thought the room was never used on Sunday!" Mrs. Hobson's prominent eyes took in the table and rested with interest upon Helen. Behind her half a dozen grouped themselves; some of the young people had followed in restless curiosity, and among them was Bec.

"Of course I never dreamed of intruding!" pressed Mrs. Hobson, nevertheless leading on into the room.

"I assure you it's only a pleasure to share this delightful view." Helen waved her hand hospitably toward the garden. "I was too tired for the dining-room, and so I had my coffee served here." She watched Mrs. Hobson's eyes count cups.

"So kind of you to let us come in. Over there"— Mrs. Hobson addressed her guests as if they were on a Cook's Tour—"you get a glimpse of the old church—so quaint!" She led them to the windows. "And here—" her hand clasped the edge of the screen: she was about to draw its folds back to make room for the sight-seers——

It was a moment for any hazard—and Helen hazarded. With ostentatious stealth she jogged Mrs. Hobson's elbow. The others were all intent upon the gardens below. Mrs. Hobson turned, stayed her hand; her eyes inquired.

Detesting the subterfuge, but driven, Helen glanced significantly toward Bequita; then lingered over a deep wink.

In delighted response to the confidence, Mrs. Hobson raised questioning eyebrows, and delivered herself of an answering wink that descended with a fulsome flap, rose, hovered, flapped again.

"Ah!" She bent close to whisper. *"Je comprends!"* Her large white kid forefinger tapped her compressed lips. "A little *tête-à-tête!* When—horror of horrors!— enters the guileless daughter! The *ingênue!* Delicious, my dear! So French! Rely upon me, you are safe!" She whirled away from the screen, giving off a vast puff of sandalwood scent with the whirl.

"And now, my dear friends, we must go downstairs, to have one more word with Mr. Sinclair before he bids us farewell. Do show the young people the way, Rebequita darling," she proposed in a sudden intimacy engendered by the complicity into which she had been drawn with Rebequita's parent. Driving her guests out ahead, she paused for one more unctuous whisper:

"Delicious, I repeat, my dear! One thirsts so for a French note in this dull American propriety! *A deux*— the sudden peril—the lovely young daughter, sweet innocent, arriving unexpectedly—exquisite! My dear, you can trust me as a sister! But I must have my reward!" She shook a playful finger. "I must hear some day who he is!" And with one more wink, which descended upon and enfolded the secret like a curtain, she rustled away.

Again the conspirators stood facing each other across the table.

"The wonderful thing about you," Helen stated, profoundly admiring, "is that you could hide behind a screen—think of it—a detestably farcical situation—you, a distinguished physician of eminently respectable demeanor—and still retain your air of imperishable dignity. Which proves that your dignity is no mere screen like some people's, behind which self may hide."

He smiled. "Probably no less a screen than others—merely less transparent. Only a very opaque one would serve in your presence, I fear."

"At any rate, you deserve a second cup of coffee. Let's both have some more!" They sank with sighs of relief into the willow chairs.

"You've got to settle down and stay, you see, until I make sure by reconnoitering that Mrs. Gwendolen Elise Hobson has left the building," she warned him.

"I'm shamelessly resigned. So let's talk. Talk about——"

"Yes?"

His eyes roamed toward the window, then returned, and rested upon her.

"About Adam and Eve," said Dr. Aspden.

IV

Helen, starting for home a half-hour later, found that Bec had already gone. The fact stirred her discomfiture; it was most unlike the child not to wait for her, or run in to say so if she were leaving with the young people. There was constraint in this silent departure; in it Helen saw mirrored her own escapade as it might have appeared in her daughter's eyes. For Bec, like Mrs. Hobson, must have counted cups!

She felt a quick heat mounting her cheeks—Helen was not of the sensitive temperament that tends to easy flushing. The very fact of the flush increased her discomfiture. She hurried off at an absurd pace to the subway, instead of the Fifth Avenue stage, impatient for the quicker conveyance. Helen Kent was far from admitting to herself, nevertheless, how very much she desired to explain her escapade to her own daughter.

"Home, youngster?" She heard the ingratiating and somewhat exaggerated cheer of her own tone, and it rang in her ears rather like Bec's voice when the youngster was seeking atonement for some misdeed.

"Yes, I'm here." The tone was colourless.

"Sorry I was late, dear, but I couldn't get away any sooner. The fact is, your staid parent, who is already far advanced in her thirties, as you are well aware, contrived to let herself in for as farcical a scrape as any high school miss. My child, hear my tale."

As girl to girl, and with the keenest relish, Helen set forth her adventure in full . . . .

"The plot thickens. My *ingénue* daughter enters, and in her I see a refuge. I feign conspiracy with Mrs. Hobson, who swallows the bait at one gulp. . . ." Unconsciously watching the gas logs' flicker, Helen was rattling on gleefully, her enjoyment growing as the whole adventure reviewed itself amusingly in her memory, when Bec's silence caused her to look up. Bec, unsmiling, was gazing at her from the aloofness of mature and critical observation.

Helen started. Here was a Bec wholly new. She knew the buoyant child of former days; she had lately come to know a depressed girl of unhappy broodings; but here, face to face, sat a woman who calmly and judicially measured her.

Helen closed her narrative briefly and went to her room.

v

Bec sat alone. She did not rise to light the lamp, though the gas logs did feeble duty against the gathering dusk. What she saw was not the darkness, nor yet the prancing flames at which she gazed. It was Helen's face that glowed into hers.

"She isn't thirty, or forty, or any age," she thought. "But she shines, the way she always said I did when the happiest things were happening. She isn't Helen to-night —not the Helen I know, that is; she's a girl, full of something that tingles, and she doesn't even know it.

"Oh, she *likes* him! She likes him terribly much! She could never look like that if she didn't!"

There was a long time that Bec stared on at the logs. Darts of emerald and sapphire and topaz and ruby and amethyst shot up from them and fell back in flickering rhythm. At last she rose, and a queer hardness seemed to rise with her.

"So! She takes *her* fun when she wants it! She scoffs at me because I like Philip so much, and she drives him off, and kills my happiness. She preaches about a fool's paradise. But if *she* wants to like one man especially, that's another matter, I suppose!"

Bec's lips drew abruptly to a tight line; she flung her head.

"She can forbid my seeing Philip, but there's one thing she can't forbid. I won't wait any longer. I'm going to do it—to do it to-morrow!"

CHAPTER VIII

BITTERSWEET ALLEY

I

"THERE'S one thing she can't forbid. I won't wait any longer."

Since Bec's night of tempest, during the days of outward passivity, a plan had hung in the air, ever present, but not quite shaping into resolve. Now at last, following the Spindle reception, all the vague dreamings and schemings had taken form.

"I'll have my dancing in spite of her! Nobody shall wreck my art, whatever happens to my life!"

It was Monday afternoon, and Bec was free. Miss Timmons happened to have been taken obligingly ill; Helen, as usual, was at the office. Nothing stood in the way. Yes, she cried to herself, Helen could tear her and Philip apart, could crush her joy as it was unfolding; but no one had the right to kill her art. Just here her sense of honour was making a curious distinction: it recoiled from the thought of a clandestine heart affair, but yielded to secrecy where art and labour, instead of the self-most personal joy, were concerned.

Yes, this plan meant secrecy. It meant that black and haunted forest of concealment hitherto unexplored, unguessed even, in the sun-flooded travelling of Bec's open road. She was turning into the forest path, was choosing its lurking presences for daily companions. She was leaving the open road that she and Helen had trod together. Hereafter, even though she return, they could never meet without some shadow of that forest entering between them. Something would be gone forever from the exquisite candour of that one-time ardent relation.

But all this Bec did not know; nor would she have halted. She only plunged ahead now, like a wild little stream seeking some outlet, dammed back but finding its channel by instinct, rushing toward its release. The unwitting Helen had cleared away the last obstruction, namely the habit of obedience. For weeks this obstruction had held, though crumbling; but now it had gone down with a final crash, while the wild little stream tore through.

"She takes her fun when she wants it; I'll have my art!"

When a stream is making its own channel it must force a bit here, a bit there, zigzag, nose, shove, creep, bound over. Its instinct is to push ever toward the first hint of an opening. And that opening to Bequita lay in remembered words:

"If only Zélie could teach you! She lives in Bittersweet Alley. . . ."

For some mysterious reason, Philip had bitten back his words as soon as uttered; but this much Bec had caught. Zélie (surname missed) must be a dancer who gave lessons. And she could be found. She could teach

Bec's importunate toes the technique for which they
yearned. That another prompting drew Bequita toward
Bittersweet Alley, her conscious mind never guessed: that
deep within her hidden soul something less obvious but
far more potent than the wish for dancing lessons tugged
her like an undertow toward this Zélie.

She was primed for the adventure. She had looked
up Bittersweet Alley on the map, had found it caught
in a cobwebby tangle of ancient downtown streets.
Thrilled at her own daring, she set out to find her way
alone in this quaint and haunted storeroom of old New
York tradition.

II

A labyrinth of small streets, "Places," courts and al-
leys stretched on all sides. Jaded and faded, the red
brick dwellings of other days now displayed faint-hearted
business signs, such as "Feathers a Specialty," or "Lunch
Room. 25 Cents," or "Tony. Ice, Coal, Wood," or
"Lamparella the Tailor. Ladies and Gents." One sign
read "Two for Tea Room," and behind the shabby ex-
terior Bec caught a glimpse of leaf-green curtains and
lavender tables in array. Once-dignified residences
sprouted dirty children at every window and door, like
garden plots given up to overriding little weeds. Strings
of parti-coloured washings hung about; lean cats skulked,
wearing an expression of being misunderstood. In the
midst of this labyrinth wandered Bec.

The map seemed to have no bearing upon the maze.
Into one letter-L of a street she would turn, down the

letter-V of another, skirting tiny "squares," as dabs of
dingy grass were named, searching signs, entering and
withdrawing from queer, trap-like courts. Over and over
she put her question—"Can you tell me where to find
Bittersweet Alley?" One old woman had declared that
it "would be just around that corner"; another had flatly
contradicted by insisting that it "was back a ways. . . ."
Ah, the sign, at a rusty iron gate—Bittersweet Alley
at last!

The corpse of a long-forgotten fountain lingered in
the centre of the "alley," which was in reality a court,
and from it grass had sprouted, grown lank and dangling
like hair upon the dead. Bec followed the cracked walk
up between aged brick dwellings; there being only a
dozen of these, it was a short matter to find the doorbell
she sought. "Zélie Barrajas" was the curious French-
Spanish combination inscribed above one of the bells
in the doorway of number 5½; and now the door was
opening to her nervous ringing, and she was making her
way upstairs.

At the head of the first flight she paused, peering
with some trepidation beyond. It was spooky lonesome,
Bec told herself. But her trepidation was not to end
with the ending of the lonesomeness. For, after a silence,
came the clattering of a door above, then the explosion
of a voice from dim regions. Like the crack of a pistol
it reported through the halls:

"Who the devil's jerking my bell, anyway?" And next,
like peppering shots, came a series of words in unknown
languages, but strongly suggesting oaths.

Bec cast her eyes up to discern a slender form in

what seemed a gypsy costume. A short, full skirt hovered above bare ankles; the feet attached to these ankles
were thrust into bath slippers, and as Bec stammered
and failed to bring forth an intelligible reply, one of
the feet gave a kick in token of impatience. At the
kick, its slipper flew; the slipper grazed Bec's cheek in
its wild descent through space, and fell on, thudding in
the hall far below.

At this the voice burst into laughter. "Nearly took
you in the eye, didn't it? Wish it had. I won't be
interrupted while I'm practising, I tell you, whoever you
are. So clear out!"

Quaking, Bec hesitated between parley and flight. But
her longing got the better of her fear.

"I—I won't detain you long!" she begged. "If only
I could see you a few minutes on—on business!"

From the explosive snort of rage it appeared that a
more violent dismissal was to follow; but at that moment
Miss Barrajas leaned over, peering more keenly at her
guest, and her mood changed like a gust of capricious
wind.

"Say, you are the peach sundae, all right, aren't you?
Who the devil are you, anyway? Come up and let's
have a look at you!"

Bec's surprising hostess led the way into a long,
sparsely furnished room and flung herself out in a cat-
like sprawl upon the couch, from which vantage-point
she studied her guest with insolent deliberation. Bec,
in turn, studied her hostess. She saw vivid eyes of a
reddish-brown cast; such an exact match for the hair

which hung loose from the scarlet twist of the gypsy cap, that Bec caught herself wondering which Nature had chosen to match the other? And next she fell to wondering how any being as "skinny thin" as her hostess could be so devoid of angles—nothing but curves from top to toe—the long, lean shoulders, stem-like arms and wrists, legs bare below the knees, without a sharp corner anywhere; all like a long ribbon that you catch up and fling out and undulate and let lie. And still she stood —not having been offered a seat—while Miss Barrajas scrutinised her.

The red-brown orbs having travelled over her face, form, hat, and shoes, they brought up at last eye to eye.

"Well—my original question still holds good. Who the devil are you, anyway?" The voice was soft now— the same voice that had exploded in a similar question so shortly before.

"I'm Bec."

"Bec. Who's Bec? Throw a light on your mysterious presence, my fair one. What brought you hither, if I may venture to inquire? Bittersweet Alley isn't in your neighborhood—that's certain. How did you hear of me?"

Bec stammered. "I—I heard someone mention you as a dancer——" She stopped in distress. She had not been prepared for this inquiry, and an instinctive discretion warned her against mentioning Philip.

Zélie noted her embarrassment with shrewd eyes, but let the matter drop. "Well, what are you after?" she went on. "Come across with it."

"It's—it's my dancing I want to talk over with you. You see, I want so much to learn! And if you'll only take me as a pupil——"

"Aha!" The voice sprang raucous, like that of a creature pouncing on prey. Bec was beginning to realise that the voice was perhaps the most astounding feature of this Zélie, leaping from mood to mood, as it did, with feline agility. "So that's it! Not much! I've got a little Russian dance job at present, though I'm still waiting for the golden opportunity—so I don't have to count one-two-three for young idiots who imagine they're the Isadora Duncans and Ruth St. Denises of the future. I suppose you want to wear a Grecian robe while you carry an undernourished jug on one shoulder and drape the other arm like a weeping-willow——"

"But I don't think you'd find me stupid—" Bec endeavoured to break in with faint protest. But the wrath of her hostess was working itself up to so high a pitch that she heard nothing. She stormed furiously on.

"I'm done with teaching forever, I tell you! If I lose my job of dancing, I'd rather take in washing—you can jump up and down on the washing's prostrate form when you feel that way. One of my pupils couldn't tell her fingers from her toes. Another one flapped her arms as if somebody had dropped her into the East River, and I wished to goodness they had. Never again, say I!"

Bec turned away in discouragement. "I suppose it's no use then. I had it all planned, how I'd pay for lessons out of my allowance, and skimp on milk chocolate and silk stockings. And it would be an investment for you, besides—I thought that when I got to earning, a percentage would come to you—perhaps five or six percent." (Thus commercial school training had superimposed itself upon art.) "But I see it's no use. Please excuse me for interrupting you." She tightened her boa for departure.

But at the "five or six percent," Miss Barrajas had burst into a revel of laughter. She flung her arms over the back of the couch; she draped her ribbon-like person over them, suggesting the sheer prostration of mirth; then of a sudden she sprang to her feet, and in one pirouetting step was across the room and pouncing upon Bec, who met the pounce in consternation. If a mountain lioness had attacked her during one of her California camping trips, the pounce and her shock would have differed very little from these.

But the next instant told Bec that her eyes remained in their sockets, her limbs were not sundered. Instead, Zélie's arms entwined her as softly as her own feather boa; Zélie's kiss alighted on her cheek and was gone. Another instant, and her hostess was standing off and gazing at her with a merry tenderness that was fairly maternal.

"You *are* a peach sundae, and no mistake! Five or six percent! Bless the baby! I suppose you see me supporting my own limousine on the interest from this 'investment'! Oh, you are in the prize winner of the Baby Show, and I can't help liking you to save my life!"

Bec's impulse was to resent this; but desire made her cunning.

"Then if you like me, couldn't you, oh, wouldn't you, give me lessons?"

Again Miss Barrajas's indignation rose. "Nary a lesson! I've got my own career to worry about, not other people's. I ought to be practising this minute!" she screamed in annoyance. She dashed to the mirror, and adjusted cap and skirt. "Where on earth's my tambourine?"

"That looks like a tambourine," Bec suggested doubtfully, pointing to a vessel from which a fat tortoise-shell cat was lapping milk.

"Sure enough! I couldn't find a dish that wasn't broken, so I put her dinner in it," Zélie recollected. Slapping away the animal, she poured from the window what scanty lappings were left, and tossed the tambourine on high. She started toward the phonograph; but at that moment something tragic in Bec's eyes, something quivering in Bec's lips, arrested her.

"Oh, well," she said. "Go ahead and show me your stunt. I know you won't be at peace till you get it out of your system. Then I can tell you that 'your talent is remarkable, but owing to many engagements at present,' and so forth. Go ahead!" With a yawn as wide and withering as that of the tortoise-shell cat, Zélie gathered that animal to herself upon the couch and lay back, fondling it so tenderly as to blot out all memory of the recent slapping. The cat, humming like an airplane, curled into her arm, and together the emerald and the red-brown eyes blinked in bored tolerance at Bequita.

"All ready! Come on!"

III

The invitation was not inspiring, and Bec hesitated. "I can't truly say that I have a 'stunt.' I've never had a teacher, and I've never been allowed to see much dancing. So I've made up things. I dance what comes into my head, but my feet are very ignorant."

"Humph! If more dancers used their heads and occasionally forgot their feet, it might be an improvement," Miss Barrajas grunted in approbation.

"But I don't know the ABCs of technique. Anybody can think up ideas for dances, I suppose."

"Anybody can't. Probably you can't, either. It takes genius to originate. Anybody with a flexible body can acquire technique."

"But the ideas just come of themselves!"

Zélie shrugged. "Well—since we're in the presence of the great idea-manufacturer, we tremble with anticipation, don't we, Villageoise?" And the cat gave back her wink. But there was malice in neither the emerald nor the red-brown eye, only half-amused *ennui*.

Although encouragement was lacking, Bequita set her lips in determination to carry out her purpose. She slipped off wraps and hat, and donned a pair of satin sandals from her handbag. "My mother gave me these long ago, when she liked having me dance for fun," she explained. "Afterwards, she never let me have another pair. I am here without her knowledge or consent," she stated formally, as though honour demanded the truth.

She was unconscious of the pathos of the outworn,

outgrown slippers.   Cousin Ress, coming upon them one
day and learning their story, had gone home to declare
violently, "They are veritable symbols of that youngster's soul-struggle!   They look as if the puppy had
dragged them over a ten-acre lot, and I'll wager her
poor little hopes would look the same way if we could
see them.   Helen Kent's the smartest member of the whole
family, and the darnedest fool it possesses."

"And now," said Bequita, shy but resolute, "I'll show
you a dance I made last summer, on the Pacific Coast.
It's different from the Atlantic.   Everybody laughs at
me for saying that you'd know the Pacific is a bigger
ocean just to look at it, but that's the truth.   They say
you can only tell its bigness by looking at the map.
But that's because most people see everything the way
it looks on a map, or in a book, or by some rule—never
the *inside* way.   I think a great ocean is like a great
person—it doesn't make as much noise and fuss as the
little one, but you feel something strong and splendid,
something that you can rest on."

"The funniest kiddie yet," Zélie informed the assent-
ing cat.

"And so," Bec pressed on, absorbed and unheeding,
"one day I was all alone on the beach—it was so sunny
that the sand looked like hot snow—and I had been
in bathing, and when I came out I lay on the sand to
dry, and I played I was kelp.   That's the seaweed we
have out there, very long and traily.   I began to *feel into*
the seaweed.   Do you know what I mean by *feeling into*
things?   Nobody ever does, though they pretend to—

they say, 'How very interesting, yes, indeed!" and then they make me *tired!*" she burst out passionately.

If Zélie understood anything of this groping, child-like mysticism; of the yearning artist imagination seeking oneness with nature, with the self-expression of the universal meaning, she gave no sign.

"All right," she said, "fire away with the reflections of a piece of seaweed on the destiny of man, and its philosophical contemplation of the whichness of the what!"

But some intuition told Bec that there was no offense in this joking; that beneath the crackling surface of it, Zélie in some way responded dimly to her clumsily expressed desire for an increased and a subtler consciousness of life in its manifestations.

"I want a simple little waltz, something as quiet as a lullaby," Bec said, quickly arranging the phonograph for herself. Then with a long, soft toss of her whole kelp-like body, she all at once flung herself, as into the swinging sea.

IV

Zélie was kneeling before Bec, clasping her waist with ribbony arms.

"You are divine! You are an angel straight down from heaven! You are the wonder-kiddie of the age!" Tears hovered against her red-brown lashes. "I kneel to you—me, what am I? As to teaching you—do you suppose I'd presume to give you a lesson?"

Bec gazed, honestly confounded. "But I don't know anything. I'm an ignoramus. I suppose it would bore you too much to give me a little technique, and I won't bother you any more by begging for lessons, but I don't think I'd be impossible if I were brushed up a bit."

"Impossible! Brushed up! Why, you're a genius, child. In heaven's name, don't you know it? You're the one to teach the rest of us. We can learn to fold ourselves like a strip of paper, and we can train our toes to stand alone like performing dogs, and we can accommodate ourselves to anything from a Chopin movement to a fandango, but how many of us have anything to tell, I'd like to know? You aren't 'expert.' But you're the kind that comes down out of the skies without knowing there are rules and regulations here below, and makes the world sit up and take notice." With this she stood off again, and again made a pounce upon Bec. "You darling!" she almost sobbed. "I love you! Yes, actually, I love you! I don't hand out much of that currency—my affection. Found long ago that the interest was never paid, and the principal couldn't be got back when I wanted it to invest somewhere else. But nobody on earth could resist you!" Again her caress alighted for an instant, then flitted away, like the lightest of butterflies.

But Bec was thoughtful. She shook her head. "It's awfully good of you to like my dancing, and to say these kind things. But I know how much I don't know."

"Another proof of genius."

"No. Only of common sense. I'm clumsy. I have the idea, I see what I want to do, but it's as if I'd been given tools that I didn't know how to handle skilfully."

Zélie nodded, though reluctant to admit any qualification of her praise. "I do see what you mean. A little technical training would help you to find muscles that you don't know you have, perhaps. Well—I feel as if my job ought to be washing dishes from the table that's set for you, but if my tips are worth anything, they're yours for the taking. I'm good on technique: I've been through the grind."

And now they fell to planning. In an ecstatic half-hour of turbulent talk the lessons were arranged. Project after project tumbled forth, one upon the heels of another. There was almost a wrangle when Zélie declared that she would take no money, "not a red cent from your blessed little pocket-book, you divine kiddie." In the end Bec sagely appeared to resign the quarrel, with an inner resolve to make her teacher take a recompense as soon as her own earnings should begin.

What hours they would spend together! Bec's school would claim only two afternoons a week after this, so she would be free during much of Helen's absence. They would go to see the great dancers. They would read together the wonderful books about dancing in other countries—books which Bec had found in the library, and of which Zélie had never heard. And how they would improvise, and criticise each other—only how could they ever criticise, when each held the firm conviction that the other was a genius? For Zélie, at her guest's urging, had given her gypsy dance, and to Bec it was the most wonderful madness she had ever seen. "It makes me feel as if I were going mad and wanted to shout to everybody to come and go mad too," she had gasped.

"That's my line—Spanish or gypsy, or any of the

tiger-cat varieties.   S'pose it's natural, considering that
my ancestors were south-Russian, Hungarian, Italian,
gypsy, Portuguese, Spanish, French, and the Lord knows
what else.   That's why I was able to say 'damn' at you
in six languages when you rang my bell. . . . Now your
line will aways be the spirituelle—flowers, spirits, dreams,
—that sort of thing.   Well—some day we'll each find
our G. O.!"   And Bec had thrilled at the delicious intimacy of thus being drawn into Zélie's slang, in which
she was often thereafter to hear sighed longings for the
"Golden Opportunity."

A feast followed.   The larder yielded only a broken
cake of milk chocolate, a green banana, and a shopworn
cinnamon bun, but the spirit of revel transmuted these
into a banquet.   The tortoise-shell cat rubbed their
ankles and hummed in ecstacy.   When Zélie flavored their
glasses of hydrant water with a remnant of *vin ordinaire,*
and the two drank to the future of fame and fortune
into which they should dance their way, the revel was
running so high that for a moment neither heard the
disturbance outside.

v

A violence of scratchy bounds against the door startled
both girls at last.   The door trembled and rattled under
the attack.

"There, there!   What's the matter with you?   I'm
coming!"   Zélie rose, still munching her last bite of cinnamon bun, and lounged to the door, while the demand
for admittance grew more and more impatient.   She

opened to a wagging, yapping, jumping, wriggling, snuf-
fling, writhing, leaping, insisting, clamouring whirlwind
of a Boston terrier, at whose disorderly entrance the cat
retreated to a corner in spinsterly disapproval.

"There! Can't you wait a minute? Anybody might
think I was your bell-hop!" Zélie scolded, patting and
hugging the dog meanwhile. "What have you got now?"
For to his neck was attached a small packet.

She held him on her lap where he revolved, a snorting
windmill, while she untied the packet with difficulty. It
proved to contain a man's glove; Zélie examined the
glove, and displayed two rips down the fingers.

"So that's the trouble! And I suppose he wants it
back by return dog. A pal of mine sent this," she explained to Bec. "This dog of his, A. D. T. by name,
carries any little message between us. He lives a few
blocks from here. . . . It must be after five now—who'd
have thought it? From nine to five he's at his office,
and it's only when he's at home that he sends things by
A. D. T. . . . Gracious—I haven't a scrap of brown
thread to mend this with!" She rummaged for thread not
only in a work-basket and a table drawer, but also in the
larder.

"I have some! This is called my Magic Box," Bec
said, producing from her handbag a marvellous sewing-
box of fairy size, but containing, it appeared, everything
for mending emergencies. It was one of the pretty trifles
which Helen's deft fingers were always fondly adding to
her daughter's possessions.

"Let me mend the rips!" She had found brown thread.

Zélie tossed her the glove. "You look as if you'd be better at that sort of thing than I am."

It was long and slender, badly worn, but the stamp of one of the best of all makes showed within the wrist.

"It's so interesting to read a glove," Bec observed, as she threaded her needle. "Don't tell me anything about your pal, and I'll tell you."

Zélie disposed herself to listen. "Fire away!"

"He is poor," proceeded Bec, driving in her needle, "but he has the finest sort of taste. And he's full of fun. And he is a great deal more in earnest than he will show." She held up the third finger, pondering. "Yes, he loves the arts—all beautiful things—music, sculpture, poetry, drama—and dancing, when it is very true and noble in its meaning. . . ."

She paused dreamily, and her needle fell. But her eyes dwelt upon the brown glove in her hand. Had she glanced then at Zélie, who lay stroking the cat with one hand and patting the dog with the other, she might have seen a swift widening and narrowing of the red-brown eyes, have caught a flickering smile and nod.

"So you're a seventh daughter of a seventh daughter?"

Slowly Bequita's voice returned, but her eyes wandered. "No. I was only—guessing. Did I—guess—well?"

"Extremely well," Zélie replied, drily, and silence fell.

Bec snapped her thread, the rips being mended, and rose. Her eyes were still dreaming. "It's late," she sighed. "I must hurry. Till Thursday, then, Miss Barrajas; and thank you a thousand times for taking me as a pupil."

Her hand slid down to the dog's neck as she passed the couch where he lay curled. He leaped on the instant to her caress, and returned it with doggish ardour.

"Good-bye—A. D. T.!" she said, softly, but she quite forgot the cat.

At the door she turned back. "Oh—I'm still holding the glove!" she exclaimed. "How absent-minded!" She held it a barely perceptible instant longer, and handed it to Zélie, who took it, with a farewell kiss on Bec's cheek.

Bec went slowly down the stairs. The revelry of a short time before was gone from her mood. The brooding fog had fallen again.

"Half-past five! I must never stay so late again! 'Nine to five' at his office, she said. That means that he may drop in here at any minute after he leaves work. And I must never, never once, run the risk of meeting him, for that would be dishonourable. It would be *clandestine*." To Bec, the word indicated the deepest abysses of sin.

So her fiercely insistent honour fought down her longings. Unknown to herself, the strongest attraction to Bittersweet Alley lay in the sense of haunting a spot haunted by Philip. But behind the pliant tenderness of Bequita lay a certain young austerity; a power of sacrifice that could be self-scourging and self-crushing.

"I wonder why he didn't want me to know Zélie?" she mused. "And somehow I feel that she wouldn't want me to know him. I can't tell why, but I'm sure she'll never mention me to him. So everything's secret—like a tight knot."

At the iron gate she turned to look back at her new world of Bittersweet Alley. "How strange," she thought, "that for weeks, months, perhaps, I shall be going there often, day after day at times, and he will never know. He will never know."

CHAPTER IX

THE TERRIBLE GODS

I

NEVER once as the weeks progressed did Bec fail to appear before the Obelisk with lesson thoroughly prepared, fingers spurred to dictation. Evening after evening she poured over her school books, and she often asked Helen to give her exercises in dictation. At last, Helen congratulated herself, the child was "leaving romantic notions behind." It was a sober Bec; coldly preoccupied, but diligent. "Leave her alone and she will come home," was Helen's summary. There had been a blow, no denying that; but the resiliency of youth, especially of Bec's youth, could not long resist spring weather.

Such inquiries as "What have you been doing this afternoon, dear?" always brought the replies, "Reading in the library," or "Studying," or "Walking in the Park"—truths that Helen did not suspect as being partial truths only. The excellence of Miss Timmons's reports amply accounted for Bec's spare time.

Even Bequita herself did not guess that in her diligence a remorseful soul revealed itself. That soul offered up sacrifice and bowed abjectly and sought to propitiate

certain vague gods in terms of Pitman and the mimeo-
graph, of balances, interests compounded, and discounts.

Always she reminded those gods:

"Just slipping off secretly while Helen's at the office
can't be wrong! She will be so glad—oh, simply delighted
about my dancing, as soon as I make a success! She
thinks it isn't practical. But as soon as I prove that I
can make a fortune, and everybody is raving and sending
me American Beauties and saying that I am the newest
note in the ancientest art—then won't she be glad and
proud!" And as the gods maintained their silence, "She
will, too!" Bequita urged lamely and in vain.

For they never broke their formidable silence, these
strange gods of her own invention. Bequita had a groping desire to approach nearer to them, a sense that somehow she might explain the situation and make them
understand her difficulties, as she sometimes did Miss Timmons, when her balances were wrong for a perfectly rea-
sonable reason. Even the terrible Obelisk would cease to
frown when Bec, with the rich appeal of her full candour,
showed her how misleading was the explanation on page
77 of the commercial arithmetic. It was something such
a situation, she felt, that now lay between her and these
dim, formless gods.

Not that she really believed in them as gods, or visual-
ized them. They were merely the undefined, accusing on-
lookers who had sprung up in her imagination of late,
before whom her perturbed conscience was continually
seeking justification. In many ways she was the child
still; and she groped, after the child's manner of con-
fusing conscience with parental rulership. To obey that

rulership or to disobey it is the child's distinction between right and wrong. Until she should find her own soul and learn to heed its dictates, she must continue to grope.

Her gods were born of this vague search for truth. Worship them she did not. In a dusk like that of primitive man, she felt something present and austere, and she feared a good deal; but far more she fumbled for the unknown something that should cast out fear. But as yet naught had been declared unto her.

There was one point, however, on which her conscience suffered no compromise. The Spartan within her held to its resolve. Her dancing lessons might be stolen by way of escapes, evasions, part-truths, excuses; but no other stealing should there be.

With what ingenuity she managed her comings and goings always to escape the time when that "pal" of Zélie's might happen in at Bittersweet Alley! He was never named by either girl; he was mentioned as a "pal" only in connection with that frequent visitor, the dog; and Bec never forgot to avoid the hours within which his visits were possible. She would snatch her wraps in the midst of the most absorbing rehearsal, with a sudden excuse for haste. Never, she held firm, should the forbidden meeting take place. She did not see even a surface ripple of that deep-flowing current, "the wishful self," that had irresistibly drawn her little craft to the same waters on which that other craft was accustomed to float.

II

Bec arrived in Bittersweet Alley one afternoon to find

Zélie scrambling into what she termed her "glad rags."

"Off for a motor ride. Can't give you your lesson. You don't need it, anyhow. You're so far ahead of me already that I might as well try to jump on a train while it's going a mile a minute."

"Nonsense! You're simply wonderful, with all those Russian leaps! All I can do is to dance-out queer things that pop into my head."

"That's the best part of it. And now (give me that slipper, Villageoise!) you're getting the technique besides—have already got it, in fact. We must begin to talk about your début. It's got to be the real thing—very dignified, and an opportunity for you to do your finest work. Heigho! Shouldn't mind having a crack at my own G. O., also. Well—here's to us both—so long! You stay here and practise, and when you go, be sure to leave the key under the doormat so the burglar won't have any trouble." With a kiss, she ran.

Bec waved her out, and turned back to the room, where she could practise undisturbed. It was like another home to her, this queer, shabby studio where for weeks her dancing had been speeding forward toward a surely mastered art.

An odd, but ardent friendship had sprung up between these two girls. Perhaps, at first, each one's unusedness to the other's world and type—a mutual curiosity as to background, vision, reactions, petty personal habits and tastes, with all their deep significance to the feminine mind—had led them to mutual investigation. Zélie drew enlightenment from many details: from the white, never blue or pink, ribbons that peeped through the film of Bec's sheer blouses, as well as from Bec's crystal gaze of non-comprehension at her teacher's occasional "pretty raw slips," as Zélie styled certain of her own phrases in self-rebuke. For all their crudeness, these "slips" always escaped actual vulgarity; there was an underlying fineness in this strange daughter of many nations. Because of that fineness, she began to set a watch upon her tongue.

"If I ever was glad that—it is—as it is," she said once when alone with the cat, "I'm glad now, Villageoise. If it—wasn't all right, I couldn't stand it when she looks at me that open way, like the sky."

Bec, in return, was alertly interested in every glimpse of the Bittersweet Alley mode of living. What charming casualness lay in Zélie's marketing—"Say, there, shoot me up one long French, and charge it to Helen Gould's account!" she might lightly call down to the baker's boy if she chanced to see him passing; and with infallible skill she would catch the crusty loaf tossed from the stairs below. And what lure of mystery gleamed from the narrowed eyes of Villageoise, the cream-fed cat, for whose sake Zélie often drank skim-milk in her own coffee—the pet who was alternately boxed across the room in a temper and consoled by the offer of an emerald velvet evening wrap for a cushion!

Zélie's toes had known dancing as long as she could remember, but her brain had paid comparatively little attention to it. The toes recalled a babyhood of blistering pavements, and the grinding melody of a hurdy-gurdy which lashed on the tired toes to quicker measure, and nights of hurting, and days of the same blistering pave-

ments and peremptory melody all over again. The toes
knew the game from beginning to end; but the brain
opened with astonishment at Bec's revelations.

For Bec had prowled in the library and had found the
most wonderful books—books that told what dancing
really meant. How it had been the expression of joy or
sorrow or praise or triumph or longing or worship to
ancient peoples. (*Worship,* pondered Bec.) It had been
their way of telling what they felt, using the motions of
their bodies like words. Reading, confessed Zélie, was
not her long suit; but Bec would sometimes bring the
books to her and read passages aloud, and sometimes
report what she had read by herself, interpreting, questioning.

That huge volume from the French of Gaston Vuil-
lier—it couldn't be taken to Bittersweet Alley, but Zélie
simply must see it—they went together to the great reference library and pored over its beautiful reproductions
of precious old paintings and sculptures. There was
David Dancing before the Ark, after Domenichino—an
Opera Dancer of the Seventeenth Century—a Sacred
Dance of Greece—strolling ballets, pastoral dances, the
seguidillas of Spain—think of how dancing spreads out,
all over the world, all over the past! cried Bec. And
a *Treatise on the Art of Dancing,* by Giovanni-Andrea
Gallini—how long ago the ridiculous dear wrote it, so
long ago that he made every *s* look like an *f*—but what
wisdom! "Dancing, like painting, can only present situations to the eye; and every truly theatrical situation is
nothing but a living picture," said Gallini in the seventeen-
hundreds. And to-day what could be more true?

Now and then, slipping away together, they saw some of the famous dancers, discussed their interpretations——

"That *Berceuse* is exquisite, Zélie, as she gives it—she dances it with her feeling, and forgets her muscles."

"Ye-es. But I like the kind with more ginger. Now, the Amazon dances from *Iphigenie* would have been corkers if the girls could only have got mad about something just before they went on."

Bec once discovered a precious little monograph on the Japanese Dance, by Hincks——

"Hooray! That reminds me! I'll take you to call on Aya. She danced near me once in a pageant."

Although accustomed to the Japanese in California, Bec had never seen a grown-up human creature so tiny and so lovely, in her own exotic way, as this Aya. She was so small that she seemed more like a little black-eyed bird than one of our kind. Her body could do things that no occidental body can ever learn to do—it could curve and ripple like water, or like young wheat in the wind.

Bec was entranced by this tiny mortal and her art, and the few Japanese words which she had acquired from Koyama, the family cook in California, set Aya into peals of delighted exclamations. Her English was almost as meagre as Bec's Japanese, but somehow the two girls made each other out. In the living-room of the apartment where this oriental household dwelt, the little dancer performed several of the ancient nature-dances of her people, explaining as she danced.

"She says that this movement shows the spring coming—flowers bloom now," Bec interpreted, as Aya seized a long spray of paper fruit blossoms.

"Now summer! See her spread her parasol!

"Autumn! Oh, charming! Maple leaves—red, and she scatters them!

"What can that white handkerchief be for? What *does* she mean?——Oh, oh—spread over her dear little head—winter, of course!"

In a corner Aya's elder sister twanged the samisen. She was hideous in her American dress, with round spectacles; she had protruding teeth and ropey hair; but she drew forth strange music from the instrument with an almost sinister skill.

Aya was struggling to explain. She talked like quick little wooden mallets clattering, and her red mouth pouted in eagerness to tell, even her pudgy nose seemed pressing forward as though it were trying to help the mouth to tell.

"So—dance say—make frower come, pretty, make frower die, make snow come, all die." Her voice drooped. Then, suddenly gay, she snatched up the pink paper blossoms again.

"Frower come—al-ways—again. Buddha!"

In the corner sat the hideous sister, and from her fingers twanged the music of the samisen, hoarse, melancholy, unchanging in its refrain, old with the age of Fuji and the hoary winters and the shifting seas.

This little Japanese was the only one of her friends whom Zélie ever introduced to Bec. Now and then she would answer some neighbor's knock; but, "Go along!

This is my busy day!" she would stamp out at the visitor, and, returning, she would cry:

"They shan't come near you! You're like a little lace handkerchief folded away in sachet!" and snatch the younger girl into a savage feline protectiveness.

III

Bequita, alone in the studio this afternoon with a luxurious sense of freedom, fell languidly to glancing over the music. None of it suited. She wanted very much to dance, but she was vague as to what—no flower or tree or element defined itself, only a nebulous unrest besieged her spirit. It was the weather, she concluded.

She dropped the music and wandered to the window. Here, even in the jaded court of Bittersweet Alley, the green was thrusting itself through crannies, poking impudent fingers amidst the tangle of dead grass that surrounded the broken-down fountain. The window was open; in sneaked a young spring breeze, and it had its way with Bequita.

"How can I dance-out anything," she demanded of it, "when I want to dance-out everything at once?"

At this moment she was interrupted by a scuffling announcement.

"A. D. T.!" she cried, flinging open the door. "A. D. T., dearest of doggies!" He bounded to her arms and she buried her face against his head. A little sob broke her voice, so near the surface flowed both pleasure and pain with the spring's melting of emotional restraint.

"A. D. T., old boy, it's the first chance we've ever had

to talk alone! Tell me—can't you tell me *some*thing? Does—does he ever say anything—as if he remembered? Have you ever told him you know me? Can't *you* say even one little word, A. D. T?"

The dog fixed his eyes upon hers. It was then that she noticed the note tied to his collar. "RUSH! IMPORTANT!" was scrawled imperatively thereon.

"Rush—important!" Bec repeated. "There's something he wants of Zélie at once, and she won't be here till late. Oh, what ought I to do?"

She pondered. To open another's letter was a liberty repugnant to all her ethical fastidiousness; on the other hand, neglect might cause serious trouble. She untied the letter, re-tied it, re-untied it, laid it on the table to wait, took it up to open, studied the handwriting, laid it down, took it up once more, and—broke the seal. This, her insight told her at last, was what the less fastidious Zélie would scoff at her for not doing. The reticence in this case was her own, not her hostess's. And now Bec read:

"I'm leaving the office early; have caught a beastly cold; am all in. Hail, gentle Spring! Be a good Samaritan and have one of your crackerjack toddies hot for an afflicted fellow-mortal, won't you? And one of your open fires? You know how to mother a chap. I'll be there at three sharp."

Philip was ill! He needed care! All the maternal in Bec's woman-nature sprang awake on the instant, responsive to the demand. Her anxious fancy leaped to influenza, to pneumonia. A mental flash even showed her herself bending at a bedside—rubbish, she knew, but the imagination can turn somersaults. But he was ill, he was coming for help, and there was no one else to give it.

Grooves carved themselves in her forehead while A. D. T. studied her face as though awaiting an answer for his master. "What shall I do, what ought I to do, A. D. T.?" she cried. "I mustn't see him—I've always stood by that. Over and over I've hurried home when I thought your master might happen in. I've held to my vow like a nun. I said I'd never run a chance of seeing him; I'd never be here except when he was at work; I put myself on my honour. But this is an emergency case. This might involve serious illness—life or death, perhaps——"

The rather debonair salutation to Spring, accompanied by the request for a fire and toddy, hardly suggested a life-or-death crisis; but just now Bec's judgment was not sober. The depths of her longing soul were sore beset, agitated like waters by a stone aimed straight into their shadowy gulfs. "Life or death—" she murmured again; then, "I *must* make ready for him! There's no other way. Then I'll go. I'll slip away before he comes."

She glanced at the clock. Fifteen minutes left before "three sharp." She must work fast. Fourteen minutes, thirteen, twelve, eleven——

Bottle, lemon, sugar, glass—she had them all together on the table, brought forth from Zélie's cupboard of marvels. She discovered, also, a shabby old afghan, and she placed it alluringly on the couch. Fortunately the fire had been laid ready for the match—now a scratch, and it was off with gasp and crackle. "Poor dear! In a chill, on this warm day!" sighed Bec the mother, and poked the logs to smarter energy.

Another glance at the clock—nine minutes yet. She filled the kettle and placed it on the gas stove, turning the flame low. And now her wraps. They leaped to her, it seemed, so swift were her movements. A moment she paused, for one searching inspection; yes; fire, couch, kettle, ingredients, all were in complete readiness. But what about an explanation? Should she leave some word concerning Zélie, or slip away like a pixie at dawn?

She settled the problem by seizing a sheet of Zélie's rose-coloured green-bordered note-paper (she had never had the heart to make a suggestion concerning note-paper) and scribbling thereon:

Zélie is away until evening. You will find everything ready. Please be very careful not to get——

An appalling problem was here confronted, spelling ever having been full of terrors for Bec; but she valiantly bearded the orthographical lion in his den, and concluded:

penumonia.

Yours sincerely——

She halted her pencil as if it were a runaway steed. How it longed to dash on, to leap at one bound to the tell-tale signature! If only she could let him know that it was she, Bequita, who had tried to "mother a chap!" But it would not do. An instant's debate, then the signature:

A Busy Fairy.

"He has never seen my writing, so there's no way he can guess. Zélie will never tell him." Bec knew this, as she had always known that the same silence which Zélie observed concerning her "pal's" name would be observed concerning her own, Bec's name. The knowledge was as intuitive as it was inexplicable.

She weighted the note in plain sight under the tumbler's edge, noted five minutes left for escape, and turned to flee. She was springing to the door in flight, her hand was reaching to the knob, when, with a mad volley of barks, A. D. T. bounded past her to the door and dashed it open.

Bequita fell back, white and still. "I—meant to—get away—in time—" she panted, and it was to the gods she said it.

IV

The dog went sharply silent, eyes fixed upon a master he did not know—a master who had no word, no pat for him: a master who only stood and stared, then darted into the room, ignoring him, pressing past him——

"But I don't understand! You—you! Here! What can it mean? No—don't tell me! I might lose a minute of the mere fact that you *are* here!" He had her eyes, he had her hands.

"I didn't mean to—oh, I meant to slip away in time—truly, I did!" she pleaded with the gods. "I tried to, but he came ahead of time—I was hurrying as fast as I could——"

It was the breaking-point of weeks of tension, and battling conscience, and pent unhappiness. With a crash of walls that crumbled, a thunder of waters that rushed through, the climax came. He drew her, sobbing, to a seat and kneeled beside her, stroking a hand which she did not try to withdraw.

"Don't, Bequita! Don't try to tell me anything about it yet. All I want to know is that you are here, and I can see you, touch you."

Her sobs were coming in big gulps now, like a child's. Bec the mother was vanished indeed.

"I've kept my word. I've never broken faith. I never stayed when I thought he might come, or sent him a single message by A. D. T.—oh, how I've wanted to tie just one tiny word to that collar! But I didn't. And to-day I hurried, hurried so hard to get away before three—I meant to do right——"

"Bequita! Bec! Please! I don't know what you've done wrong, but I know you didn't do it, because you couldn't. And if it's the gods you are pleading with," (ah, how he knew exactly, how he laid his finger on the pain and eased it by his mere touch—was this all a part of the miracle of his being *he?*) "let me tell you something I've found out about them in a good many dealings."

He rose, and gazed down at her from paternal heights. "It's this, Bec: they're not anything like such old tyrants as they try to make us believe. They frown terribly, like schoolmasters over their spectacles, but in the end they give a chuckle and say, 'Oh, well, boys will be boys, we suppose!' And how much more must they forgive girls for being girls!"

Her hysteria fell back exhausted, and she looked up and met his look. "You're so comforting. How can you tell so well—so exactly—what to say?"

"It's not because of any rare wisdom, dear child. It's

only because—O Bec, can't you see it, feel it? It's only because you are you and I am I!"

She gasped as he struck her own thought like a bare nerve.

"I don't understand the situation at all," he went on, "how you came to be here instead of Zélie Barrajas, and how fate has led me to tumble in upon you—but at present I don't care. It's enough, simply that it *is*. Please let me look at you. And then look at you some more. And keep on looking. And look again. And continue to look, without ceasing. Just because it *is*, Bequita!"

She was drying her eyes now, and a smile crept through the last of her tears. How could tears survive, when she found those whimsical eyes waiting for hers? There were so many things in them: pleading, and mischief, and longing, and make-funning—and that other thing—that thing until recently known to Bec in her dreams alone— that mystery which awaits girlhood at the shrine of life. She did not name it as yet even to herself. Her gods of terror she might daringly face, but before Love she bowed her head, inarticulate.

"Yes—Philip," she murmured. "You may look." At this he drew up a chair, and his whimsical eyes never loosened their hold. "I wouldn't have you not look. We must both look very hard." Her smile faded at this. "Because we can never look again. It wouldn't have happened this time except by accident."

"Bec! Don't say it can never be again!"

"But it's true. We are forbidden to meet—yes, I know all about your coming to my home." She forestalled explanation. "I'd rather—not talk about that—

and what happened—because it hurts. But since I'm
not allowed to see you at home, I can't see you anywhere else, because that would be clandestine." The word
was barely whispered, so profound was her sense of its
dreadful portent.

He smiled gently as if he found her quaint; but the
smile seemed on the outside, behind it lurked a shudder.

"Let's ignore the precarious future along with the
cold-hearted past—for to-day. For to-day, let's merely
be alive. Isn't it good just to be that? And to realise
it? Plenty of people waste time by never finding it out
until it's over. My dear child, let's escape at least that
charge when the account comes to be taken." And once
more that paternal smile bent benignantly upon her, and
made her laugh despite her woes.

"You're so funny and grandfatherly to be only——"
She paused.

"Twenty-four," he finished for her. His eyes queried,
"And——?"

Bec's lashes drooped an instant, as if all maiden revelation lay in her reply. Then she breathed it tremulously: "Nineteen." They had "told ages!" With a
thrill she realized the fact. To tell ages was to have
reached a stage of intimacy so far advanced that the
thought dizzied her. And they were "calling first-
names"—had never done anything else, in fact. It had
all come about without preliminaries, all of itself, as if,
like the entire relation, it simply *was;* with no beginning,
no upleading steps to further the acquaintance.

"We say 'Philip' and 'Bec.' " She gave voice to her
thoughts.

"Do you mind?"

"No. It was natural——"

"As natural as your being you and my being I. And the only unnatural thing is your being here. No, don't tell me yet—explanations take too long when time is flying. Let's hurry away." His glance covered the dingy, ill-kept room; its baronial chairs inherited from the photographic studio where Zélie once had posed as a model, their carvings grey with dust; the broken couch and faded afghan; the gas-smeared ceiling; and the two-plate "cooker" on which Zélie was wont to prepare erratic meals.

"Come, come away!" he cried. "You don't belong here. You mustn't stay another minute. You belong to woods and waters—I have seen the wind frolic with you while you breasted the waves—I have seen you fluttering with the snowflakes and joining their romp. You are a child of nature, you are lyric, and you shan't stay another minute in Bittersweet Alley! We fly, and at once!" He held out his hands to her like a merrily luring faun, mocking his own sentimentalities with his own whimsical eyes, and yet somehow conveying the information that while he laughed at himself for saying it, he nevertheless meant all he said.

Before she knew it Bec's hands had met his, and with a laugh of sheer faun frolic they whirled for an instant of mad rhythm.

"But your cold!" she suddenly remembered.

"Cold? My cold?" He was at a loss.

"And you came to be nursed!" She explained her rôle in the drama.

"Honestly, I'd forgotten it entirely. You see you've done what all the afghans and fires and toddies in Christendom could never have accomplished: you have cured me instantaneously. Not a sneeze left to tell the tale! Did you know yourself for a miraculous healer? Let's put out the fire" (with a dash from the pitcher this was accomplished) "and return the bottle to its shelf; and—why, here's a note——"

Bec stood silent while he read it, shy eyes evading his. When he had finished,

" 'A Busy Fairy'," he repeated, slowly, and again, his voice going low, " 'A Busy Fairy.' "

There was a long pause. Then, very gently, and without mocking himself at all this time, he pressed his lips to the words. From an inner pocket he drew one of those receptacles which dwell within the inner pocket of every man—leather, always rubbed to grey about the edges, always redolent of tobacco, always stuffed to bursting, always subtly maintaining their air of sacredest privacy—and into this receptacle he folded the rose-coloured green-bordered note.

"I've an idea," he observed, meditatively, "that a message like that—merely the careless scribble of a Busy Fairy—might tide a chap over a good many bad quarter-hours in that afore-mentioned precarious future. Fairies so seldom indulge in letter-writing that even a hurried line from one is worth preserving. And now——" with a brisk slap of the pocket which seemed to cry Hence! to cloudy meditation, "We must be off without further delay. I will summon wings to carry us to the woods, where all fairies, of course, really belong. What do you say to flying as swiftly as possible to the upper end of the Park, and there descending to earth, and trying which of us first shall discover the spot where the Snow Fairy once danced?"

"Oh, we can, we must! Surely we shall find it, and see how it looks in its new spring dress!"

In a whirl of laughter, with cries of gaiety, they were off, A. D. T. leaping between them, barking an accompaniment to their May madness. Not once did Bec protest; she did not so much as waver. The great tide of life had caught her up as though she were no more than a petal to offer resistance; had swept her to itself, was bearing her onward with unswerving mastery out toward far waters.

v

At an upper entrance of the Park the taxicab deposited them. It had writhed its way through blocks of traffic; amidst the cloppings of hoofs, the raucous warnings of motor-cars, the clangings of trolley bells, the roarings of elevated trains, the muffled growlings of subways; blocks, miles of this; and here, all at once, as at the waving of a wand—here was Spring.

She danced forth riotously to welcome them, with a fling of skirts and a clatter of tambourine. The Park, city-girt and elderly, was joining in the dance; it had decked itself in the yellow of forsythia, the purple of wistaria; it had sleeked down its green silken hips; and now it made as if to step forth jauntily, extending hands to them, while Spring shook loose the rhythm from her tambourine. "I am as young as you—yes, younger!" the elderly Park might have been crying to Bec. "For no youth is as young as age renascent. Dance as gaily as you can, and still I shall out-dance you; for across the path of youth the future must ever and again cast a shadow; whereas, a future that lies behind cannot be feared."

So they met, Bec and her lover and the Park and Spring. It was a meeting of mad pulses.

"And now for the Snow Fairy's dancing pavilion," he cried, as the path folded them away from every contact of the city. "Can you recall——"

"I haven't the least idea—except that I entered by that path. But I wandered. Let me see. . . ."

"In that case," he said with guilty demureness, "I win. For I've been here so many times since, hoping that fate might again arrange a meeting, that I can show you every landmark!"

And to that confession she made no reply. But, impulsively, she held out her hands to him.

VI

"Ah, here's the clump of bushes!" he pointed out.

"The very bushes! Where is the squirrel that——"

"Cleaned me out of——"

"Peanuts——"

"And revealed his true character——"

"So that you revealed yours, by calling him names——"

"Which he richly deserved."

"Pot and kettle! As if you weren't quite as much of a

fraud as he, when you pretend that your cold is cured!"

"But I swear it! Can it be, O Lady of Magic, that you are unaware of your own powers?"

The tossed chatter fell, like a ball; Bec had failed to toss back.

"I'm more aware of my lack of powers," she mused aloud. "Somehow I used to think that life was—I mean, that one could do—anything—have anything—one set out for. And nowadays it feels as if there were walls all around, like those around a blindfolded person, and he goes ahead without seeing them, and all of a sudden he goes *bump!*"

He gazed down in long reproach. "Bequita!" he rebuked, at length. "When to-day we have come here merely to *be!*"

She could not realise how precociously mature was his knowledge of the evanescence of joy, that he held it so fiercely sheltered for the brief hour.

But she turned penitent. "Forgive me! But, do you know, Philip, I'm beginning to think that perhaps I'm really grown up!" Thus she interpreted her despondencies, the growing-pains of the soul.

"Never! You couldn't be!" he smiled. "A fairy dwells in a changeless world of un-grown-up-ness. And now—ah, now! Here is the very spot, the tree under which the snow dance transfixed the gaze of mortal eyes, casting over the mortal owner of those eyes a spell from which there is no escape."

"It is, it is the very tree! Men have a much better sense of locality than we. Don't you think it's nice of me to own it?"

"I think everything's nice of you.   And look!   Hush, A. D. T.—no chasing!"

Straight up to them came a squirrel, scanning them so diligently as to lead to the belief that he recognised old friends.

"The little rascal!   Of course it's he!   It's perfectly evident, Philip, that he knows us."

"Let's put it to the proof.   If he rejects a peanut, he's a stranger.   If he accepts it, then of course——"

"Of course!"

With a flash of swiftly manipulating paws the peanut was snatched.

"Identification   complete!"   Philip   cried,   and   with laughter they swung off, out of the sunshine into the sweet enfoldment of a deeper, more lost path.

Their talk rambled on irresponsibly, touching here, there, everywhere, as the talk of lovers will, as though time spread before them like a boundless park through which they might wander without arrest.

The news they had for one another was endless.   They could have talked a week, a month, a year, it seemed, and then have paused only for lack of breath.   He must tell her of his new work, and of the bachelor rooms he had acquired in a most inexpensive block, along with a jani-tress known as the Dutchess, who retailed romances of her one-time carriage and pair while on her knees with scrubbing-brush poised.   Bec, in the tumbling-forth of her news, found herself picking up all the unimportant items first: she had learned skating the past winter, such a wonderful out-of-door novelty to a Californian!   And a canary had joined the family, a legacy from its mistress, a lovely California girl who, dying in the influenza epidemic, had asked that the bird be sent all the way from San Francisco to Bec's tender care. And oh, the one important thing she had forgotten—her Roof o' Dreams!

"Roof o' Dreams? The very name enthralls me!"

"High above the city I gaze forth over all the world, and dream dreams——"

"And weave spells, fair lady!"

"In a wonderful dream house, set round with daisies and pansies and geraniums and forget-me-nots." And she went on to tell him of the little canvas shelter which Helen had devised for Bec's out-door hours, an awning above a steamer chair and flower boxes, erected on the roof of the apartment building.

"The mere picture sets me dreaming, too!" he declared.

When he told her the tale of the cabby "who risked a smash-up and wouldn't take a cent, that I might find my Cinderella," Bec listened enraptured.

"What a man he would be to know!" she sighed. "For he is evidently an idealist, and idealists are so uplifting!" Occasionally Bec exposed doctrines not derived from Helen's teachings. "And you've never seen him again?"

"Ah! There begins Chapter II." And he related the sequel. It seemed that he had run across the cabby again, one stormy winter day, had paid the delinquent bill in full, much against Mr. Popp's (for that was his delightful name) wish, and had wound up by calling at the Popp home, as full of grandchildren as a nest of young birds.

"Poor old chap, he's hard up. Can't work much, on

account of rheumatism.   And yet he rejected my cold
cash on that occasion!"

"Oh, what fun it would be to play fairy to all those
darling little Popps!"

His eyes rested upon her, and a tender reverence filled
them, the sort of reverence with which we grown-ups regard a child when it is borne in upon us how much nearer
than we it is to the inner secret of things.

"You shall see them some day," he promised.   "And
now let us be very businesslike, and discuss the future."

The words startled her; she glanced at her watch.   "I
must go.   And there isn't to be any 'some day,' Philip.
I've been forgetting."   Her voice sagged.   "I've been
imagining that all this was real, instead of a tiny, short
dream, tucked in between years and years of realness."

He drew her to a seat upon a fallen tree.   They might
have been in the depths of a forest for all they could see
now of the city.   On every side they were enclosed by a
mist of young green through which the black trunks, not
yet concealed by the new foliage, showed in decorative
upright lines.

"Bec," he said gravely, "do you suppose that I am
going to abide by any dismissal that is not of your own
volition?"

She was silent.

"Until to-day," he went on, "I did not know but that
you also, on second thoughts, dismissed me.   But now
I believe that your will would be to see me again.   Am
I right?"

Her eyes answered that.

"Then," he went on, still in that slow, sure, grave

voice, "no one can prevent our friendship. We men that were in France learned not to take a 'no.' I intend to see you again."

"No, no, Philip! Promise you won't try to meet me at Zélie's! It's a matter of honour to me. Promise!"

"I promise that, for I hope never to see you there again. And now will you tell me how it happened?"

She told him briefly of her acquaintance with Zélie, of the lessons, the plans for a career. He listened with growing astonishment.

"You don't mean to say that you've been studying under her constantly for weeks?"

"Yes, for weeks."

He compressed his lips and knitted his brows, as though endeavouring to solve a mystery. "When I found you there I never dreamed but it was some strange accident for the once. How can it be that——" He broke off. Then, almost angrily: "And to think that one stray remark of mine, a remark I snatched back as soon as it escaped, should have——" Again he broke off. "Look here, Bec," he began, authoritatively, and in that tone Bec had her first taste of man's protective proprietorship, which we ever resent and for which we ever adore him. "You must call it off, and right away. Zélie—well, Bittersweet Alley isn't the place for you."

"But she's a friend of yours!"

"So she is, a loyal little old pal. But—well, my dear child, you can't understand these things, but Bittersweet Alley——"

She rose, flushed and on the defensive.

"Give up Zélie Barrajas? Indeed I'll not! If you

think I'm going to give up a true friend, just because her note-paper and her apartment are different from mine——"

He had risen, too, and he stood looking tenderly, wisely into her face. Her words resounded in her own ears. Actually, she was quarrelling with *him!* It came to her then, never to be forgotten, how easily the bells may be put out of tune.

Her hands went out to him. "How could I—to-day!"

"You are right. We'll drop disagreements for to-day. But as to the future—you won't tell me where I may find you?"

"There isn't to be any future, for—us."

He did not reply. The spring day's brilliancy was softening toward twilight as they emerged into the crowded drive. Behind, woodsy fragrances reached out after them like soft urgings to return, but Bec faced steadily outward. The precious, tiny noises that a few minutes ago had surrounded them—a breeze in the leaves, birds' wings, the scamper of a squirrel—these had vanished, lost in the city's din.

At the corner she gave him her hand, but she did not look up. Her "good-bye" was hardly more than a choking whisper. "It's—for always," she breathed. And the crowd had surged between them.

CHAPTER X

ZÉLIE FACES THE INEVITABLE

I

ON the same evening, Miss Zélie Barrajas, having dined frugally to atone to her purse for "one high-fly afternoon" on Long Island with a party of convivial spirits, settled down to domesticity with Villageoise.

"Sorry for you, my dear, that it had to be weak-fish instead of halibut steak," she apologised, hunting for something to dry the dishes, and discovering a soiled and stringless apron which would serve very nicely as dish-towel. "I know your preferences. Same here. But you're a wise one. If you can't get halibut steak you'll give an extra clean lick to your dish to make anybody believe you really like weak-fish the best, after all. That's what I call the sporting spirit, Villageoise."

Villageoise accepted this compliment to her philosophical nature with superb indifference, and continued to pursue the last particles of fish over the edge of her plate with long, sidewise reaches of a sinuous pink tongue.

"You're a better dishwasher than I am, Madame Cat," Zélie's sociable chatter continued while she inspected her own superficial results. "I suppose domesticity never was

my long suit. All the same, if Somebody was to come
along and remark, 'Zélie, my dear, what'd you say to a
little apartment with all modern improvements, including
shower-bath, kitchenette, and marriage certificate framed
on the wall?'—I said if Somebody was to, Villageoise, not
Anybody, you understand—oh, say, Villageoise, would
you go along to purr the hymen-eel anthem, I guess
yes!"

Zélie drew a long sigh and her eyes went dreamy. She
turned toward the open window, her improvised dish-towel
slung like a dancer's scarf over her shoulder. The warm
weather loafed with invitation.

"Yes," she rambled on, "there's something about domesticity that sort o' comes out in the Spring, like violets
and monkeys on hurdy-gurdies. You don't think much
about it till the weather gets hold o' you, then you begin
to see how you'd look at a cute little white sink, with
ruffles on your apron, or putting away the cream in an
icebox just big enough for two. . . . Come in!"

She swung about at the knock, a quiet, purposeful
knock; then, with a joyous start, swept forward, hands
out.

"Honey, old boy! Why didn't you give your three-
rap signal? Say, but it's good to set eyes on you again!
Been motoring on Long Island—some class, eh, what?
Say, Philly, dear, that new suit sure has got the style,
there's no doubt about it, and brown certainly is your—
say, what's the matter, anyhow?" She had come to
silence abruptly at last, halting with hands on his shoulders, pushing him off to arm's length for better inspection.

There was no response: he was restrained and sober. And now she realised what his look held: in it she read criticism, and austerity; something that was not exactly anger, but more alarming: something that she stumblingly defined to herself as "a sort of cold far-off-ness." It was as if, it seemed to Zélie, he had passed beyond her, into some rarer atmosphere. Her lips lost their mischievous smile. Something that had shone in her eyes from the moment he entered went out like a blown flame. Slowly, very slowly, as if numbed, her hands fell from his shoulders; slowly her eyes ceased their merry, tender scrutiny. She turned, and, picking up Villageoise from the easiest of all the uneasy chairs, she buried her face for a moment in the tortoise-shell fur.

Only Villageoise heard her whisper.

"It's come," was what Villageoise heard. "I always knew it had to come."

II

She rallied vigorously. "Villageoise, I'm ashamed of you! Give the gentleman a seat!" With a padded thud the cat was dumped upon the floor. "Here, Phil, make yourself comfortable. You'll excuse me if I finish the dishes, won't you?" She twirled toward the cupboard.

Zélie could feel ungovernable contractions of her face going on, as if the face were turning somersaults. It seemed to her that her lips were jerking, that her eyes were twitching, her forehead knotting; but a glance at the mirror showed none of these nerve-writhings recorded on the surface. Only a queer, dry glitter of the eyes, a hot reddening of the lids with no sign of tears, and an unnatural pallor through her swarthiness. Yes, she would pass muster as to looks, she reassured herself.

"Sit down, do!" she urged again, hanging the one be-handled cup upon its hook. *"Tra la la, tra la lira!"* She hummed a bar of her Spanish dance with laborious lightness. "Long Island's great this time of year. Say, you ought to have seen the way we speeded. You couldn't have told us from a torpedo shot from a submarine. Reddy said that new hat of mine sure was some periscope. Oh, *tra la la, la lira!* Say, listen——"

Philip had not taken the seat vacated for him. Instead, he had thrust his hands deep into his pockets and was pacing up and down the long room, his eyes raking the floor. At length he halted near her—she could feel him there while she went on arranging dishes, rearranging them, *tra-la*-ing inconsequently. . . . If only her face would stop those somersaults—surely they must show now! And her heart was pumping up, up against her chest——

"Zélie!"

"Present! Well, what, honey? Don't set my heart to pitty-patting like that! When you employ that tone o' voice, I can't tell whether I'm to be court-martialled or proposed to, and the suspense makes me nervous." With an *insouciant* flip of the improvised dish-towel she went on putting away dishes, as though they were the primary concern of life.

"As soon as you're through, I'd like to have a talk."

"Talk on, sweet babbling brook. Oh, *tra la lira li*——"

With an impatient expelling of breath he turned on his heel and paced the floor again. Her pretense fell away of a sudden, exposing all the pitiful fright beneath it. She laid aside the dish-towel, closed the cupboard door upon her labours, crossed directly to him, and waited, her eyes squarely meeting his; for that second she wore the look of the brave facing execution.

"Well?"

"We might as well sit down to it," he said, quietly. "I want you to tell me the whole story, please, to begin at the beginning." (If only he wouldn't be so quiet about it, so dreadfully gentle and self-contained!) "Please tell me how you came to take Miss Kent as a pupil?"

Zélie shrugged, and with an effort regained her flippancy. "I didn't 'came' at all. She did it. She came here hunting for me and begging me to teach her as if I was Pavlowa and all her future hung on the guidance of my master hand—or master toes, eh, what? It was my busy day, and I pretty near kicked her downstairs, but when I got a look at her I had to have a heart."

"Rather!" she heard his aside. Aloud he went on questioning: "So this has been going on for weeks?"

"Correct, my bright lad."

"And you never once mentioned to me that you had a pupil, that you knew Miss Kent, that——"

Zélie ostentatiously rounded her eyes to saucers. "How was I to know there was any need to mention it? She never spoke of knowing you!"

"Let's be honest, Zélie." (Ever more dreadfully quiet he grew—if only he would lose his temper!) "It's pretty evident you did know something, or you would never

have kept so still about the whole affair, considering that
I see you every few days, and we naturally make a pretty
exhaustive interchange of news of our doings."

"I don't recall that *you*'ve ever mentioned her in all
that 'exhaustive interchange'!"

At least she had made him wince. "There's been nothing to mention," was all he could say. "I've not seen her
for weeks until now. But you—teaching her—being
with her day after day—you never *happened* not to
speak of her. You had a reason."

If his rebuke for her failure in the candour of friendship had been less gentle it might not have stung her
to such sharpness of retort. "Prob'ly I had," she snapped.
"I usually have a reason for my conduct. But considering you hadn't seen her for weeks, I take it you hardly
know her. So why the deuce you should get so fussed
up over it I can't see."

He did not reply to this, but sat looking straight
into her eyes, and all at once she recognised in that look
—pity! *That* she could not bear. Her lip shook, and
she bit it wrathfully in its weakness; she squinted back
the hot tears that started.

"Zélie, we've been good old pals—" he was beginning,
and he laid a hand on hers. But she snatched her own
away.

"You can have the whole story, and welcome! since
you've got the curiosity of a cat! Miss Kent came to
me for lessons, and all she said was that she'd 'heard
someone mention me as a dancer.' When she pretended
to describe you from your glove, I tumbled as to who
the 'someone' was, but seeing she didn't care to talk

about it, I just laid low and held my tongue. I knew
you'd never have advised her to come to me" (a bitterness shadowed her face for a moment), "so I figured it
out like this: Prob'ly you'd happened to mention me
and my dancing to her, and prob'ly she'd burst out, in
her way, that she wanted to know me, and then you'd
regretted what you'd said, and told her not to look
me up. That, I figured, was one reason why she kept
so quiet about you. So you see, naturally, I wasn't going
to give her away."

Perhaps he was reflecting on how uncannily accurate
her surmises were, as is so often the case with creatures
as primitive and intuitive as Zélie. Perhaps he was
debating how to meet those surmises. At any rate, he
did not reply for long moments, while his hands hung
locked between his knees and his stare saw only the
floor.

Then he sat up with a gesture of final resolve, but
his voice was gentle.

"Zélie, it's got to come to an end."

She felt as if something within her were turning white:
her very heart, like her face. But she mustered a debonair
lift of the eyebrows.

"An end? You've got another guess coming, sonny. I
didn't want her at first, but now I've got her career on
my hands, I'm going to put it through till I see her
launched, believe *me!*"

But he shook his head. "It can't go on, Zélie. I am
the only one of Miss Kent's friends who knows of her
coming here, and that's why I feel that it's up to me.
I appeal to you; do you think that Bittersweet Alley

is the place for a girl so young and utterly inexperienced?"

"You mean—you mean——" She was only breathing it, her voice seemed to hiss in her throat. She had said the thing herself, but now that *he* said it, rage choked her.

"You mean that—that you consider me——"

He swung about in his chair and laid both hands upon her arms, holding tight when she tried to jerk from his grasp. And now his eyes struck straight into hers, not with austerity or coldness or even gentle pity, but with a world of frank and tender friendship.

"No, Zélie Barrajas, that is not what I mean! I know you through and through, and I know what you are, and I count knowing you as one of the worth-while friendships of my life—the friendships that boost our belief in human nature, and give that belief something to fall back on now and then when it feels the need.

"I saw you come to this city. You had never had any teaching, anybody to bring you up; you were alone, nobody to care, without a cent, and handicapped by much charm and prettiness. It looked like a foregone conclusion. But it wasn't. There isn't one girl in a thousand in just your situation, and with just your vagabond background, who could have kept straight. But you have. When a girl like you comes his way, any man that's worth the name takes off his hat."

She had ceased to fight for her freedom. She sat drinking in his words, quivering in the pain of the joy they brought her.

"But it's Bittersweet Alley, Zélie," he went on. "You

and I know what this particular type of 'Bohemia' stands
for.   It isn't the true Bohemia, which should be a centre
of care-free gaiety and the good old eat, drink and be
merry spirit of let-the-morrow-worry.   This is ugly and
festering.   It's sordid and morbid and slimy.   *You* can
take every type into your good, warm friendship, welcome them all, and march on straight in your own way;
but do you think that such an environment is one that
a man can bear to think of in connection with the girl
he——"

She waited for it, as for a stab.   It came.

"He cares for," he finished.

There was a very long silence.   She slipped her arms
from his hold.   She was struggling again with that queer
feeling of having turned white inside, as though her heart
were as white as her face.   Yes, she had known it all
along, her brain was trying to tell her, but——

"You needn't be afraid," she heard her voice say at
last.   It sounded a long way off.   "I've always thought
of—her—as a little lace handkerchief to be folded away
in sachet.   I've watched myself—my talk—I've never let
her meet any of the crowd, with their raw stories, and
their ways.   I've sheltered her, always.   Can't—can't you
trust her to me?   If you can't, how am I to believe what
you say of me?"

Very strange her voice sounded to her: it seemed to
have gone humble, and it ended almost on a sob.   Still
his gaze was full of frank, tender friendship, and now
something within him seemed suddenly to give way.

"Yes, Zélie, you *can* believe that I believe in you!   I'm
ready to prove it.   Now that you tell me this—that she

is under your protection—sheltered from the things that surround her here—then I trust her to you. I have no right to say that," he added, "except—that I love her, whether she lets me or not."

The words, slow, low and distinct, fell into a silence like a pool. It was as though the ripples they caused faded ever so slowly. Zélie's face was averted. It was a long time before she spoke. She said then:

"I sometimes think"—she was speaking to the world beyond the window, not to him—"that nothing could harm her anyhow. It's as if—as if—well, nothing could soil a star that was shining down on Bittersweet Alley, but we'd all be shined up a lot by that star."

At that he did a strange thing: he kissed her on the forehead. Then he went.

Zélie rubbed the spot curiously.

"I know what cheeks and lips are for, Villageoise," she observed, "but that's a new one on me. It made me think of church."

III

He was gone.

As he closed the door and went down the stairs, Zélie had a sense of clinging to each sound, as one clings to words of the dying. To be sure, he would come again. That is, the shell of him would. But the Phil inside that shell, her own, as she had counted him in friendship, was gone, she knew, forever.

"He's always played fair—don't you dare say he hasn't!" she cried now to Villageoise, as if that unwinking observer had uttered blame. "He never led me on; he always made it plain we were only pals. But as long as there was nobody else——"

Villageoise's silence was perhaps construed as criticism, for Zélie burst out:

"Oh, I always knew I was a fool! But I couldn't help it! Who could? With his fun, and his little ways of doing nice things for a person, and his loyalty, and his squareness. He hasn't got a fault I ever could find— and I've hunted for 'em—except the way he keeps himself poor trying to support everybody that's in trouble. I've even got my suspicion that he was back of that lady who paid my hospital bill last winter. He knew I wouldn't let him help if I knew it."

Villageoise remained non-committal. "Well, suppose you were me!" Zélie cried to that stony silence. "Suppose you'd been born a vagabond, and the world had played ball with you, and then one clean man liked you the straight way!"

Her own words broke her down at last; she ran to Villageoise, and flung herself, sobbing wildly, against the tortoise-shell fur.

"My God! Why don't I hate her? Why don't I twist that yellow hair around her neck so tight that she never breathes again? Why can't I? Because I love her, I tell you! I'm going to see her a success, if it takes all the fight there is in me. Oh, I'm a fool, I know it, a fool! I'd like to hate her, but you could easier hate roses and stars."

Her wild sobs and cries, elemental, undisciplined as the cries of some creature of the woods, rose higher and higher until they beat themselves out in sheer exhaustion. No sound remained except the flapping of the court's iron gate which Philip had left open; rusty and hoarse with age, the gate squawked mournfully back and forth.

CHAPTER XI

ROOF O' DREAMS

I

ON that same evening, Bec pushed aside her dinner plate in languid distaste.

"Please, dear!" she begged off. "It's too warm for anything but the salad and fruit."

Half dazed by all that had happened, she had hurried home from the park to greet a depressed and preoccupied Helen. For a moment, this mood had caused Bec acute anxiety; Helen was not herself; could it be that she in any way knew——?

"The country must be lovely. I've been walking in the Park now, to play I was out of town," she had said, nervously forestalling questions.

Helen had made no response to this. An instant of panic-stricken self-consciousness had caused Bec to flush deeply; then her own preoccupation had surged back, washing away every other thought. If only she could escape, could think alone!

"I'm rather tired. I'll go to the roof and rest." She was leaving her strawberries unfinished.

"Take your sweater. These spring evenings are treacherous."

Bec went for it. She always wore it on the roof. But now, as she met its frank boyishness, it repelled her. A sweater didn't belong to her mood to-night. It was angular and efficient, it suggested enterprise, the day's work capably abetted by its snug fit and free arms. No, she couldn't bear a sweater to-night! She must have some languorous wrap—a clinging oriental shawl for leaning and dreaming would be the thing, but only old ladies wore shawls nowadays . . . ah, her evening cloak!

She drew it from its hanger. It was a marvellous frosty green, pale as a Luna moth's wing. Luxuriously she nestled in the folds of its silken lining. She started for the roof.

Helen's finely cut nostrils dilated slightly at the sight.

"A sooty roof should improve the appearance of a pale green evening cloak!"

"I'll be ever so careful, truly. It won't get a speck, and if it does, I'll clean it myself, with gasoline."

"It will be done by the dry cleanser for five dollars."

For a moment the girl swerved. The old Bec would have gone back for the sweater; but now came the thought, it was her own cloak! To be sure, she had not bought it, but neither had Helen; it had been a gift from Cousin Ress.

"If it does have to go to the cleanser, I'll pay for it out of my allowance," she said coldly, and went.

Alone on her Roof o' Dreams, Bec drew a long breath of release. At last she was high above the turmoil of life; at last she could think. And yet how could she

think, in the face of all that had taken place? Any
attempt to readjust her mental world at present was like
trying to pick up a town and set it back in place after
a cyclone's visit.

She walked restlessly to the parapet. Far away the
lights of the city's heart made a murky glare. Nearer,
she could trace the bright lines that were busy thorough-
fares, the duller channels that were less-frequented streets.
Dim towers pricked the twilight sky here and there; even
the looming tanks and pent-shafts on near-by buildings
took on a certain dignity, sombre monoliths rearing themselves against the sky.

Her steamer chair awaited her under its canopy. She
sank back against its cushions. She was exceedingly
weary from the day's excitement, but weary beyond the
point where rest ensues. Her brain was agitated to a
keen wakefulness.

That adjustment to the inevitable which nature so
mercifully arranges for us had helped Bec over the weeks
during which she had looked upon Philip as lost. But
now all the longings had been roused again, and to an
intensity tenfold greater than before. As the swift heat
had released the ready leaves into sudden bursting, so
those afternoon hours had forced into a full blooming
her pent emotions. She was no longer vaguely dreamy.
Her overwrought brain teemed with vivid memories of
each minute incident, each insignificant word.

All the occurrences of those brief hours whirled before
her, as if they were a reel in which the same pictures repeated themselves endlessly. Over and over she saw Philip

as he entered Zélie's door, and stood dumbfounded at
sight of her; the squirrel coming to meet them; A. D. T.
barking at it; Philip as he walked beside her in the woods;
Philip as he drew her down to the log——

And so it went on. Each scene, each word repictured.
And, forcing their way as they never had forced before,
the longings now seized upon her: longings for that perfect companionship which she visualised; for relief from
that loneliness of intellect and soul which Philip's absence
now meant to her.

Was it wrong, she paused once to ask herself, to long
so desperately for her lover? Was it unwomanly? Could
it be true, as the novelists would have us believe, that
maiden charm and dignity consists in sitting remotely
aloft upon a pedestal of ice?

Unenlightened, pitifully new to life, from which her
mother had "shielded" her for nineteen years, Bec heard
her strange gods speaking through Helen's voice alone,
condemning to outer darkness all the pure and womanly
passion of youth, leaving it to cry alone in that darkness, unheard. And, seeking in blind obedience to obey
those gods' teachings, she wrestled there alone with her
tortured emotions. They cried out in their pain; they
claimed their own; they struggled to assert their purity
—a purity founded on the truth that is the very essence
of life—but Bec fought on. At last she conquered. Little
by little they fell back. She had found rest at last—
the rest which despair brings, a rest in which the heart
sinks with the sagging muscles, and the sense of oblivion
follows the desire for it.

II

Helen lingered alone over her coffee, forehead in hand.
"Matter with you, Nell?"

She had not heard the doorbell, so deep was she in
troubled thought. And here was Ress bustling in, more
than ever cheerful, more than ever be-figured over with
a new foulard design of uncommonly ample size.

"Good!" she greeted her cousin. "You look like a stiff
breeze to blow away glooms. I'll have fresh coffee
brought."

"I made a point of being in time for coffee. Don't
dump any worries on to me till I get it—then, Barkis is
willin'," she offered, in the idiom of an earlier generation.

"You shall have a dozen cups and not a single worry.
I've no desire to spill over."

Nevertheless, at the end of the first cup, Ress displayed
sympathy. "Work going badly?"

"Going wonderfully, on the contrary. Mr. McNab
owned to-day that the experiment already looks like a
brilliant success."

"I always knew it would! Well, then, there's only one
other problem that could drive you to the point of wearing your prettiest filet collar crooked—namely, Bec.
Where is she, by the way?"

Helen reached up in startled fastidiousness to adjust
the collar, and shrugged at the same time to indicate
that no disturbance lay in Bec's direction.

"On the roof. We're moody this warm weather. We
wander in the Park and don't want dinner, and we de-

part in our light-green evening cloak to commune with nature." Again Helen shrugged. "I suppose there must still be glooms at times, when she happens to remember the lovely boy doll that was snatched away before she had a chance to play with it."

Miss Clifton seemed to be weighing some question. "You've never described the youth to me. Do you mean that literally? Is he a boy doll?"

"Well, no. I was indulging in a figure of speech. He isn't."

"What type is he?"

Helen sipped her coffee. Then she faced the older woman with a fling of defiant honesty.

"He's altogether as manly a type as you're likely to find. I've happened to meet his Chief, Mr. Frost, who bears out my impressions. The boy is of fine stock, well educated, clever, and with a certain quality that makes for success—it's a poise, a quiet daring, an instinct to master the situation rather than be mastered by it. In short, he's a very dangerous variety, and I'm only too glad that I nipped matters in the bud."

For a long pause they sipped in silence, Cousin Ress dissolving two large lumps in her *demi-tasse*, Helen drinking hers in lean absence of sweetening. But something was swelling within the be-figured foulard bosom. There came an outburst at last.

"Nell Kent, sometimes I think you're actually crazy —ought to be confined where you couldn't do damage! You've hugged your own trouble till you can't see anything else. 'Just because *you* picked a rose that held a bee that stung your nose,' you want the rest of the

world, in particular your own daughter, to stop picking
roses, do you? For heaven's sake, if there isn't anything
the matter with the chap, why couldn't you let the poor
child have him?"

Helen played with her spoon and did not look up. Her
lips were vanishing within, as a grim determination drew
them closer and closer.

"Haven't we thrashed that matter out enough, Ress?
You know my intentions."

"We'll never have thrashed it out enough till you
come to your senses. Why in the name of sanity you
want to spoil what might have been a perfectly good love
affair——"

"That's exactly the point. She may have all the young
men she wants for friends. But this would have been
genuine, no transient flirtation. I felt it in both of
them."

"Then you're a fool. I'm not sure but you're worse.
Maybe you're a murderess. To kill anything as pure and
alive as young love——"

Helen turned angrily. She was white.

"Kill it? I'd risk everything I might ever possess to
kill it—before it should have a chance to kill my child!
Do you suppose that fragile, lovely soul of hers would
ever survive the nightmare of disillusion that love is?
She's as sensitive as a flower; she lives in her imagination; she's as fine as poetry or music. When the awakening came, it would kill her outright! I'll save her, I
tell you!" Her voice shook with passion. "I'll save
her from it no matter what it means to accomplish the
rescue! How would that sensitive plant ever survive when

I—I, as hard as she is soft—I, made of steel and tempered by years—am no stronger than *this!*" She pointed to her left hand, which trembled where it rested.

"It's been shaking like that ever since noon," she went on, torn by her own white violence. "And why? Because, as I came out from the office, I ran across someone who resembled—a memory. The likeness at first glance was so striking that I started as if I had come upon the dead walking. At second glance there was no similarity, of course—only a forlorn, middle-aged man —the resemblance was elusive, something in carriage, gesture, expression—but the shock of that instant's fancy has left me a wreck ever since. And after nineteen years! Ress Clifton, can you wonder that I'd give my life to save the one creature on earth that I love with every breath I draw—to save her from what I have been through?"

III

An hour later Miss Clifton said good night and entered the elevator. Helen had accompanied her to its door, had rung the bell, and now saw her started on the journey down. But no sooner had the cage been swallowed from Helen's view, than a purposeful pucker drew Miss Clifton's neatly moulded little mouth.

"Now," she instructed the elevator girl, "you may reverse, and take me to the top floor."

The girl turned to stare at her erratic passenger, but her hand obeyed the remarkable order.

At the top floor Miss Clifton alighted, and proceeded

up the one flight of stairs to the roof. She had never
visited the roof of an apartment building before; she
had supposed these retreats given over to the hanging
of washings and the *affaires-du-cœur* of maids and hall-
boys. Now, some hundred feet above the city, she stepped
forth into an amazing sweep of sky and stars and tower
tips and clean night air. "No wonder the child comes
here for refuge!" she commented.

Her comment was quickly altered, and she lifted her
skirts gingerly as she felt the tar of the roof clinging
with affectionate warmth to the Louis Fifteenth heels
of her new colonial pumps. And her beautiful foulard
would probably be ruined by melting tar—that design
of floral wreaths could never be replaced in these post-
war days of difficult shopping! How preposterous to
have followed her impulse and come to this outlandish
place! An idiot she was, to be sure, forever going off
half-cocked!——At that moment she came upon Bec.

The girl was leaning back wearily in the steamer chair,
her loose hair blown about her face. In the darkness
she looked pale and dim, a ghost-girl. The pansies gave
off a faint, sweet odour in the stirring air. The edge
of the canopy kept up a small flapping noise, like feeble
wings in troubled beating. Cousin Ress caught her
breath.

"It's all very lovely, child!"

Bec turned languidly; then, recognising her visitor,
sprang up. "Cousin Ress! I never thought of anyone
but the elevator girl coming here. Helen never comes—
she thinks it's sooty, but really it isn't—much." Bec

had her guest plumped into the steamer chair, and was perching on a stool at her feet.

"Cousin Ress, dear, I don't mean any disrespect to the cloak you gave me by wearing it here," she poured forth in apology. "I'm taking the best care of it. It's so lovely—and up here, with my flowers—somehow I couldn't resist it!"

"Humph!" responded Cousin Ress. She did not enlarge upon the monosyllable at that moment. She was engaged in solving the problem of making herself at ease in the steamer chair, where she poised uncomfortably in rocking roundness, about as able to recline as an apple. Settling as best she could: "So it wasn't approved of— your wearing it up here?" she inquired.

"I suppose it did seem foolish," was the extenuating reply.

"Humph!" said Cousin Ress again. "Isn't it an evening cloak? And isn't it now evening? You wouldn't wear it on Fifth Avenue at the lunch hour, I hope." She changed the subject with alarming abruptness. "Look here, Bec; who's the young man you meet up here?"

"Cousin Ress!" The mere exclamation was indignant denial. Bec rose, quivering, panting. "What can you mean, suspecting me like that? I've never spoken to a soul up here, I come to be alone——"

"There, there, child, sit down. Goodness gracious, don't I know it! It never occurred to me that Tom, Dick or Harry popped up from a trap-door to join you. But when a youngster of your age comes off by herself time after time, it's not to be alone—in her thoughts." She had drawn Bec back to the stool at her feet, and now she laid a hand upon the girl's shoulder, clasping it with her fat little fingers upon which numberless rings twinkled.

"You're meeting some young man—in your thoughts, my dear, I repeat. Oh, I may be a spinster and fifty-nine, but I'm no old fool," she continued. "Sometimes I think that the only women who know anything about either their own sex or the other are the spinsters of this world. A married woman has lost her broad, flying bird's-eye view; she huddles in her own little nest and peeps with one eye cocked now and then. To my way of thinking, nobody knows as little about marriage as the married. But those of us that roam the sky with unfettered wings"—in illustration Cousin Ress flapped two fat arms—"we keep our sense of perspective."

Bec was listening intently, and as Cousin Ress's defense of the single state drew to a wheezy close, she suddenly flung her arms over the older woman's knees, and searched her round, sagacious little face.

"Cousin Ress, dear! I always felt that there was something about you like—like—" Bec stumbled. "You won't mind, will you? Like a pillow made of the warmest down, so that one just longs to snuggle and cry it out into the pillow. I mean that your *heart* is like that— you understand, don't you?"

"I quite understand, my child, that no allusion to my figure was intended." Cousin Ress drew her closer. "Bless your poor little heart—snuggle then, and cry, if you want to."

"I don't. But I'd like to think I might; if—if ever——"

"Here's my hand on it. Bec, do you want to tell me anything?"

Face hidden in Miss Clifton's ample lap, the golden head was shaken in negative.

"All right. I won't ask. But you can count on me."

The head nodded.

At length Bec raised it, and said, "Isn't it queer, since there isn't any God, as of course we all know, that sometimes it should feel exactly as though there were one?"

Miss Clifton locked her lips. She and Helen had had *that* out long ago.

"It's since I've been up here alone so much, near the sky, that I've noticed it. When I'm down below, I know that it's an illusion. But up here, when I come with—troubles—I get a feeling that somebody—no, rather some*thing*—is listening and wanting to help. As though it would help if I knew how to give way, and let it. I don't know how to describe it; it's not like a person, but it's a big, soft something that seems to flow all around, like some finer kind of air. Sometimes it carries me along, as if I were a little boat sailing on that air, and as long as I let it carry me the little boat can't be tipped over or harmed in any way. . . . Oh, dear, I'm mixing my metaphors dreadfully!" she sighed. "I suppose it's the same sort of illusion that has kept people duped all these centuries, don't you?"

Miss Clifton's lip smarted where she was biting it. Long ago Helen had exacted her pledge of non-interference on this matter. She rose.

"I must go, child. But my advice is: stick to your

roof.   Oh, by the way, I want you to use this green
cloak up here—in fact, I'm very particular that you
should.   You need it these cool evenings.   I shall send
you another wrap for parties."

"Cousin Ress! You darling, *darling* DEAR!"

But Cousin Ress waited for only one hug of thanks,
which she curtly returned.   Lifting her Louis Fifteenth
heels over the tar with the dainty flicks of a cat minc-
ing through dampness, she hurried away.

CHAPTER XII

SPRING LAYS A TRAP FOR HELEN

I

IT was three days since Bec's adventure with spring, and the warmth still held. Helen rose lazily from her office desk and threw open the window. Across the languorous air a whiff of violets flitted to her. She looked forth between dun, perpendicular walls; they rose like fastnesses to imprison dream and desire; but in spite of them, the view beyond beckoned. Grass showed green in the old churchyard, tourists were loitering among the headstones, reading famous inscriptions with leisurely pleasure. Even lovers were enticed here by the tripping spring; a pair of them clung openly in the churchyard.

"Young idiots," Helen observed. Unable to direct her observation to the lovers themselves, she used Miss Muldoon as target.

"It's the girl, however, who's the chief idiot," she elucidated.

"So I understood you to mean," Miss Muldoon responded demurely, her eyes bent upon a carbon copy. "Yes—I understood what you meant. What I don't understand——" Here she broke off with a blush, and fell

220

to correcting the blurred carbon copy with sudden zeal.

Helen noted the broken question with languid interest. "What is it you don't understand? Whatever it is, you ought to. You're at the idiot age yourself."

Miss Muldoon bit a red, smooth lip and hesitated. Then she lifted her eyes and met Helen's fully.

"With all your talk to us girls all the time like that, Mrs. Kent—how we're fools to fall in love, and all like that—you never said—what I mean, however do you expect" (Miss Muldoon's blushing had become furious)—"expect the world to keep on, if we don't be that kind of fool?"

Helen smiled. "You sound like some wrinkled, distraught old celibate sociologist, my child. The professors are so anxious over the abstract question of what's to become of the world, that they lose track of such concrete questions as what's to become of Maybelle Muldoon. Apparently a small matter; but I beg to remind them that it's the multiplication of the individual Maybelle Muldoons that makes up half our population. As for the other half, since its desires lead to our undoing —why should we care? All of you young fools will walk into the noose, will you, and so perpetuate a race of unhappy women?" she demanded, sharpening. "Since marriage inevitably brings unhappiness to a woman, let us bring it to an end! Nature can't force upon us a world that is not made to fit our needs—there's no obligation on our part to accept such a world by perpetuating it."

"But I know some married women that are happy—" mildly protested Miss Maybelle Muldoon.

"Bluff, my child. Never believe *that* lie. So, as to the world and women—let those of us that are here get what we can out of it, as I tell my daughter—and that's a good deal, if we crush out illusion. As to the future, let the race die for want of replenishing, since nature's trick for replenishing means wreck to woman."

Miss Muldoon mused a pace. She was recollecting a brief visit that daughter had once paid to the office when Helen was absent. . . .

"Oh, Miss Muldoon, you ought to be married and have a darling little house to do such things in! It's wicked for you to be wasted on an office!" The subject of cooking had chanced to come up, and Miss Muldoon had revealed her profound and affectionate knowledge of the art.

"Miss Kent! What would your mother say to that!"

Hesitation—a flush—then, breaking loose——

"Oh, dear Miss Muldoon, don't let my mother—I—I mean—you ought to be happy, no matter what anybody says!"

What a queer person this Mrs. Kent was, anyway, ran the inward comment now of Maybelle. Anybody might think she was crazy, the way she was always preaching against marriage to the girls of the Monroe —and maybe she was, and no joke! She was the smartest woman that Maybelle had ever known, took your breath away when she handled insurance, but smart people could be batty on one subject—she had heard this often, and she almost believed it! Like Miss Clifton, she knew nothing of psychology, but she did know a thing or two about what she believed this world was designed for.

She turned to her employer and met the jetty eye without flinching.

"Sociologists, and perpetuating, and those kind of things are Greek to me. All I know is, I've got a hope-chest home. I sew for it every night. I've finished the doilies and centrepieces and guest-towels and napkins. And now I'm doing the—the darlingest—little Gertrude petticoat. I'm scalloping it." And Miss Muldoon bent in final surrender to the blushes which were now over-whelming.

II

Helen "humphed," and turned once more to the open window. She must take up this matter again on some day when the weather did not so conspire with youth against her. Again that sharp sweetness of violets came to her, bringing with it deeper stabs than its own fleeting beauty. She had climbed California fences at eighteen to rob purple beds of their bloom. It had been one of the popular university pranks to steal violets where they could be had for the asking, and she and Vernon had thrilled at the adventure on those spring days—"just twenty-one springs ago," she caught her thoughts saying, and she shrugged at the sentimentality. And again that scent came to her from somewhere—that scent than which none is more fraught with the meaning of spring, more exquisitely alive, more subtly sad in its suggestion of evanescent loveliness, like certain music—Grieg's *To Spring*, for instance. . . .

Minutes later Helen became aware that Miss Muldoon

was replying to a knock. "I've been wool-gathering,"
she accused herself. "Yes, come in, do, Dr. Aspden!"
As he entered from the main corridor, "I hope you are
feeling chatty. There really isn't any work *in* me this
demoralising day!" She closed her roll-top with a gesture of despair.

"I came to say that my car is at the door, and I should
be glad to drop you at your home." Looking down upon
her gravely from his austere height, he might have been
offering a prescription.

She smiled up at him as the desk lock sprang shut.
"It's outrageously early for me, but I'm reckless. I
don't care what becomes of anybody's policy. I have
no business to leave this office, but I'm going to. Miss
Muldoon, do you do likewise. If you stay on toiling, you
will haunt me like a memory of guilt. Go forth and
do anything—anything conceivable, this intoxicating day,
except fall in love!"

Miss Muldoon rose with a demure "Thank you." Her
blue orbs paused, regarding first her employer, then her
employer's guest, and returned to rest upon Helen. And
the gaze cast by Miss Muldoon was profound and enig-
matical.

Miss Maybelle Muldoon turned back to close her own
desk. Making ready to leave it, she took from its small-
est, most secret drawer, a thimble and a pair of fine
embroidery scissors, and slipped them into her handbag.

"So she even snatches off-hours at the office for it!"
Helen groaned inwardly; but her thoughts could spare no
more time for the hopeful Miss Muldoon.

"You shall see how quickly a woman can get ready,"

she boasted to her guest. Opening the wardrobe, she took down what Bec called her "tall" cape, the crisply wing-trimmed hat, the gleaming summer fur that shone like her own jettiness. "You're so lanky-lovely and slippery-black in all these togs, darling!" Bec had cried in a moment of impulsiveness like that of the old Bec, holding Helen at arm's-length on the day when the spring outfit had been completed. "You look like one of those long, thin jet sequins that dangle on your own evening gown."

A few deft movements now, and she was done. "Ready!" she smiled up at Dr. Aspden.

Miss Muldoon was waiting to put the office in order. "I forgot to say," she said as Helen was departing, "that a gentleman called up while you were in conference."

"No message?"

"None whatever. He did say something that sounded funny, though. I said, 'Will you call again?' and he said what sounded like, 'That depends on fate,' and when I asked him 'What?' he rang off."

"How ridiculous!" Helen dismissed the matter with a gesture. But, in the hall, some caprice of curiosity led her back.

"Did it sound—old or young?" she inquired, and wondered why.

Miss Muldoon paused to consider. "I should say about—about—your age—that is, I mean——" she stumbled.

Helen laughed. "That is very definite, my child. I am a lady of no uncertain age. Now run along and play." Closing the door behind her, "Don't you think," she demanded audaciously, with a defiant flash into the eyes above, "that thirty-nine, which happened to me last week, brings me to a delightfully certain age?"

"Less certain, I should say, than twenty, but far more delightful. Do you find that my additional eight years puts me into the class of hopeless senility?"

She thought at that moment that she had never seen him look less those additional eight years. The spring was capering, somehow, even though his incorruptible dignity—a dignity that she had seen put to the ultimate test.

"Now," she told him, "as Bequita says, we're friends, because we have told ages." And they laughed together after a manner not noticeably older than that of Bequita herself.

He excused himself for a moment to slip back from the corridor into his own office. He returned at once bearing a great bouquet of violets.

"How's this?" she cried. "I stood at my window and smelled them, and now they arrive by another route. Have they some occult power of projecting their astral scent?"

"Their only power is to show which way the wind blows, I fancy. They have been in my window, awaiting the hour when I might offer them." With them he presented the long purple-headed pin of the florist's convention.

She took them with an inward smile at the bachelor reticence that had held them back in Miss Muldoon's presence. "They have been teasing me sinfully," she said, as she pinned them boldly, the great mass of purple, against her breast. "They and the south wind together have driven work altogether out of my head. Oh, it's spring!" Impetuously she gave vent to a full stretch; the movement was like a strong light suddenly cast upon her long lines, her freedom of posture, the clever leanness of her costume, her own vivid black-and-whiteness with the daring contrast of purple flowers. And from the austere gravity of long bachelorhood, Dr. Aspden looked down upon her.

III

He was driving his own car that afternoon, and he tucked her in beside him. Broadway choked their progress for a space; but he wove skillfully, on through the maggoty swarms of Washington Square, past the stately old red-brick aristocracy near by, into the congestion and buffetings of the shopping district, crossing, writhing, emerging, and—the river at last. Here was space; here was a toying air; here the wide sweep of water giving back blue for blue; here the abandon of spring in every loitering woman slowly pushing a baby-carriage, in all the bud-like burst of clamouring youngsters. It was as if, with a playful shove, spring were crying to everyone, "Off you go!"—and off, indeed, you must go.

"Do you wonder that I chose these parts for my abode?" she asked him. "Look at my glowing nineteen-year old, and tell me, as a physician, if I didn't choose well!"

"I should like to look at her. Although in the same room, I have never seen her, you know, owing to the

interference of a screen." It was more than a month
since the two imps within two pairs of eyes had met
at the Spindle, but of a sudden they gleamed a recognition.

"Although we have had amicable business relations for
some time," continued Dr. Aspden deliberately, "you have
never invited me to call!"

"I've never had a chance in our hurried business inter-
views. This, remember, is the first time you ever brought
me home!"

"I suppose, my dear madam, I should be looking a
gift horse in the mouth to complain that this ride is
the first when it might have been the seventh. Exactly
six times have I stopped at your door and offered to
spare you the subway jam."

"Yes," she admitted, "and exactly six times have I
refused. I counted them, too," she twinkled.

"Then, may I ask—idle curiosity—is there some magic
in the number seven?"

She laughed and shook her head. "No. But the day
caught me this time. That south wind—and the violets.
I didn't care whether school kept or not—to-day."

"The car would have waited any day until school was
out. You have not yet explained those six refusals. If
you don't fear subway suffocation for yourself, at least
let me save that charming hat from destruction!" And
the bachelor of forty-seven beamed with a sudden startled
delight at his own words. He had done it very well! he
congratulated himself.

But Helen was silent, her eyes lost on the Palisades
beyond. For all at once it had occurred to her to won-

der, herself, why those six refusals? Some inhibition that
she half detected but could not have explained——

"This is my street," she roused to say.

He slowed down the car. He turned to her, and his
eyes fixed themselves very firmly upon her eyes.

"This, you say, is your street," stated Dr. Aspden
deliberately.   "But we may not see another genuine
spring day for a month. You have already renounced
work. And so have I. And——" To the right lay
Helen's way, hemmed by tall apartment buildings, wall
upon wall of cliff dwellings. But ahead curved the Drive,
on as far as the eye could reach, flanking the blue spring
river——

"Let us suppose," continued Dr. Aspden, "that at this
point the car becomes unmanageable, refuses to turn to
the right, forges rapidly ahead, and cannot be checked
in its course."

IV

Across the snowy table of a brisk wayside hostelry,
Mrs. Kent and Dr. Aspden faced one another. And
imp met imp once more, as old-time fellow-conspirators
now, and between these imps there passed a significant
"*Well?*"

"It is really a perfectly fair return," he said. "You
cannot deny that you abducted me the first time—and,
being true to the original Eve, you will not attempt
to deny it."

"But does that justify you in abducting me now?"

"I think it does. It is only fair that Adam should

tempt the woman and that she should eat—" with a ges
ture that covered the crisp club sandwiches at that moment appearing above a solicitous waiter.

"And anyway," he pursued, watching the shining tea
service being spread before her, watching her long, deft
hands draw cups and pot toward her—every movement
quick, distinct, purposeful, shorn of all needless han-
dlings and bustlings, as clean-cut as her incisive brain—
"anyway—do you greatly object to being thus stolen and
carried off from town—on such a day?" His eyes led
hers to the freshly green lawn and the restlessly sparkling river spread before them. Not even glass interfered
with their view; the cosy table stood in the front window
of this old colonial residence turned restaurant, and
the room was thrown open to the spring.

Her eyes swept the river, the lawn, the trim beds of
tulips, the stately old pillared veranda, and returned
to the peeping lettuce leaves between golden-brown tri-
angles of toast.

"Although thirty-nine and a cynic," said she demurely,
"I admit the charms of folly—on such a day." And
unconsciously Helen Kent's eyes rested on the fragrant mass of purple bloom against her breast.

"On such a day," she said later on, while pouring
him his third cup of tea and recalling with a secret smile
his former distaste for that beverage, "I am tempted to
the bucolic life and commutation. But it tired my nerves
even in California—they could never stand it in New
York."

The physician's swift scrutiny raked her. "You look
as if the foundation were firm. If the nerves tire, it's

more because they have been overstrained than through
any fundamental weakness."

"Yes. They went through a good deal—once upon
a time. But that's over."

He made no reply, only continuing to look into her
with that wise penetration which is in itself sympathy,
because of its profound understanding. For a minute her
eyes strayed out over the river, to the dusky beauty of
the other shore, shadowed against a western sun; then,
astounding herself, she turned abruptly to him, and said:

"I went through a prolonged hell. My husband gam-
bled himself into poverty, drank himself into loathsome-
ness, and wound up by offering me the ultimate insult.
I struck out with the baby. I've gone it alone ever since.
He died a few years ago. That's the whole story."

Never before in all the years had she said as much
to any save those persons intimately concerned in her
affairs. As the facts fell from her, stark in all their
brutality, she realised this; and next she realised the
wonderful perfectness of the man's silence. Any word—
a step in any of the possible directions, toward expression of pity, or surprise, or blame, or inquiry—would
have turned her confession to a weakness in her own
eyes and have moved her to detest herself for it. But,
instead, he was still. It was as though he offered her
that stillness like a strong arm. . . .

She went on. "I sometimes think it was better, after
all, to learn the truth so early—that man, as a husband,
is impossible—that 'love' is a delusion, and that marriage is the tragedy of woman's life. Most girls have
to come to it later—they are kept longer in the clouds,

where they are unable to see anything clearly. It's to spare my child what I went through—the finding out by bitter personal experience—that I've brought her up to know facts as they are. I've called a spade a spade to her. She has been taught to realise that her one chance for a successful life is to avoid the romantic moonshine known as 'love.' We're going to live an ideal life together, free, as woman should always be free."

She glanced up to find the serious grey eyes fixed upon her with an odd look. It was a look neither of approval nor disapproval: it was both penetrating and kind, almost pitying. The thought crossed Helen's mind that it was the look of a physician studying sympathetically a grave case. And still he maintained that stillness, so queerly like a strong arm. . . .

As the car whirred its way home through the delicious chill fragrance of late afternoon, "To return to the subject of commuting," said Dr. Aspden. "I have never fancied that daily leap for life myself. But I have cherished another fancy. It is to possess myself of some rambling, homey old farmhouse, far from the madding crowd—quite lost, in fact, so that only a few intimate friends shall know its whereabout—and there make unto myself a dwelling for whatever times and seasons the whim shall prompt. Run out to it for a week-end or a fortnight's vacation, or desert it for months at a time if I please—but always know it is there, snuggled in some valley, and awaiting me."

He turned to her just then, to find her face alight.

"What a dream of bliss! To be able completely to

'shake' humanity, at such times as it becomes insufferable! To commune with one's percolator and one's cigarette in heavenly solitude——"

"Exactly!" His own enthusiasm ignited at hers. "Spreading rooms—the house touched up only enough for perfect comfort, nothing done to spoil its mellowness, for in that will lie much of its healing power—easy chairs, of course, shaded lamps, books, curtains, cushions——"

"And a dining porch thrown out to the east——"

"Good! What sort of table ware?"

"Blue-and-white Japanese. It's the coolest for summer breakfasts."

"Blue-and-white it shall be. The same east porch will be ready for loafing on hot afternoons and evenings. A Gloucester hammock——"

"And steamer chairs."

"With cushions. And I must be ready for cold weather, too. On sharp October nights, and later, when the leaves take on those fine, rich browns of old tapestries, I want to be able to draw up to my fire——"

"Before a huge fireplace built of the native stone——"

"With Stevenson or Conrad for company——"

"Stop thief!" she cried at that. "For it is nothing less than thieving thus to rob me of smug comfort in my small urban apartment!" The car was drawing up at her door.

Alone, Helen entered the elevator in a preoccupied sparkle. Her brilliant eyes were seeing a long way off, apparently; they did not note the new elevator girl, the maiden in high French heels and abbreviated skirt.

The girl, unacquainted with tenants, continued upward.

"Floor?" she inquired at length, having reached the top.

Helen roused. "No, no—the fourth." At her own door she did not ring, but entered with her latchkey. Not until she had walked in silence the length of the hall did she see——

It was a flash of rose colour that recalled her to her senses—Bec, in her new evening gown, the pink Georgette which Helen had designed with such pleasure—and now, beyond Bec, she saw the dining-room. Its table was charmingly spread—the French china, the cut glass, a favourite drawn-work centrepiece, a simple cluster of blush roses——

"Helen! Oh, my dear, is that you?" It was Bec crying to her, sweeping her up as into the heart of her rose-like self. "I've been so frightened, dearest! I telephoned the office, and they said you had left long before, and Miss Muldoon was gone, and nobody knew anything about you. I couldn't tell—I imagined things—you might have been in some horrid accident—I was sure you would always call me up if you were detained very late! But I got everything ready. It's time for them now. Is the table all right?"

Helen's voice was halting somewhere in the depths of her throat and refusing to produce a sound. For the first time she remembered that a party of old friends from California were to be her guests at a half-past-seven o'clock dinner!

"The table is simply charming," she brought forth

at last, conscious of a remarkable huskiness in her struggling voice. "And you were an angel to make it so.
You're perfect yourself, too, dear. I'm so sorry you
worried—I'll explain later. I must leap into an evening
gown now."

Helen rushed to her room. She did not hear, "Put
the big yellow rose on your shoulder, darling!" She
heard only the confusion of her own brain-hammers
pounding, a multitude of them, in her ears.

What did it mean, that the intoxication of this spring
weather could trick her, Helen Kent, into such childish
folly—to forget the passage of time, and a social obligation, like some heedless schoolgirl? She, who always
held social obligations card-indexed and filed for ready
reference! Could she be ill? Seriously, was some fever
brewing, that she could thus be driven to lose her rational
efficiency, her commanding poise? What would Bec say
if she knew? And what could she say to Bec, when
guests were gone and the time for chatting privately
should arrive?

There! A snapper spread, and refusing to snap! How
fingers turned to thumbs when one hurried!——The doorbell!

Could she tell Bec, indeed? She had come home with
the impulse to pour forth laughingly the story of her
jolly ride with the once-curt bachelor. But how explain
her oblivion——

Again the doorbell! Would that slipper never go on
at the heel? Where *was* the shoe-horn?——

She loathed subterfuge. Of course she must be frank,

must tell the whole story, confess her shameful forget-
fulness——

The last snapper was fastened now, her hand was on
the doorknob. She could hear Bec's voice in charming
welcome to Mrs. Elmore.

For an instant Helen paused to regain breath and
emerge unflurried. And in that instant an astonishing,
irrelevant thought flashed through her mind. It was an
impertinent thought, rudely pushing its entrance where
it was not invited. The thought cried:

"He must have the willow furniture stained black for
the big living-room with the fireplace, and get cretonne
of a deep, dull blue combined with dahlia reds. I'll
tell him to-morrow."

She snatched open the door and went forth, quick, vivid,
definitely silhouetted. "I'm so sorry!" she cried, both
hands out to them all with a dominating cordiality that
commanded forgiveness. "That I should have been un-
avoidably detained this day of all days! Has Bequita
told you how delighted we are, and how we have looked
forward to this informal little gathering, for auld lang
syne?"

v

"Darling, to think I've got you again, and safe!"
Bec was perched on the arm of Helen's chair; her hands
drooped against Helen's shining hair, her olive-white
neck; the caress was like that of a lost lover restored.
Whatever resentments had been breeding during recent
weeks were dispelled for the time, at least. In that hour

of Bec's panic at Helen's absence, all her old passionate
devotion had surged back in an overpowering tide.

"I'm so sorry. I didn't realise that you would worry so.
It was very careless of me not to telephone." Helen
halted. Yes, it was time for the explanation. The guests
were gone. "Very careless," Helen repeated.

The soft, bare arms, still thin with the thinness of
youth, clung about her shoulders. She could feel the
beat of that young, fragrant breath against her cheek.
It had been weeks, weeks, since she had known the sharp
sweetness of those old, impulsive caresses. She had not
realised how she was suffering from their absence; but to
feel them again, the warmth of them, the dearness of
them——

Before Helen rose a picture of the Bec who, on one
occasion, had gazed at her with the coldness of a critical
maturity.

"The child cannot understand," she thought. "If I
tell her, she will again place some absurd misconstruc-
tion upon my act. Perhaps she is jealous. At any rate,
it's no use. Better not try to explain."

"I won't be so careless again, dear. I had to go—
that is, I went—up beyond town, and I took time to
snatch a bite, which made me late——"

Like wings the caresses hovered about her hair, her
neck. Helen closed her eyes, drinking in their delight.
The constrained coldness of past weeks was gone, like
the bleakness of a dreadful winter; here beckoned the
seduction of an exquisite warmth. . . .

She shook herself together. She, Helen Kent, to pur-
chase back even these beloved caresses at the price of

a weak subterfuge, a silence amounting to falsehood! Scorn of herself made her voice firm.

"In fact," she stated, "the once-crusty Dr. Aspden asked me to ride this afternoon, and we had tea at a restaurant up the river. That was how," Helen persisted distinctly, "I came to be delayed beyond my time." And she sat apparently unmoved as the arms fell from her neck.

VI

As Helen's brief explanation unfolded, Bec had felt as though a hand seized her throat. Her heart seemed rending—she felt about to shriek, and she felt struck dumb, both at once. For seconds she stood in locked silence; then, with a rush of escape, she fled to her roof.

And now she stood there, face to face with the sky, and she cried to it. No voice could have been heard; her words did not rise above a whisper; and yet to her they were cries that rent the darkness, that shrieked and beat with their wings up against the bars of the sky above.

"I want my own! I have a right to it now! She has forfeited every right to forbid me! She—who does as she pleases, preaches one thing and practises another, who forgets every responsibility while she flirts away an afternoon, who tries to kill my happiness while she looks out for her own——"

Bitter cries, furious, despairing, they stormed forth in the night; they beat themselves to exhaustion; they fell back and rose again:

"I am going to have it, I tell you!" "You" was perhaps the sky, or Helen. "I'm going to take my happiness—it's mine—I have a right to it! I don't care how, clandestinely, any way. She's forfeited all right to my obedience. I told him good-bye forever the other day; but now, now—I'll call him back!"

There in the starlight her cloak floated like the wings of a great moth, frostily green, fluttering, opening, hovering. Like the trapped moth that, elementally possessing the powers from which man has educated himself away, summons its mate over a score of miles by a soundless call that is nothing more tangible than intense longing projected——

"I'll call him back!" whispered Bequita. "But how?"

And then, suddenly, Bequita fell upon her knees. For the second time in her life, she prayed.

"O God, bring him to me! Bring him back! He's the only person that understands. God—I don't know who you are, and of course I don't believe in you, and I know that you're nothing but a delusion like Santa Claus, but I *feel* you! It—you—are something that flows all around like air, and it goes everywhere all at once, and so it must reach everybody, as if everything were *one*, and so why can't it go to him, and tell him, oh, tell him— to find me! Keep her from separating us ever—ever again!"

She knelt, not knowing why; nor why her arms flung themselves toward the sky above. She was merely obeying instinct. And yet that untaught instinct had already strangely found its way from a pleading with vague plural gods, like those of the barbarian, to a crude con-

ception of Unity.   There on that city roof, above the
head of Helen Kent who, for nineteen years, had shielded
her daughter from every outward approach of dangerous delusion, that daughter knelt before a Power that
approached from within.

On the following evening she arrived to find a dim
figure on a near-by roof.   At her appearance, it crossed
rapidly over the two intervening roofs, and took her into
its arms.

"I—I'll—be able—to talk—in a few minutes, Philip.
The—the reason you—you frightened me so, was that
the thing I expected really happened."   Her words,
naïvely unconscious of their world-weary humour, were
panting themselves out against his breast.

"Then you knew I would, must come?"   He was holding her from him now, the better to realise her actuality
with devouring eyes.

"I called you," Bec said.

And to her it was always to remain that she had called
him and he had answered, despite his explanation of
his mysterious appearance.

"The day after seeing you, I began my series of charges
upon innocent housewives throughout this vicinity.   I
have spent all my available time since in scheming, trickery, coercion, assault and battery, to get a room in
some apartment beneath one of the contiguous roofs;
and without success until this evening, when one Mrs.
Coon, three doors away, yielded at last at the point
of the bayonet and for a fabulous sum in advance.   And
all this, Bequita *mia*, that I might perhaps only once
tread this sky path to the Lady of My Thoughts upon

her Roof o' Dreams, once see her among her flowers and stars. Perhaps I shall be summarily dismissed. My fate lies in your hands." Again he drew her to him, her face turned up to his; his own bent nearer, his lips approaching.

She did not resist; but from the curious miscellany of conduct rules pathetically gathered here and there and heaped within her untaught mind, a faint protest voiced itself.

"But people don't—don't kiss each other until they're engaged!"

"Then the sooner we settle the preliminaries, the better!"

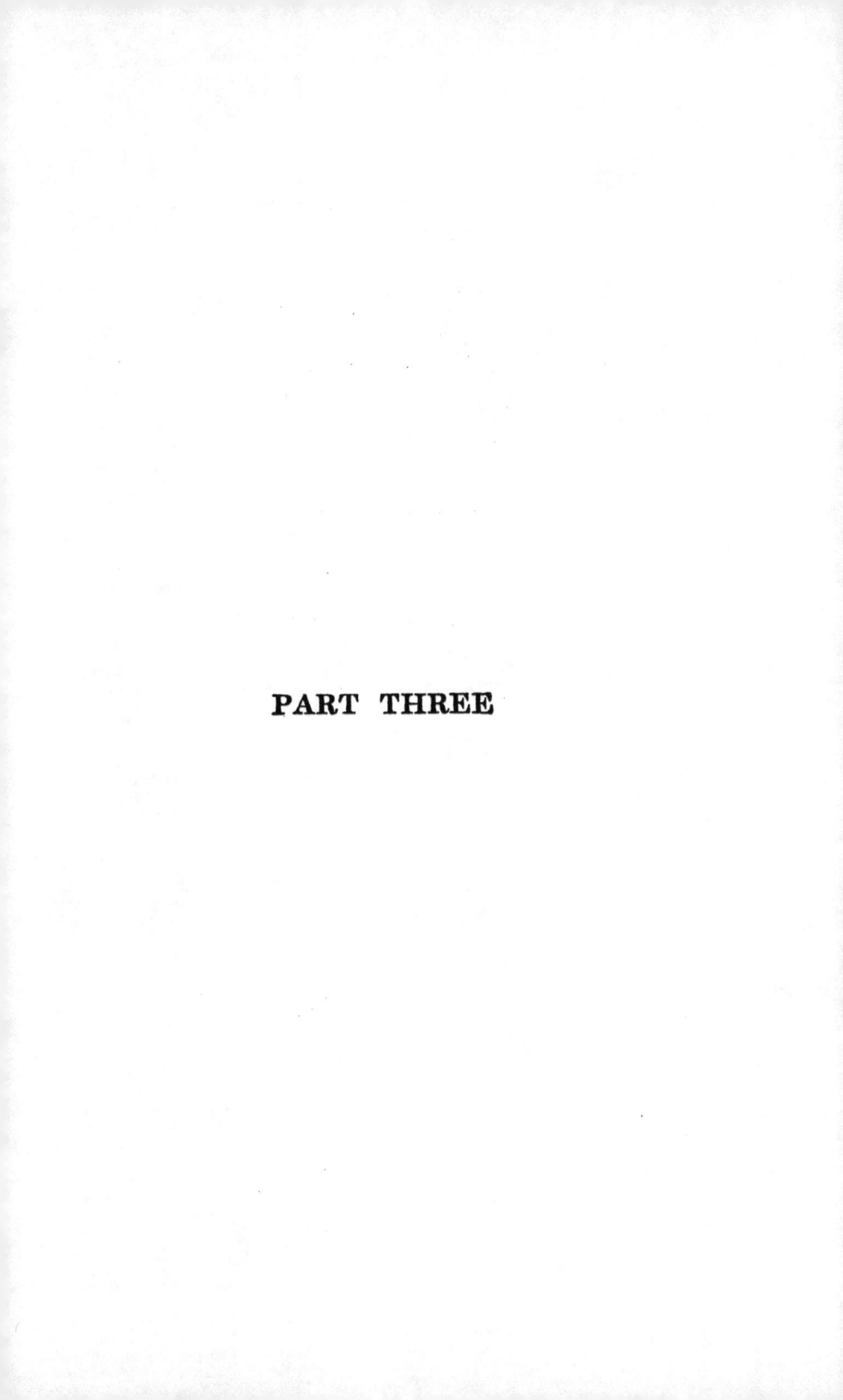

PART THREE

CHAPTER XIII

BEC ENTERS A STRANGE GATE

I

HEAVEN and hell awaited Bequita. By the same gate she entered them, and found them one.

It was heaven always at the trysting hour. Whenever that might be—in the late afternoon, when the full sun beat down upon her little awning, and, in its shade, a cool breeze shook loose the mignonette's fragrance; in the early evening, when the gilded red sun, like some giant Christmas tree ball, plumped itself into the Palisades; later, when winky stars brightened in a sky that looked like Cousin Ress's sapphire-colored velvet gown— Bec went to her trysts upon the Roof o' Dreams with a strange new light in her eyes. They shone blue as the heart of a flame, and they were wide with the abnormal calm born of excitement's fever heat. She perceived through senses that were given a new awareness. The feeble but lovely scent of pansies; the blue porcelain glaze of a wind-burnished sky; the gentle melancholy of the far-off tower clock's stroke, reaching her now and then from Madison Square; the cool, elastic touch of the earth in her flower-boxes—all these perceptions and a

245

thousand more, long familiar, became suddenly keen, as if heretofore her senses had been asleep to the delights that lay open to them.

At whatever time her "slip-away" chance offered, she would go to meet her lover. There under the little canopy he would come to her, and all heaven would open wide and dazzle her with its splendour and drug her with its rapture.

And then—a talk, a walk if possible—the meeting would be over, and she would part from Philip dreamy, under the anesthetic of ecstasy. She would return to her normal routine—study, dinner, chat with Helen, shopping, a party, perhaps—in this half-dazed condition. Gradually the anesthetic would wear off, and in its place would come the inevitable depression, the nightmare hours that were her hell.

There were various chambers in this infernal abode. In one, hopelessness hung like grey curtains and there was no other furnishing.

Another chamber was possessed by fear. In this, unreasonable panic would seize her—terror of losing her lover, morbid anxiety lest some misunderstood word of her own should turn him from her. Had he thought her cold at parting? She had said a curt "good-bye" and had run without a backward glance—perhaps he had thought her angry over their difference concerning free verse, whereas of course she wasn't, but what if he should fail to come the next evening because of her curtness? Should she write and explain? No, that wouldn't do. But if he should never come again. . . . And so on, overwrought to an almost neurotic condition, she would be distorting the situation all the evening in her mind, while holding an unseen book before her eyes.

Or, fear would clutch at some careless phrase of Philip's, and spend hours in futile twistings and turnings of it. What had he meant by saying, "There is a certain quality in first love that can never be found again?" Had he loved previously? Until three or four o'clock in the morning she might lie torturing herself with such frights.

In still another chamber, remorse brooded; here, most dreadful sight of all, her eyes fell upon herself. Was it she, indeed, Rebequita Kent, who was living this life of vile duplicity, of sinister evasions as bad as direct lies, of clandestine meetings, of reckless disobedience? Rather, it must be some base creature, deaf to any voice but that of her own driven desire. Some girl that had never been taught. Some girl devoid of honour. A being despicable, low, unashamed. At such moments she stood off and looked upon her actions in horrified detachment, as though they were no more real than a delirium through which she had passed, like the queer things she had dreamed of doing during scarlet fever, years before.

Still she saw through a glass, darkly; still she groped in that half-light of childhood where obedience to parental rulership stands for conscience, where the soul has not yet seen face to face. One mind within her was seeking the truth; but her other mind still clung to the habit of discriminating between right and wrong on a basis of Helen's approval or disapproval.

And the constant fear of detection, the starting at a sound, flushing at some ambiguous remark of Helen's, guessing at what reservations lay behind some silence of hers! Either Helen was inexplicably blind during these days, or she had her reasons for saying nothing, Bec often thought. This, her own cowering, was to her the vilest of all.

There would be hours of these churning reflections, then a sudden, heavy sleep of exhaustion—a weary dragging back to consciousness—a forenoon of clogged brain —a sloth gradually wearing off as excitement returned with the approaching hour. . . .

And the Roof o' Dreams kept its own counsel.

II

Each tryst brought its new delight. Once, for instance, it was Philip's idea to inspect the morning world from their eyrie. They met before Helen was even awake.

"I'm glad you made me come for this!" Bec's glance and gesture swept the sun-shot river, the clean morning green of the Jersey shore, the streets below, all dapper in the untarnished freshness of the new day. "I might have gone on forever and never have known what it looks like before people take hold of the day and handle it, and it gets mussed."

He laughed—that was the way the adorableness of her affected him, he always told her, it made him want to laugh out of sheer delight merely because of the wonderful fact that she was she.

"Not a thing out of order yet. Even the fussy little tugs and the clumsy barges are almost pretty at this hour," she went on, perching herself with a spring that

was hardly more than a flutter upon the parapet.   He
offered a hand in vain.

"Thanks, but I'm not the sort of girl one need offer
a hand to, because, you see, when I pick the place I want
to go, I *fly* to it."

"Fairy style, of course.   And whither, O more than
mortal being, do you propose flight this afternoon?   It's
mine off."

"But Saturday is—is not free for me."   What Bec
really meant was that this was Helen's afternoon at
home; but so acute was her sensitiveness concerning the
whole situation, that she rarely spoke frankly of its
duplicities.

"Isn't there any way?"

Bec pondered.   "I can't say now.   But I'll leave a
note with Toby at noon."

Yes, there was a postoffice: a ravishing toy, the droll-
est old Toby that Philip counted one of his priceless
treasures.   Nothing less would be worthy the sacred
trust, he had said.   They had buried it in a corner of
one of the flower-boxes, covered it with a veil of ivy;
they spoke of Toby as their postmaster, and entrusted to
his pottery protection from wind, moisture, prying and
theft, their daily correspondence.   What secrets did the
genial old wiseacre tuck away beneath the sturdy breast
of that ancient blue coat!

And Philip, home at one-thirty that day, slipped up
to his own roof, quickly crossed that of the intervening
house, and on the Roof o' Dreams, stooped and drew from
Toby's hold the promised scribble.

"Can come after two o'clock."   The note did not add

the information which had been imparted to Bec over the telephone: that Helen was to drive with Dr. Aspden that afternoon, and would not be at home until dinner time. Bec had hung up the receiver with eyes angrily brilliant, lips a hard line. These drives were becoming frequent, as were the Doctor's calls at the little apartment; he had plainly made an effort to win Bec's liking from the first, but in vain. She viewed him with thinly veiled hostility.

This afternoon's freedom meant, for Bec and Philip, some uncommon adventure, what was known as a "very special" journey. The journeys were few, usually brief, but always unforgettable. They were as wide as the world and as long as eternity, or so they seemed, until suddenly the stroke of the clock would end that seeming. To avenge themselves they made verses at it:

> "Twinkle, twinkle, little tower,
> Always harping on the hour!
> Up above the world so high,
> Batting now and then an eye!"

They might wander for a priceless half-hour among those hilly paths of Riverside Park, where dirty babies toddle among clean babies; where shrubs and trees and grass and flowers play at bringing the country to city folk; where the river, in sphinx-like silence, observes the loves of this year as it has observed them for several centuries along the same banks, even from the days when some Hiawatha wooed his Minnehaha in their shade— and with the same bored incredulity in its impassive grey gaze.

Once they re-trod the old Central Park path, charged already with memory; so short a space on the calendar

of lovers does it take to hang the hushing sign, "For Old
Times' Sake" before a gateway!

"Think of it, Bequita—we might have spent thirty,
maybe forty-five minutes more of our lives together if it
hadn't been for those bushes that hid you from me!"

At times they fell sober. Bec was nowadays becoming obsessed with curiosity concerning "that thing some
people call God." She had questioned various persons,
from Russian Anna to the Obelisk, concerning their attitude; but with Philip she hesitated, because of their very
closeness of spirit, The question urged, however.

"Philip, of course you don't believe in what people
call God?"

He, too, hesitated. At last he said:

"I was in France."

He hesitated again. Then, "Before that, I didn't
think about such things—I didn't exactly disbelieve, but
I didn't bother about them. But in France—well, a man
didn't have much if he didn't have some kind of—well,
Something to hang on to."

. . . Always they found the breath of spring and the
soul of the open in the heart of our densest city.
Whether on the Roof o' Dreams, or in one of the thronged
parks, the city became lyric at their touch. Especially
they liked little Morningside Park, that glowing treasure
tossed into the lap of a crowded uptown, comparatively
unsought by the multitude, content to lie in the sun and
fling back its light joyously from green facets. It was
there they discovered the Wishing Stone.

Fortunately, they found it on the long afternoon above
mentioned. It was Bec saw it first: "This shall be our

Wishing Stone!" she cried, and ran toward a boulder that humped itself in the midst of the green, and sat upon it, and closed her eyes for better seeing.

"I wish—" her roaming ideas began, "I wish——"

"Be careful!" Philip warned. "For it's sure to come true, you know, uttered on a Wishing Stone." At that moment, he could easily have believed it. Looking at Bec on a day like this, he told himself, one could believe anything. It was a day when the heavy, sweet fatigue of spring merges into summer. Beside the winding walk pink blossoming shrubs stood up stiffly like quaint bouquets, and starry yellow blooms lay scattered on the path. He had swayed with a strap in the hot elevated train shortly before; he had observed women leaning from windows as if stifled forth from their tenements; but here, in this green strip overbosomed by motherly old rocks, Bec wrought for him all the magic of spring.

"The trouble is, I can't put my wish into words. It's so big it hasn't any outline. It seems to be something like sailing away and away——"

"I don't know anything to offer but an ocean voyage. Will you take one with me?"

"The very thing!"

He looked at his watch. "We can just make it, to secure passports and get aboard," he reported, with a business-like air of competent seriousness. Twenty minutes later, when he led her, panting, wondering, sparkling, guessing, upon an excursion boat at its uptown landing, he drew a long breath of satisfaction and observed:

"So the Wishing Stone functions."

"Perfectly! And now we have nothing to do but think up wishes, and run down to Morningside, and sit on the Stone, and—presto!"

"Presto!" he echoed, with a gesture of happy finality, and they sought deck seats to watch for foreign lands.

When, at the boat's Battery landing, they disembarked, it was to exclaim at the marvels of an unknown city in a strange country.

"How tall the buildings are! The natives must always be striving to climb on top of one another," ran her make-believe observation, and:

"Don't you notice that over-eating must prevail among the inhabitants?" he inquired, as they chanced to pass three fat men and one super-fat woman in succession.

"Horrors! You don't suppose we've landed on a cannibal island by mistake?"

So, laughing, nonsense-ing, they caught a subway express back uptown, and planned another voyage of marvels for the next opportunity. Thus did make-believe strangely blend with the deepest realities of life.

III

For the realities were ever-present. Bec, perplexed and inexperienced, tried to push them from her mind. Philip, wiser than his years, wanted them faced down.

"It can't go on this way, Bec. If we had been permitted to see each other normally, I shouldn't have talked of marriage for many a long day yet, till I could offer you the right sort of home. But you're not happy as it is. Wouldn't you rather make the break? And let us work up together. We've a sense of humour, which solves most difficulties, and gives flavour to a diet of bread, cheese and kisses."

Always at these urgings she turned to him a longing, pitiful face.

"You know I'd rather, Philip!"

"Then let us, at once!"

But always debate came to the same end. "No, no, we can't! She would never consent."

"Let me go to her openly, and have it out with her!"

"No, no—never! You don't know her!" Overwrought, Bec would fall into panic at the thought of disclosure to Helen, who hovered like a Nemesis nowadays in her daughter's imagination. "She would separate us forever if she knew!"

"Well, then, there's the other way—take it on ourselves, go ahead on our own responsibility. You say it is what *she* did."

But at this proposal Bec's panic would only increase. Somehow, she could not tell how, but *somehow* the Nemesis would follow.

IV

On a day when they could both steal an hour at noon, Philip kept his promise to introduce Bec to the Popp family, who lived on the East Side uptown.

"It's like calling at the home of one's fairy godfather," she declared. "To be sure, he failed in his efforts to bring us together, but he *meant* to godfather us. And perhaps his wish had something to do with its coming

true, after all. Do you know," she meditated aloud, "I
believe that every wish pushes in the direction it wants
to go—gives either a little push or a big shove, according
to how hard it is."

The delicate mysticism of her nature always found a
response, though usually a silent one, in him. He never
laughed at these fancies, if fancies they were. And that,
Bec told herself, was a part of his being *he*.

They found the crowded nest of Popps in a clamour
of young chirpings and older twitterings. They were
welcomed almost to suffocation.

"How fortunate that you had such a bad attack of
rheumatism to-day, Mr. Popp," Bec rejoiced, "because
otherwise I might never have met you."

Mr. Popp bowed magnificently, scorning the twinges
that such ceremony cost him.

"This hour, Miss, is one of the memorable hours of
my life. Never did I think that such a reunion as this
would take place. I done my effort, that was all. I
knowed that if I could but bring two young and beating hearts together, it was mine to do. Little did I
dream," rolled on the eloquence of Mr. Popp, "of ever
seeing them young hearts again. Instead of which, I owe
to Mr. Oliver here all——"

Philip interrupted. "Miss Kent is very anxious to
see the photograph of you and Mrs. Popp as bride and
bridegroom," he declared, whereupon Mrs. Popp bustled
forward, beaming, and the topic was shifted. Twice
later, Bec observed, did Philip break up the conversation
in similar fashion.

It was very hard to leave, Bec found. She lingered

longest over the tiniest bird in the nest; it whacked its
fists about without aim, and said "goo-goo" as though
"goo-goo" were really an important statement.

"I wish I could take it along," she said to Philip, who
was holding open the door for her.

He looked at her with one of his long, still looks,
as if something had stirred deep wells and left him inarticulate. And the same thought came to each, although
he did not know that the night before Bec had dreamed
of a baby that nestled squirmily in her lap, curling its
pink toes into droll little fists.

Not until the following week did she understand
Philip's curious interruptions of Mr. Popp's discourse.
Then, slipping over to the East Side home one afternoon
all by herself and unknown to him, she descended upon
the chirping nest with a basketful of toys and candy, a
wonderful Santa Claus pack, bought with the hoarded
allowance.

"I couldn't wait till Christmas," she explained, passing
out tidbits to the deafening chorus of cheeps. "It's more
than half a year away."

"I do declare, you'n him's just alike in the goodness
of your blessed young hearts!" cried Grandmother Popp,
and forthwith proceeded to recount the way "that grand
young gentleman kept us all from being dispossessed
last winter when Pa couldn't work and we thought the end
had came, and if he didn't send around dinners, and
pay the rent, and he won't let Pa pay back a cent till
he's well enough to work reg'lar."

And Mr. Popp himself, returning at that moment,
joined in the praises of the grand young gentleman.

"And, Miss, if there's ever a way I can serve you, remember the word of John Jenkins Popp," he offered solemnly, and Bec pledged herself to remember his pledge. Neither guessed how soon it might be ratified.

As she was saying good-bye, the queer obsession seized her even here—the insatiable desire to know what everyone thought concerning her newly awakened questionings.

"Mr. Popp, excuse me for seeming personal," she apologised, "but would you object to telling me whether you believe in what they call God? I'm sure you are a profound thinker."

"In God, Miss?" His eyes rounded in surprise. "And why wouldn't I, seein' what your grand young gentleman done for our family when we was at the limit?" With which simple logic, Mr. Popp covered ground upon which philosophers have squandered volumes.

"Thank you," Bec replied. "I'm glad of your opinion, at any rate. Good-bye!" she cried to all the nest.

Thinking of the revelations concerning "the grand young gentleman," Bec went away with a feeling of something newly warm deep in her heart. Heretofore she had known Philip as he was to her; now she had caught a glimpse of his other side, in contact with an outer world.

v

In reality, the hours given to these lovers' meetings would have totalled a pauper's allowance. Rarely twenty-four hours passed, to be sure, without a moment's glimpse together of the Roof o' Dreams; either in the early morning, or late afternoon, or at night, when Bec

would flit up to her flowers like a great moth on frosty-
green wings; but often the meeting was one with the parting.   All told, a record of their excursions would
not have covered the fingers of her hands.   But the
impression of each was so vivid that Bec could live on it
for days together, storing every word, every minutest
incident, for her hours alone.   The fact that so much
of the lovers' communion never passed beyond her world
of dreams, explains to some extent Helen's surprising
blindness.   Moreover, that dominant person's conviction
of her own mastery helped account for it.   She took for
granted, largely, that her child could not disobey.   But,
nevertheless, Helen Kent's perceptions were far too keen
to escape the sense of events in the air, had her own
mind not been extraordinarily preoccupied during these
days—more and more preoccupied with every day that
passed—by a new element in her life, which was closing
her eyes as effectually as a new element in Bec's was
opening hers.   Were the emotions roused in the two women
essentially different? one might have wondered.   Or does
the same emotion produce blindness in the neighbourhood
of forty, that at twenty makes for clear-seeing?

Summer entered, and Bec's schooldays came to an end.
She had more than "passed," her examinations having
borne fruit in marks little short of perfection, those
marks having ripened under the most rigid scrutiny of
the terrible Obelisk.   Helen shone jettily in complacent
pride, and gave her young graduate a box party at the
most charming musical comedy in town, with a restaurant
supper following.   Both the lobster *à la Newburg* and
the *parfait* were heavenly, the graduate declared, roused

to her old-time sparkle for once; indeed, she showed such a wealth of Bec-ishness, that one of the youths, a romantic aviator, fell hopelessly a-mooning. Helen observed him with the lazy glint of luxurious amusement. Her property was safe from the air-raids of *those* eyes!

"Now for a long summer's rest," Helen said that night in the confidence of the bedtime hour. "We shall spend July in the mountains, and you shan't begin the new work until autumn. Then for the great career! Then begins the famous partnership for fortune! Miss and Mrs. Crœsus—here's to them!"

And even while Helen raised her midnight coffee-cup with a gesture that claimed the future for her own, her daughter was inwardly revolving the problem which had been growing more and more pressing of late: how was the great début to be accomplished? For:

"There's no use my giving you any more lessons," Zélie had said. "You're more than ready. But how the dev—I mean, how on the green apple we're going to find a chance for you to star in a performance of the highest order and in the most exclusive sassiety, is more than I know. Fair one, we've put in a pretty large order."

"Yes, it's almost the impossible." But Bec had nodded with an odd show of optimism.

"You said it."

"And yet I'm certain it's going to come true. Because we're wishing it so hard. I'm sort of *calling* for it, inside me, all the time. I'm finding out queer things," she had gone on sagely. "There's a way to make things come true. I seem able to catch the way at times, but

then I lose it again. But I've found out this: there's
a way to wish a thing, very, very hard, as though you
were telling someone—not some*one*, either, but some
great, floating power—all about your need, and explaining very clearly why you need it; and then forgetting
all about it, as though you had written a letter and sealed
and posted it and sent it off to its destination, and all
you had to do was to wait for the answer. Oh, I can't
explain it!" she had cried, "but I can feel it!"

Thus Bequita groped. It was as though, thirsting in
darkness, she fumbled over the face of unseen rocks and
now and then caught the plash of the crystal cascade
upon them, and touched her lips to it and was revived.
But only for instants; no light as yet shed its ray to
guide her steadfastly.

Zélie, in meditative amusement, had gently pulled the
tail of Villageoise.

"The funniest kiddie yet, isn't she, Vill?"

But Bec had not heeded. She had pushed on. "Zélie,
do you believe in anything—I mean anything like what
some people call God?"

Zélie had fallen silent, continuing to annoy Villageoise.
"Considering the way I was brought up," she had observed at length, "in everything from a gypsy camp to
the family end of a saloon, it can't be called surprising
that I never folded my little hands in prayer in the infant
class of Sunday-school." She had mused again.

"And from what I've seen of this world for twenty-
five years, I can't say I'm particularly stuck on the idea
of a world-to-come-life-everlasting. I guess I'll have had

enough of living by the time I'm through with three-score-years-and-ten of the job." Again musing—

"I suppose what I believe comes to about this," she had concluded. "That there's Some Reason for being square."

"S-s-s-s!" hissed Villageoise. There is a limit to the long-suffering of even the most patient of tails.

CHAPTER XIV

ADVENTURES TEMPORAL AND SPIRITUAL

I

BEC'S brain-racking on the subject of the début led her by devious ways to the one person besides Zélie who had shown a critical and detached interest in her dancing: McNab. He had seen and been impressed by it; he was a practical and influential man of affairs; might he not help her art to find a way out? She had never met him since his one call at the apartment, but surely he would remember. . . . With a sudden access of desperate courage, she dashed one morning to the telephone.

She had grasped the receiver when a horrid wobbliness came over her, purpose and all, and she fled to her room. She was all at once very much scared of what she had intended to do. The busy, important Mr. McNab! Of course he would not remember her! And even if he should, how it would annoy him to be interrupted!

The telephone bell rang. Someone wanting Helen, no doubt. Bec returned to the hall and pleasantly inquired "Hello?" welcoming the distraction.

"What number did you want?" It was the hall-girl. Her instant's hold of the receiver had registered, after all. Her reply was surprised from her, and before she knew it she had said "St. Paul 3000," and then was left staring at that small apparatus of metal, gutta percha and green cord as though it were a dragon.

But she had said it, she must go ahead now. "Number?" the operator was chirping, and she heard the repetition—it was swift, like being passed along from room to room and having no power to escape the final tribunal. . . .

"Monroe Mutual," came with crisp finality.

"Surely he won't be in his office," Bec's hope now murmured to her. "Helen says it's almost impossible to catch him——"

"*Monroe Mutual.*"

"Is—is Mr. Charles Mack McNab in?" Why hadn't she hung up, and ended it all? Her original purpose was functioning like a mechanism which, having once been started, she was powerless to check. Instants more —purrings, clickings——

"Hello, hello!" pounced at her.

"Is—is Mr. NcNab—in?"

"You're talking to him right now." There it was—no escape. Meet it, meet it square in the face!

"I'm—I'm Bec," she panted.

"Who? Didn't catch it."

"B-Bec. Rebequita Kent. Mrs. Kent's daughter. You met me at my mother's. I suppose you've forgotten —I know you're so busy. I danced a daffodil for you——"

"Oh, say, I get you now! Miss—Miss—sure, I remember!" His voice was cordial, but it was odd, his not

repeating her name.   Had he really forgotten her?
Helen was always talking about the preoccupied New
York business man who had no time for "outside" mat-
ters.   And how "outside" a matter was she, indeed!

"I—I'm afraid I ought not to have bothered you," she
murmured miserably.

"Oh, that's all right.   What can I do for you?"   Then
his voice turned aside and said to someone, "Just be looking over that report, won't you, and we'll take it up in a
minute."   He was engaged, then, and no doubt impatient.
Oh, why had she ever——

"It's only—only about a little matter of my own, and
I'm sorry I took up your time, and please never mind!   I
thought if I could have a little talk with you about my
dancing—but *please* don't think of it again.   I know how
busy you are!"

"Hold on—wait a second.   I could meet you at—let
me see——"

Now that she had gone so far, she rallied her pride;
it would be less weak-minded to see the thing through,
much as she regretted her act.   She would be very business-like and hasten the interview.

"I thought of—the Public Library," she ventured.
"There's a marble bench in the north corridor."   Once
she had seen a couple meet at this marble bench and sit
upon it to confer.   The aspect had been eminently proper.

"The—*what?*   Oh, say, wouldn't that chill you, eh,
what?"   He was taking a moment to think.   Then it
came:

"Be at Westbridge's at one-fifteen," he said with quiet
definiteness.   "Good-bye."

It was a restaurant! He was taking her to lunch! But one mustn't go to lunch unchaperoned with a man one knew but slightly! And in secret at that! It was impossible! But this was the situation. The appointment was made; he had rung off, without waiting for her reply. Yes, this was the situation, and Bec sank into a chair, her face flaming with the conflagration of knowl‑ edge that she had brought it upon herself.

To be sure, she had never dreamed of a lunch with Mr. McNab. So clearly had she visualised the chaste corridors of the Public Library, the icy sedateness of that marble bench, that possibilities of this kind had never entered her head. But she had opened the way to this invitation, she had been wholly to blame. And now—what was she to do about it? Should she call up again, and make excuses? But that would be contemptibly silly! She could see Helen shut her lips in a tight line and say, "You let yourself in for the thing. You've got to go through with it." Even Helen would say that, scorning.

The clock—half-past twelve already! And she must dress from pumps up. Yes, the only thing to do was to go promptly, be very business-like, and close the interview as speedily as possible. Business-like—that must be the keynote. Very, very business-like. . . .

"The white linen blouse looks most so." She ran over the row of lifeless forms hanging from sachet-padded stretchers in her wardrobe. "The white linen. But——" She hesitated. Eve throbbed within her breast.

"But the flesh-coloured crêpe-de-Chine is more suitable for a smart restaurant."

Again she hesitated. Again Eve, the woman within her, claiming her dower of loveliness, throbbed and cried out softly. From among the lifeless forms of silk, linen and cotton she took down the pale rosy crêpe, and a minute later it was endowed with breath. Into its arms she infused her own free-stretching movements, movements that seemed to seek and reach toward life; its numb bosom was no longer numb, it beat to her own pulse, It warmed, it stirred, it took on exquisite form. Its tint responded to the delicate warmth of the cheeks above it, emphasised the faint honey-colour of the throat upon which it parted in a deep point.

"I'm—very nice," Bequita commented humbly, and her mirror gave silent acclamation.

II

"Good for you! On the dot of one-fifteen. Little sport, all right, aren't you?"

McNab had met her with a vigorous handshake, had quickly steered her to a quiet table, past a gauntlet of eyes, and now he was settling down opposite with a long smile of satisfaction. If her interruption had annoyed him this forenoon, he certainly seemed far from annoyed now! She breathed deep at last. A soft burst of chords rose from a little jungle of palms, caught up the last vestige of her fear, flung it away, laughing after it.

She pulled off her gloves, and gave a light toss as if some harness were removed, shaking her shoulders free. Her eyes took in the luxury of palms, glittering tables, deft waiters, sophisticated costumes.

"It's heavenly!"

"Glad you think so."

"I really do. Helen says it's silly to call things heavenly, but sometimes they simply are!"

"If you say so, heavenly they are. You're right every time when I'm the judge!"

Bee drew back almost imperceptibly. Again she was not quite at ease.

The waiter approached.

"What's the good word?" McNab inquired. "Dry Martini? Bronx? That's about right, strikes me. Orange gives a ladylike, dressy touch."

"Oh, not any—not any kind!" she protested hurriedly. "Just lunch, please. We must get to business, so as not to detain you. I never drink cocktails—that is, I never did but once, and it made me feel awfully twinkly."

But in spite of her protests, McNab had aready given the order, and now he laughed in a delighted, leisurely way, and leaned forward slightly across the table.

"'Awfully twinkly' would suit to a T. Twinkle, twinkle, little star, twinkle right here where you are."

She drew back perceptibly now, and he seemed not obtuse to the movement. He became at once brisk and to the point.

"Now what shall we have? Iced consommé? You must be warm after hurrying all the way from uptown. Sorry to ask you to come so far, but my time was cut out for me."

"Oh, I'm the one to feel sorry," she insisted, reassured. "I was so ashamed after I'd—well, roped you in."

"Never mind, so long as the victim enjoys his lasso."

Now *that* smile was all right—it was friendly and fraternal, and made her feel comfortable.

"I'm afraid I sounded pretty short," he went on, as they sipped the cocktails. "But when you called up—well, what do you suppose the situation was?"

"I can't guess!" Already the sensation of twinkliness was beginning; she felt more interested in everything, less self-conscious and afraid.

"You see, I got the idea right away that this little matter was—well, between us two."

She nodded.

"And while we were talking about this appointment, who should be seated at my elbow but your charming mother!"

"Oh, she didn't—did she?—hear——"

"Not a word. I caught on in time to keep from repeating your name. Have one"—he passed her a delightful nest of a basket in which snuggled a whole litter of rolls, no two alike—"and now let's hear about California. I never had time to get away from Broadway long enough to see it."

The twinkly sensation was making her very comfortable now, it seemed easier than usual to talk, and she had a consciousness that she was being interesting. Soon her tales of California were in full swing—how she had dived into the Pacific after a goldfish as big as a mackerel when she was not much bigger herself, thinking that she could pick up the fish like a kitten, and how she was nearly drowned . . . how she had often gone camping in the redwoods with other girls, wood-nymphs in serge bloomers, who slew their own bear once on a time. . . .

"Gosh," he muttered, half aloud, "that's the life! I'd like to get away from Broadway long enough to be human for awhile—camp out, swim, fish, play and sleep afterwards, instead of play when you ought to be asleep. . . . It's clean, that is. . . ."

Bec heard him muttering to his own thoughts, but did not heed, for a sudden anxiety had seized her. Here they were at the dessert, and the business of the occasion had not yet come up. How broach the subject? He was bolting his ice—he must be in a hurry to get off. The interview would soon be over, and in vain. . . .

His ice was gone. He fumbled in a pocket. With a sudden movement of relaxation he settled back, opening his cigarette case.

"And now," said McNab, "we're ready for the conference. Just what is it you have to tell me about your dancing? How can I help?"

And in that moment's rush of reassurance, the glow of hope reborn, Bec learned for all time the lesson that every woman learns sooner or later—to trust all, biding at peace, to the striking of the match.

III

"Then the proposition is this," he summed up, as, at the end of her eager narrative, she came to a breathless halt. "What you want is to chuck the typewriter for good—trip forth, light fantastic and all that——"

He was regarding her with a smoky gaze. It seemed to be endless, this far-away and yet very-much-there look. Under the length of it her eyes fell at last. . . .

"Cat has to be away now and then—business demands absence—one mouse calls another on the 'phone—other mouse says 'Come on and play!' Where's the harm?" Apropos of nothing, apparently, he was murmuring on. "Say—great idea that—I like the picture of me as a mouse at play."

He leaned across the table. Her eyes rose with a start.

"Say, Miss Bec, look here. I liked you a lot from the first minute when you danced that daffodil thing, though I haven't shown it by calling—busy man, and all that. But why can't——"

"Oh, I'm always busy, too!" she broke in. The comfortable twinkliness had gone, she was conscious of acute nervousness, and the wish that she could somehow push his eyes away. Dimly, she was aware of something crucial in the moment. Her poise quivered, righted itself——

"Mr. McNab," she went on, "it was what you said of my gift that really gave me my start. From that day I resolved some time to carry out my wish." She met his eyes safely, with sincerity in her own; the moment was past.

He looked at her still, but differently. The smoky look somehow faded out. And she had a conviction that what he said in the end was not at all what he had intended to say in the beginning.

"Do you know, Miss Bec, there's something about you that makes a man want the decent things. Would—would you mind if I dropped around sometimes, at the apartment?"

And at this, very unskilfully but very honestly, Bec said:

"I should like to see you often, Mr. McNab. You are so kind and I like you so much. But I'd rather you knew that—that—I *belong*."

And McNab tightened his lips with a sudden indrawing of breath, reddened, tensed; then, his fat little immaculate hand out:

"You're *all right*, Miss Bec! And good fortune to you—and to him, the lucky dog! S'pose you're not—not announcing it yet?"

"No. No one knows." At that moment she met a thing in his gaze that she had always wanted. It had something to do with brothers, she fancied.

"I am going to tell you his name. It is Philip Rodney Oliver. He is an architect."

"What! Phil Oliver?" broke from McNab. "Why, I knew that chap in France—haven't seen him since, but I'll never forget that night. . . . He made a swim under fire, to rescue a wounded man—gosh, but I never saw anything to beat it while I was over there. And he'd had the reputation of being a bit slow on the job—not that he failed anywhere, but he had a lazy way of laughing at the others when they roared about capturing the Kaiser's whole army, and all that. And then, when his chance came"—McNab paused and shook his head as if to express the unutterable—"well, he *showed* 'em, believe *me*."

The little man fumbled for one of the immaculate and high-priced handkerchiefs which he always produced in foldings unbroken, and mopped a warm brow.

"If it's Oliver's won you, I say he's the chap to deserve his luck, that's all. . . . I'll put you into a taxi, if you'll forgive my hurrying to an engagement. And I'll be thinking about a chance for your dancing—if there's anything I can do, you can sure count on me!"

He had helped her into the cab when she delayed him.

"Oh, by the way, excuse my hindering you—but I want so much to ask—do you think there's anything in the idea—the thing, whatever it is—that people call God? You're a practical business man, I thought you might know."

McNab stopped with a jerk of surprise, then he laughed.

"Afraid I'm a poor adviser on that matter, Miss Bec. I've always said that most people don't believe it, but they aren't quite sure enough it's a fake to be as bad as they'd like to be. . . . You'll hear from me if anything turns up. Good luck!"

As she rode home Bec thought it all over, and recalled the way the smokiness had risen in McNab's eyes, and the way it had faded, and she knew intuitively that she would never see it there again.

IV

Adventure had come to fill Bequita's world. Where the temporal ended the spiritual began.

What were churches like, after all? she found herself wondering, and one Sunday while Helen was driving she slipped off to the one nearest at hand, and tucked herself away in an obscure corner.

Something welled up in her at the music—she could feel it in her throat—but all the welling died down at the sermon. It was about money. The congregation were not giving enough, they came and took home food, food for the soul, a hungry-looking man told them, and failed to pay for the food. How was this church to continue? How was this edifice of worship to be supported? The preacher seemed to grow thinner and sharper as he said "edifice of worship," and he sounded like the Obelisk when she found that the whole class had flunked in compound interest.

And the prayers mourned in Bec's ears. "Oh Lord, have mercy!" they besought, as if the people were being punished and were begging that the lashing be stopped. She was horribly mortified when the plate was passed, for she had not brought her purse, never thinking of a collection—but afterwards she consoled herself with realising that she had not received any spiritual food, so that she didn't really owe anything.

But whenever the music rose again that choky, wonderful, hurty feeling of joy welled up in her. If only worship were all music . . . it was the music that brought the Thing nearer; that scolding sermon, those mourning prayers only drove It off. . . .

On her Roof o' Dreams she pondered over all the opinions that she had been gathering, sorting them, peering into them, piecing together broken bits, guessing at what lay behind them.

Zélie didn't seem to have much use for creeds, but she had half confessed to a sense of Something—the same Thing, Bec supposed, that she herself felt so curiously in the air. And Mr. McNab's attitude seemed very much the same.

And Mr. Popp—"Why wouldn't I believe in God, seein' what your grand young gentleman done for our family when we was at the limit?" It was as simple and sincere as the statement of a child who believes in Santa Claus because his stocking is filled. After all, why wasn't that a perfectly good reason? To be sure, there was no more a great ruler sitting on a throne and wearing a beard than there was a fat little Saint driving reindeer, but why might there not be a sort of force, this queer Thing that she felt, moving people to act as agents, either to fill stockings or to rescue the Popps?

It turned out that everyone she had questioned, no matter how little they followed the rule of churches, had owned, after a fashion, to a belief in Something. Cousin Ress wouldn't talk about it because she had promised Helen, but Bec knew very well that she did believe, although she always motored all Sunday and said that church played the devil with her neuritis. . . . Little Aya and her Buddha. . . . The Obelisk and Russian Anna were both punctilious church-goers, therefore Bec gave less heed to their opinion, for she suspected that it had been accepted by them like a hand-me-down coat without scrutiny of the fit. But when people had looked at the Thing with a sceptical eye, and even so were partly convinced. . . . Philip—even Philip, who hated talking about it—he was very gruff and growly about it, and yet he admitted that in France, at least, he had found Something. . . .

That was the amazing thing to Bec, in the face of all

that Helen had taught her: the discovery that all sorts of people, in diverse walks, people taught and untaught, reverent and irreverent, some far from pious, very worldly, in fact, possibly rather naughty—people who made fun of you at first when you wanted to talk about it seriously—nevertheless, in the end, if you pinned them down tight, admitted at least a suspicion that there was Something. They didn't, in short, feel ready to accept Helen's theory that we are no more than miserable mechanical toys, "wound up like the cocks that the venders show on Forty-Second Street, to fight each other until the machinery runs down or goes to smash."

And now, in so sweeping a review of her universe that she felt like the Locksley Hall gentleman, Bec fell to wondering whether Helen's professors in that great, far-visioned western university had ever taught or thought what Helen believed? She had always been quoting them —"survival of the fittest"—"ignorance of the law excuses no one"—phrases that sounded cruel enough—but didn't the cruelty lie in Helen's perversion of their true meaning? Bec had listened to these same professors now and then in her childhood; words that had passed over her head at the time returned to her with the noblest significance.

"The law of survival of the fittest is never to be read in a crude and physical, nor even in a cold-bloodedly intellectual sense. Only in the subtlest ethical meaning does its truth lie. The fittest are, indeed, the conquerors of the earth; but their fitness is that of right, not might."

One of the professors had said that.

No, it was not the university that had been responsible

for Helen Clifton's doctrines. It was something inside Helen herself. How Bec wished that she might return now, grown-up to understand, and find help in that great, free institution which had so bravely shaken itself loose from dogma more than a quarter-century ago. . . . More and more she was coming to puzzle over Helen's point of view. . . .

In her new spirit of zeal Bec visited several churches of various denominations; but although some of the preachers were agreeable, and some of the prayers impressive, she never found what she sought. One day it dawned upon her——

"They all treat the Thing like an outsider. They talk about Him, or pray at Him, as if he were somewhere up above all the time, instead of a great air floating all around them—more than that—something *inside* themselves."

She was fumbling—getting closer—almost she had it——

"More than *inside* themselves—why isn't it *themselves?* Why isn't God *all of us?* What if He is? What if He is what does the things we do—the best things? When I dance, what if it is God dances? The Obelisk would call that frightfully irreverent. But suppose it was really He writing plays when they called it Shakespeare, and travelling to America when they called it Columbus —moving, acting, doing things to make the world grow, all the time, through all of us, as though we were fingers. . . .

"If that could be true, then what we pray to would be Ourselves. . . ."

V

Bec was to see an instance of that obscure law which, once you start cause moving in one channel, brings about effect in a channel wholly different. She had rolled up her sleeves, so to speak, when she had sought McNab's influence; and now not that gentleman, but Zélie, was to prove the agent of her directed energy.

"Well, my child, something's doing at last."

Bec arrived at the studio on a rainy June day to find Zélie, who had summoned her, pacing the floor with long sinuous strides that made no more sound than do the strides of one of her feline relatives over a bed of forest leaves. Something was worrying her, Bec was sure; but Miss Barrajas refused to admit it. "Never felt more cheerful. Why shouldn't I? I've landed your G. O.!"

"I always knew it would come!" Bec breathed. She caught the other in a smothering embrace. But, to her surprise, Zélie drew back.

"Sit down, kid," she instructed bluntly. "I haven't time to spare for any ecstasies."

It was astounding, that touch of cynicism, almost bitterness, in Zélie's manner. How could she not burst into ecstasy, after all their hoping and striving?

"Now then," Zélie went on with business-like curtness. "You're going to Manito Summit Park for your outing?"

"Yes. It's settled." In the sadly degenerate Catskills a few lovely refuges still remain, and Helen had chosen one of the most delightful of these.

"O. K. Dovetails exactly. Now for it. The

high-mucky-mucks of Eagle's Eyrie Park, a few miles
beyond, are getting up a sort of pageant—*some* class,
believe *me!* So se-lect that none of the Great Majority
could get an eyelash through the gates. But money—
why, kid, it's to flow like champagne the last night before
the Drys take over the earth! They've got Edmund
Lyall Van Buren to design the whole thing, costumes and
all—the artist that's doing 'em for all the new plays.
He's making the paintings for it now. What do you
know about *that?* And——"

"But—but what——" Bec panted, fumbling for the
connection between this event and her own fortune, too
incredulous to dare see——

"You'll learn in time, my child." Zélie's haste seemed
to have passed. "To resume: this show is to represent
some American Indian legends. Very appropriate and
all that, in the wilds of nature *et cetera.* And the *pièce
de résistance*"—Zélie paused impressively, and fixed her
eyes upon Bec's—"is to be—" she went on with tormenting deliberateness, as though dangling a tidbit just beyond
the reach of a famished victim—"is to be the scene where
the White Maiden, a Spirit of the Waterfall, appears
to the Indians who are dying of thirst, and leads them
to the cascade. She flits up to them through the woods,
then comes to the edge of the gone-dry waterfall, and
there she dances—*dances*, mind you—oh, hey tiddlety,
tiddlety tee!—a dance that represents the bubbling,
leaping cascade—do you get me? And that dance is
expected to be some punkins! The Indians sit around
gaping, audience ditto. Everybody spellbound. At the
end, as the sun sets, she smites the rock—bing!—and the

waterfall gushes forth—whish!—then she waves—ta-ta!
and vanishes."

To an imagination like Bec's the picture, even through
the medium of Zélie's slang, was vivid as light. Zélie
paused to meet her dead silence. Bec could hear her own
heart like a clock ticking in the night. Could it be that
—no, no, she mustn't believe—and yet——

"You can't mean that—that—O Zélie, don't torment me! Who—is to be the—White Maiden?"

For answer Zélie picked up a hand mirror and held
it before Bec's blazing eyes.

Bec saw in it a face pale with excitement; eyes that
burned more black than blue in their fever; lips a livid
coral; a mass of foaming gold hair escaping under the
broad straw hat. Bequita Kent would have fallen far
short of intelligent womanhood had she not recognised
the fact that, for all the faulty features, here was beauty
—the sort that burns its way from within, and flames in
the outward expression of face, in the arresting grace
of every posture.

She covered the face, bowed it, in a sudden overwhelming humility.

"It's all too wonderful! But what if I should fail?"

"Rats! Buck up, my fair one. You won't do a thing
to that dance!"

"But, Zélie, why not you?" came the next amendment.
"It's so generous of you, but you're waiting for your
G. O. as well as I!"

Again that shade of bitterness surprised Bec. But
Zélie replied briefly, "A nice White Spirit I'd make,
wouldn't I? No, lamb, the tiger-cat is my style. Now

then, I suppose you want a few items. The long and
the short of it, then, is that some of the bunch happened
to—well, to ask me to recommend someone for the said
White Spirit. I saw it would work out A number one
for you, with you staying near enough to slip over on
the quiet for rehearsals. We'll talk about the details
later. All that's needed now is your official acceptance.
Do I convey it, *Mademoiselle la Premiére?*"

"Zélie! The idea of asking! And that you should
contrive all this for me, to make my dream come true!
O my dear, how I hope that your own G. O. will come
running after it!"

The reply was a trifle snorty.

"Now beat it—skiddoo! I've got to go and meet the
committee, to give 'em your answer."

But, left alone with Villageoise, Miss Barrajas sank
into one of the baronial chairs, and for long minutes
she did not stir.

"Well—my G. O. waves to me and flits," she sighed
at last, rising heavily. "That's all right. She has
everything ahead, and she deserves it. As for you and
me, Vill, we might lose our heads with too much prosperity. You might take to champagne instead of cream,
if you could get it, and I might acquire the vicious habit
of cutting my old friends of Bittersweet Alley."

She rose with extreme lassitude, put on her turban
at a recklessly don't-care angle, picked up two unmated
gloves, and prepared to set out.

"She'll never guess the truth—don't worry. Everybody that might let it out is going to be pledged not to.
Otherwise, she'd break her little generous heart. So—

it's all right all 'round. And if you ever catch me being sorry I did it, just kindly claw my eyes out, will you, Madame Cat? So long!"

VI

Turbulent with the great news, Bec sped home. And here she was at her own door, in a turmoil of excitement; how should she crush it down, drive it from her eyes, her cheeks, her voice, her panting breath? She must not rouse a flicker of suspicion in Helen. What a campaign, indeed, lay ahead—all the preparation for this marvellous début, without once giving the secret away! Impossible, and yet not impossible, because what must be done could be. And when the great triumph was won, Helen would be convinced at last—how she would shine with pride——

So, her thoughts tumbling in exultant confusion, Bec entered the apartment. Helen was out.

Bec learned this with a sense of relief, for now she would have time to cool the fever of her excitement. She entered her own room. On a chair, neatly set forth, lay one of her party gowns, and the sash and slippers and stockings that she wore with it, and a wreath of tiny ribbon buds to trail over her shoulder. Until then she had forgotten the dinner-dance at Adelaide Matcham's.

Helen had put everything in exquisite order—had made the gown look like new, with its fresh garniture. Bec sank into her easy chair and gathered all the charming follies into her lap. Their gaiety, their luxurious charm, blended somehow with all her joyous turbulence of new hopes—with her thought of Philip, too, who might at this moment be awaiting her. How could she tell him the whole wonderful news in hours, even, let alone a few snatched minutes? Philip, pink buds, Spirit of the Waterfall, rosy Georgette crêpe, all shimmered like some blending stage spectacle before her intoxicated mind. . . .

Anna was handing her a letter. "Man bring," explained the absence of a stamp.

No letter such as this had Bec ever received. It was addressed to her in the laboured handwriting of an ignorant person. The envelope was of cheap paper, and smeary about the flap. Bec turned it over and over, in feminine fashion, wondering who could have sent it. And at length she was driven to that ultimate resource of opening it.

There, alone, Bequita read her letter. She read it slowly, from first line to last. She read it staring, unbelieving, puzzling, rejecting, doubting, shrinking, confounded, defying, scorning, wilting, and in the end returning always to one agony, which was a powerlessness to disbelieve. The letter would not be disbelieved, try as she might. Subtly it insisted upon its own authenticity. There was that in it which rang true. That ring—yes, that was the thing which testified. Something that lay between the lines. Although she cried in white silence against belief, Bequita knew. The letter told the truth.

On the floor at her feet were strewn the pretty follies that she had gathered into her lap. The rosy froth of the gown, the shimmer of silk hosiery, slippers, adornments—all lay in a tumble, slipped from her hold. All that they stood for seemed to have slipped from her hold, as well—their unshadowed youthfulness, their fragrance of wishes and blitheness and gaieties and allurements and sweet credulities—all their meaning seemed to have slipped from her along with them, and to have crumpled, and the soul within her seemed to be sitting there as the body sat, a mussed sort of soul.

Her eyes fixed upon the fallen wreath. There it lay, overturned, and the wrong side of it lay uppermost—a mesh of wires and long stitches. Were all lovely things like that if you turned them over? Helen would reply, "Of course"; would explain that the right side, as we call it, the pretty side of life, is nothing more than the appearance of things, and that you only get at the truth when you turn them over and look at the stitches and wires.

So this—all that the letter revealed—was the wrong side, the ugly side, the true side of life. . . .

But the instinct for action was strong in Bequita, for all its immaturity. The question now faced her: What was to be done?

CHAPTER XV

"GHOSTS RISE"

I

O N the afternoon when Bec was learning from Zélie her great news, Helen had gone forth at a curious request from Dr. Aspden. He had entered her office that morning (by way of the general corridor, of course) as shyly as some overgrown, gruff boy, and had gingerly put his request.

"Would you, on some convenient day, do a kind act for a lone and ignorant male creature?"

"Doing kindnesses for male creatures is not in my line," she flashed gaily, "but out with it! We'll see."

"I want your judgment on some furniture and curtains."

Her eyebrows curved in delighted surprise. "Is the house found—the long-anticipated refuge for every grouch?"

"Not yet. But I've decided to select the furniture and perhaps that will bring the house—the old principle of 'Get your spindle and your distaff ready,' you see."

She laughed. "Nothing gives me greater pleasure than minding other people's business," she assured him. "Miss Muldoon is away—tonsilitis—so I've got to omit some of my work to-day. Let's go this afternoon."

284

"Really?" He beamed quite as though her prompt response were too good to be true.

Departing, he involuntarily seized the knob of the sealed door, the direct route to his own office, and met its sturdy resistance.

"Absurd! Force of old habit!" he exclaimed, and there showed a flush of annoyance at himself as he turned.

The lady's eyes awaiting his, and the gleam of amusement in them, by no means decreased his flush. But there was more than amusement.

"Our two departments have, perforce, a great deal of communication," she observed. "Don't you think it might facilitate matters if—" She paused, quizzically eyeing him—"if the carpenter were called to unseal our door?"

For a long moment of embarrassed recollection, amusement, and pleasure, he regarded her. Then, "Really?" he asked again, as though this, also, were too good to be true.

He picked up the telephone extension. "Send the carpenter here at once," he directed.

II

Helen had various home matters to attend to on that day, and, as she was to give the later afternoon to Dr. Aspden, she decided to run up home for lunch, and let him come for her at half-past three at the Spindle Club, which was within the shopping district.

She must make ready for Bec's dinner engagement. Helen assiduously cultivated the frolicsome side of her daughter in these days, believing it to be the safety valve for romantic broodings. Yes, she must be sure to repair the pink gown, to freshen its trimmings, so that Bec would look her most charming.

She found that Bec had already lunched and gone when she reached home, so, having sewed for almost an hour, she set forth the costume as temptingly as a wily shopkeeper displaying his wares, and started for the Spindle.

The thought of the Club, of finding Dr. Aspden there, brought back to her with fresh vividness that day of her imp's escapade, which had sealed their friendship. Here, crossing Fifth Avenue, she caught herself smiling with a gleam of remembered mischief, and she bit her lip, trying to drive the smile back, and was made aware by the impertinent glance of a passing male that the smile still incorrigibly lighted her eye. What a jolly beginning it had been, and how comfortably the friendship had grown apace ever since! Men might, indeed, be delightful comrades on the basis of cool friendship, once kill out romantic nonsense for all time!

She had several blocks to traverse in the rain—a compulsion that, on another day, might have been disagreeable. But to-day nothing was disagreeable. Quite unrealized by herself, a glamour was cast this afternoon over Helen Kent's world. Strolling easily under her red umbrella, she looked forth with delight at the picture the Avenue presented. A host of other gorgeous umbrellas had blossomed there—blue and red and green and purple—like great exotic flowers all coming forth at once in the moist warmth.

She even loitered before shop windows. Here were imported perfumes in bottles of irresistible design; toilet waters; exquisite soaps and powders: all the delicately sensuous luxuries of the toilet table. Helen lingered, seduced by their charm; they played upon her senses, and so did the warm, still rain, and the gay blossoming of umbrellas. . . .

Here she was, at the cross street of the Spindle. Five minutes later she was greeting Dr. Aspden.

"You are altogether too kind to a lone and perplexed man, to help him out on such a day. But you shall be kept dry in the car."

Her smile was, to him, inscrutable. But no less inscrutable were her thoughts to herself.

"To-day, I seem somehow to like even rain," was what she said.

III

Bec, alone in the apartment in the later afternoon, sat staring out at the river and her question. What was to be done?

For something must be done, and immediately.

Or, on the other hand, should nothing be done? Should she disregard the letter's request, tear it to bits, refuse to believe its statements, blot it from her life? That, she knew, was what she would like to do. But that was impossible.

Should she wait, and turn the matter over to Helen?

But Helen had left no word concerning her return; she might be dining out, going to the theatre—hours might elapse if Bec waited for her. And besides, if she heeded the letter's warning—"Say nothing to any-one"——

There before her, on the laboriously written sheet, were fullest instructions. The address was clear; the request was, to come at once and alone. Should she follow these instructions blindly, implicitly?

Her decision began to swing like a pendulum. She would dash for her wraps—throw them down—pin on her hat—declare that to go was madness, that to heed such a letter from a stranger was preposterous——

And the letter, poor and brief and dingy, silently regarded her.

There was a long minute that Bec stood dead still, her fists drawn tight.

"I'll—go," she said, and she said it to the smeared sheet as to a human being awaiting her word. It seemed almost to sigh its relief.

But how? The locality named was strange to her, the afternoon was growing late, and the rain had brought an early dusk. Could she find the way? She was afraid —so afraid that her eyes brightened with dread, her muscles grew rigid. And then, all at once, in the midst of her fear, a recollection sprang forward.

"Remember the word of John Jenkins Popp!" it seemed fairly to cry aloud.

Her problem was solved. On this strange, terrifying mission, good Mr. Popp would guide her, care for her. He had insisted upon her having his telephone number. . . .

In an incredibly brief time Bec, huddled against the

rain and the dismal twilight and her fear, was being driven through unknown and sinister ways under a care as cherishing as it was reverential.

"No harm shall come near you, Miss; I am your servant to the death," Mr. Popp had assured her eloquently; but, unlike some eloquence, she knew his to be sincere.

Huddled in the depths of the cab, Bec sat rigid and white, her hands gripping each other for support. Oh, would her courage hold out? cried her thoughts. Could she face it? Could she, oh, could she "see it through?"

IV

The address proved to be that of a dreary old brick house in a dreary old street, shrunken by the overshadowing of a great hospital. The hospital buildings humped themselves in the rain, grey against grey; the house shared their despairing bleakness.

"Shall I—ahem—would it be more agreeable to you if I was to accompany you inside the door, Miss?" Mr. Popp delicately inquired. At sea as to the nature of her visit, he hovered anxiously over it like a nervous old hen. She had told him, merely, that she was obliged to pay an unexpected call at a strange house, and would be grateful for his escort.

"No, thank you, I must go in alone. But I shall know that you are waiting outside, Mr. Popp."

"Till the crack of doom, if need be, Miss!"

And then, in swift sequence, she had been ushered into the dingy rooming-house, had found the landlady, had been led to that person's dining-room.

"I'll have him come to you here," said the landlady. She stared dully at Bec through jaded eyes, and kept trying to button her olive-green wrapper while she talked, apparently unaware that the button was missing. The room smelled of soup and an uncleaned carpet and the rusty gas heater and years of non-ventilation.

"Then he isn't ill?" Bec asked in surprise. "Your letter said that he would probably not live long."

"He thought so. So'd I. Heart," replied the landlady succinctly. "But got a lot better quick. Won't last, though. Liable to go any day. He's up now. Got clothes on. . . . I take 'em in here a lot, when they're discharged from hospital," she added in explanation.

"He has been in hospital, then?"

"Yep. Alcoholic." With which brief report, she left Bec to await the meeting.

v

For minutes Bec was left alone. Then the inner door opened, and a man advanced toward her. He paused, studying her face; he shut the door behind him, so that the two were now enclosed together; still keeping to the opposite side of the room, he scanned every line of her face as one devours a letter to get the gist of the message. So long did this fierce scrutiny continue that Bec, meeting it intently, dumbly, had opportunity to seize upon all that went outwardly to make up the man: the nerve-racked thinness of the whole body, called to her attention by the blue-veined emaciation of the wrists, by the fleshless neck; the haggard youth of the face, a boy-

ishness that seemed somehow to be beckoning through
the wreckage, as if a sinking ship hoisted its signal and
waved gallantly to the last. Above this queerly old-young
face the close cropping of hospital regulation was already
being defied by a curly mop which was springing anew—
and as white as old age. But the blue eyes, brilliant as
water under sun, held to youth; the eyes, and also a
certain movement or attitude of the body—some turn, or
swing, that still had a lilt in it.

After moments of this face-to-face scrutiny, he said
brusquely:

"Turn your profile."

Still dumb, Bec obeyed.

At last he summed up his conclusions:

"You haven't a trace of her about you, except in the
chin and line of the jaw. There you show her determination to do what you set out to do. Otherwise, you're
me all over—and may the Lord help you!"

Bec felt the blood rushing to her face at last. Even
that was a relief, after the whiteness of dread of which
she had been conscious. Yes, the suspense was over in
a way; at least, there was no more speculation concerning the personality. This was all she had to meet—
a white-haired wreck of a man, with blue eyes no older
than her own.

He seemed to be waiting now for her to speak; to speak
out of the void of almost twenty years of silence and of
complete strangerhood. And still she stood without a
word; what could the past, the present, or the future
offer these two in common?

Perhaps seeing her embarrassment, perhaps overcoming a timidity of his own, he drew forward a chair for her.

" 'Rebequita,' " he said, as though trying its sound. " 'Bec,' " we were going to call you. You're still called that?"

"Yes."

He repeated the name musingly. "It's been six years now since I saw you last. Then you were hardly through being *little* Bec."

"Six years!" she puzzled aloud. "But we've never met since I was a baby!"

"Oh, yes, we have." He laughed deep in his throat; almost a muffled groan, his laugh was. "We met six years ago on Sutter Street in San Francisco. I was in no danger of being recognised, but I saw. You wore a long braid—it wasn't 'done up' yet—and a lot of buttercups and daisies and things on your hat."

"I remember the hat," murmured Bec.

"Looked like the wreaths a little girl would make herself, out in the fields, in summer. If she went walking, maybe—with somebody—her Daddy, say——"

His voice was drifting away as his eyes were. They strayed out over the grey hospital walls rising in tiers, over the roofs now dun with the rain's twilight.

"Those California fields—they can put it all over this, can't they?" He came back with a sorry little cornerwise smile.

He took a seat now near Bec's, but no nearer than a formal caller might draw to his hostess. In fact, there was no familiarity whatever in his manner; rather, a suggestion of maintaining a respectful distance, like one entitled to nothing more. But on the other hand, this

manner did not shade by a hair's-breadth toward cring-
ing; in fact, it was that respect for another which is
one with self-respect. Whatever else had gone to wreck
in body, intellect, or soul, she felt intuitively that one
quality stood upright, like the tree left standing by the
tornado: that quality was personal dignity. It sur-
vived even here and now, in the midst of all that was
sordid, at the close of a detention in the city's psycho-
pathic ward.

"I suppose," he began at length, "you'd like a brief
explanation, inasmuch as you've regarded me as dead for
the last four years or so." His inflection was a query;
the only answer she could make was to nod assent.

"I can cover the story quickly. History's a bore, so
the sooner it's done, the better. Of course, as you've
always known, no doubt, I went from bad to worse.
After I'd drifted into Idaho, and was running with about
the lowest-down gang in the Rocky Mountains, it happened that I acquired a pal so like me that our own
wives could hardly have told us apart. Charlie and I
used to palm ourselves off for each other, just to see
the fun."

He paused, drawing the long, tired breath of a sick
man.

"Don't tell the story if it tires you," Bec put in, her
woman's instinct to the fore.

At that he regarded her keenly again. "You're sympathetic, aren't you? . . . No," he went on musingly,
"you haven't got anything of hers but her chin.

"Well," he picked up his narrative, "something—never
mind what—took place about four years ago that made

it advisable for me to disappear as promptly as possible." He gave a short, harsh laugh. "And, very conveniently, and to show how obliging a good old pal could be, Charlie happened to get killed by a drunken Indian at the same time. So—well the details don't matter, but the long and the short of it is that another good friend arranged to have it understood that I was the one killed, and that Charlie had gone to Alaska. It was especially easy, in that no one wanted to investigate—my relatives were all pretty well satisfied to accept me as dead and gone, and no chance of my disgracing them any further." He shrugged and fell silent, again gazing out at the dun twilight.

"Have you been—long in the East?" hesitated Bec, caught by an odd sense of delicacy at pressing for more information than was offered.

"Longer than you. I resurrected myself and worked my way here at once, after I was killed." Again that queer, half-flippant, half-tragic smile curled the beautifully cut lips. They were the lips of a child or a poet, Bec noticed; more beauty than strength in their modelling, but a charm only outdone by that of the boyishly blue eyes.

"I've always kept track of you. Once in a while I used to see you, when you lived near the University——"

"How? Where?" her wonder broke forth.

He laughed dully. "Never mind how. I knew when she was in San Francisco, and I managed to slip around where I could catch a glimpse of you. Once I met you with a beau, and I wondered if you'd every marry, and what luck *you*'d have at the game. The Lord knows *she* drew a blank."

Neither broke the silence for a long time. After awhile:

"Another day I followed you secretly when you were out in the country," he resumed. "You walked over the hills to a lonely spot under the live oaks, and there, all by yourself, you danced. I don't know what the dance was, but it made me think of a mariposa lily— a butterfly attached to a stem. If you hadn't been attached, I kept thinking, you'd make a clean getaway from this earth."

Bec's exclamation leaped at the surprise of this. "I remember the day perfectly! You don't mean that you were there watching?"

"All the time. I dodged behind trees, or a wall. Oh, I've never quite lost you. I knew when you came to New York, and I've seen you here, though only at a distance. And the older you grow, the more you look like me."

In the gathering dark they gazed for moments each at the other face so strangely similar. Yes, it was true; for all the snowy hair, the marks of sickness, the lines of hard living, the likeness still was insistent.

"I suppose you'd like to curse because it's so?" he flung out.

At first she did not reply. Bequita's world was too much overturned for her as yet to find her position upon it. That the dead lived; that she had a father; that he had sought her; that he was this derelict, here before her eyes, sick, broken, branded, low—by all these facts she was too much confounded for speech, for approach of any kind, either of blame or sentiment.

But at last words came: words that surprised her as much as they surprised him.

"No. I wasn't wishing I looked unlike you. Somehow, I think—I'm not sorry at all. I was just feeling that—that if we had met before, we might have—got acquainted. Maybe there's something alike—something, I mean, more important than the colour of our eyes or that tweak in our noses."

She could see that he flushed at this, and a longing sprang into his eyes, and he made an impulsive move toward her; but at once he crushed back the impulse, as if disciplined by a grim resolve.

"The one kindness I've ever shown you was to keep from getting acquainted. For nineteen years I've kept from disturbing you, and this is the last time as well as the first. I wouldn't have done it now if I hadn't known I'm done for, and I gave way to my great desire to speak with you once — and I was ashamed the minute I'd done it."

Amidst all the chaos of her thoughts, Bec found one. "I'm glad you did. I shall always be glad."

He looked at her gratefully. "Thank you for that. I don't know why you should say it, but you seem to mean it. Perhaps you prefer to know the worst at once," he smiled quizzically. "And since we are not to meet again—oh, don't fear, I haven't butted in on your life to spoil it, like an impolite skeleton stalking out of his closet in the midst of an afternoon tea—I'm going to drop out, you see, just as I did before—so let's understand a few points clearly. First, don't say anything to her about this."

He had not once spoken Helen's name. And without knowing why, Bec fell into his pronominal mention.

"But I shall have to tell her."

"Why?"

"Because—oh, because——" She fumbled for a reason. As always it was, in fact, the long habit of submission to a dominant nature.

"Don't do it," he said with quiet finality. "It's better not, all 'round. Once I thought I'd get in touch with her myself—a mere freakish impulse. I telephoned her office, but she was out, as good luck had it. I had caught a glimpse of her one day—hung around when she was coming out at noon. After that one look in her face, I might have known we'd better never meet. . . . She grows handsomer—she's the type to reach her height in maturity. Now you're different; youth is your long suit, you are the spirit of youth, spring, blossoms, all that sort of thing. . . . Well, I don't wish her anything but luck, God knows, and I wouldn't add one pain to all I've caused her, by letting her know of my existence. And there's nothing in it for either of us. So don't tell her, Bec."

Though troubled, she felt obliged to yield. Unknowingly he had added another burden to the load of secrecy that she, open as the day by nature, had by such complex devices of circumstance been trapped into carrying.

"And don't try to come again yourself. As I said, I'm ashamed that I asked it of you at all—I'd never have done it if I hadn't thought I was dying at the time I got the woman to write, and my good resolution gave way that once. But I shan't last much longer, any-

way; and you're to keep on thinking of me just as you
have been doing all along—as dead and gone."

"But I might do something for you!" She swept up,
in her glance, the poverty of background, and dwelt at
length upon the aspect of the man's own misery.

He smiled, as though pleased. "I neither deserve
nor need doing for. No; I insist; leave me alone, Bec, in
every sense of the word. Forget me. I prefer to drop
out again, and let the world wash over. It's going to
mean something to me that you offered, though. And
now you must be hurrying back."

He was dismissing her, exhausted by the long interview which had been little but a monologue; but she did
not go. Still she was all confusion, stunned by the whole
situation, unable to formulate her own emotions. Impulses pressed forward, then fell back, puzzled and afraid.
In the pause of her failing to go, his eyes and thoughts
strayed once more. Suddenly they turned to her, alert
with a question:

"I suppose you've been taught that there's nothing else
—nothing beyond, above, I mean?" His gesture indicated some vague space, such as the sky.

"You mean that there's no God?"

"Well, yes—God, by way of attaching some name
to it."

"Of course. I was taught that from the first."

He drummed on the arm of his chair, staring at the
floor.

"And you believe that?" he demanded at length.

Her lips began to form "Of course." Then they
halted.

"I've always *known* there was nothing but cold-blooded law of nature, that everything else was a delusion. But sometimes—oh, sometimes, it *feels* as if there were something else!" She pressed toward him eagerly, subjectively aware of response in his silence. "Do you (you do!) know what I mean?"

"Rather," he answered drily. Then, "Bec, if I didn't know, I'd have put a bullet here" (touching his temple) "fifteen years ago. You may say that I'd better have done it. But I kept from it because, in spite of everything, I always felt—well, what you feel. I don't bother about the churches. She always said that the church was like the spinning-wheel in having outlived its usefulness, but the difference was that the former hadn't the grace of the latter to stop whirring," he observed with a parenthetical smile. "No—it's something bigger than churches that I mean. And as for the name 'God,' that's just a handle to try and get hold of it by. It's something bigger than such a name implies."

"I know!" Bec breathed. "More like some wonderful kind of air, that flows all around us, all the time and everywhere."

"Yes. That's what I mean. The people that say 'God,' instinctively see a sort of super-person—and it isn't that. It's spirit, force; and the essential point I'm making is that it is not cold-blooded force; it is of the nature of love, and it recognises individual need."

The awed stillness of revelation seemed to fill the darkening room. "Oh, I'm so glad that you've told me; that you feel it, too!" she whispered through the hush.

"You'll remember it sometime. It's the word of a

derelict, a down-and-outer, and a rotter—and perhaps it carries all the more weight for that reason. That force, or spirit, or love, or what you will, is the only living thing that ever kept on believing in me in spite of what it saw of me."

He paused, and his eyes, grey now, rather than blue, as though shadowed by gravity, rested upon hers with profound significance.

"Bec, remember this, too: you've got to learn to go by what *It* tells you, not by anybody else's orders. You'll never know right from wrong so long as you let somebody else be your conscience. You need to remember that!" He smiled with curious emphasis.

The door opened to the landlady, bearing a smelly oil lamp.

"Saves gas," she remarked.

"Good-bye," Vernon said.

Bec turned to go. Their hands hesitated, then met in a mutually shy clasp.

It was over. The grey street received her. All the words said and unsaid, the spectral appearance, the strange mutualities, above all, the revelation of those long years of a secret, passionate, shyly pursuant love that had never quite failed to follow her, lay as yet like the dim forms upon a negative, unseen but present, in the future to be developed to clearness in the dark room of lonely wakings, by such chemicals as| love and pity and suffering and maturer vision.

But as yet it had all been too swift, too startling. Her thoughts remained a chaos. Mr. Popp was holding the umbrella with the clucking tenderness of a hen that extends its wing to a dazed chick.

Bec sank back, exhausted, in the cab's remotest corner. "Home, Miss?"

The faded voice of Bequita murmured, "Home."

VI

The long drive uptown was grey, like everything else. To Bec, the world seemed faded out to one bleak colour, the colour of the rain and the sky. All the vividness that had shone for her a short time before had been blotted out by this tragic experience. Like her first walk alone with her lover, like the first kiss, it was to become one of the few immortal experiences that go to make up a life; but as yet she found in it only confusion and numb misery. She had forgotten the gay party to which she was to have gone; the dazzling prospect of her début; even the moment she was to have had with Philip. She seemed to be sitting alone in the midst of infinite grey rain, eternal grey rain. . . .

She entered the apartment with her own key, wondering vaguely whether Helen would have returned, and whether it were time for dinner or long past, and how it would feel to go on knowing that she had a father, and in the same city, and whether she should ever know more——

The living-room was softly bright with candles—she recognised the candle-light even here, in the hall. Helen must have a guest, then: alone, she chose the stronger lamp-light for reading or sewing. But there was no sound of voices. And yet, by that sixth sense which occasionally imparts information to each of us, and which is particularly acute in such natures as Bec's, she felt that some visitor was there——

Puzzled, she paused. And now, after a charged silence, someone was speaking—a man, in a low, intense voice:

"Mrs. Kent, you can't mean what you say! Surely this bitterness of yours is a cloak to hide your deeper feelings. It is impossible—a woman like you can never hold that there is no such thing as love; that it is, as you say, 'the erotic moonshine of sickly youth,' and 'a perilous infection'—in short, only a vicious delusion. I won't believe that you believe it! Mrs. Kent——"

For these moments Bec had stood as if in shackles, powerless to move, to disclose her presence. But now her forces somehow rallied; all at once she was alive, burning with haste. This terrible thing—it must be stopped—Helen must be told! In the face of this situation, Vernon's request for silence was as nothing. It was impossible to heed it. To what length might Helen, ignorant, go? leaped Bec's imagination (which had construed the Doctor's words as "love-making")—even to marriage, perhaps——!

White and panting, she stood before the two. Her hand was out to them, as though to ward off some catastrophe.

"Don't!" she cried, breathless. "You mustn't go on! You don't know! Helen Kent, don't let that man say another word of love to you!"

Aghast, the two stared at her. They had fancied themselves to be engaged in abstract argument.

"You don't know!" gasped Bec. "Oh, you don't know!"

The two had risen, dumbfounded, and still they did not speak.

"He—he—oh, he *isn't dead*, Helen! And his hair—it's so beautiful, and snow-white! And he looks like *me!*"

CHAPTER XVI

THE STORM

I

IT was the end of July. New York's midsummer hung heavy in the storm-breeding air. Helen, having done with the last detail of tickets, baggage expressing, Pullman reservations and time-tables, sank into a chair beside the open window. And, as always nowadays—during day and night, whenever alone—she fell to reliving all of those crowded hours of one June night, weeks in the past though it now was, and all the subsequent days. . . .

Again, as though it were happening at this instant, she felt the numbing shock of that terrible news which Bec had brought. She felt the push of events that had followed, carrying her, dazed, upon the current of their haste. Again Bec stood before her, white, insistent; again she was crying out in fear:

"He isn't dead!"

There followed the silence that seemed never to be broken; then the rapid, chaotic questioning; then the whirl of happenings in which Helen appeared to herself merely a leaf picked up and borne along.

It was Dr. Aspden, quick, terse, masterfully helpful,

who was directing these happenings. He was putting his car at her service; she saw the three of them again as they entered it, caught the smell of leather within its closed depths, sealed against the rain. That smell was in her nostrils still—what was there that clung so about the memory of any odour, she wondered? And then the long, eternally long drive, although he drove as fast as permissible. Oppressive stillness held them, save when now and then some suddenly-thought-of question darted from her to Bec. . . . The bleak house at last; the unbuttoned landlady at the door, peering past her noisome oil lamp; pelting queries; the landlady's succinct reply: "He's took worse again. You kin go up."

They were in the hall. Helen turned to the others. "I wish to go alone."

Alone, then, guided by the landlady's lamp, she was finding her way once more to the "top-floor rear"—she was entering—he was turning feebly upon his pillow——

"Oh! So Bec told, after all," he murmured in a tone that bespoke disappointment in Bec.

"She did only what she was—or imagined she was—compelled to do, because of unexpected circumstances," Helen replied in prompt extenuation. "Naturally, when I learned this, I felt obliged to come and see for myself. She might have been duped."

Even then, upon that sick face, there was an amused curl of the beautifully cut lips, the curl that she remembered, as he asked:

"Well—are you satisfied that she was not 'duped'?"

She did not reply. She had seated herself near the bed, but in no contact with anything pertaining to the man before her. The two regarded one another. At last he smiled again, but this time one could not have said whether the smile was droll or sorry.

"Well, Helen," he observed, "ghosts rise, you see!"

The smile faded, the eyes wearily closed. She sat there still, noting every feature, above all the snowy crop of hair, thick and clustering in curls. It once had been the yellow mass in which her fingers had lain tangled. . . . A faintness came over her, and she closed her eyes for minutes. When she opened them, he was dead.

II

And now, whirling on, swift as the processes of a dream, followed all the events which together made up the fog of dreadfulness that had surrounded her, black, impenetrable. In it she could distinguish nothing clearly; it was hideous and enveloping. Although her freedom was now as complete as she had all along supposed it to be, somehow the revelation of that night seemed dragging her back, away from daylight, into its own sordid gloom, a gloom that she felt she could never escape. . . .

And then, breaking the fog ever so gradually, at first only faintly discernible, came light. And that light was shed by the most perfect friendship that she had ever known.

The perfectness lay in many things. For one, the unquestioning silence through which Cuyler Aspden had somehow conveyed a sympathy such as she had never felt before in either man or woman. It was the sympathy of complete understanding. As a physician and a friend, he had taken upon himself all the dreary duties —such matters as decent burial, supervision of bills, notices forwarded—all the bleak and usual formula. He had headed off a multitude of annoyances, had anticipated her wishes at every point. Yes, that unfailing service was another phase of the perfect friendship.

And then, too, the still, masterful gentleness of him —never intruding, but just quietly *there*—a thing stout as a wall for shelter, and yet as unobtrusive in its strength, a wall that smothers itself in the softness of ivy to conceal its own stoutness. Yes, these all went to make up the perfectness. . . .

And there alone in her living-room, gazing forth at the still river which for so long a time had received her daughter's confidence, Helen Kent made her confession: "I don't fool myself any longer."

She hardly knew whether this fact were chiefly terrifying, or amusing, or humiliating, or loathsome. She only knew it to be true; she "didn't fool herself any longer." And that, in summary, was the significance that the return of Vernon Kent had held for *her*.

Up to the moment of Bec's dreadful announcement, she had fooled herself completely, duped by her own cynical bravado. She had believed herself invulnerable. The idea that Cuyler Aspden, any more than any other man, could pierce her armour, would have been preposterous. And she had chosen to assume the invulnerability of his long-confirmed bachelorhood as equal to her own. It was only on that June evening, for the first time,

that he had shown otherwise; returning home with her
from their shopping excursion, he had, under the guise
of abstract argument, sounded the note which so alarmed
Bec; Helen had been making return, however, in her old
satirical vein.   And then the whirl of confounding
events. . . . It had been like his delicacy to leave the
subject dormant so far.   But he would return to it, she
knew; how could she again meet it?   For she "didn't
fool herself any longer."

It was not mere friendship.   It was the other thing.
It was the thing at which she had sneered and scoffed
for a score of years.   It was the delusion against which,
in her daughter, she had fought as against a devouring
enemy.   It was the prime peril of womanhood; it was
that which devastated happiness, wrought ruin for a
lifetime.   Yes, she recognised it; looking back to that
June night she knew now that, in her subconscious mind,
she had recognised it at the moment of learning that
she was still a married woman.   She had not had the
slightest desire to marry again; she would have railed
angrily at the suggestion; but the revelation that she was
not free to do so, briefly as it lasted, had opened her eyes.
She had felt herself turn ashy at the sudden sight of a
barrier between herself and Cuyler Aspden.   Vernon
Kent, rising from the dead, although so promptly returning, had shown her the truth.

Well—what of it?   Crush the thing, of course!   It
was astonishing and humiliating to find that the automatic reactions of even *her* nature could still be subject
to so human a weakness.   But in her clear knowledge
lay safety.   Will power was everything; will power could

be relied upon to stamp out this fancy as it had stamped out headaches or cured her of influenza. And a friendship so invaluable should not be sacrificed to any insane emotionalism. Reason should carry the day, and matters should stand exactly where they were——

"There! My trunk's done." Bec emerged from her room.

"Thank fortune, we're leaving for the mountains tomorrow. The weather is really intolerable. I hope Dr. Aspden and I shan't be caught in a thunderstorm today." Helen scanned the sky.

Bec's languid glance seemed to Helen to comment upon the frequency of these drives with Dr. Aspden, but at once she rebuked herself for self-consciousness.

"Are you driving far?"

"Several miles up into Westchester County. The Company is arranging for a hospital, and the Doctor wants me to look over the ground."

"Then you won't be home for dinner?"

"There he is now!" Helen observed, catching sight of the grey car below. "Yes, dear, I shall be home for dinner," she turned to reply. "Unless a storm should prevent."

Helen paused. Then, "Bec, won't you go along today? You know Dr. Aspden always wants you—as do I."

But as always, Bec shook her head. "No, thank you, Helen. I'm going to the roof to look for a breeze."

Before the Doctor was announced, Bec had slipped away.

III

Slipping away made it easier to dodge the Doctor's invitation, for one thing; Bec always dodged when possible. But, moreover, she had her own plans for this, the last afternoon before the month of absence. She hurried to Toby; there, beneath his blue coat, she found the brief message which told her that Philip would meet her in Riverside Park at two o'clock. It was to be the longest afternoon they had ever had together.

The mass of blue-black in the west claimed her notice.

"It looks dreadfully near!" Her hope fell, dismayed.

But the next instant the sun had broken through, and hope with it. After all, it didn't look so much like a storm; and it was a shame to change the plan for a mere fear. Philip would be frightfully disappointed; a man never thinks it is going to rain! In the end, the Doctor and Helen having departed, Bec hurried downstairs to dress for the expedition.

IV

They set sail *via* the Fort Lee ferry. An old brown boat like a beetle waddled with them over to the Jersey shore, and recalled for them the morning, now more than a half-year ago, when another brown ferryboat had served as their meeting-place.

"The horse—oh, do you remember the horse?" she cried. "Pickles!"

"And caramels!"

"And gulls——"

"And, all on a wintry morning, came 'spring-wind like a dancing psaltress.'" And he quoted the lines, telling her how she had "exercised such magic as to call Browning back to life, which is going some," in his irreverent modernity.

The air was breathlessly still, even on the river, but not a cloud was to be seen now. "To think that I was afraid of the weather!" Bec laughed at herself, and, exulting in the wonder of the sunny day, they landed and began their trolley ascent of the Palisades.

"Let's get away from the beaten path and the madding crowd," Philip proposed at the top, and with that they broke into the woods, and the world was lost.

The green was deep, and through it they could now and then catch far-below glimpses of the light-speckled water. At moments they would see the whole breadth of the river spreading to the New York shore, littered with craft—tugs, barges, a long excursion boat, small pleasure boats, a destroyer. Again the trees would be drawn like a curtain, and they would know the river's presence only by the distant dg-dg-dg-dg of a motor boat's throb. Gradually, as they zigzagged northward, the river grew farther below; when they approached the Palisades' edge, it was to look off from the pinnacle of some sheer cliff abutting at what seemed mountain height. These cliffs became more barren, more formidable; the trees that clung to them were like terrified living creatures dizzily awaiting their fall.

"Ugh! Let's get away from the edge!" shivered Bec. "This is as scary as our western mountains." Again she shivered. "Philip, it's getting dark, too! There's

something queer about this still air. I believe, after all,
a storm is brewing."

"Then we'll find shelter. We're really not far from
habitation at any point, although the woods seem so
isolated. You're nervous, Bec."

"Thunderstorms always frighten me. It's not so much
the storm itself that I mind, as it is that sense of fore-
boding it brings—I feel that some dreadful thing is
going to happen. I never saw a thunderstorm in California."

"Little pagan! What a beauty-drenched life you led,
in that world of summer and flowers! But there's nothing to fear, my child; it's all a case of nerves. What
you have been through would account for anything."

For there was no detail of her experience in discovering her father which Philip had not heard; that it had
been intolerable until she could tell him was perhaps the
supreme proof of what she thought of as "his being *he*."
She would always suffer torments until she could tell
him everything, happy or terrible; and the knowledge that
he would always exactly understand was a thought that
opened like a harbour to her stormy tossing.

"You haven't told me all about the perfected arrangements for the wonderful début," he reminded her now,
and the cloud passed.

There was much to tell, for this was their first long
talk for a fortnight. Actually, the plan was working
out to perfection, incredible as it seemed. Helen did
not show a sign of suspicion.

"The rehearsals were what stumped me. If all those
people who play the Indian rôles should see me once,

the cat would be out of the bag. But an understudy takes my part at rehearsals, and meanwhile, the director is to train me privately. A few lessons will do it— I can slip away to him and Mrs. Van Nuys, at her cottage in Eagle's Eyrie Park. She is getting up the whole affair, and only one or two others are in the secret. I'd never have managed, if I hadn't impressed Cousin Ress and Mr. McNab into service. They've been darlings."

The masculine expression, to a more practiced feminine eye, might have indicated dissatisfaction in hearing Mr. McNab called by this endearing epithet; however: "Just how are they working it?" Philip inquired with interest.

"Well, as you know, I asked each one privately to conspire with me, and they more than promised. I think, to tell the truth," reflected Bec aloud, "they rather enjoy the joke on Helen."

"Doubtless."

"Cousin Ress is a friend of Mrs. Van Nuys, you see, so she could explain my whole situation, my reason for acting secretly, and enlist her sympathy. And of course we all realise how proud and glad Helen will be," she insisted, "when she sees my triumph. Think of it—never a suspicion—and suddenly she will realise that it is her own daughter who is the star of the occasion!"

Bec was silent after this. Whether, in her deepest thoughts, there were misgivings; whether she failed to find joy in the prospect of Helen's delight, she perhaps did not know herself.

"As for Mr. McNab," she went on, at length, "he made

the whole plan possible by getting Helen to change her vacation from July to August. The pageant was set for the last week of summer, and that was an obstacle that I couldn't surmount. But he invented business reasons for the change, and—there we were. I'm afraid it upset some of his arrangements a great deal more than he would admit, but he insisted—'Nothing too much trouble if it boosts the show, not on your life!' " Bec flawlessly imitated Mr. McNab's rotund and genial manner. "He was a perfect dear about it all," she continued, naïvely unconscious of the very wry face that her companion was struggling to conceal.

v

The faraway shriek of an interurban trolley car roused Bec to the thought of getting home.

"Surely we had better be starting soon, Phil, if we're to walk back the way we came."

But they lingered wistfully, loath to see the afternoon slipping through their fingers. Procrastinating, they watched a great brown hawk circling above the water; they listened to a shrill tune piped up to them from an excursion boat.

"Si-ilver threads among the go-old."

"Not yet awhile, my friend," Philip debonairly addressed the distant musician. "Silver threads don't frighten us." His eyes rested upon the gold escaping under Bec's hat-brim.

"But some day we shall both be snowy and doddering!" she laughed, as though, for all her jesting words, that were a quite impossible future.

And so they made talk, and lingered, clinging with an undermining dread to these last minutes of this last walk. But: "We *must* start!" sighed Bequita, and faced determinedly homeward at last.

At that instant the bushes parted with a crashing sound, and forth upon them rushed a tall, powerfully built man, villainous of aspect, and strangely garbed in a costume of some century and a half ago.

Bec's voice started to scream, then turned into a pealing laugh, as a red-coated British officer and a Continental in cocked hat sprang forth to meet the villain, followed by a puffing, portly gentleman in modern garb and a temper.

"What the h— are we going to do?" demanded the portly gentleman. "Miss Mannerly's sprained her ankle and she can't take a step, and here we are with the sun nearly gone and that picture due!" He gave vent to his disappointment in terms not intended for a lady's ear. Catching sight of Bec, he closed his mouth like a trap, then apologised.

"I beg your pardon—but we're up against it, and I guess my language was getting pretty hot. You see," he explained to the highly interested observers, "this picture has to be rushed through to-day. (*Janice's Revenge*, a story of Revolutionary days, and it's a winner, believe *me*.) And now the star's had an accident." With that he caught his breath; he fell to staring at Bec.

"Say—do you know—look here, boys! Ain't this lady the dead ringer for Marian Mannerly? Look here!

Oh, say, what do you know about *that*——" He stammered.

He vanished, and reappeared with a rush, carrying a woman's scarlet cape. Puffing, purple with haste and excitement, he flung it around Bec's shoulders.

"Janice to the life! Now, let your hair down—it's got to hang loose and blow when you run—here are her slippers—all you have to do, Miss, is to run lickety-split while this chap here runs after you—he's one o' the Pine Robbers, Tory agents they were—he's going to stab you because you're onto his secret. Then you fall on your knees—up rushes Captain Perkins, here, also Captain Montague——" Puffing furiously, the apoplectic director of the moving-picture had already wrapped Bec in the enveloping scarlet cloak——

"Oh, but the young lady can't think of it! Sorry, but it's quite impossible!" Philip was interrupting authoritatively, but Bec, radiant, thrust his protests aside.

"Of course I can! Why, it will be one of the most thrilling adventures of my life!" She was jumping into the quaint slippers, tearing out hairpins, letting down the long light hair, "exactly like Miss Mannerly's!" the actors all cried, adding the assurance that "the face wouldn't show much." Philip's protests were carried completely off their feet.

Hurried by the photographer, who was hastily summoned, and the panting director who kept shouting to everybody, even the escaping sun, the play began. After one swift rehearsal, Bec was pronounced ready to make her run for life.

It was as thrilling, she told Philip later, as though she

had really felt the Pine Robber's knife descending. How she ran! Her long hair blew out behind, the cloak flew with her like her own terrified wings, the villain pursued, knife flashing. She dropped to her knees—up rushed both British and American heroes, as they had nobly pledged themselves to do——

A flash and a crash broke terribly through the woods. The deluge came.

"Get it?" gasped the agonised director.

"Yep," replied the photographer, and a long-pent breath of relief heaved through the company.

They all fled to shelter now, and huddled under trees. "Nothing to do but strike out for the trolley," the director said. "I sent the motor-car on ahead with Miss Mannerly. Sorry I can't offer you a ride home, after the way you've saved us," he regretted to Bec. "Best I can do is to offer you our camp. Wife and I have a little place over here—gives us an outing now and then while I'm on the job. Make yourselves at home, and use whatever you can find."

The two welcomed his offer, there being no sign of a lull in the storm, and, as it was time for the trolley-car, and the moving-picture people were obliged to take it, Philip and Bec refused to permit him to escort them to the cabin. They would find it easily—no, indeed, Bec would not think of letting the director mail her a check —it had all been great sport to her—yes, Philip would return the cabin's key next day—another terrific thunderclap, and the parties separated without further talk. Phil seized Bec's arm, hurrying her through the woods and into the cosy cabin, while the others set out for their long, drenching walk over to the trolley track.

Safely housed at last, the two stood and peered about through the dusk. The cabin consisted of one large room with a wide fireplace built of stone. Dim objects loomed: Philip's matches, and the candle which he eventually found, revealed these as comfortable chairs, a broad couch before the fireplace, a table, and an oil cook-stove. Gaudy cushions littered the couch, a multitude of moving-picture performers smiled and strutted and struck poses upon the walls. Altogether, despite the lack of taste in furnishing, a warmth of hospitality glowed toward them.

"Can't you see his wife in that row of saucepans?" cried Bec. "Fat, and motherly, and petting all the young actors and actresses."

"They probably live in a duplex apartment on Riverside Drive, and never know true bliss until they cuddle down here for a week, and recall with happiness the days when they didn't have a fat salary to spend, while he gets off his coat and lights his pipe," Philip went on with her sketch.

"And she bakes a pie in that oven—such a pie!" Thus they were conjuring up the picture of their host and hostess, when, "Oh, look!" she exclaimed, for the first time realising her costume. "I'm wearing the cloak still! We all forgot it in the hubbub."

"We can dry it by the fire." Philip was kneeling, coaxing the logs to flame. "And leave it here, along with the slippers, which, fortunately, you are carrying."

Bec had changed them for her own shoes. "I'll leave word where they are when I return the key."

But Bec stood for moments without removing the wet cloak. It clung to her with a chilly hold; not sufficiently wet to have darkened, it glowed vividly scarlet as she stood beside the now-leaping fire. The room behind gloomed dusky; shadows skulked, lean and creeping, in far corners. But Bequita stood staring at the scarlet cloak. It seemed possessed of some sinister charm, a spell to bind her senses. . . .

The scarlet cloak held terror and fascination at the same time. It suggested dreadful things that she had read and heard; things unspeakable, things unthinkable. They were like ghostly presences; like the disembodied forms of sins long dead, sins strange to her, sins of women unknown and for ages forgotten. With a shudder she turned her eyes from it. . . .

VI

They had dined frugally but with enthusiasm upon the canned Italian spaghetti found in the larder and the cake of chocolate found in Philip's pocket. So far, excitement had carried Bec. But now that they settled down before the fire, listening to the ever-renewed crashings and lashings of the storm, silence fell; and, with it, dusky fears, like a night gathering about her spirit.

Watching the flames, these fears gathered more and more thickly with the passing minutes. What if the storm failed to detain Helen? they nagged. Very likely she had returned to the apartment in time for dinner.

Bec saw her growing alarm as she waited, pictured her going to the telephone, calling Cousin Ress, Adelaide Matcham, other friends. What would Helen do then? What would she say? Most dreadful of all, what would she think?

A panic seized Bec, and she rose abruptly. "Philip, Philip, you *must* take me to the car! Helen is almost sure to be at home. You must, you must—if you won't, I'll have to go alone. Philip, please—right away——"

Her pantings were half sobs. Astonished, he laid a quieting hand upon hers.

"Bec, you can't go now, child! It would be the dickens of a risk. You'd almost certainly be ill after a long trip home in clothing drenched through. I can't let you——"

In fresh panic she tried to snatch away her hand. "Let me go, you've no right to keep me, let me go, Philip Oliver, let me go!" she was crying hysterically.

He drew her into the shelter of his arm. Here was refuge. He piled up cushions behind her shoulders. His brown cheek brushed her pale one as, side by side, they stared on at the fire. For the time she gave way to the lull of it all: the stillness of perfect companionship, a stillness enhanced by the drive of the storm without and the tiny crashings of the fire within. The candle had burned out, there was no oil to fill the lamp. Only the fire pierced the darkness. Behind, the skulking shadows, creeping silently in their far corners; but here, vivid in the firelight——

It had caught her eyes again, had seized upon them in their flight, dragged them back. The scarlet cloak

would not be eluded. Its flaming colour held her with
sinister fascination; it terrified her with its innuendo of
things unthinkable. It raised ghosts. Ghosts of sins
long dead, of unknown women's sins——

"Philip, Philip, take me away! I'm afraid!"

He turned to her. He dropped his arm from her, and
drew away. He was almost harsh.

"Bec, you look as if you were afraid of *me!*"

She fought back tears. "No, Philip, no! But I'm
frightened, like listening to a ghost story even though
you know it's only a story—don't you see? The night,
and our being off here alone—the things it seems *like*—
the dreadful stories it suggests. How can I make you
understand? It's the *seeming* that frightens me, that
I loathe—the secrecy, the darkness of it all—it's like
going through a black alley with wicked faces leering at
you——"

He had risen, and he stood before her with his hands
defiantly thrust into his pockets; defiant, Bec felt toward
all the opposing forces of the universe.

"Then why don't we come out into the open?" he
demanded.

He had asked it many times before; he had urged,
and she had fairly fled from the urging; but something
newly roused within her listened now.

"If you, the real *you*, ever turn me down, I'll quit. But
it isn't you. It's what somebody else thinks that an-
swers me through you. You don't honestly think it would
be wrong to take matters into your own hands and marry
me. You're letting somebody else be your conscience."

She was listening. Strangely his words seemed to

echo that warning which Vernon had uttered so significantly weeks ago:

"You've got to learn to go by what *It* tells you. . . .
You'll never know right from wrong so long as you let
somebody else be your conscience."

They had sunk back into their seats before the fire,
and, side by side, they were watching the flames again.

"I think I'm all mixed up about right and wrong," she
said, and the words gave vent to all the sorry grop-
ings of her bewildered spirit. "Our secret meetings have
tortured me—while I'm with you I'm mostly happy, but
when I'm alone and think it over, it seems wicked. When
I stop thinking, and simply feel, it all seems to come
right—as if a nice, elderly, purry voice were telling
me that there can't be any wrong in such a great true
love as ours."

The rain still fell, but the storm's anger had died. . . .

"You've got to learn to go by what *It* tells you. . . ."

Again she recalled the landlady's dismal room, the
dying day, the white-haired wreck of a man from whose
eyes the boy looked forth—again she heard the voice,
broken but full of charm:

"By what *It* tells you. . . ."

Suddenly a strange, unforgettable thing occurred. It
filled only a few swift instants; no one but Bec knew
of it; Philip remained gazing into the fire. And yet it
was always to remain for her one of the supreme occurrences of a lifetime.

Afterwards she was to wonder if it hadn't all been
fancy. But at that moment it semed as though the broken
figure actually stood before her; that the boyish blue eyes

once more met hers; that he spoke, repeated the warning, smiled, understanding and wanting to help. . . .

The moment had passed. Ages of stillness. Only stillness, and dying rain, and dusk interwoven with threads of firelight. And to Bequita, the crucial hour; as though being led to the forking of two roads she had seen where each led: the one to blind, perilously easy slavery of the spirit, the other to hard-won liberty. And she chose.

The rain had died. "I think we can go now," Philip said, rising.

She made ready and they set out, over the soaked ground, between trees that scattered cold, fragrant drops upon them. Neither spoke until just before the car came. Then Bec, self-contained and low-voiced, said:

"I'm not afraid now. Because there never was anything real to be afraid of, only ghosts, and if you don't go into dark places you won't see ghosts. And I'm going to come out into the open. If I go by what the thing inside tells me, I'll know that I haven't done wrong, and I'm ready to face whatever comes. I wonder," she added paradoxically, "if the wrong isn't in not believing what you really do believe?"

She had passed through her spiritual conflict and had conquered fear. She was ready to battle at last for her own conscience, for her right to assert the truth for herself. But, although Bec was girded for the issue, the hour for that issue had not yet arrived.

Helen had been detained by the storm and was still absent when her daughter reached home.

CHAPTER XVII

THE SPIRIT OF THE WATERFALL

I

MANITO SUMMIT and Eagle's Eyrie Parks were a-hum with the great event. It was the end of August, and the famous pageant, to which all the season had been breathlessly leading up, was ready. From cottages and hotels people thronged—people who wore delightful clothes, and talked in stylish voices, and hub-bubbed agreeably in the pitch of well-bred society.

Helen came downstairs. Below, in the hotel lounge, Cousin Ress, Mr. McNab and Dr. Aspden awaited her. They had all "run up" for the week-end to witness the far-heralded performance; the day had turned out perfect, and now they were all congratulating themselves smugly on their luck, and giving way to the fiesta spirit all around.

Miss Clifton led off with Mr. McNab. Dr. Aspden joined Helen. "And the daughter?" he politely inquired.

"Can't we start without our young chaperon?" The imp flashed at that instant.

The imp, in fact, showed symptoms of especial unruliness to-day. A month of rest had made Helen fit to a degree; the fiesta spirit had taken hold of her; and now, after a month's separation, she was once more enjoying the companionship of this handsome, distinguished, devoted friend, who had never possessed, in her eyes, a serious fault except his fondness for frayed scarfs in a life of busy preoccupation—and of late weeks, for some reason, he had abandoned these for the most perfect made-to-order scarfs, as her fastidious shrewdness detected. Yes, to-day, she felt, she could hardly be responsible for what the imp *might* do.

"Surely Miss Bec has not condemned us as too elderly for playmates?"

The Doctor uttered it solicitously; but behind the tone, Helen detected a boyish, sneaking hope—almost a sigh of relief, in fact, smothered but distinguishable. He had never won Bec's friendship, despite persistent efforts, and her attitude toward him was that of a disapproving chaperon.

He continued, "We can't be any older than we feel!"

"That's accepted as true for your sex, but, by the same proverb, a woman may be only as young as she looks!" On the instant she wanted to recall it, as shamelessly bald; but he merely looked the flattering rejoinder without uttering a word, thus absolving her in her own eyes. Mirrors, indeed, had showed her that day all that his most ardent flatteries could have declaimed—lines as long and slender as on the day when her two-stepping had snapped a provocative whip to younger passions; eyes brilliant, though with a keener, harder brilliancy; costuming far more seductive in its mature daring and authority. "I am power, I capture, I subdue!" the mirror had proclaimed.

"Bec has joined some still younger friends, and is going to the pageant with them," she explained. She, too, was conscious of a certain relief in this fact. It was always uncomfortable to stand between her friend and her silently disapprobative daughter, no matter how keenly she appreciated the humour of the situation; she had accepted Bec's apologies for absence so readily that she had barely waited to hear them. This arrangement made for comfort and pleasure all around; she had congratulated herself. And now, having set off with her tall escort in gala mood, she gave way to it completely. Her daughter's existence was almost forgotten for the once. Bec had gone to join friends in Eagle's Eyrie Park where, near the ravine, the performance was to take place. No doubt she was prowling among the actors at this moment, as children always do, occurred to Helen once on the drive over, and then she thought of Bec no more.

The stage was a bit of clearing close beside a ravine, the woods serving as stage-setting. As Dr. Aspden guided her to a seat in the foremost row of spectators, perfectly placed for seeing the performance at its best, Helen felt the admiration that followed her, as though it had been an utterance. "This thing of renewing one's youth shall not be cornered by the eagle alone," observed Helen Kent, in inner colloquy with her imp; and the imp echoed, "Not by the eagle alone!"

And now the drama was beginning. Weird Indian music struck up, a long file of braves advanced slowly through the woods.

"Clever work!" Dr. Aspden whispered, as the opening scene disclosed itself.

"This is perfect!" Helen's reply murmured—a reply that vaguely embraced weather, front seat, companion, music, stage-setting, actors, and her own gown. Helen's earth was whirling to a completely harmonious rhythm at that hour; a rhythm which moved on as smoothly as though it were never to be broken.

Casually, as the play proceeded, she observed several small matters which at the time bore for her no significance whatever. Once Miss Clifton left the group and slipped away—Helen wondered if she had a telegram —felt reassured, upon that lady's return, by the satisfaction which sat upon the plump countenance. Again, Helen's eyes roamed in desultory fashion toward a slender white figure apearing for a moment in the woods—as she looked, the figure disappeared. . . .

They were but some of the flotsam and jetsam thoughts that the mind's tide flings up on the shore and forsakes. The tide of Helen's mind was really concerned with only one great fused delight: the delight of a remarkably beautiful spectacle enjoyed in company with the one person who could completely round out her pleasure. The splendour of colour displayed against the sombre forest background—a carnival of red, purple, green, blue, yellow; the cadence of Indian music droning on, rising, dying, blaring, softening, wailing; the presence beside her—all wrought upon the senses to intoxicate, to conquer.

And so Helen's afternoon glowed on. The play was

drawing toward its great scene, where thirst, like a pestilence, descends upon the tribe. The song of sorrow began:

> "Ha go wa nah u na
> Ha go way nah u na ha ha ha go way"

With the rest of the audience, Helen sat transfixed. There was a hypnotic spell in the scene, in the cadences rising, mourning away down the aisles of that primeval forest.

"This is ripping!" she heard Dr. Aspden's murmured enthusiasm beside her. And,

"Ripping!" echoed Helen.

II

Bec, meanwhile, waited in a cottage near by.

Her hour was almost here. It was to be the hour for which all the artist soul of her had bided; the hour for which body and brain and will had toiled; the hour which was to open to her the gate into that great world of consecrated work and fame, the world of her long dreams.

The shadows of afternoon deepened among the pines, charging them with mystery. As the day waned, a hint of autumn crept in, adding to the sombre spell of the haunted woods. Here and there a flaming sword was brandished by some maple or oak; already the raucous chirp of crickets, the rude controversy of katydids gave warning. The sulky blaze of fire-weed, the still sulkier of Joe-Pye, mingled with goldenrod along the path. The

year hung in that glowing, breathless suspense which
is as exquisite a beauty and as exquisite a pain as the
last days on earth of a beloved.

Bequita, at the window, gazed forth upon it all in the
awe and exaltation of one who witnesses a noble death.
It was her first death-bed watch; the seasons of her
California had wrought no tragedies. But this dying
summer—she felt a new, a poignant agony as it slipped
from her grasp, and a more acute sense of beauty than
she had ever felt in beauty's security. The day and her
mood flowed back and forth into one another, merging
like waters. There was the stillness of exaltation in both;
and the breathlessness of suspense.

The door was stealthily opened. "All right, child?"
whispered Cousin Ress.

Bec nodded.

"Not scared, are you?"

Bec did not reply in words; but her eyes must have
answered as they met the other's with a long, full gaze
that was like still water. At that hour she was above
fear; she stood on a plane where the excitement of elation was so intense that it stilled itself, like the heart
of the whirlpool.

Miss Clifton took a rapid survey with her shrewd little
eyes—a survey that included every detail of the White
Maiden's marvellously wrought costume of floating
gauze which parted upon faintly discerned rainbow
gleams, the willow wand, and the Maiden's eyes "large
and glowing like those of a fawn at night," as the legend
ran, her skin "no less white than the snow in winter,"

and cheeks "like the first coming of the sun on mornings when the corn is ripe."

"Quite so," Miss Clifton snapped out her brisk conclusion. "You're altogether as you should be. In fact, my child, you are doomed to success—and may the Lord pity you in the tribulations which *that* brings! Now—it's time for you to slip out to your place in the woods, ready for your entrance. Good-bye—and keep your nerve!"

But, as she turned to go:

"Cousin Ress!"

"Well?"

"Where is Helen?"

"In a front seat, looking perfectly stunning and in a mood to be delighted with anything, for she's got that Doctor dangling. He's a fine man, and I wish to goodness she'd drop her tommyrot about 'romantic delusions' and marry him, like a sensible woman, and not set herself up as knowing such a darned sight more than her great-grandmother Eve."

Bec was grave. "I hope she will be happy when she sees my success. I wish that Helen and I might—" a wistful shadow crossed her face—"might understand each other better again. If only the old days could come back!"

Miss Clifton again eyed her sharply. "You're not going to be afraid of what she thinks, are you?"

"I'm not afraid of anything any longer, except of being untrue to the truth." Bec left the cryptic little phrase unexplained; but Miss Clifton read finality and self-sureness in her quiet tone. "I'm ready for—whatever comes."

III

Bec waited in her hiding-place in the woods behind the stage. Unseen herself, she could watch actors and audience. Here, almost beside her, on the cleared stretch of ground which served as stage, the Indian figures moved back and forth in the sombre fire of the setting sun.

Artist brains had conceived a spectacle of rarest beauty, and lavish purses had spared nothing to carry it out. The spirit of the mountain legend had been captured. At that point of the story, where the tribe, stricken by thirst, made a plea to its deity, one felt the wild appeal of such worship as belongs to the childhood of a race.

The chant of suffering and prayer mourned in strange cadence. The woods took up the moaning and echoed it. The Indian women and children lay upon the ground, exhausted by thirst; now and then a woman would raise her head and feebly join in the chanted prayer which the men were still able to utter, as they stood with arms raised to the heavens, their figures outlined in a melancholy picture, like drought-smitten pines against the darkly burning sky. The acting was superb; actors themselves were under the spell of the scene's illusion, and one watched in a trance, doubting his own calendar, here in the surroundings where just such a scene might verily have taken place in the forgotten centuries.

The stage was met at the rear and on one side by woods; on the other side it came to an abrupt end at the edge of the ravine. This was the precipice, a sheer drop of rock wall, greenish with slimy growth, where the little waterfall was wont to cascade in lithe leaps to the boulders at the foot.

But now no cascade was to be seen. By a clever bit of trickery, abetted by a genuine drought which had greatly reduced the water's volume, the small stream had been dammed back and temporarily deflected at some distance to the rear, so that it seemed verily to have vanished off the face of the dry earth. Its release was to be so timed that at a smiting of the White Maiden's wand it would gush forth to its fall over the rocks. To the minutest detail this pretty deception had been worked out so that not a slip could occur.

Bec's alert eyes noted the spot where her wand was to strike as a signal, and the curtain of branches behind which she was to vanish at the water's release. Her eyes travelled on to the audience. No figure in it was discernible from where she stood; it appeared but as a mass of mingled colours, broken by the dark lines of men's garb.

"Ha una ha na ha ah,"

droned the chant. One of the braves collapsed, fell—another. Their dying groans rose, desolate echoes of the prayer that the survivors still raised to a merciless deity.

"Na sa ha nee ga ha do wayhe ah——"

Bec was lost now to every thought save the reality of the entrancing scene. She strained forward, listening for a moan of wind in the forest, which was to be her cue.

"Ha u na ha ah ha——"

A weird sound rose. It was the cue. The moan of
wind was caught up by the actors, and it pierced the
woods like a chorus of lost souls. They roused to join
in it, where they lay exhausted and dying, as if it were
their last utterance on earth. The three who remained
standing raised the cry to a shriek, hands uplifted, and
fell. The cry died, whining slowly to silence. It seemed
a world of the dead. . . .

Bequita raised hands that were thrilled beyond the
weakness of trembling, and parted the leaves. She was
conscious that a shaft of light sought her between the
pines; that, as she moved slowly forward, the light seized
and swept her all at once into full view. For a long
pause she stood motionless; the blackening woods, the
deathlike forms, were background for the vision of un-
earthly light that she presented. She saw herself, as
though she stood outside and looked on: she knew that
her supple whiteness of limb, her gleam of draperies, her
floating glory of hair were the cause of that sudden
stop. It was a stop that she felt as though the audience
were one human pulse and her finger were upon it. It
seemed as though their common heart ceased to beat, their
breath to come and go. It felt, thought Bec, as if the
last trump had sounded, and people were waiting to see
what would happen. . . .

She began, now, to move forward. She seemed to herself to be gliding, as if she made no motion to propel
herself but were carried by a greater force, as wind or
water are carried. She approached the unconscious

Indians; she gazed down upon them benignly. At that moment the rendering of this myth was as real to Bequita as though these men, women and children were in fact Indians, actually perishing of thirst, and she were their sole deliverer.

Raising her wand, the White Maiden gently waved it. The Indians' eyes opened, a vague wonder stole into their faces. She flung her arms to the sky, invoking strength from some source of strength. Then her arms reached out over the dying, with a movement that suggested cherishing wings; eyes were fixed upon her, the Indians slowly, feebly rose. Still her succouring arms reached forth to them. Bequita herself was so charged with the sense of saving these people in their extremity, that she conveyed her meaning to her spectators as if it travelled directly from mind to mind. Only art that is great enough to be artless can rise to this height; only when the artist is so transported by his meaning that self becomes non-existent, does he reach the plane where the medium of expression becomes negligible, the direct trans-mission of thought seems to transcend expression.

One by one, at her gesture, the stricken Indians rose to their feet; first a child, staring at the vision, then another; men and women followed. The group stood gazing at the White Maiden as though heaven had de-scended to earth.

And now she flung off the spell of awe. With a swing of filmy draperies she sprang to the edge of the precipice. A moment she paused there, her eyes sweeping the audi-ence; still no individuals detached themselves from the mass. The assembly was one to her—one straining expectancy.

Instinct taught her, artist that she was, precisely how long to hold that tension. Her arms were extended motionless, the cloudy white floated out from them. Then, with a leap as light as the tossing of water, she broke into her dance—the dance of the waterfall, the dance that sparkled and frothed and tossed and tumbled and foamed and twinkled and cascaded and splintered into rainbows.

To Bequita it was as though *she* were not dancing at all—something within her was what danced, the soul of the waterfall which had entered her soul. She felt herself the water; she seemed to be frothing over rocks into green, deep places; to be laughing in tinkles; to be breaking on the rocks into a thousand glintings; to be tossing upward in foam. And in the midst of the sheer joy of water at play, she was conscious still of that deeper, more solemn joy: of delivering a stricken people at the brink of death.

On foamed the dance. The dancer hovered on the dizzy brink of the precipice; she retreated only to spring forward again, poising on the rock that jutted over the gorge, leaping free in the air and alighting on the brink once more. She seemed as unconscious of peril as the darning-needle that alighted beside her; as sure that the air would support her. Now she bent forward, covering her head with her white draperies, imitating the foaming fall; she drooped far over the steepest rocks, hung there in limp grace. Now she tossed herself erect again, and pirouetted on the ledge. She was no more conscious of

technique than a waterfall itself. She was like one of the
elements, swayed only by a vast Thought. Dimly she
knew this; not explicitly, but in some cellar of her consciousness. She knew, too, that this dance was supreme,
that she had never before reached such height of beauty
in her art's expression, perhaps never again would reach
it.

The taut silence intensified with the minutes. In it,
Bequita could feel her conquest. She knew that she was
dancing as these people had never seen anyone dance
before; that they were strung to a pitch of dumb wonder
which spelled her complete triumph. Behind her, the
Indians were pressing closer; even they, her fellow-mum-
mers, shared the astonishment and forgot feigned wonder
in genuine.

With a final spring and a movement of tossing foam
which released rainbow flashes, the dance reached its
height and stopped abruptly. In the absolute stillness
the White Maiden paused on the ledge. There was to
be a long-drawn moment of suspense, then the smiting
of the rock, the gushing forth of the stream, the grand
finale of praises from a delivered people, the Maiden's
vanishing in the forest.

She paused. Every nerve of her body was tuned to
perfect pitch; she could feel to a nicety the hold she had
upon that audience's tension, the instant at which she
must break it with the great climax. She stood poised
on the lightest tiptoe, her hand holding forth the willow
wand——

She faced her spectators. The mass of blended
colours met her eye—but now, for the first time, an in-

dividual figure stood out as a strong bar of light struck
it.   The figure seemed to Bec's eyes to detach itself from
the mass until it was the only thing seen.   It was standing; it was in the front row, and had stepped a trifle in
advance of the others; it leaned forward intently, eyes
riveted upon the dancer. . . .

And now Bec met those eyes.   Even at that distance,
not a shading of their jetty glance failed to reach her.
Narrowed to mere flashing lines, they seemed to Bec at
that instant more terrible than she had ever dreamed
they could be.   At the instant when, poising on the edge
of the precipice, she met them, she felt her beating heart
turn to ice and go thumping down within her. . . .

For a sick moment she struggled to recover.   Her
whole body was numb; her will was like her heart, merely
a lump of ice, with no power left to direct her actions.
She tried to drag her eyes away from those dreadful ones,
and was unable to release them.   She thought, flittingly,
of tales of evil spells. . . . Her arm made a dull reach
forward, automatically obeying its training, and with a
lifeless stroke she smote the rock, and was aware of the
sudden gush of the fettered water.   With a surge it
leaped forward, cries of joy broke from the Indians; but
still her eyes were held prisoner by those other eyes. . . .
She made a clumsy step backward as the water burst
forth; she was losing her power of balance, overwhelmed
as she was.   She knew only that her step backward
seemed at a loss for foothold, that it groped behind her,
stumbled.   In the instant when her balance wavered
on the edge of the precipice—when she saw, yawning like
measureless space, that sheer pitch of slimy-green rock

below; in that instant life and death hung in the scales, and a life and death no more of the body than the spirit.

IV

Except to rise to a standing posture, Helen had been rigid since Bec's entrance. She had not felt the questioning glances that Dr. Aspden had cast toward her at this unexpected dancer's appearance; she had known nothing but the fact of that appearance. At first, as the plot had broken upon her, she had passed into rage like a trance. She had been bound by the terrible spell. Years passed before her in the minutes of Bec's performance; she saw the dancing baby in a California garden; the yellow-haired child pleading for lessons; the girl tingling with art's urge; later, the woman of defiant silence, which she had so blindly failed to interpret! And at last before her eyes, her daughter, her flesh, who had secretly defied and outwitted her, and now triumphed in her very face. . . .

During these moments her impulse of anger was so strong that she forgot the selflessness of her motive in denying Bec a career of art. She was conscious of no definite purpose to defeat the girl; her wrath (which, in truth, was more at her own blindness than at Bec) simply burned through her eyes like a conflagration through windows; and she was aware of its blazing its way to Bec, as though she stood watching an unchecked fire speed toward its victim. She exerted no volition to drive the fire; it followed its own course. And she knew when

it reached the victim.   She saw the fright leap into
Bequita's eyes, saw her swerve, weaken. . . .

And at that moment Helen passed from one trance
into another; from that of blind rage into that of blind
terror.

The girl was stumbling—she was losing her balance!
And there, on the very edge of the gorge!   It had taken
the nicest equilibrium to dance in that perilous position,
and now that she was plainly bewildered . . .

Dumb with fright, Helen could not look at the swaying
figure.   Her eyes riveted themselves upon a white birch,
upon the initials "A. C." and "J. S. M." carved within
a heart upon its maiden flesh.   The letters were mean-
ingless—only the knife-scribblings of some vanished young
vandals—but in her hypnosis they impressed themselves
upon her brain as though they had been carved there,
instead of upon the tree.   Helen was never while she
lived to forget those letters—"A. C." and "J. S. M."—
carved black, and girdled by a blacker heart upon the
ravished white birch.   They gave back stare for stare
while she waited; it seemed to her that her breath, her
pulse, had stopped completely; that heaven and earth,
too, were stunned to silence, and held their breath.   She
knew only one thing: that, impotent, she waited.

V

With   the   uncanny   swiftness,   the   instantaneous
thought-flashing of such moments, Bequita's mind took
in all that the situation meant.   It was the crucial moment of Helen's dominion over her.   Give way utterly

to those terrifying eyes, and catastrophe awaited—at least the collapse and fiasco of what might have been her artistic triumph; perhaps a fall to death, overwhelmed as she was by fright. Or—throw off the eyes' power to terrify—defy them—rally her forces, her poise —and something told Bec that their power would be vanquished for all time.

Still that hideous bewilderment, that sense of physical collapse—a complete giving-way. And the slimy cliff— infinite, yawning space. . . .

"You've got to learn to go by what *It* tells you. . . ."

How strangely actual the remembered voice seemed, the gravely shadowed blue eyes. . . .

The green, yawning rocks. . . .

"What *It* tells you. . . ."

A deep breath seemed unclenching her tight body, as if breathed into her lungs by some gentle, relaxing power. She inhaled it fully. Her body drew itself erect with slowly recovered ease; as gracefully as that of a wind-bent tree her balance was recovered.

The Indians' song of praise rang loudly.

She waited, smiling now as these actors pressed forward to drink. So swiftly had her crisis passed that the break in her dance had been barely noticed by most of the spectators. In another second she had gathered her draperies for the sweeping fling of the dance's brief finale; a flash, a triumphant whirl of rainbow shimmers, dizzying movements that were all light, joy, victory—and the Maiden vanished into the forest.

She was deeply hidden in trees when the storm of applause burst. Even there it was deafening.

"Come, come on out, Miss Kent, they want you, they've got to have you! You've scored—it's the biggest thing anybody's seen for many a day!"

"Listen to *that!* They've gone crazy! You've got to come out——"

"They'll storm the place if you don't——"

Actors, managers, a horde, it seemed to Bec, were trying to draw her forth to meet this thunderstorm of applause. But the Maiden, with "eyes large and glowing like those of a fawn at night," fled like the fawn of tradition. The forest received her, enfolded her; like the Spirit Maiden of the legend, she had appeared, enthralled men, and vanished from mortal sight. Far within the dusk of the trees she heard the calls and clapping, all the mad turmoil that crowned her success in art. But her deeper victory was unknown to those who hailed her.

PART FOUR

CHAPTER XVIII

DEAD LEAVES

I

HERE'S a new tonic that Dr. Aspden has sent for you, dear," Helen said with forced cheerfulness, entering the little blue room that looked out upon the autumn river. "Now I'm sure you'll soon be yourself again!"

But the face that Bec turned upon the pillow was white and pinched. "I don't think the tonic matters," she responded; her voice sagged, lifeless. Not a ray of the old Bec glowed in eye or face or voice or motion. Something deeper than physical weakness showed here: there was an apathy, a weary hopelessness, that bespoke a sick soul.

For Bec had been very ill. At last the crash had come; months of the straining effort toward art's success; the unnatural excitement of her relations with Philip and the mental turmoil they had caused; the final supreme triumph as a dancer, bought at such a cost to her nervous endurance—altogether, the crash was inevitable. She had broken completely, and now for long weeks had lain dragging back to a life that she did not want.

For what was there to get well for? her misery kept

asking.   Not in all these weeks, since she had been brought home from the mountains, had a word come from Philip.   What did it mean, this silence that hung like death?   During her absence from town it had been understood that he was not to write, for the thought of continuing a clandestine correspondence had become loathsome to her, and the time to "tell" had not then been ripe.   But, having laid aside secrecy at last, she had written to him three times, propped up and struggling with a pencil that made wobbly characters in her poor wobbly hand.   She had given the letters to Helen to post, and, when at first there had been no reply, had made sure that nothing had happened to Philip by getting Russian Anna to telephone to his landlady and inquire.   And days, more days, days that mounted into weeks, had gone by, and still no word!   She realised fully, at last, that all her happiness depended upon him; that her life, except the mere existence of the body, lay in his hands to cherish or crush.   Hour after hour she watched the wan scattering of dead leaves beside the river, and thought of her hopes as being like them, blown to the four winds.

II

At first Bec had lain dangerously ill.   Dr. Aspden had fought for her life and health as though she had been his own.

"I used to think you were horrid—wasn't that the funniest thing?" she had observed to him one day, and then they had shaken hands and laughed over it.   Why, he was one of the friends that she classified as "very special," nowadays. So growly at times—she had always liked men to be growly, and to twinkle behind the growliness!

Helen had fought at the bedside night and day, ignoring sleep, fanning the spark which had so nearly flickered out. And then had come the dreary convalescence. In it, Bec and Helen had talked quietly and at length.

The story of Bittersweet Alley had been told in full—not at Helen's solicitation, for she had put no questions, in fact, had urged that the matter be left until Bec's strength returned. But there had been a chafing. "I think I'll breathe better when it's told," Bec had sighed. "I'm so tired"—panting—"with carrying heavy secrets so far."

The confession had been in no way an apology. Cool and level-eyed, for all her weakness, she had made *that* clear. "My dancing was not wrong. I've had time to think over everything, lying here, and I know more than ever that I had the right to develop my gift—indeed, I had no right *not* to—just because it *was* a gift, and I was meant to make the most of it. But there was a wrong in my acting secretly. That was because" (she had met Helen's eyes with unflinching steadiness) "I was afraid. Cowardice and secrecy are wrong. . . . But it's all over now." She had fallen back wearily.

"You had better have your nap," had been Helen's only comment.

A week later Bec had said, "I didn't finish all I had to tell you the other day, Mother."

It was one of Helen's secret pangs that she often heard

the name in these days. It carried always a sense of distance, a lessening of that close bond of·sisterhood which formerly had been the joy of their particular relation. But, with firm cheerfulness, she replied:

"Talk away, youngster, if you think you had better."

Again Bec was level-eyed in calm fearlessness. "It's not that this thing was wrong in itself, any more than my studying dancing was wrong," she proceeded clearly. "It's only that being clandestine about it was wrong. But somehow I got into it. It was as though I had strayed into a dark alley, and then I didn't know how to turn around and go back. It never was like me to be underhanded, but I wonder," mused Bec aloud, "whether most people don't, sooner or later, find themselves trapped into doing something that they can't believe of themselves when they stand off and look it over? The thing I'm referring to," she resumed, "is my secret meeting, for many weeks, with Philip."

Silence met it.

"For a long time I obeyed you," ran on the revelation. "But after I realised that you—were in love with Dr. Aspden," pronounced Bec, hesitating but distinct, "I didn't care."

She sank back. She was physically weary and mentally overwrought. Helen was beside her in an instant.

"Leave it all, Bec, till you are well!" She was kneeling, a strong arm encircling the girl's waist.

But Bec struggled on, like one climbing an appalling mountain and compelled to reach the top.

"No, don't stop me, please. I want to finish. What I want to say is this: That, since I've laid aside fear and secrecy, knowing them to be wrong, I'm going on openly hereafter. I love Philip and he loves me, and I am going to marry him. I wish you might agree to it. I'd like to think that we could be sisters again, in the old way." Her voice was wistful at that. "But if we can't, why then, I must go on alone."

Again she paused, fatigued painfully; but, resolutely, she finished.

"I've had to live so much alone—that is, the real *me*. I had to go alone to my Roof to get acquainted with It. By It, I mean the Thing that you don't believe in. Vernon and I know about It." (The tense was as unconsciously present as if she spoke of a living comrade.) "I half believed before that there was Something; and talking with him made me sure. It's so big that I can't make out very much about It yet, and I don't thing It's at all like what people have always imagined—I know It's not a big man on a throne, or anything the least bit like that—but, whatever It is, It seems to take a sort of personal interest in me. I'm hoping for a better acquaintance with It," concluded the daughter of Helen Kent.

And at that moment Helen felt as though her last fortress had fallen. She had built her redoubts to protect her child against art, love, and faith; and the enemy, in every case, seemed to have beaten its way through in spite of her.

III

But Helen fought on. She would not acknowledge

defeat. One chance was left, and she clung to that.
If she could ward off the romantic affair for a period,
it yet might die a natural death. When Bec became
able to scribble a bit, and asked for pencil and paper to
write to Philip and tell him of her illness (what must
he have thought at not hearing in all this time? she
wondered), Helen humoured her, and brought the pretty
willow bed-tray, note-paper and pencil. But the letters
were never posted. Doctor's orders, Helen explained to
herself, justified her in this course. These orders had
been for complete rest—nothing that could cause the
slightest excitement—no communication with friends—the
complete laying-aside of all interests until the nervous
prostration was over.

For the same reason Helen, receiving Philip's inquiries
suavely, frankly refused to pass them on. Any exchange
of letters or messages surely made for excitement, she
argued, and must be forbidden.

For Philip had heard of the alarming illness and had
come to Mrs. Kent directly, throwing aside secrecy with
honest impatience.

"You are so kind to show such interest, Mr. Oliver,"
she had invariably thanked him. "My daughter is improving, but will be unable to receive guests for many
a long day." And always the lady's baffling courtesy
had bowed him out.

IV

But Helen realised, as the weeks went on, that her
efforts to keep the lovers apart amounted only to tem-

porising. At present, while Bec remained an invalid, it was necessary (so said Helen's self-justification) to protect her from all excitement; and surely any message from her lover would be excitement in the highest degree. But the end would come. Her only hope lay in prolonging the separation indefinitely—then, trust the fickleness of youth to do the rest! It was after turning away the persistent Mr. Oliver for the seventh time that the solution occurred to her. She strode to the telephone, and rattled the hook in savage haste to reach Miss Clifton.

After a brief but enthusiastic conversation with that lady, Helen hurried to Bec.

"You're to go with Cousin Ress on her long tour, my dear! What do you say to that? I've arranged to send you with her, for the sake of your health. Think of it—two years of globe-trotting! Won't that make you well? I shall miss you terribly, but the business career can wait—you'll be all the more ready to make a success of it after a long vacation.

"I haven't told you the news about the business," she went on, watching eagerly for a sign of response to her delight. "You haven't been well enough to think of such things. But the proud fact is that my department, having grown like a green bay tree, is to be greatly enlarged. I'm to have a suite of several rooms, a corps of assistants, a whopping big salary, and some day, when she is well and ready to take up her career, Miss Kent is to have a fine position with me. Now! Isn't that a dose of news by way of tonic? And aren't you delighted to travel with Cousin Ress?"

Bec tried to rouse from the despairing apathy into which she had fallen. It was weeks since her return from the mountains—and three letters she had sent to Philip, pleading letters, begging for a word in her illness— and no response! He didn't care, he couldn't care! And what could life mean to her any more, but a dull round of empty days—days all alike—days like grey sand, like the Mojave desert—days that would reach into dreadful, endless years. . . . So her thoughts ceaselessly ran. . . .

"I'll travel, if you want me to. It doesn't matter to me."

As to the "career," that was too far in the weary future to be debated at present. Just now, she could not picture herself ever dancing again. Bequita's eyes turned back to the wan scattering of dead leaves beside the autumn river.

CHAPTER XIX

ROOF O' DEAD DREAMS

I

ON a certain Sunday Philip Oliver strode beside the river. A. D. T., following in dumb devotion, shared his master's gloom. The world was a monochrome: grey sky, grey river, grey trees, grey ships, grey thoughts. The thoughts ran turbid, a sombre stream bearing Philip on faster and faster. He found himself walking as though in a hopeless race, block after block shed off behind him—and still no goal attained.

He had reached the point of despair.

This trap-like situation—how escape it? He darted from side to side within it, fought for release, pounded and shouted, and still it closed upon him inexorably. It had closed, apparently, forever. The more he thought, direly striving to see a way out, the tighter it closed. And now, worst of all, had come self-blame, that torture from which there is no relief.

All his fault, he told himself. The fault of that damnable procrastination of his—the curse of his temperament. Always he let things slide on too easily before he woke up and *did* something—"got busy."

Usually, to be sure, he did get busy in time, after all, before it was too late.   His temperament had a trick of catching at an opportunity just as it was getting tired of waiting for him, was giving him up for good, and departing.   And he did manage to snatch it then, at the eleventh hour.   In fact, he usually made up for lost time by more than succeeding.   But this time—this time it was too late.   And this was the one time in all life that really mattered.

He had, reflected Philip, let the woman he loved slip from him forever.

Why had he permitted those spring and summer days to pass and nothing *done?*   Week after week he had dallied on, making love, sunning himself in its warmth— as though love's winter were never to follow!   He had fallen in all too easily with Bequita's protests—had let her put him off, had abided by her panic-stricken wish that he should not have it out with her mother.   Why had he not taken matters into his own hands, thrashed it out with that formidable lady, and, in the probable event of her persistent refusal, have married the girl high-handedly?   Things were already going well with his business, and promising much better—he need no longer offer a diet of bread, cheese, kisses and humour alone.   And yet he had let the weeks slip away, and now——

Now—all was lost.

No moated princess could have been more inaccessible than was Bequita to her despairing prince.   In her illness she had passed completely under her mother's dominion.   Over and over he had called at the apartment;

over and over that lady had offered refreshment and a
chair, along with her own excellent company, and Mr.
Oliver, his teeth clinched, had invariably declined.

No use—as well give up and acknowledge himself
beaten.

The grey autumn day, all the greyer for being Sunday, when work could not offer relief, dragged miserably.
Despondent, he brought his walk to an end, and sought
the small apartment bedroom whither last May he had
gone to dwell in such discomfort and ecstasy, all because, by way of it, he had found his path to the Lady
of his Thoughts upon her Roof o' Dreams.

Roof o' Dreams.

In all these weeks alone he had not visited the spot.
He had not been able to bear the thought of that haunted
garden. Not since a certain summer twilight that
he recalled—the last meeting there—when, under the
fluttering shelter of the little canopy, he had held her
for long moments in his arms. . . .

He would go there now!

Suddenly it came to him that he must go. Why, he
could not have told. Hitherto, in his solitude, he had
shunned the place; but now, on this melancholy autumn
day like a twilight, something urged—something that
would not be denied, a compulsion of mysterious forces.

II

The garden was dead. Weather-stained, the barren
flower-boxes were a bleak sight, with brown, crumpled
leaves and bare stalks their only display. The gay little

awning had been removed, along with all the pretty furnishings—willow chair and stool, cushions, and the like—they had made a veritable summer parlour of the tiny pavilion. Only the drab, stained boxes, and the crackle of dead vines blowing in a grey wind. . . . Dead, all dead. . . .

A small wooden bench remained. He sank upon it, and stared out at the gloomy sky. The sky seemed to give forth a deathly chill. Once it had been like a summer lawn—velvety and star-strewn; once flowers had given off warm scents, mingling in the tender night; once the canopy had fluttered softly, like little hovering wings. . . .

He could feel it all again, vivid to the point of agony —that lovely young form against his breast—the beat of her pulse—the movement, in his arms, of her deep sigh— the silk of her hair against his cheek, the perfume of it, like flowers——

His face contracted in the torture of exquisite happiness remembered and lost. Forever lost, said his thoughts.

And then, in the bleakness, something came to him. It was a resolve. It seemed almost as though, through that dead and haunted garden, her dear ghost passed, and, passing, waiting for a pledge. Was it for this, he wondered, that he had been prompted to come?

Yes, he was pledged now. He had drifted far too easily, too long, but delay was over.

"She's got to let me see Bec—she's got to! For I'm primed now. And I'll fight!"

III

"Really, my dear Mr. Oliver," Mrs. Kent was saying that evening, as she and her caller faced one another, "I think I have listened very patiently to your very impatient demands to see my daughter. In fact you have almost—shall I say it?—harangued!"

Philip stifled a snort of exasperation. As ever, she was eyeing him frostily, playing with those everlasting jet beads that glittered like her own diabolical jet eyes.

"Mrs. Kent, if I have been rude in any way, I apologise. I came simply to present my case once more, and ask for a fair show. In brief, it sums up: that I love your daughter and want to marry her; that, formerly, she cared for me; and that I consider it only fair that I should be given one opportunity to see her. Perhaps she would be indifferent—perhaps not. It's fair to try the thing out. By this time she must be strong enough to receive me." He recognised in himself a new force; surely Mrs. Kent must give way at last before his reinforced purpose!

"She is strong enough," Helen replied. "She has improved so rapidly, indeed, that (I should have told you this at once, but really this has been my first chance to interrupt your stream of demands)—she is so much better that—" the lady paused, narrowed her eyes to gleaming lines, and fixed them for long moments upon the young man.

"That," she went on, "since Miss Clifton had reasons for starting on her world-tour rather suddenly, I have let my daughter start with her. They left this morning."

She felt the recoil of her own shot, so terrific was its force.

"You say that she—she has gone on a *world-tour?*" he breathed.

"Yes. They have left for San Francisco, and from there they will sail immediately for Honolulu, and so on around the globe. They will be gone two years."

It was met with a silence so dreadful that Helen herself almost shuddered. Somehow the silence was like a face—drawn, agonised. . . .

Moments passed. It was as if the victim of some catastrophe were struggling back to life. Then, ghastly and rigid, Philip rose. He went with the merest "Good night."

Two years! his youth was echoing over and over. Two years! Two years! As well say forever! Two years—an eternity at twenty-four. . . .

A swirl of leaves, black in the darkness, crackled around him and made him shiver, with their suggestion of death. Dead leaves, dead hopes, dead dreams, dead love. . . .

CHAPTER XX

PARADISE AND HELEN

I

IT had come, Helen realised.

Sitting there alone with Cuyler Aspden, in the living-room of the little apartment, shut in by the autumn night, she met his eyes for an imperishable moment and knew that it had come.

"Everything has been changing for me so rapidly that I have hardly made out the situation yet," he had said, as he hurried in. "May I tell you my news in this hour before my train leaves?"

That was all. But, meeting his eyes, she knew that she could no longer hold it off. It had been bound to come, some time.

She felt her throat tighten. Sooner or later she would have a direct question to answer. . . . Would she have the strength to meet it defiantly?

How often she had vowed that she would meet it, overcome it, and triumph. She who knew all the bitterest that experience had to teach—no walking into a noose for her! Insight and will—Helen had drawn her hands to fists, tensed her lips, and her eyes had brightened with resolve—insight and will were her sword and buckler.

Yes, she would be ready! She could meet the question, laugh in its face, scorn its human weakness, come off victorious—and keep her hold on this valuable friendship into the bargain! Trust the skill of a woman-of-the-world for that! Thus she had boasted.

"Nothing appeals to the solitary as does news," she replied to his words, not his eyes. "I was sure something 'thrilling,' as Bec says, was on foot when you ran up on a Monday." It was the evening following Philip's visit, and Dr. Aspden had just learned with surprise of Bec's sudden departure.

"Let's have a cup of late coffee as accompaniment to the tale." She touched to flame the spirit-lamp under the gleaming brass pot. Her sharply defined, skilful motions held him, as always, with the fascination of their delicate mastery. If it were only to drop a lump into a teacup, or poke a log to brighter burning, she never wasted a movement, each was aimed with grace born of sureness. Ah, her sureness—it was with that he must battle, and to-night!

II

"Monday's for luck," he quoted in response, and left the statement unexplained. He did not, just then, begin his story. His glance roamed over the room, softly bright in the lamplight, with cushions and curtains of warm browns and yellows. Books and fresh magazines lay about, a mass of autumn foliage and berries shone above the fireplace, comfort, charm abounded wherever he turned his eyes.

"It is such a room as this," he murmured, "that I
have visualised. And such—companionship," he concluded resolutely, and his eyes gripped hers.

Again Helen felt her throat tighten. Formerly, she
had sworn she would meet it with every weapon ready, not
a loose buckle in her armour. . . . Again reprieve.

"A great change has come to me," said Dr. Aspden.
"After so many years with the Monroe that I looked
upon it as for life, I am taking a very important new
position which means a broader scope in every sense.
It has all been so rapid, my decision had to be made in
a day. . . . In brief, I am to be at the head of the great
new hospital at L——, near New York. It is a
tremendous opportunity." He halted, but only a moment. "Helen," he said, "will you come with me?"

In the end it had come so abruptly that she was unpre-
pared, and she met it with silence. He waited, as silent
as she. He was not the man to urge and plead, to add
coaxings and wooings to his blunt question. He had
flung it down for her to take or leave.

"You know my belief on that subject," she said at
length.

"I know your unbelief. It is purely negative. A
negative isn't even worth combating."

She smiled slightly, but shook her head. "It is far
too positive to be regarded in that wise. I've told you
more than once that I have no illusions concerning what
is called 'love'—the alleged basis of marriage. Romantic
love is a world-old delusion, nature's trick to gain her
ends. Instincts over which we have no control set the

trap. But if we can't control the instincts we can dodge
the trap."

Her lips were uttering the old formula, the tenets
of a lifelong creed; but suddenly, looking into his face—
passionate but self-mastered, awaiting her word with that
man's control of self that was so infinitely more intoxicating than the hotly impetuous pleadings of a boy
once had been—Helen gave way. The truth tore from
her, an elemental thing bursting bars.

"Oh, I don't pretend to be proof against feeling!" she
cried. "Old as I am, nature fools me yet! Here I am,
thirty-nine, with hell's torments behind me, and still, if
I followed my impulse, I should plunge in again! But I
know what it would mean. A few months—say a year—
of glamour. Then a lifetime of disillusion."

"But you can't think that I——"

"Oh, of course, you wouldn't be a brute. You'd be a
dutiful husband. There are various forms of misery.
With you, it wouldn't be a gross, overt form. But that
doesn't matter. Disillusion—the death of glamour—petty
irritations that become maddening in their sting—ennui,
perpetual grinding-out of the days—bleak commonplace-
ness where once was magic—what a long, grey tragedy!
Might it not be even worse than the spectacular cruel-
ties?"

"Decidedly worse. In fact, I can imagine no torment
like that you picture. But my picture is different. I
see years, not of the infatuation of twenty-year-old children, to be sure; but of a delightful, mellow companionship, a keen mutual interest, the pleasure of building
together, travelling together, reading together, enjoying

friends together, settling down together in a charming
room beside a fire——"

He looked up to discover that Helen had covered her
face with her hands as though to shut out the picture
he drew.

She was not meeting the attack.

Where was her once-boasted defense? Some buckle in
her armour must have been left loose. Somehow her
sword must have failed of sharpness. She felt an incredible weakness, a sense of surrender creeping upon her.
What could it mean—why was she not springing forward
with her counter-thrusts of laughter, of irony, of ready
wit and baffling coldness? Why was she not rising to
complete refusal, settling the question then and there, as
she had so clearly foreseen?

Instead, she was begging for time! She, Helen Kent,
undecided, pleading for time like a tremulous girl!

"Please—please go!" she was begging. "I can't think
now! I must have a chance alone—to think."

He rose. "It is time for my train, and you shall think
alone. I am leaving for Chicago to confer with a great
surgeon about joining me. May I find your answer upon
my return, Saturday morning?"

"You shall have it then."

He went quickly, with only a friendly hand-clasp.

III

The little home lay in deep silence. The city's noise
had died from its hearing. How still the apartment was
without Bec! Only a cricket's voice was heard; the small

creature had arrived with the branches of autumn foliage, and had taken up its abode with Helen. It was argumentative. It stalked forth into sight now, and took a position facing her, as though in alliance with her thoughts.

The clock ticked off the minutes and multiplied them into hours. Still Helen's noisy thoughts and the noisy cricket argued on.

It was madness, madness, madness, cried the thoughts.

"Madness, madness, madness," rasped the insect.

The whole thing was out of the question, as it always had been. Why had she made trouble for herself and for Cuyler Aspden as well, by thus delaying her final answer? She must write at once, must prove to him how positive was her rejection. . . .

Thus ran the determined thoughts, formulated under the old creed; and each time that she declared herself thus finally, there arose a picture: friends, books, fire, home, *together*——

"It's a delusion!" cried Helen Kent, and she cried it aloud. It was two o'clock in the morning, and she was worn to pallor by the battle of her mind, but her eyes shone vivid. "The thing couldn't last! It's a delusion—don't I know?"

And then she crumpled. She went down in a conquered heap, her arms out upon the table, her head upon the cross they made.

"My God!" she said, and she was unaware of the grotesque irony of the familiar phrase upon her lips. "It's a delusion, and I know it—but—friends, books, fire, home—with *him!* It would be paradise! The

glamour would end in a year, and thirty years of disillusion would follow, but what would the thirty be if
I'd had the one? I'd rather have that year," she cried,
"rather have it, knowing that I faced thirty years of
misery ahead, than anything that life could send! It
would make all the past and all the future worth while.
I'm no longer young, I should go in with my eyes open.
And in spite of that—I'll face a lifetime of purgatory.
For first I shall have had my year!"

Helen flung herself erect; she seemed to be addressing
the raucous insect as though the tiny, violent creature
embodied her own protesting thoughts:

"The delirious passion of youth is no more than a
surface bubble upon such waters as these! Paradise is
worth any price! Who cares for the cost of buying
heaven—with him, with him!"

Paradise; paradise. It was like a tune that her mind
sang over and over. . . . She sat gazing on into the
autumn night beyond the window. . . .

The irascible insect had fallen still. . . .

The sudden determined resumption of the creature's
argument roused her. It was turning to leave; but it
could not go without a last word. Like a loud warning
it suddenly uttered its thoughts; the warning, as it scurried away, bore a ridiculous likeness to:

"Bec-c-c-c-, Bec-c-c-c-, Bec-c-c-c!"

IV

Bec!

How, in this blind hour, had she for a moment lost
sight of the relation of all this affair to Bec? How had

passion so swept her, like devouring flame, that she had
seen only her paradise, awaiting and shining? Her longings had bounded over every obstacle, had not even observed that the obstacles were there. What had she been
doing, thus to dream, madly, madly. . . .

Bec!

Helen herself might steer in perilous waters, after her
long and dreadful schooling, and with her steelier temperament to guard her; but Bec! That sensitive plant!
Why, the child would wither under the certain disillusion
that marriage would be to such a little idealist, like a
flower in the desert wind! The first blast would kill her,
kill her very soul!

Bec had admitted that her belief that Helen was "in
love with Dr. Aspden" had prompted her to a clandestine
affair. And how could Helen forbid her daughter to marry
if she herself should yield to marriage? Impossible to
explain that what might be safe for her was peril to
another!

"Friends, books, fire, home, togeth—" sang her mocking thoughts.

"Don't—don't say it again!" she cried, as though
someone had spoken. "Not *that!*"

A queer little visitor rose capriciously in her memory
—an ungainly insect scurrying away in irascible protest, crying its disapproval in sounds that ridiculously
resembled:

"Bec-c-c-c, Bec-c-c-c, Bec-c-c-c!"

"It was to have been black willow furniture and dark
red and blue chintz—friends, books, fire, home. . . ."

Her silence, with eyes closed, with that tense pressing

against self that made every muscle rigid, was as long as another woman's prayer. When it broke, there was no further protest against the powers, no despairing pleas. Helen Kent merely picked up her gold pen, took out agreeable grey note-paper, and wrote.

There were expressions of gratitude, esteem, and friendship. Following these:

"Of course, knowing my attitude, you cannot be surprised at my final and positive refusal."

Five minutes later this reply fell, with a flashing whizz, down the slide and into the hands of a postman who happened to be collecting mail in the hall below. The die was cast.

"She would give her all, she would sell her last chance of happiness for Bec." How often she had used the phrase! . . . Paradise. . . .

The stroke of a pen. . . .

v

The Chicago train was not crowded that night. It offered comfortable roominess to the reflective Dr. Aspden, enjoying an excellent late cigar in the smoking-car, or strolling thoughtfully through the aisle to his own section, where he sat long, in the solitude of others' slumbers, to watch distant lights scurrying to cover away from the flashing train.

Again he saw Helen's gesture—covering her eyes, as though to fight off the vision of home—a home together. He heard her tremulous (yes, tremulous!) pleading:

"I must have a chance alone—to think!"

To think!

What was she thinking—to-night, as the train and the hours sped on with him? Was she awake? Was she still undecided? Or had she settled the question for good and all? Had she determined upon her answer——

Her answer!

With the human instinct of self-protection against hope, he tried to push away the thought; but it was too strong for him. It thrust its way in, past the barricade: it cried: "Her answer—it means happiness! Don't you know it? She sees, she sees!"

Long ago he had made his diagnosis of the "case" with professional self-confidence.

"Of course, one of my profession must look upon her morbid obsession with complete understanding. Complete understanding. The shock of girlish illusions wrecked—repeated shocks—ideals. shattered; bitterness and a hatred of all men are the natural consequence. Such obsessions are by no means uncommon. And they can be overcome only by a thorough comprehension. A physician," continued the Doctor in soliloquy, "comprehends."

He recognised the note of assurance creeping into his own inner voice, and again he attempted to rear the barrier against hope. But hope was arrogant. "Her gesture, her tremulousness!" hope cried.

"Such a case must be handled with skill. Violent siege would have driven her to still more violent dislike of our unfortunate sex. Oh, it was necessary to be patient—and wary. Never to press the matter. Slowly to build up confidence, friendship, esteem, intimacy." (How

"slowly" may a few months of waiting pass, even at forty-
seven!)

Again he saw her gesture, her tremulous indeci-
sion. . . .

Her answer—even now it might be determined—he must
ward off hope. . . .

And at that he gave way.

"I can't ward it off. I saw her gesture. I heard her
voice. I can't help it—I believe that she sees, at last,"
said Dr. Aspden, and the dark car window reflected a
face in which confidence triumphed.

VI

Helen had renounced paradise, but she was at peace
with herself. She had seen Bec on her way to the ends
of·the earth. She had seen Philip crushed by despair
at the knowledge of miles and years between them. But
she had not seen him an hour or so later on that Sunday
evening.

It was after leaving her that the great idea had come
to him, driving like a furious spur.

"My romance began with mad pursuit—let it end so!"
the idea had shouted in his ears. "It was useless before
—it's probably useless now. But in any event, I shall
have fought it through!"

CHAPTER XXI

PURSUIT

I

HE had walked the most of the three thousand miles across the continent, Philip felt, when the train snorted into Oakland. For days and nights he had placed the aisles much of the time; had savagely endured passivity, the inability to get out and push the wheels faster; had slept barely at all; had visited the dining-car only to bolt a cup of coffee and turn from food; had smoked incessantly; had stared from the observation car's rear platform wondering if he couldn't run faster than the train if he should jump off and try it. . . . San Francisco at last! And six hours behind time!

Practically, he had already lost. Only by some stroke of unheard-of luck the Hawaii-bound vessel might be late in sailing. He had the barest possible data to go by. Mrs. Kent had said that Bec was to sail "immediately"; quick queries in New York had developed the information that the first Honolulu sailing after what must be Bec's arrival in San Francisco was the following day. After a mad race of preparation—telephone consultation with his "Chief" (who had proved "great" be-

370

yond words), packing, ticket purchasing, all frantic as a whirlwind, he had caught an early morning train for the Coast, on the chance of arrival before that sailing.

And then—washouts, interminable delays, the Overland standing in the middle of a desert as idle as a painted ship upon a painted ocean, insane speed to cover the loss of time, a breakdown, and the upshot—six hours late!

But, up to the last, he would fight. He would die sword in hand. A taxi was summoned—a volley of orders, and he was off for the pier. It occurred to him that, had Mr. Popp been in charge, he would have arrived in time. But even then, in the midst of pursuit, he recognised its futility. He could not dash up a gangplank, cry to a departing passenger, "Marry me!" and snatch her ashore to the altar. His only chance had lain in a quiet talk previously. . . . And still he pursued, and arrived to see the Hawaii-bound boat steaming forth blithely into the sunlit waters of the Golden Gate.

There were minutes in which the most insane visions rioted through his brain. On, on, he saw himself journeying—to Hawaii, to Japan, perhaps, or India, or China —strange lands whither the whim might be carrying these two travellers—learning at every port of their departure, catching a clue only to lose it again. . . .

But utter brain- and body-exhaustion overcame him. Why had he not realised all along that the whole pursuit had been for an *ignis fatuus?* He might go on indefinitely, missing the travellers here, there, everywhere; and, on the other hand, what? Might not time have killed Bec's feeling for him? He was disheartened enough to credit any calamity. In his despair he pictured her love as dead as the garden where it had flowered.

It was then that Philip Oliver gave up. "A hotel—any—I don't care which," was his only order. A little later he found himself in a dingy old hostelry of cracked wallpaper and stuffy atmosphere, a melancholy survivor of the Fire; and in a dismal and enormous room he sank into a chair and felt the chill of final hopelessness fall upon him like an enveloping cloak. It was over, and he had lost. To-morrow he would return to New York.

The paralysis of gloom conquered. In a sleep more like lethargy than the normal man's rest, he forgot hope, longing, passion, sorrow, even hopelessness.

II

Philip woke to a chaos of whistlings and siren shriekings in the harbour. The room was dark; he had slept on into the evening, it seemed, in his numb exhaustion. Evidently something was the matter; he shook himself together and went downstairs.

"There's been some sort of accident to a boat," the clerk told him. "She's putting back in for repairs. She'll be able to start again by morning. It's the one that sailed for Honolulu this afternoon."

Philip felt himself tighten in every muscle. "And the passengers—hurry up! What about the passengers?" he demanded, thrusting his face toward the clerk.

That person coldly stared, as though the man were a little mad. "Oh, they're all right. Nobody hurt. All back in port by this time."

And then Philip recognised, emerging from the confusion of swift impressions, guesses, perceptions, reflections, that the gods were holding out something to him. That something was—another chance!

And a last chance. By a miracle of delay, Bec was now in the city with him, and the guard was absent!

How find her?

That had been his previous problem, while he had raced across three thousand miles in the wild hope of arriving before his Princess should vanish. He could but try at each hotel. And suppose the capricious Miss Clifton happened not to choose a hotel at all—she might be dropping in upon relatives, for instance! . . .

"All I can do is to begin, and go down the hotel list," he told himself, seeking a telephone booth. "My first guess is the Castle. That's expensive enough for Miss Clifton, and has the tradition of age. Elderly people like elderly things," he assured himself, with the satisfied sapience of youth.

But the Castle registered no "Clifton" or "Kent."

"Stupid! I might have known that the adventurous spinster would choose the most up-to-date!" he swung about. He had met her once at Mrs.' Kent's and had formed rapid opinions.

He called another, the height of modern fashion and fabulous prices. A "no" from the clerk. The E——, the H——, the C——, and the W—— followed in turn. He had exhausted the list of famously excellent establishments; he began on the simple, quiet, little known "family hotels." In vain.

Baffled, he returned to his own dismal headquarters.

It was past ten o'clock. The vessel, he had taken time to make sure, would be sailing early the next morning. What, in a few hours of night, could he do?

Leaving the elevator, he walked down the long and dreadfully red-carpeted hall. He was slow with misery. His eyes were bent to the floor. Raising them, he faced Miss Clifton.

"*Here?*" was the one word that found its way from his lips.

"Here, of course," replied the lady crisply, holding out her hand to him. "Where else? I always stop here. There isn't another chef on the Coast who thoroughly comprehends the subtlety of a cracked crab."

"*And?*——" He was clutching the hand she had given him, as if it were his one hold on hope, impaling her eyes upon his own.

"*And?*—— You mean, I suppose, young man, that you'd rather hear about my youthful cousin than about cracked crab just now." So she knew!

For a moment of frowning study Miss Clifton waited. She shook her head, she pondered, she pursed her lips, she stamped her foot at her own thoughts. Then——

"Come along!" she cried, and it was the voice of anarchy. "I suppose I ought not to—there'll be the devil to pay—but I'm sick of this whole inquisition. That's what it is—rack and thumbscrew applied to young love. . . . Young man, come with me! I have a romantic soul, and from this moment it takes the bit in its teeth!" With which remarkable flow of rhetoric, she led him down the hall and threw open the door of a private sitting-room.

Beside the table Bec sat reading. She looked up languidly—then, as amazed recognition flushed her cheeks, widened her eyes——

"I've got business to attend to downstairs," said Miss Clifton. "It will take me quite a while."

CHAPTER XXII

HELEN REFLECTS

I

ON Saturday morning Mr. McNab briskly led the
way down the office corridor, and, with a vast
display of pride, flung open a door to an alertly
masterful lady who entered, smartly fur-swathed to the
chin.

"Behold! What do you say to *that? Some* suite, eh,
what? Think you own the Monroe, directors and all,
don't you! Maybe you'll be satisfied *now* for a week or
so, before you order a building all your own!"

Thus with cheerful persiflage Mr. McNab introduced
to Helen her new domain. It was a kingdom. The two
suites which formerly had been her own and Dr. Aspden's had been thrown together, and two more rooms
added, to give the women's department the scope it re-
quired. The smell of varnish arose, pungent and delicious in its suggestion of freshness; everywhere shone
newly papered walls, newly upholstered furniture, reno-
vated ceilings and floors and woodwork. Two great
potted rubber plants gave the final touch of impressive-
ness to the dark-blue and mahogany grandeur.

"Can't you say 'Thanks' to the gentleman, and make
a pretty bow?" prattled the irrepressible McNab.

"It would be so inadequate that I haven't the courage to say it," she told him, smiling her delighted pride into his fat, shining little face. "I'll say it in terms of the annual reports—wait and see!"

"I see already! You're a winner, Mrs. Kent, if ever there was one. My money's on you every time. Oh— by the way—we'll have to be looking up a new secretary for you. That little Muldoon just up and resigned yesterday—going to be married. Don't know what's the matter with 'em all, but it's epidemic. Lost two cracker-jack stenographers last month, and my best bookkeeper's given notice, and I have suspicions of another. Always noticed it breaks out in waves, like influenza. . . . So long! Luck!"

Alone in her splendour, Helen moved about restlessly, like a queen becoming acquainted with a new domain. It was Saturday—the agents and assistants would not be reporting for duty until next week. She loosened her wraps, at last dropped into a vast cushioned chair in her own old office, gazed about.

It was empire.

Even her fondest visions had not pictured such proud achievement as this. Success was written in every detail of costly furniture, of spaciousness, of desks and equipment with their implication of "big business." Achievement, success—no longer an inexpensive apartment, no longer a Russian Anna blundering to the door. . . . And she had won it all herself! By dint of concentrated effort, the steady driving of brain and will, she had more than "made good." Far sooner than she had ever dreamed, she had "won out."

The thought occurred to her:

"I've got what I went after."

Somehow there was a curious lack of elation in the thought.

II

Helen rose, and moved restlessly about the rooms. Her thoughts reverted to Bec. She had not received the expected message, but of course the child was already sailing safely toward Pacific islands. Helen would not permit herself to feel anxious.

She strolled toward the adjoining room, but suddenly she turned sharply, and closed its door behind her—the once-sealed door. (At that moment Cuyler Aspden might be reading her letter!) There was a ghost in that room. The ghost chanted in her ears the refrain which all one night she had battled to drive out: "Friends, books, fire, home." That room should be turned over to her assistants for the present, until her nerves stopped their nonsense. Nerves! What traitors they were!

She wandered to her own desk. Beside it stood the deserted typewriter of one Maybelle Muldoon. Married! In Helen's memory rose a familiar thimble and bit of embroidery, the blushings and snatched seconds consecrated to the hope-chest.

It was at that moment, as she sat in lonely state and thought of Maybelle Muldoon, that the sense of futility began to move in Helen's mind. It began almost imperceptibly, as does the avalanche: a slight downward slide, a slight gain of momentum——

What an effort she had made on Miss Muldoon's behalf, to root "nonsense" out of her mind, to make the deluded young idiot see that "men are all right until you marry them," that her interests lay in business! And so, too, she had worked with the other office girls. And in spite of it, marriage had become epidemic among them!

How the world seemed bound over to its delusions after all, Helen reflected. (The sense of futility was gaining momentum with every instant.) Here was this matter of belief, too. When *she* had been a girl, at the end of the nineteenth century, she had supposed that the broader thinkers were getting bravely beyond the old horizons, were "dropping poppycock." But on all hands nowadays were signs of a curious change. Not, she realised, a movement toward the church of old days, but a tendency to reach toward something not demonstrable in the laboratory. (To Helen this indicated a return to old horizons; she failed to see in it a movement still further beyond those that formerly had been "broad.")

It was queer. Everybody was saying that the war had done it. Here a distinguished middle-aged author of cynical tendencies was publishing a book about "God," having just made His acquaintance; there a throng of eager suppliants found standing room only in their rush to hear a famous thinker discourse upon life after death. The soldiers themselves had developed an amazing interest in various forms of religion. These were signs of the times; Helen could not fail to see them. Old formulated orthodoxy was, perhaps, fading away; but on every hand she recognised a rising tide of interest in things not material. . . .

Words of Cuyler Aspden recurred to her. They had been in response to asseverations of her own.

"I recognise the failures of the Church as you do," he had said. "But—well, as a physician of many years' experience I have witnessed death hundreds, yes, thousands of times, and from the most materialistic standpoint, as a physician must. I have seen that, as far as I could prove, death meant the cessation of pulse, of respiration, of cerebration, and nothing beyond. And in spite of a quarter-century of this disillusioning experience, I still feel that there is something that my signature of the death certificate fails to cover."

Her reflections were broken. Three telegrams were handed her.

III

The first one opened was signed "Philip Oliver." This fact surprised her; would the young man never have done with his pleadings? With a bored impassivity she began to read; an impassivity that turned first to incredulity, then to alarm.

"San Francisco
"Overtook your daughter here. She consents marry me"

Its frankly succinct statement was as much as to say, "I give you fair warning!"

He had pursued Bec to California!

Helen felt a sort of dizziness, as if all her world, which

she had so carefully mapped and laid out, were dancing about in topsy-turvy fashion before her eyes. Why, she had arranged everything! She had packed Bec off to safety, she had informed the young lover that his game was up, she had settled the future irrevocably. And now——

Clumsy with bewilderment, Helen fumbled at opening the second message. It was from Cousin Ress:

"No use your being fool any longer. Face the music. I would not be fat old maid to-day if my father had not interfered. Oliver fine fellow. Doubt if will ever have money. Not mean enough. But will keep her love. That better and more unusual. Will be married here immediately. Have waited long enough, poor things. Honeymoon Southern California. I will see them through."

Helen's sense of a world whirling dizzily about her was increasing. Groping for foothold upon it, she opened Bec's night-letter. It was even lengthier than Miss Clifton's and showered with an extravagant abundance of connectives:

"Dear Helen,
"Philip is here, and we are going to be married at once. I wish I could think of you as happy in my happiness, but I suppose it is no use. It seems as if you might understand my love because of your own for another man, but you never have. I wish you would marry Dr. Aspden, for I would like him for a relation now that I know how nice he is and he is so pleasant behind his growliness and we are congenial on the subject of dogs. I am no longer acting clandestinely, but I must decide for myself, and there is no wrong in Philip's and my great love. Cousin Ress has ordered the most wonderful wedding cake, with frosting like that snowstorm in New York last winter. Please try to understand me and love me if you can, and give the canary lettuce.
"Your Bec."

The crumpled papers slid from Helen's hand. That sense of futility which had been growing within her had indeed become an avalanche. Down, down it went sliding, carrying with it one purpose after another, crushing them, crumbling them to atoms. Helen saw herself as a creature thwarted, failing in every effort save the material striving. *That* was triumphant; in terms of rich blue upholstery and mahogany and potted plants it flaunted itself. But in the other strivings—nature had beaten her.

That was what it came to. Nature had gained her every end. In spite of Helen, Bec had developed her art to exquisite perfection. And that sister to art, romantic love, had persistently refused to surrender. Even the world-old delusion of faith had snatched her child from under her vigilant eyes.

Art, love, faith—in spite of her, Bec had found them all. They were Nature's decree, and Nature had won.

Futility dominated Helen's mind now. She had made her sacrifice—her last, supreme effort, and she had failed. Nature and youth's instinctive belief in life, were stronger than she and her unbelief. She was beaten. . . .

And paradise. . . .

Her breath stopped as realisation broke upon her. Her happiness—she had renounced it all for nothing.

She might have had her paradise after all. Upon this she fell to brooding.

IV

Far into the forenoon she sat alone in her splendour, brooding into vacancy, held by an inertia of misery. It was almost noon when someone knocked; when, to her

"Come in," Dr. Aspden entered, she seemed to realise his presence only dimly, like a sick person. She did not even wonder at his coming when he must have received her letter.

She looked up dully. Then, picking up the telegrams, she handed them all to him.

He read them without exclamation—read them slowly, fully. Then, very quietly, he made brief comment:

"Well—it is the law of life."

There was a long silence. At length, raising her eyes from the sombre study of vacancy into which she had again fallen, she found the grave grey ones awaiting them.

"This morning I received a letter signed by you," Dr. Aspden said. "But I feel that your inmost, truest self did not write that letter."

His grave eyes blazed. He stepped toward her, made as though to take her hands, a vibration shook his low voice:

"Helen, Helen Kent, was not that letter of yours false? Your bitterness must be only a black cloud through which you have looked wrongly upon life! Happiness is for you, if you will only let yourself take it! Learn the truth from little Bec—she recognises life, and reaches out, and takes it! I came back resolved that if you didn't already see, I would make you see—I would fight down that false fear of yours—for it is, in reality, only fear—Bordeaux's 'La Peur de Vivre'—I will overcome it for you, with you—you wonderful, loving, courageous, bitter, self-deluded, glorious woman——"

For the moment, something within her vibrated in re-

sponse. For that moment it seemed that a fog was
rolling away: a fog of morbid doubt, of life-long dis-
trust, of black hopelessness. As if light were breaking
through a veiled sky. . . . The fog again . . . closing
in. . . .

Her eyes fell away from the hold of his, a muscular
depression caused her whole body to sag. Again she
was gazing greyly into vacancy. He barely made out
her words, for her voice, too, fell with her falling spirit.

"It's too late," said Helen Kent.

"I'll be frank with you," she went on sombrely, still
speaking into the grey void. "I did have a few hours
of illusion. Human weakness—I'm not above it. Things
looked rose-coloured for awhile. I resolved to take it—
to take the illusion of paradise, even knowing that disillusion was to follow. I was mad for a few hours. And
in the end I cast this fancied happiness away to save
Bec. I thought, by setting her a good example, I could
make sure of her renouncing marriage, which would mean
her tragedy. I made what, at that hour, was the supreme sacrifice of my life. I watched gates swing shut
on paradise.

"Well—I didn't save her. . . . Oh, yes—" she put out
her hand as if to push away his expected protests, "you
think that releases me. It does. No use of the sacrifice
now. I'm free.

"Free." She rose wearily. "But it's too late. I was
mad for a little while, drunk with the thought of a brief
paradise, ready to face any misery for the sake of it,
but now——

"That's over. I've come to my senses. No, don't

urge. It's no good." In grey heaviness she drew on her wraps. "I'm thirty-nine, and I can't begin to acquire illusions, at this stage of the game." She snapped a glove-fastener and laid her hand on the door-knob. She turned, as if to speak; hesitated, then——

"Oh, I wish," broke from her as she met his eyes for a single instant, "I wish it were not too late!"

V

She was gone. Every impulse of his desire, his will, his resolve moved to follow her, to protest, to conquer, to capture; but some opposing force chained him. He must seize her, draw her back, crush her—he who had resolved to fight her obsession to the death—why was he standing dumb and motionless?

And as the door closed upon her he realised that it was because somehow, at last, he *knew*.

He knew that a lifetime of battle would be no use, for she would create the very unhappiness that she anticipated by her fixed belief in it. She was not the victim of a mere passing doubt; rather, the soul of doubt was inherent in her, it was the very essence of her nature. As Bec was the eternal affirmative, the spirit that takes life on trust, letting what may follow, so Helen was the eternal negative, disbelieving at every turn. They were like the two great world-forces, the eternal Yea and Nay, the Nay ever futile against the onward stream of life.

Irrelevantly he observed to himself:

"I'd like to know that young man who's carried off her daughter. . . ."

"Too late to acquire illusions." It had always been too late. His self-confident diagnosis of her "case" and his projected "cure" returned to him, fatuous and smug in his ears. He, who had been so sure of himself, of his power to fight to a finish, was left standing alone, impotent, beaten along with Helen herself, fellow-victim of her unconquerable disbelief. Once, in her girlhood, that disbelief must have failed her, he knew; but equally he knew that it would never fail her again. It had all along been "too late."

The accident of an unhappy marriage had not made Helen Kent the doubter she was; rather, the soul of doubt within her had moulded her. The tragic experience had not been the cause of her scepticism; could her scepticism have been in any way the cause of her tragic experience? oddly occurred to him. Could it indeed be true that "the soul contains in itself the event that shall befall it?" A sweeping statement, that, of the poet. . . .

"How are you, Doc?" McNab's entrance came like a crash upon his reverie.

"I came to get some papers I left in my hurried departure. Here they are. I shan't be in again," said Dr. Aspden.

CHAPTER XXIII

AUTUMN SANDS

I

THE autumn blue of Santa Barbara's sea—a particular blue which it is said that no other water but the Bay of Naples ever achieves—glinted in their eyes, giving off the sun's reflected light like metal. The sand lay warm beneath them; the slight, very slight breeze bore from the land a fragrance of late roses to mingle with the sea smell of naked kelp.

"Helen came here, too," Bec said musingly, after a long silence through which she had absently built ramparts of sand and demolished them.

"You mean when they, too, were just married?"

"Yes. She told me all about it once. They went often to the Mission, just as we have done. That very, *very* old Padre, humped almost double, poor dear, in his brown robe—the one that showed us the illuminated volumes—I have an idea is the same one who showed them to Helen—and Vernon."

"Dear, don't think of anything that makes you sad," Philip begged, noting a catch in her voice.

She turned full upon him. "I'm not sad about Vernon, even if I did wink a tear. I feel richer, somehow,

387

because I know him now, and he understands me and I understand him." Always the tense was present when Bec spoke of her dead father. "As for being sad about *any*thing," she went on, "—Philip, I'm so happy—so happier than I ever dreamed that mortals on this mere earth could be—that nothing in existence, or in imagination, could possibly make me sad. But, just because I'm so happy, I'm *still*—inside, as well. as out. Do you know what I mean? It's as if I'd found the great final Heaven, and there could never be any more worry or even wishing—there's nothing to do but sit still and think about how nice it is, forever."

"Flow-ahs? Ros-es? Cah-nations?" sang a little Spanish flower-seller along the beach. Philip bought a great bouquet, "for my wife," he observed with unction. Such terms as "wife," "husband," "married," and the like throb at every utterance while the honeymoon is young.

"You're already almost as pink as these," he declared, as Bec pinned the roses against her white gown. "By the time our fortnight is up, and you're back in New York, your mother won't know her invalid." It had only wanted happiness for Bec's complete recovery.

"My mother," Bec mused. "I hope she and I can begin all over, like sisters again. I mean to try. I suppose it's hard to put things back as they were before. But I've blotted out all my old resentment."

His eyebrows arched involuntarily. In time, he trusted, he would learn forgiveness; but encounters with that jetty lady still rankled.

"I know," said Bec, "that I've never understood her.

But I think she has understood herself still less. And it's because she didn't understand herself, that she couldn't understand me. At any rate, I know that her one motive was always a passionate desire for what she believed would be my happiness. Cousin Ress talked to me about it."

"Miss Clifton, bless her! She's the sport *par excellence!*" His favoritism was patent. "Wasn't she great —to put off sailing till the next boat so as to get us up a jolly little wedding right in the hotel—cake, flowers, and all—and to ship us off here, crying, 'Bless you, my children,' wheezing like an automobile all the time———"

"I've always felt that Cousin Ress must have a love story of her own tucked away in her heart, or she couldn't be so romantic—considering how fat she is," murmured Bequita reflectively.

II

There were fourteen untarnished golden days of blue water, late roses, sands that held the sun-warmth in their hollows, idle strolls to the Franciscan Mission where the brown-robed Padres welcomed them under the ancient bell-tower, loafings in a hotel garden of rustling palms and bamboo. With exquisite emphasis each day repeated the beauty of the preceding, until the fortnight became like a chime.

Gaiety was not the pitch. It was all, as Bec said, too happy for that—it was so rapturous that it was *still.* They talked even soberly.

"Dear me, I must write to Zélie. I've been neglecting her dreadfully," she repented one day, when buying post-cards of the Mission.

Philip started to reply—thought better of it—checked himself abruptly; but Bec had caught him.

"What is it—do you know anything about her now?" she asked quickly.

He hesitated. "No," he said at length.

But, loafing on the sand later on, she took it up.

"Phil, you do know something about Zélie. Tell me. I've never had a word from her since I told her good-bye upon leaving for the Catskills, August first, though I wrote and wrote."

He thought. "I believe I might as well tell you," he said at length, "although it may cause you sadness. But sooner or later you'd find out."

"Phil! Is it something dreadful?"

"I don't know even that. I only know that Zélie's gone."

"Gone!"

"Vanished. Completely. I called a few times and couldn't get in, and at last I hunted up the janitress. She says that, early in August, Zélie paid up every bill in her square little way, took Villageoise, and went. No-body knows where. The studio stands forsaken gather-ing dust, poor old baronial chairs and all."

"Phil! Oh, what can it mean?"

Again he hesitated. "I think it means that Zélie saw a task she had set herself accomplished, and that then—she was through."

"My dear! You mean her seeing me launched?"

"Her seeing you launched."

"But it's as though I had driven her away, some-how."

"Don't feel that. It was her great desire—and she's a vagabond by instinct. I wasn't going to tell you what I have learned about her. But I believe, on second thoughts, I will. . . .

"It seems, Bec, that she gave her G. O., as she al-ways called it, to you. I've found this out only very lately, inquiring here and there, putting two and two together. She kept it a secret. But—she was chosen in the beginning to dance as the star performer of the Pageant—the Indian girl. It was at her suggestion that the Indian girl was cut out, and the dance and stellar rôle given to the White Maiden. . . . Bec! Don't, dear, don't!"

"I can't—can't *bear* it, Philip!"

"In time you can—for you will realise that to a nature as rare as Zélie's, such sacrifice is the supreme happi-ness. It hurts, I know—it hurts me, too, for I share with you. But think what it is always going to be to both of us to have had her as a friend—always to have her, in memory. . . ."

III

At the end of the fortnight they jumped up and down upon their trunks, to make the stubborn lids shut upon all the treasures they had bought.

"We have *some*thing, anyway, toward furnishing an apartment," Bec observed with grave satisfaction. "That

Navajo blanket will be a great help in the living-room. And the bronze Japanese lantern—and there are two dozen cakes of that wonderful soap made from the native olives—and—let's see—how many tins of clam juice did I get?"

"I feel," solemnly responded Philip, "that the apartment is practically equipped for housekeeping already, with a Japanese lantern, a Navajo blanket, two dozen cakes of soap, and some clam juice—to say nothing of a dog awaiting us in New York——"

"Dear A. D. T. !"

She waxed suddenly grave with responsibility. "And now that I'm well, and crazy to dance again, I shall be able to help along——"

"Now look here! My wife doesn't 'help along'—is that clearly understood? To be sure, I'm no tyrant of an earlier generation, and I don't intend to slaughter an artist to make me a helpmate, and if she wants to dance for her own and other people's pleasure she can dance till the cows come home. But not to pay for my porterhouse." His chest inflated. "Perhaps *this* will 'help along,' instead," and he handed her a letter just received from Mr. Frost.

"Your Chief—oh—oh—*Philip Oliver!* Congratulations, and a *raise!* Phil-*lip!*"

Their hands clasped, and he whirled her, dizzily, to the tune of her enraptured squeals.

"Darling! *Now* can't we have an electric toaster?" was her passionate request. And:

"An electric toaster shall celebrate the first breakfast at home of Mrs. and Mr. Philip R. Oliver. And you may burn the toast, dearest, as much as you desire," was his promise.

And so they made ready, after the way of the world, to build and feather the nest. Helen Kent, more than twenty years before, had done the same. And the outcome for Helen Kent's daughter lay, as it had lain for her, on the knees of the gods.

END

There's More to Follow!

More stories of the sort you like; more, probably, by the author of this one; more than 500 titles all told by writers of world-wide reputation, in the Authors' Alphabetical List which you will find on the *reverse side* of the wrapper of this book. Look it over before you lay it aside. There are books here you are sure to want—some, possibly, that you have *always* wanted.

It is a *selected* list; every book in it has achieved a certain measure of *success*.

The Grosset & Dunlap list is not only the greatest Index of Good Fiction available, it represents in addition a generally accepted Standard of Value. It will pay you to

Look on the Other Side of the Wrapper!

In case the wrapper is lost write to the publishers for a complete catalog